10-6-2021

Love Sign
Susan Kirby

Books by Susan Kirby

Love Inspired

Your Dream and Mine #64
Love Sign #127

SUSAN KIRBY

has written numerous novels for children, teens and
adults. She is a recipient of the Child Study Children's Book Committee Award, and has received
honors from The Friends of American Writers. Her
Main Street Series for children, a collection of books
that follow one family through four generations of
living along the famed highway Route 66, has
enjoyed popularity with children and adults alike.
With a number of historical novels to her credit,
Susan enjoys intermingling writing and research
travels with visits to classrooms across the country.

Love Sign
Susan Kirby

Love Inspired®

Published by Steeple Hill Books™

STEEPLE HILL BOOKS

Steeple
Hill™

2 in 1 ISBN 0-7394-1782-7

LOVE SIGN

Copyright © 2001 by Susan Kirby

Printed in U.S.A.

For in Him we live and move and have our being.

—*Acts* 17:28

To Levi
You're a patient sounding board
a storehouse of ideas
and a constant source of joy.
What more could a mother ask?

Chapter One

Shelby Taylor awoke ahead of her alarm. She slipped out of bed and onto her knees. Words were slow to come, but time spent with God quieted her hurting heart. She rose to turn off her alarm and open the drapes. The bedroom window of her third-story Lake Shore Drive apartment overlooked Lake Michigan. A kiss-me red sunrise splashed rosy hues over whitecaps, gulls and bobbing sailboats. Shelby dawdled, combing her fingers through short red-gold tangles and admiring God's artistry as if it were an ordinary Saturday and as if time were a luxury she could afford. But her calendar told a different story. She flipped the page to July, covering the unnecessary reminder of what was *not* going to happen this last weekend in June.

Shelby plugged in the coffeemaker, showered, then swung her closet door wide. White satin and lace spilled out and tickled her in the ribs. She stood clutching a damp towel, waiting for the aftershocks to subside. She should do something with the dress.

But what? Shelby retreated to the kitchen, braced herself with coffee and returned to the closet. She skimmed past the wedding gown and retrieved a streamlined skirt and silk blouse.

Patrick Delaney, a corporate attorney, had been a part of her life for three years. Shelby had come to appreciate him as a realist who knew his limitations. *Until he called off their wedding with only a week left on the clock.*

Shelby didn't plead or storm or try to bury him in guilt. An only child with busy parents who were intent on not spoiling her, she had been conditioned at any early age to hold back the little actress within. "Scenes" belonged in childhood plays and daydreams and storybooks.

It was a lesson that served her well as an editor, as a writer and even as a jilted bride. While juggling wedding cancellations and a nightmarish problem with an author who was threatening a lawsuit because she didn't like her book cover, Shelby had hugged the small consolation that someday, this week of horror would provide grist for the mill. That, God's grace and the promise of the only thing she hadn't canceled—weekend reservations at Wildwood—had kept her going.

Chosen initially as a honeymoon getaway, Wildwood was a downstate bed-and-breakfast with cozy cottages off in the pines. She prayed it would prove the perfect hideaway to the plot her new novel, which hereto was not stewing so well.

Shelby lifted her eyes to the shelf on the wall facing her computer. Her Bible was there, and five teen novels with her own name on the binding. If not for the meat-and-potato necessities of the real world, she would be writing full-time.

Shelby packed light and pulled her game face from her cosmetic bag, beginning with sunblock. Hazel eyed and fair skinned, she burned easily if she spent much time outdoors. While that hadn't been a problem in some time, her new laptop computer gave her options, sunshine among them. Feeling more composed, more focused and better equipped to cope, she donned a pair of trendy platform sandals and pearl earrings. Shelby finished her coffee standing up before stuffing projects from work into an oversize book bag. *Anesthesia, should her own fiction fail her.*

A fresh breeze whisked through Jackson Signs South. It diluted the blended odor of dust, engine grease, sweeping compound and banner ink. Jake Jackson hit the remote. The overhead chain-driven door shuddered up the track. Jake shifted the fifty-foot ladder truck into gear, then braked for his twelve-year-old niece, Joy, who blocked his way with her skinny arms outstretched.

He cranked down the window. "You trying to get run over, blondie?"

Straw-haired and freckled, Joy wrinkled her nose at the outgrown nickname. "Just checking your brakes. Is Mom around?"

Jake jerked his thumb toward the back room where his oldest sister, Paula, was bending neon. "Thought you'd be in the field."

"Mr. Wiseman never showed up. We waited an hour."

"Something must have kept him." Jake anchored

the stack of service orders on the seat beside him with a phone book. "Move it or lose it, kiddo. I have a bank job waiting."

"How about a ride home?" Joy asked.

"Okay," Jake agreed. "Update your mom first, and let's go."

Joy flung her hoe on the back of the flatbed crane truck, trotted into the neon room and was back in short order. "Can we swing by the sign first?"

"What sign?" Jake played dumb.

"*Dad's* sign."

Jake was concerned over Joy's johnny-come-lately fascination with her absentee father, Colton Blake. Fifteen years ago Colton's image had gone up on the billboard on the outskirts of Liberty Flats after Wind, Water and Sky Outdoor Gear chose him for their advertising campaign. Clad in jeans, flannel, leather boots and a distinguishing red voyager cap, the Voyager, as Colton was dubbed, had become a North American icon in the intervening years—all due to that one billboard image of him paddling a canoe along a wilderness stream.

"Satisfied?" Jake asked as they cruised past.

"Thanks," Joy said, attention riveted on the bigger-than-life portrait of the father she had never met. "Uncle Jake?" she began. "Dad has a right to know about me, don't you think?"

"It's not my call," replied Jake.

Joy flopped against the seat. "You're a big help."

Jake took her mood shift in stride. She had been underfoot since she could crawl. But then with Colton gone and her mother sharing the sign company partnership, where else would she be?

* * *

The interstate highway gave way to a fair-size city 150 miles south of Chicago. Shelby spotted a bank from the off-ramp. A lighted message board spelled out generous savings rates—the decimal point was missing.

A sign truck turned into the lot just ahead of her. It rolled to a stop and parallel parked at the curb in front of the bank. The driver cut the motor and climbed out, a lanky, wide-shouldered, long-waisted man in jeans and T-shirt, dark glasses and a baseball cap.

Shelby circled the lot once before finding a space. She searched her shoulder bag for her traveler's checks, only to remember they were in her suitcase.

The sun was hot and climbing as Shelby opened the trunk. She grabbed her suitcase, returned to the front seat to retrieve her traveler's checks from within, then locked the car, leaving the suitcase on the seat with her laptop.

The sign serviceman was up on the back of the flatbed truck raising his hydraulic ladder as Shelby approached the curb on the heels of a heavyset fellow in painter's garb. "Better buy CDs. The rates are about to take a dive," the sign man called to the painter.

"Go home, Jake, you old spoiler, you," replied the grinning painter, then held the door for Shelby.

Waiting in line, Shelby's attention strayed inward to that place where stories were born. First, a name. Something catchy for the heroine. She entertained a dozen possibilities in the time it took to cash a traveler's check and let herself out again. The ladder on the sign truck stretched to the roof of the building.

Shelby cut around the truck, off the curb and onto asphalt.

"Look out, lady! Stay back!"

Shelby pivoted to see the sign truck's hydraulic ladder swing away from the building, leaving the sign man on the roof, waving, shouting a warning. Alarmed, Shelby leapt back onto the curb and watched the unmanned ladder sweep the air twenty feet above the parking lot. All at once, the boom toppled. It came down like a limb in an ice storm and unbalanced the truck. The truck tilted, then fell over on its side. The boom crashed into Shelby's car with a stomach-turning crunch of steel and shattering glass.

When the dust settled, what lay beneath the crane more closely resembled a crumpled soda can than a car. The air fizzed out of a tire, rupturing the caught-breath silence. Shelby wheeled around, tipping her face to the sign man hunkered at the edge of the roof.

"It's never done that before," he said, peering down at the damage. "Some kind of malfunction..."

"*You* or the crane?" Shelby cut in.

"Toggle switch, I'm guessing." He shifted to his feet and planted his hands on narrow hips. His sunglasses and the brim of his cap shadowed a tanned and wary demeanor. "I'm sorry. I don't know what else to say."

It was a car, not a human being. *Or a relationship squashed like a bug.* As Shelby struggled with herself, the young man palmed his cap and dived tanned fingers through short-clipped sun-bleached chestnut waves. "I hate to ask. But could you help me down?" he ventured. "There's a rope there—fell off the deck."

"Deck?"

"Truck deck," he amended, pointing.

Shelby cast the less-than-stable-looking truck a doubtful glance. "It won't roll over on me, will it?"

"It shouldn't."

Peachy. The rope had fallen on the pavement when the truck spilled over. Shelby gripped her purse under one arm and picked up one end of the rope.

"Can you throw me one end?" Sign Man called from the roof.

Shelby gave it a go. The rope uncurled like a striking snake. It climbed half a story, then dropped and nipped her on the noggin. Her second effort was better, but unsuccessful. She put her shoulder bag down on the curb.

A pickup truck pulled into the parking lot. The man inside assessed the situation and climbed out. "Anyone hurt?" he asked.

"Just my car," said Shelby ruefully.

"Here, let me," he said, and took the rope.

Relieved, Shelby backed out of the way and dusted her hands.

The man coiled the rope a few times and tossed it skyward. Sign Man caught it and anchored his end. The muscles in his arms bunched as he eased himself down the rope and to the ground.

He was thirtyish, clean-shaven with strong shoulders and tall enough so that Shelby had to look up. The sunglasses still screened his eyes. He pressed his lips together, and dimples emerged then went into hiding again as he shifted his attention to the man who had come to their aid. With tanned and capable hands, he slipped the sunglasses from his face and into his T-shirt pocket as he thanked the Good Samaritan.

"The hydraulic lever stuck. I figured the crane

would circle around and come back to me," he explained. "I didn't think about it jerking the truck over."

"Did you set your outriggers?" asked the other man.

"Just on the driver's side. I know better. I got distracted and broke my own rules." Sign Man's glance shifted to Shelby. His eyes, a striking blue, enhanced prominent cheeks. His jaw sloped to a nicely carved chin that jutted slightly as he asked, "Are you in a hurry to get someplace?"

"No. Not now," replied Shelby.

"I'll call one of my men and get this truck upright," he said. "Then I'll see what we can do about getting you wherever you're headed."

"Wildwood," she said.

"Vacationing?" he asked.

Shelby nodded, and glanced at the Good Samaritan who was walking away. Sign Man noticed, and called after him, "Thanks, man."

The man waved and drove away in his pickup truck.

It wasn't long until a second sign truck pulled into the lot in answer to Sign Man's phone call. With the help of the crane, the truck was soon upright and the boom off Shelby's car.

Sign Man retrieved Shelby's purse from the curb on his way by. "Here you go," he said. Faint creases tugged at the corners of his morning glory eyes. "I'm Jake Jackson."

"Shelby Taylor," she returned.

Jake started to offer his hand, then checked the impulse. He turned up a grease-smudged palm and asked, "So how upset are you?"

"I'm sorry I snapped at you." Lamely, Shelby offered, "It happened so fast."

"Kind of caught me off guard, too." He spared her further apology and glanced back at her car. "I'll call my insurance company, see if they can get you something to drive," he offered.

Jake called on his cell phone and returned with word that his insurer would send an adjuster out. "He'll see about a loaner car once he has taken some pictures and squared away the paperwork. Like I said, I'd be happy to give you a lift if you don't want to wait on him."

At a loss as to how else she was to reach the cabin at Wildwood, Shelby accepted.

"Need anything from the car?" he asked.

"My laptop and suitcase from the front seat. Grab my cell phone, too, would you? Oh! And my book bag, please. It's in the trunk," she said, and gave him her car keys.

Jake jerked a thumb in the direction of the bank lobby. "May as well wait inside where it's cool," he said.

Thoughtful, as saboteurs went, noted Shelby as she retreated to the lobby. He wasn't long. Her suitcase swung from one hand, her laptop from the other. He retrieved her cell phone from his shirt pocket. Their fingers brushed as it changed hands.

"Can you get along without the book bag? I didn't have any luck popping the trunk lid," he said.

Reluctant to leave unpublished works behind, Shelby wondered aloud, "Could we pry it open?"

"I thought of that. But the adjuster may want to snap his pictures before we tear into it," he said.

Conceding his point, Shelby followed him to his

truck. He checked the oil, then wiped his hands on a towel that lay in the seat. Except for some scraped paint and a broken side view mirror, the truck appeared sound. The engine coughed a time or two en route to the sign shop. But they covered the short distance without incident.

Shelby's gaze swept twin steel buildings, a hodgepodge of equipment emblazoned with the Jackson name, and a graveyard of old signs.

"It's a family business," Jake explained. "We have a shop south of here at Liberty Flats. Wildwood's just a few miles farther on. Hope I haven't fouled up your vacation too badly."

"It's a working one, anyway." Shelby accepted his help out of the truck. He had a steady hand. Durable fingers, a callused palm and a measured grip. She turned to collect her things.

"Let me." Jake reached for her suitcase and laptop.

Shelby followed him to a sporty four-wheel drive vehicle and stowed her things behind the seat while she climbed in.

"There's a bookstore nearby. You want to pick up something to read?" he asked as they got underway.

Realizing he had misunderstood about the book bag, she said, "Thanks, but it isn't leisure reading. The bag contains manuscripts."

"You're a writer?" Jake winced as she conceded as much. "Can't say I'd want to leave *my* life's work in the trunk of a wrecked car."

"It isn't mine." Seeing his confusion, Shelby explained, "I work full-time for Parnell Publishing, and write part-time. What will they do with the car?"

"Have it towed, I suppose. I'll phone the insurance company again and explain about the manuscripts. They could take it to my shop. It'd be easier for you to access than at a salvage yard.''

Jake made the call while waiting for a light to change. Traffic flowed once more. He resumed their conversation. ''What is it you do at Parnell?''

''I'm an editor.''

''Really! Can't say I've ever met an editor.'' Jake threaded his way along busy streets. ''What kind of books does your company publish?''

''We do a variety of nonfiction titles—self-help, how-tos, food and cooking titles, home and family, travel and guidebooks. That sort of thing,'' said Shelby.

''And your part-time writing—is that for Parnell?''

''No. I write romance mysteries for young adults.''

''Is that right?'' His smile deepened, his eyes reflecting a sunny twinkle. ''Thomasina's a real fan of romance novels. Out at Wildwood,'' he added. ''She and her husband Trace have transformed that old farm into a real cozy vacation retreat.''

''I've heard nothing but good things about their business,'' said Shelby as Jake took the interstate south out of town. ''I look forward to meeting them.''

''You'll have to stick around a couple of weeks, then. They left for the southwest two days ago for their third wedding anniversary.

''Oh.''

''How about you? Are you married?'' he asked with a glance from those vivid blue eyes.

''No.''

''Seeing someone?''

"No." The word to Shelby's own ears, clanged like a metal gate. She twisted the strap of her pocket book, and fell silent.

They passed the next dozen miles in silence. Jake flipped the air off as they exited the interstate, trucked past the Voyager billboard, and rolled down the window as they skirted Liberty Flats.

"Too much wind? I can roll it up," offered Jake, as the breeze riffled Shelby's short curls.

"No, don't. It's fine," she said and lowered her window, too.

Jake stole a sidelong glance, admiring the wind in her hair and sunlight dancing on flawless skin. But he couldn't remember when he had seen such a soft round face look so long and weary. His carelessness had complicated her vacation plans, big time, that went without saying. He thought about apologizing again. But then, what good did that do? They hurtled along the country road a few miles, then Jake slowed for Wildwood Lane.

Shelby draped her arm out the window, letting the air blow through her fingers. In the air there was a fragrance of green growing things and of sun-warmed earth. She breathed deeply, filling her lungs with clean country air, willing the stone to roll off her heart. Time, that's what she needed. Anonymity in which to lick her wounds until she had ceased to flinch at words like *marriage* and *anniversary*.

The lane ended in front of a two-story farmhouse. The house, freshly painted, gleamed like a pearl amidst blooming gardens and barn-red outbuildings. Reprieve was so close, she could almost taste it.

"Go on and get squared away. I'll bring your things," Jake offered.

The path to the front office was bordered by a bright tangle of nodding flowers. Inside, flowerpots filled the office windowsills. Trailing plants spilled from the pots onto a battered drop-leaf table. There was a coffee urn and cups and glasses and iced lemonade beading a carnival glass pitcher. Shelby pushed the bell. Chimes rang through the house. She helped herself to a glass of lemonade. A young woman came in response to the bell. "May I help you?" she asked, her hoop earrings jangling.

"Yes, I have reservations." Shelby gave her her name.

The woman sat down at the computer and hit a few keys. When she lifted her yes again, her smile had faded. "I'm sorry. But I don't seem to have any record of it," she said.

Shelby set down the half-drained glass of lemonade to retrieve the confirmation number from her checkbook register where she had written it on the day she and Patrick finalized their honeymoon plans.

The young woman typed in the number. Frown lines creased her forehead. "You're marked out."

Startled, Shelby protested, "There must be some mistake."

"Forgive me, you're right, it wasn't you." The young woman turned from the screen to a lined tablet. "It was a man who called to cancel. I wrote it here somewhere." She ran a finger down to the middle of the page and looked up again. "Patrick Delaney."

The name washed over Shelby in a bone-skinning tide. Tears threatened. She batted them back, struggling to make mental adjustments. "If the cottage has been rented, a room will do."

"I'm sorry, but we're booked here at the house, too."

Jake was a dozen steps from the house when the front door spit Shelby out onto the garden path. Her cream-colored silk blouse and a fitted skirt molded nicely to feminine curves.

She was almost upon him before she saw him and skidded to a stop. Clouds darkened her eyes. She pressed her full lips together. A pulse hammered at her smooth, white temples.

"There's been a mix-up. I hate to ask, but could I please have a ride back to town?" she said, and reached for her laptop.

Her effort to keep it together as the morning went from bad to worse put a commiserating knot in Jake's gut. But her guarded facade warned him against a barrage of questions. He passed her the laptop. Fumbling to take the suitcase, too, she shifted her pocketbook and reached for the suitcase handle.

"Go on, I'll bring it," said Jake quickly.

She nodded and turned toward the drive. Jake watched the hem of her skirt trail over tall flowers that sweetened the path. She crossed crushed rock, climbed into the Jeep and settled there, hugging her laptop. Jake rubbed an uncomfortable sensation in his chest, then set her suitcase down and went inside.

"'Morning, Annie."

Antoinette Penn smiled a welcome from behind the desk. "Hello, Jake. If you're looking for Trace, he's not here."

"I'd heard they'd taken off," he said and took off his cap. "What happened with Shelby Taylor's reservations?"

"A guy called this morning and canceled the reservations," explained Antoinette.

"But if *she* made the reservations..." began Jake.

"For all I know, they made them together," Antoinette interjected. "Honeymoons are usually planned that way."

Startled, Jake blurted, "Honeymoon? She's getting married?"

"Not anymore. He called it off. That's the reason he gave for canceling."

Shelby's fragile state fell in place like a key fitting tumblers. "So what's she doing here?" he asked.

"I don't know, Jake. All I know is the honeymoon cottage is taken."

Jake swung around and looked out the window. Shelby's slim arms were still wrapped around her laptop. He had done all he could. And yet...Jake shifted his feet. "How about a room here in the house?"

"Sorry. It's like I told her, we're booked."

"What about Trace and Thomasina's room? They won't be needing it," he reasoned.

"It's full of their stuff!"

"Under the circumstances, she may not mind."

"I wasn't talking about *her*." Antoinette drew herself up. "What're you trying to do—get me fired?"

"Oh, come on," Jake cajoled. "What's the point in being in charge if you can't make an executive decision?"

"Save your breath, Jake. I am *not* booking Trace and Thomasina's bedroom. And you can quit looking at me like that, it's not my fault," huffed Antoinette.

"She's shell-shocked," Jake said. "Jilted, canceled and I dropped the crane on her car."

"You what?"

"Never mind. Guess I better drive her back to town."

"I wish you would," said Antoinette, rubbing her temples. "She's making my head throb."

"Mine, too," Jake said. Though on closer accounting, it was more of a burn than a throb and it wasn't confined to his head. He rubbed his chest again, reached into his pocket for an antacid tablet and left Antoinette muttering.

Chapter Two

Jake was gone so long, Shelby grew restless. She climbed out of the Jeep and was almost to the farmhouse screen door when she overheard his parting exchange with the desk clerk. He swung out onto the path before she could patch her expression.

Jake blinked finding her there and tipped his cap back, a gesture Shelby was beginning to recognize as habitual.

"No vacancies," she filled the sudden caught-breath silence.

"Antoinette told me. I said I'd get that," he said and reached for her suitcase on the walk where he had left it.

"I had a thought while I was waiting...perhaps a room in Liberty Flats," said Shelby, following him toward the Jeep.

"There's no motel. It's a pretty small town," he said.

Shelby raked her fingers through her curls. Anxious to find herself a place before he began to regard her as a pup he had orphaned and could not leave to fend for herself, she asked, "What about Bloomington?"

"Sure. There are plenty of rooms there if that's what you want to do," he said, and opened the Jeep door for her.

Shelby plucked her laptop off the seat and slid in. Jake circled to the driver's side and put her suitcase behind the seat. He would have stowed her laptop there, too, except she had her arms around it again. "Wherever you want to go. Just name it," he said, as he climbed behind the wheel.

"Somewhere quiet where I can work. Speaking of which, I'm keeping you from yours," she said.

"I was due for a morning off."

"Not like this," said Shelby.

"We've had a nice ride so far," said Jake.

"Thanks," she said with a wan smile.

"For what?"

"Being such a gentleman."

Her attitude caught Jake off guard. Feeling all the more responsible for her predicament, he said, "There's plenty of room at my grandmother's house. You'd be welcome to stay."

"Oh, no. I couldn't impose," she said hastily.

"You wouldn't be. Gram Kate likes having company."

"That's kind. But it's too much to ask."

"You didn't ask. I offered." Hoping she would accept and relieve his conscience, Jake stopped at the crossroads just shy of Liberty Flats. His turn was dependent upon her decision. "Would you like to have a look before you make up your mind?"

Shelby's head was pounding. She anchored the

laptop between her feet on the floor and reached into her shoulder bag. "Here," she said, and uncapped a bottle of aspirin.

"What's this?"

"For your headache. Mine's splitting, too."

Chagrined Jake rubbed the back of his neck. "You have good ears," he said finally.

"So I've heard." Shelby shook two tablets into her palm and offered them, saying, "My treat."

She was a treat, dressed all in cream. All that kept Jake from telling her so was the pain in her doe-soft hazel eyes and a mouth that was too grave. That quick, she got to him. *An almost-could-have-been-should-have-been-married woman.* He thanked God she wasn't, and gestured, saying, "You first."

Shelby tossed the tablets back. They burned all the way down. She coughed and rubbed her eyes. Jake pushed a box of tissues her way. Hoping for the chance to know her better, he made the turn into Liberty Flats. "I'll get you something to wash it down with."

The shady streets spanned a time line of American housing, from Victorian to cheerful bungalows to ranch-style homes to imposing Cape Cods on manicured lawns. At the center of town, Jake circled the village green. It enfolded a bandstand, picnic tables, a memorial stone honoring war dead and a flag pole. Old Glory rippled in the breeze, a twin to the flag jutting from the brick front of Newt's Market across the way. The remainder of the business district consisted of boarded-up buildings, a few of which leaned like stacked stove wood.

Jake turned the Jeep up the alley and parked in the driveway of his timber-framed shop. Shelby spotted the sign company logo above the overhead door. The Jackson name was also lettered on the side of the building. "You live here, too?" she asked.

"I have lately. Gram's memory isn't what it used to be," said Jake. "My sisters have families to look after. All but the youngest, and she just got married. I was the logical choice. Come on, and I'll get you that drink."

His amiable smile tweezed the thorn that had cropped up at Shelby's realization the house he referred to as his grandmother's was his home, too. She climbed out and paused for a closer look at the house. It was a two-story arts-and-craft home with clean lines and deep verandas. The slate roof sloped away from a catwalk enclosed by a wrought iron railing.

Jake knocked the dust off his feet on the back veranda and waited for her to catch up. The back door opened into a eclectic kitchen that spanned a generation. *Good bones, nice texture.* In her head Shelby heard her mother accentuating the positive.

"Tea? Juice? Soda?" Jake offered, his footsteps ringing over vintage pine flooring.

"Water's fine." Shelby dropped her head back, admiring a high ceiling sectioned by hand-hewn oak beams. The room was long and wide and graced with deep windows. Fresh flowers adorned a table big enough for all the king's horses and men. Handicrafts decorated the walls—a framed wood-burned copy of the Lord's Prayer, a plaque inscribed Friends Are Special People. The napkin holder had rust spots, and child-size fingerprints glazed the cookie jar.

Jake drew her a glass of water, waited as she drained it and returned the empty glass to the sink.

"It's a restful house. Don't think I'm not tempted to accept your hospitality," Shelby began. Then Jake's beeper cut in. She gestured, saying, "Go ahead. Don't let me keep you."

Jake excused himself to make a phone call.

After the chaos of the morning, the quiet house was to Shelby what oil was to chafed skin. Her eye skipped from child-crafted refrigerator art to toast crumbs on the counter to the yellow energy efficiency rating sticker, the grease-splattered corners of which curled from the surface of a new stove. *Ordinary folk, cutting corners rushing through ordinary days.* It wasn't like her to impose on the kindness of strangers. But then again, she hadn't exactly been herself lately.

"Shall I bring in your things, or do you want a ride back to town?" asked Jake, returning.

"Are you sure I won't be in the way?" Shelby asked.

"I'm sure," he said.

"I can see you're a busy man. I won't be a pest," she promised.

Jake smiled and excused himself and returned moments later with her belongings. "This way."

Shelby let go the last vestiges of convention and trekked after him through the kitchen and dining room. Their footsteps fell to a whisper on the rose carpet that spanned the staircase. The woodwork was dark, the walls embossed, the decor turn-of-the-century elegant, though with a nice splash of modern graces.

The guest room at the top of the landing was spacious and homey with quilts and lace curtains and woven rugs. Shelby circled the room, absorbing it with an appreciative glance that didn't escape Jake. "My mother would love this. She works with Harbor House, restoring old houses for low-income families," she said.

"And your father?"

"He is a plastic surgeon."

"I'll bet even he couldn't put a pretty face on this day," said Jake in open sympathy.

"I should have seen it coming," she murmured, then flushed at his confusion. "Oh! You mean the car."

He nodded. "What'd you think?"

Patrick. She thought he meant Patrick. Embarrassed, Shelby averted her face.

"Can I get you anything?" asked Jake.

"I'm fine, thanks," she said, gripping her pocketbook.

"Okay. I need to be going. But if you need anything, my sister Paula is out back in the shop," Jake told her.

"I'll be fine," she said. "Thank you, Mr. Jackson."

"Glad to help," he said, and stopped in the door to look back. "And make that Jake."

"Jake," Shelby amended, meeting his gaze. His smiling eyes begged descriptive notation: *Pale tropical waters splashing at sun-browned banks.*

No wastrel of words, Shelby filed the line away for literary use. She rubbed her throbbing temples, slipped out of her platform sandals and stretched out on the bed. It was plush and cozy and comforting. But she couldn't relax. She hadn't in days. Locking her hands behind her head, she invited a story line to wander in and make order of her muddled thoughts. But before she could conjure up any story characters a slim, attractive, auburn-haired woman in a cotton shirt and jeans knocked at the open door.

"You must be Shelby. Don't get up. Just popped in to say hi." A smiled warmed her face. "There's ham and fruit in the refrigerator. Help yourself when you get hungry."

"That's kind of you, thank you, but I'll get something out."

"There is no 'out.' Except Newt's Market, and you'll soon tire of that. I'm Paula Blake, by the way. Jake's sister."

"He mentioned you," Shelby said. She introduced herself.

"Jake says you write and edit and all sorts of interesting things," Paula continued amiably. "Excuse me while I get that."

Shelby swung her feet off the bed and into her shoes as Paula crossed to the nightstand and the ringing phone.

"I'm sure there's a perfectly logical explanation, Joy," Paula said. "Give Mr. Wiseman a break, would you? No, Dirk can't come over. I'll see you at four. I love you. Bye-bye."

"My daughter," Paula explained, hanging up the phone. "She's doing some field work over her summer vacation. Or supposed to be. Her boss didn't pick her up this morning. His van is gone. She can't reach him on the phone, now she's conjuring wild scenarios. He's sick. He's lost. He's fallen and can't get up," Paula ticked Joy fancies off on her fingers and rolled eyes as blue as Jake's. "Kids! Now be sure and eat something," she continued without stopping for breath, and backed out of the door, still talking.

The silence in Paula's wake was nagging. Shelby found her way to the bathroom, tidied up and went downstairs. She made a sandwich, washed it down with a soda, then returned to her room and set up her laptop. Once upon a time...she told herself, fingers poised and waiting. The anticipated lights did not flash. No icons. No whirring. Just a black screen.

"Come on, come on," murmured Shelby. "Give me a break. Please?" she muttered. But the screen remained dark and cold. At length, Shelby gave up. She fished pad and pen and dime-store reading glasses from her shoulder bag, took a seat and tried to recall the idea she had had before Patrick pushed the lead domino and brought her well-ordered future tumbling down around her. But her thought screen was as blank as her computer screen.

Shelby grumbled and wandered to the window and hiked it. She tapped folded glasses against the frame. Voilà! As if by design, a girl rode into the alley below, then flung her bicycle down. A skinny, sunburned, straw-haired preteen in cutoff jeans, she pinched off hollyhocks greens with bright-tipped fingernails and left a shredded trail of leaves into Jake's shop. Moments later, she reappeared with Paula at her heels. Paula turned the girl toward a vegetable patch and gave her a nudge.

"But Mom! I don't even like vegetables." The girl's voice carried through the open window. "Yikes! A bee! I think I'm allergic! Well, I *could* be. M-o-o-o-m!" she wailed, hands on skinny hips. "Oh, all right! How much are you paying me?"

"A nickel a weed," Paula said.

"A nickel? Is that all?"

"Make it a penny," Paula returned.

"Mom!"

"Keep whining, Joy, and you'll be weeding for free." Paula retreated into the shop.

Shelby pressed her nose to the window screen and watched Joy flounce over the garden. She plucked a weed here, a weed there, all hop-and-stop energy with no logical system. It was hard to picture a girl like that willingly weeding fields that ran on for acres and acres.

So what made Joy tick? What movements turned behind those eyes and turned-up nose and sullen brow? Shelby played what-if until a distant rumbling broke her concentration. Cool air rose from a vent on the floor below the window. Air-conditioning.

Shelby closed the window, took the chair again and balanced the pad on her knee. An opening sentence trickled across the page to be joined by more words, inserted here and there until it became a nice fat paragraph. She reached for her glasses.

Cranes, crushed cars, trapped book bags and blue-eyed men retreated as a Joy-like girl in frayed shorts and peeling freckles appeared on the lined yellow tablet. A Patrick-like guy took shape beside her. The resemblance startled Shelby from fiction to reality. She hadn't deliberately chosen him for inspiration. It was automatic. Finger memory, like a pianist's hands finding the right keys when the pages to a familiar song fluttered shut.

Shelby marked out the Patrick clone and reeled through male acquaintances, seeking hero inspiration elsewhere. None seemed to fit. Again, the Patrick-like character beckoned. Stubbornly resisting, she stirred from her chair and paced to the window. Sunshine glittered off the nearby building, lighting the lettering on the side of the building: Jackson Signs South.

Jake Jackson. He had been kind. Helpful. Patient. A gentleman. The heroics of everyday life. And he had those arresting eyes. Here, here! Her heart might be curled into the fetal position, but she still had her story world. A world with a voracious appetite, it fed indiscriminately on new situations, new people, fresh material to keep her upright and writing. That was the upside of this unsettling, upside down day. "This is the day the Lord has made."

The snippet of verse ran through Shelby's head. Not the day she had expected or long anticipated, rather a day marked by adversity. Yet in God's hands, even shrapnel was a windfall, a deposit, a hedge against creative bankruptcy.

Shelby added Jake to her characters cast. She reshaped him into a seventeen-year-old in studious dark-rimmed glasses with a knack for mystery solving and a love for dirt-track racing.

A leggy raven-haired beauty barged onto the page. Tara. Before Shelby's delighted eyes, Tara challenged her Joy-like character for the hero's heart. Sparks flew better in triangles. No sparks. No conflict. No story. Not a problem today. The words flowed, the headache fled.

Thank you, Lord. Thank you. You always know just what I need.

Chapter Three

It had been a while since Jake had met a woman who interested him enough to make the day stretch long. He played catch-up all afternoon and fell several jobs short of completing his service calls. By the time he returned to the Bloomington shop, his crew had left for the day.

Two brothers-in-law worked with him in the erecting and servicing of signs. A third oversaw the computerized banners in the Liberty Flats shop while Paula shaped neon for custom-made signs. It was a skill both she and Jake had learned from their father, John Jackson.

A two-car automobile accident had claimed Jake's parents' lives when Jake was nineteen. Colton, Paula's husband of just a few weeks, had been at the wheel of the second car, and had escaped with minor injuries. With his parents gone, and Paula's marriage on the rocks as quickly as it had come together, it was only by the grace of God that Gram Kate had kept the family together, and the sign company, too.

Now, a dozen years later, Jackson Signs was thriving.

Recently Paula had transferred all their records onto computer. She had taken some classes and was at ease with the new system. Jake wasn't. But he did appreciate the options gained by linking the sign shops and their home offices. Now, he could go home and relax a while before entering the day's business.

Jake locked up the shop, stopped for chicken and the fixings, then took the highway south. Once home, he put supper in the oven on low, set the table and climbed the stairs. The second-story landing circled past the guest room. Shelby's door was closed. Jake grabbed clean clothes and closed himself into the upstairs bathroom to shower and change.

The whistled rendition of a catchy advertising jingle penetrated Shelby's subconscious. By and by, the hum of an electric razor muted the cheery tune. Shelby sank back into to her story only to emerge again when the whistling ceased. The razor was quiet, too. Focus broken, she rose on cramped limbs and crossed to the door.

Jake was at the top of the stairs. A short-sleeved navy-blue shirt hugged the contours of muscles that flexed as he tucked his shirttail into his jeans. The denim, faded and softened by wash and wear, suited the lean, fit lines of his body as he turned and surprised her watching him from the open door.

"I heard you whistling."

"Was I?" He smiled. "Hope I didn't disturb you."

"Not at all," Shelby said.

His dimples deepened. There was a sheen to his clean-shaven jaw that caught the light. His hair was damp from the shower and bore the tracks of a comb. "Are you ready for dinner?" he asked.

"If you'll let me help," she offered.

"No need, it's on the table."

"Next time, call me and I'll help," said Shelby, flushing. "I guess I should have warned you—when I'm writing, everything fades away. Time. Good intentions, everything."

"It'll stand you in good stead in this house," Jake replied. "Family tracking in and out at all hours. It can turn into a regular zoo if you don't hold your mouth just right."

Shelby noted his was nicely held. His eyes, too. The dark shirt heightened their striking hue. The observation was part of her craft, a writing thing, as natural as breathing. She smelled soap, and something else, too. Something tantalizing. *Or was that dinner?* Since the breakup, Shelby had almost forgotten what hunger felt like. Her stomach gave a sharp reminder. "I'll be right down." Quickly, she retreated to tidy up after herself.

Jake waited for her, watching from the open door as she gathered the paper wads strewn about her chair. In contrast to those carelessly scattered papers was the precision with which she aligned her notebook, pen and reading glasses on the dresser.

"You write in long hand?" Jake asked as she snapped off the reading lamp.

"Not as a rule. But my laptop is on the fritz."

"Not another crane casualty," he said and clucked his tongue.

"There's not a scratch on it," replied Shelby. "It

may just be a glitch. I'm not much good at trouble-shooting.''

"I'll take a look if you like," he offered.

"Would you mind? I'd really appreciate it," Shelby said.

"After dinner, then. I hope you like chicken," he added.

"I do," she returned, closing the door behind her. "But you shouldn't have gone to so much trouble."

"I didn't. It's carryout. Except for the tomatoes."

"I noticed the garden from the window," Shelby told him.

"Green-thumb therapy," Jake said. He held up his thumb and motioned for her to precede him down the stairs. "What about you? Do you garden?"

"I live in a third-floor apartment. But I planted blue lobelia and vincas in a window box this year."

"Flowers, right?" he asked, and followed her down, momentarily distracted by the muted flame of red-gold curls against her slim white neck. He caught himself wondering if her skin was as soft to touch as it was to the eyes, and admitted, "Mostly what I know about flowers is that mowing them down gets you in trouble."

Flowers. They had been Patrick's passion. Shelby caught herself one foot down memory lane. She took her mind by the edges, gave it a shake and followed Jake into the kitchen where he introduced her to his grandmother, Kate Grisham.

Kate had hair like spun wool and a round face, powdered and wrinkled. Her lips were painted outside the lines. They tilted as she greeted Shelby, saying, "How lovely to meet you."

"Shelby works with books," Jake told her.

"You're Jake's bookkeeper!" Gram Kate set a pitcher of tea on the table and came to Shelby with hands outstretched.

"She doesn't work for me, Gram. We met at the bank." Jake went on to explain about the accident.

"Thank goodness you weren't hurt," Gram said, slow to release Shelby's hands. "Jake, dear you must be more careful! Why, I hate to think what might have happened if that... Joy needs... Next time you mustn't..."

The flow of Gram's words stopped. She peered more closely at Shelby, dismissed her lost train of thought and patted her hair.

"Ready to eat, Gram?" Jake asked gently, and seated her. Declining Shelby's help in transferring food from the oven to the table, he seated her, too, and when the food was in place, took his own chair.

Shelby spread her napkin over her lap. Gram Kate reached for her hand. "Would you ask the blessing for us, dear?" she asked, and patted Shelby's fingers.

Shelby tucked her chin. "Heavenly Father..."

"Dear God," rumbled Jake.

They both stopped and looked up.

"Don't tease your sister. Take her hand, now Jake, and say grace before the ice me—me-malts," said Gram Kate, her tone sweetly chiding.

It was no hardship for Jake. He took Shelby's hand, and thought it a nice perk to accompany the dinner blessing.

Jake's callused palm imprinted itself upon Shelby's skin and her thoughts, too. This was to be her wedding dinner. *Her wedding night.* And here she sat with a sweet dotty old saint who thought she was family and a stranger with a foreign touch.

Jake began passing dishes her way, giving her
hands something useful to do and her thoughts a safe
place to light. The chicken was moist and tender, the
potatoes delicious and the sliced tomatoes, wonderful.

"Did you remember crochet thread, Wendy?"
asked Gram Kate, looking at Shelby.

Shelby paused, fork in hand and lifted her eyes to
Jake.

He smiled reassuringly and said, "I'll put it on the
list, Gram."

"Thank you, dear. Have another biscuit. It's my
special reci— Tea. More tea? You must have another
piece of chicken, you're a growing boy."

Gram Kate passed everything Jake's way. He set
the tea pitcher and the serving dishes to the center
of the table, but she kept returning them to him. At
length, he transferred the dishes to the counter.

"I'll wash," offered Shelby, coming to her feet.

"No need. I'll put them in the dishwasher later
after we've had coffee," Jake replied and waved her
down again.

Shelby was nursing a second cup when Paula and
Joy let themselves in the back door. Paula was carrying a chocolate cake. Joy bumped Jake's chair and
held out her hand.

"You owe me for fifty-seven weeds, Uncle Jake."

"She has been paid. Don't even think about it,"
Paula warned, as Jake reached for his wallet.

"Fifty-seven cents. You call that pay?" complained Joy.

Jake fished a five from his wallet.

"I mean it, Jake," Paula asserted.

"It isn't for weeding, it's a consulting fee. This is

Shelby Taylor. Shelby, my niece, Joy and my sister, Paula.''

Paula exchanged smiles with Shelby. "We met earlier.''

"I heard Uncle Jake wrecked your car,'' Joy said, a lively interest in eyes a shade darker than Jake's.

"Her laptop was in the front seat. Seems to have suffered some injuries. It's upstairs in the guest room,'' Jake said. "Take a look, would you?''

"I'll go with you.'' Shelby thanked Jake for the meal, excused herself, and followed Joy up the stairs.

Jake loaded the dishwasher, left Gram in Paula's capable hands, and joined them there.

"Any luck?'' he asked.

"Not yet,'' Joy replied. She poked keys in a free-wheeling frenzy.

Shelby stood by looking on, lip caught, expression apprehensive.

"Relax,'' soothed Jake. "Blondie's a regular computer chip.''

"Not tonight, Uncle Jake. I can't get this thing to chirp.'' Joy glanced at Shelby, "Sorry, Miss Taylor.''

"Please call me Shelby,'' said Shelby. "I appreciate your efforts.''

"Me, too,'' chimed Jake. "Thanks, sport.''

"It sure pays better than weeding your garden.'' Joy tugged the wrinkled five-dollar bill from her pocket and gave it a snap.

"Any word from Mr. Wiseman?'' Jake asked.

"Not yet. We drove by his house on the way over. His van is there, but no one answers the door.''

"Joy got a job cutting weeds out of soybean fields. But her boss seems to be lost,'' Jake explained.

"He owes us for sixty hours," Joy said. "Dirk's steamed."

"Who's Dirk?" asked Shelby.

"One of the guys on the crew. He's betting we've seen the last of Mr. Wiseman. Gave me a funny feeling right here," admitted Joy, hand on her midriff.

"You sure it isn't chocolate cake weighing you down?" teased Jake.

Joy twisted in her chair and tilted her chin toward Jake. "Did you try it?"

"Not yet."

"Chocolate's your favorite, right?" she asked.

"Second only to lemon chiffon," he claimed.

"Last time I baked cherry chip, and you said it was your favorite second only to chocolate," Joy reminded him.

"That so?" Jake grinned and said, "How about you, Shelby? You ready for dessert?"

"Maybe later. I'd like to work a while."

"I have a computer downstairs. You're welcome to use it," Jake offered, seeing Shelby reach for her tablet.

"You wouldn't mind?"

"Not at all," Jake answered. "I'm not up to speed on it, yet. But if you have any questions, Joy can help you out."

"Sure. Come on. I'll get you started," agreed Joy.

The word processing program was strikingly similar to Shelby's. With Joy's help, she soon had the basics down well enough to work.

"Keep it, Uncle Jake already paid me," Joy reminded, when Shelby tried to pay her for showing her the ropes.

"I want you to have it," Shelby insisted. "Please? It'll free me to ask again, should I need more help."

"All right then." She thanked Shelby, tucked the money into her pocket, and ventured in the same breath, "Winny Penn's mom says you were supposed to get married this weekend. So did you change your mind or what?"

Chapter Four

Jake walked through the garden, then moved the lawn sprinkler close enough to give the tomato plants a good drink. He glanced toward his lighted office window and returned to the porch to take off his damp boots. Paula joined him on the steps.

"Gram's tucked in," she offered. "Her eyes were closed almost before her head hit the pillow. What's this about your houseguest getting left at the altar?"

"Who told you *that?*" Jake asked, sitting straighter.

"Antoinette. I saw her at the store, and mentioned that you and Gram had a guest. It put her mind at ease to hear it. She felt terrible over having to turn Shelby away." Paula slid him a glance and ventured, "How's she holding up, anyway?"

"Couldn't say," he replied evenly.

Paula's gaze lingered, but she let the subject drop.

Dusk fell over the yard in deepening shades of purple. The shadows brought to Jake's mind the bruise of broken promises that lingered in Shelby's eyes. She was having a hard time of it, yet she didn't complain. There was nothing of the pathetic about her. He liked that. Liked her manner, too, how she had taken Gram's mental lapses into stride without comment.

Paula spoke up, asking about Joy's employer, Mr. Wiseman. "What do you suppose happened to him, anyway?"

"He'll turn up," Jake said.

"It is peculiar, though. And speaking of peculiar, what's this about you driving Joy to the edge of town to check out Colton's face-lift?"

"You mean the sign? That wasn't *my* idea," Jake answered.

"I guessed as much." Paula sighed. "She asks about him all the time lately. She can't understand why I never told him about her. She badgered me until I finally told her that as far as I'm concerned, Colt wouldn't be in the dark about her if he had stayed home where he belonged. It's the truth," she added.

Part of it, anyway. Calling the rest to mind served no purpose. Jake asked, "What'd she say?"

"'Get over it, Mom.'"

"She's just testing the stretch in your apron strings," Jake said. "You're doing just fine. Blondie's a good kid."

"By the grace of God and a lot of help from you." Paula patted his knee and came to her feet.

"Where you going?" asked Jake.

"Home. Joy's a bear to get up if she isn't in bed by ten."

"I'll get her for you," Jake offered.

"Thanks, Jake. I'll see you at church tomorrow." Paula crossed the yard to her car.

Jake dropped his boots inside the door and trekked through the house in his sock feet. The door to his office was open, the desk in full view. Joy and Shelby were side by side at his desk, facing the door. The computer monitor partially hid their faces.

"So how come he walked out on you?" he overheard Joy ask Shelby.

"He had his reasons," replied Shelby.

"Good ones?" pressed Joy.

"I suppose they were to him." Shelby glanced away from the computer screen and saw Jake. Dusky eyelids fell behind the lenses of her reading glasses. Color swept up her pale cheeks.

Jake's gut clenched at the humiliation in her swiftly averted gaze. "Your mom's waiting in the car," he said to Joy.

"But I'm showing Shelby how to..."

He cut her short. "I'll show her."

"Retrieve from the trash? You don't even know yourself, I'll bet," replied Joy, tipping her chin.

"Go home," he said.

"I was *trying* to help," she huffed.

"Some help," Jake muttered as Joy passed him in the door.

Joy made a face at him. He crossed to the desk, wondering whether to apologize to Shelby on Joy's behalf or pretend he hadn't overheard. He was opting for pretense when Joy called to him from the open door.

He pivoted to see her hand over the light switch.

"Nighty-night," she said as the room went dark.

"Turn it on, Joy," ordered Jake.

She snickered instead and closed the door behind her.

"Sorry, I don't know what gets into her," apologized Jake, though under the circumstances, darkness wasn't all that unwelcome.

"I gather she heard things," Shelby said.

"Not from me," he said quickly. "There's a remote switch. Reach into the desk drawer."

"Which drawer?"

"Top," Jake replied, though he could have as easily crossed to the switch. The drawer squeaked as she opened it. He heard pencils rub pencils, the metallic sift of paper clips and other desk drawer contents shift beneath Shelby's unseen fingers. The darkness amplified the cat-paw soft sounds of her search. That, and the silence to which Joy's cheeky question clung like a fly caught on a glue strip. No use ignoring it.

"I'll tell Paula to talk to her," he began.

"Please don't," Shelby interjected. "You've done enough."

Jake twitched, certain she believed him the source of the *things* that had piqued Joy's curiosity.

He circled the desk. "Slide back. I can put my hand right on it." In the absence of light, he misjudged her position. His hand skimmed her curls in a chance touch that tickled his palm and his fancy, too. "Sorry."

"My fault," Shelby murmured and rolled the desk chair away from the desk, giving him more room.

The darkness heightened her flower-sweet fragrance. Feeling enveloped by it, Jake's hand closed over the remote in the drawer. "Those your toes I'm walking on?" he asked, in no hurry to shed light on the room or the inspiration behind an unorthodox and not-so-chance but gentle collision of feet.

"No harm done," she said, and withdrew them.

Jake's sock-clad feet begged to disagree. The harm was a sweet ache that started in his feet the moment she pulled hers away. Jake swallowed a sigh and hit the remote. Light flooded the room. Her silk-stocking clad feet were tucked beneath the chair. He reached to close the yawning desk drawer and in so doing, noticed her shoes neatly aligned beneath his desk. They looked good there. Like small white hens come home to roost. Foolish to think it, much less want to say so. He moved to one side, making elbow room for her as she put on reading glasses, tilted the lined pad beside the keyboard and began typing.

"Ready for some cake now?" he asked for want of a better excuse to regain her attention.

"Thanks, but I'm not hungry."

Curious as what so firmly held her focus, Jake reached for her tablet. His finger barely touched down when she whisked it away. He blinked, cupped his elbow in one hand and rubbed his chin. "So, what's this you're writing?"

"Not much at the rate I'm going," she said, her fingers poised over the keyboard.

Jake leaned in, trying to read the screen. Her silky lashes swept upward, lush and long and thick. Strained patience flashed in hazel depths. "Sorry," he said, and backed away.

"For what?"

"Well, I don't know exactly. But I didn't get that much of a reaction when I dropped my crane on your car," he said, wincing.

Color flooded Shelby's face. Grabbing the tablet

was pure reflex. Just as strong was the urge to erase the screen with a keystroke rather than to let him read her work before it was finished and polished. Unwilling to admit how raw and inadequate her first drafts seemed to her, and how she cringed at the thought of anyone else reading them, she swept a curl behind her ear, and explained, "What I'm working on is a rough draft. If I let you read it, it weakens my motivation to finish the thing."

"Top secret, eh? Now I *am* intrigued."

"You have no hang-ups?" she countered quietly.

"Classified, like your story," he claimed.

His gentle jesting cooled her rising hackles and left a foolish grin on her face. She wiped it clean, curled a leg beneath her and offered, "Shall I have my publisher send you a copy?"

"Will you sign it for me?" he pressed, mouth tilting.

"If you like."

"Just your name? Or could I have an inscription, too? Something like, 'To Jake, You Have My Number.'"

"I sure do," she countered.

He laughed and she smiled and the anchor eased its grip on her heart. But only for a moment. The interest flickering in his eyes reminded her that Patrick had once looked at her that way, too. Rejection, like honeybees, left the stinger in. Shelby averted her face before the heat of that bite brushed her cheeks.

"What's it take?" asked Jake. At her blank glance, he propped a hip on the corner of the desk and added, "Time wise, I mean."

"From here to here in a year." She tapped her

temple, then spread her hands as if she held a book. "Unless I get stuck."

"I better go then, and let you get back to it," said Jake.

Her smile, though fleeting, did nice things to her face. Like the blush on a peach. Though on closer scrutiny, Jake found that pinch never quite left her eyes. Her lashes came down, closing the beaches on those hazel seas. Intrigued, he wondered at her thoughts. That, at least was rational. The impulse to sweep her out of her chair and into his arms to kiss those pinch lines into retreat was not.

"I'll see you in the morning," he said, and came to his feet.

"Good night. Thanks for everything," she called, breathing easier now that he was leaving.

Jake wished she would use his name. He hesitated a moment, realizing he hadn't used hers, either. It formed on his tongue. But already, she had shut him out. Her white fingers were over the keys, skipping like whitecaps. Divorce, Jake had heard, was second only in trauma to suffering the death of a loved one. Where, then, did getting jilted rank? Somewhere in the ballpark with desertion, he wagered. He was still seeing the consequences of that in Paula's life, and Joy's too, as she struggled to fill the void left by a father who didn't know she existed.

Jake checked on Gram before turning in. It was a long while later when he heard water running and knew Shelby had called it quits for the night. He rubbed one eye and peered at the illuminated dial of his alarm clock. It was 3:00 a.m. And after the day she had had. She had stamina.

Jake rolled over and slept until the aroma of perking coffee stirred him awake. It was six. He could have grabbed another hour of sleep. But these days, Gram and the stove were an unpredictable mix.

Shelby smelled coffee and heard voices. In the time it took her to get her bearings, she remembered she had no car, and nowhere she had to be today. On that note, she dozed off again and got up a good while later to an empty house. A shower and a dash of lipstick helped a face in need of some color. She rubbed scented hand cream from elbows to fingertips and went downstairs.

There was coffee in a carafe and cold bacon and biscuits on the kitchen table. Shelby made a biscuit sandwich and poured coffee. She ate quickly, carried her dishes to the sink, turned on the tap and her thoughts, too. By the time she reached the study, words were crowding, wanting out.

Ringing church bells drew Shelby to the window at noon. Moments later, Jake's Jeep turned up the back alley and parked in the drive alongside his building. He climbed out loosening his tie and circled to help Gram Kate from the front seat. Three more cars pulled in behind him. Doors flew open and a blend of Jacksons piled out. Shelby assumed they were Jacksons—lanky frames and blue eyes were in the majority. She watched Joy turn down the alley. A boy pedaled toward her on his bicycle. Joy hurried to meet him. They slipped out of sight behind Jake's sign building.

Jake climbed the stairs to change out of his suit and saw the guest room was empty. He returned downstairs and found Shelby at his desk. Her fingers moved over the keys. She paused, lips pursed, and typed on, unaware of him in the open door. It was the sort of concentration he looked for in crane operators. He could have used some of it himself yesterday on the bank building, letting his eye stray to a pretty woman climbing out of her car in the lot below. For all the good it did. It was plain to see that her heart was still attached to the one who had cut her free.

Smitten in spite of himself, he called to her, "How's the story coming?"

She glanced away from the screen. "Pretty well, thank you."

"Doesn't seem like much of a vacation, closed in with your work."

"It's a treat not to have to squeeze it in between my hours at the office." She pushed her chair back, and rose smoothing her dress. It was sleeveless, with a fitted yoke, brown as toast. A drift of yellow pleats fell from the bodice.

"That's a nice sunflower dress you're wearing," said Jake, though the loose fit left a lot to the imagination.

"And you said you didn't know flowers," she countered.

Jake grinned. "No, but I've pulled enough weeds…"

"It's a weed? A sunflower is a weed?" she said doubtfully. "Are you sure?"

"Look it up." Jake reached for his favorite gardening book on the desk, and pushed it her way.

Shelby thumbed through dog-eared pages and plunked back into her chair. "You're right."

His mouth tipped at her disheartened sigh. "I haven't ruined it for you, have I?"

"'A rose by any other name'..." She set the quote adrift, and tucked a curl behind her ear. The pencil tunneled there wobbled and fell in her lap. "How was church?"

"Crowded," he replied, and ducked under the desk to retrieve the pencil. "But we would have made room for you."

"I overslept. By the way, I've been thinking about that loaner car. Perhaps it's time I phoned *my* insurer."

"No use trying on Sunday," he told her, fingers brushing hers as he returned the pencil. Her nails were trimmed short, but neatly curved and tinted ivory. "Anyway, I checked with my agent last night. He said he would have a car for you sometime tomorrow."

"Fine," Shelby said. "I'll stop by your shop then, and get the manuscripts out of the trunk."

"If they're that important, we can go today," he offered.

"Could we? I wouldn't bother you with it, but I'm responsible for them," she explained.

"We'll go after lunch. My sisters brought covered dishes for lunch," he said.

"What can I do to help?"

"You're a glutton for punishment, aren't you?"

She smiled and followed him into the kitchen where he made introductions, then slipped upstairs to change out of his suit.

There was enough physical similarity between Jake's sisters that Shelby had a hard time remem-

bering who was who. It was even more difficult with
the children. Shelby counted seven boys and six girls.
Then Joy came dashing in, flushed and fresh as a
rosebud dressed all in pink.

''Where you been?'' asked one of her cousins.

Joy pinched his arm.

''Ouch!'' he squealed. ''Quit it, Blondie Blake-a-
cake,''

Joy's giggly cousins shouted with laughter and
took up the chant: ''Blondie Blake-a-cake! Blondie
bake-a-cake, Blake-a-cake,''

''You better quit calling me that or you won't be
eating any of *my* cake,'' warned Joy with a lofty
sniff.

''Another cake? You're turning into a regular Sara
Lee,'' Jake said, joining the teasing.

He had changed into khakis and a loose-fitting
shirt that suited his eyes. The writer in Shelby made
mental notes. Preoccupied with the process, she saw
his smile shift to silent inquiry and realized her gaze
had lingered too long. His smile came on again as
their eyes met. The glow of it spread heat within,
like bottled sunshine. Startled at her instinctive response, Shelby averted her glance and finished setting the table. When the dinner call came, Jake held
a chair for her, another for Joy, and settled between
them.

The family joined hands for the blessing. Once
again, Shelby found herself comparing Jake's broad,
callused palm to the one her heart knew so well.
With an effort, she focused on the bountiful table and
the congeniality of Jake's family. The adults were
welcoming, the children boisterous and lively. The
meal, right through to dessert, was seasoned with hu-

mor and affection, and a balm to Shelby's bruised spirits.

"Scratch chocolate. Lemon's my favorite," Jake told Joy as he dribbled warm lemon sauce over his slice of lemon cake. "Second only to butter bean."

"Butter bean? I never heard of butter bean cake," said Joy.

Everyone laughed.

Joy's cheeks turned as pink as her dress. "You made that up," she accused, and flipped her braid over her shoulder.

"It's served in all the finest restaurants," claimed Jake. "A real delicacy. Isn't that right, Shelby?" he prompted with a gentle elbow and a blue-eyed wink.

Shelby indicated her mouth was too full to answer.

Thwarted, Jake wagged his head. "And here we were about to cut you in on our after-dinner baseball game."

The children gulped dessert, grabbed their baseball gloves and tramped out, arguing over teams. The men followed. Shelby stayed behind with Jake's sisters to clear away dinner and learned how to load and start the dishwasher.

Afterward Paula, Wendy and Jake's other sisters joined Gram Kate on the veranda. Shelby slipped up to her room for her notebook. She was on her way down to the study when Jake met her on the stairs.

"You're not going to spend your afternoon working, surely," he chided.

"I'm behind," she explained.

"Good position to be in." Grinning, he pivoted on the step. "You won't go wrong. Fall in behind me, and I'll take you out for some air."

"I meant behind on my work," she protested.

"Even God rested from His work on the seventh day."

His plainspoken logic nudged Shelby's conscience. But it was his coaxing smile that tipped the scales. "You're right, you know." Capitulating, she followed him downstairs.

"You want to pitch?" he asked on the way outdoors.

"No, thanks. Words are the only game I have any success with. Anyway, I'm resting. Remember?"

Jake chuckled at having his own words fed back to him. He left her with his sisters, and joined his team of Jackson progeny waiting in the yard. Shelby shaded her eyes and watched from a wicker lounger a makeshift game of men and kids and elastic rules that stretched to accommodate the smallest among them.

"So tell us, Shelby. What is it you're writing about?" asked Jake's youngest sister, Wendy.

"Teens," Shelby said.

"Joy's twelve, and already, I feel like *I* could do a book on teens!" exclaimed Paula.

In the company of her sisters, Paula was just one talker among many. Shelby's gaze returned to the game, and Jake, now hunkered down behind home plate with a catcher's mitt in hand.

"Hey, batter, batter," he chanted as a young nephew toddled up to bat. After the second strike, Jake dropped his glove and helped the pint-size batter swing.

The little guy was stunned when the bat cracked the ball. "Jimmy hit!" he cried. "Jimmy hit!"

"Run, Jimmy! Run!" hollered Jimmy's father, Curtis.

Jimmy froze, clutching the bat. Jake scooped him up and ran the bases with him. Jimmy was still clinging to the bat when they crossed home plate. He beamed as Jake set him down amidst his cheering teammates.

"Jimmy hit," he said again.

"Jimmy sure did!" Jake heaved Jimmy aloft and onto his shoulder and ran a victory lap.

"Jake needs a family of his own," Wendy commented.

"Wendy hasn't been married long," Paula said to Shelby. "The blush is still on the rose."

"But the kids do love Jake," pointed out Jimmy's mom, Christine. "Joy thinks the sun rises and sets on him."

"She should. He's always been there for us," Paula stated.

"That's all good and well. But it's time he was thinking about a nest of his own." Wendy turned a beaming smile on Shelby. "Say! Do you have any friends we could set him up with?"

"I could probably think of someone. But it would be a long drive for him," Shelby replied, rising from her chair. She caught Paula rolling her eyes, and angled for the door, adding, "Excuse me, would you? I left my sunglasses upstairs."

"That was real subtle, Wen," Paula chided Wendy.

"What?" protested Wendy with feigned innocence. "All I said was, did she know anyone."

Restless, Shelby retrieved her sunglasses, and on impulse, phoned her parents. No one answered. She wasn't surprised. They were very busy. Even in childhood, it was a catch-as-catch-can proposition.

She left a message explaining the circumstances that had forced a change of plans, where she was staying and how to reach her. As she did so, she could almost see them trading benign and somewhat surprised glances at her bid to reassure them she was fine. It wouldn't occur to them to think otherwise.

Ball game forgotten, Shelby let herself into Jake's study, closed the door and turned on the computer. Time fell away as she polished her first chapter.

THE FIELD
Chapter One
The sun was rising as Cheryl gathered with half a dozen sleepy-eyed teens beneath the park pavilion. Yesterday's rain had distorted the bill of her Weed Buster's cap. Her sneakers were stiff with dried mud and the edges of her cutoff shorts were unraveling.

"So where's the boss?" she asked one of the boys waiting there.

"Who cares? he said. "Waiting's easy cash."

Cheryl wished she could be so carefree. She looked up the empty street, then sat down on a picnic table to wait. As the minutes stretched into half an hour with no sign of Mr. Weedman, the rest of the kids picked up their lunches and hoes and ambled away, Dudley among them.

But Cheryl stayed, pacing now. He would be along anytime with a logical explanation. He would apologize for keeping her waiting. They would round up the other kids and go to the field.

Seven-thirty and still no Weedman. Where was he? Why didn't he come? She needed to work. Needed the money. Needed to kill weeds and self-doubts. Blue-eyed dirt-track speed-demon Jack Cook, in not exposing her, had given her purpose. She wanted to be who he thought she could be.

Seven forty-five. Get a brain, Cheryl. He isn't coming! She picked up her lunch cooler, her hoe. And yet...what harm was there in waiting a few more minutes?

Eight o'clock. No Weedman. Cheryl was angry now. And scared. She tried to reason away the fear. But she was cold inside. Cold with the growing conviction that something was terribly wrong. That she had seen the last of Wiley Weedman.

And she was dead right.

"So here you are! Why aren't I surprised?"

Shelby looked to find Jake leaning in the door, a grass stain on one knee of his khakis and his baseball cap in hand. "Who won?" she asked, her eyes returning to the screen.

"Hard to say when it erupts into a brawl," he said. "I called the game. Gram separated them as best she could, put them in their cars and sent them home."

"Hmm," Shelby replied, struggling against the gravitational pull of her story.

"It tuckered her out, until it was all she could do to climb in the last car out the drive. She said don't wait supper, she'll make them feed her before she comes home." Jake crossed to the window and lowered the blinds. "If you can find a stopping place there, we'll go into town and rescue your homework. May as well eat while we're at it.''

''Is it that time already?''

''Getting close,'' he said. ''If you're not hungry, we could go for a walk.''

''After an afternoon of baseball?'' Trying to talk words at odds with the words she was typing was too much. Shelby looked up just as Jake perched on the corner of the desk and reached for her hand-scrawled notes.

''Please don't...''

''...read your stuff,'' he finished, withholding the tablet.

Shelby restrained herself from leaping across the desk and wrestling her tablet away. His baiting smile triggered heat, which she strove to hide, even as she tried to divert his attention from her scribbled notes. ''About this walk. Would it take us past Mr. Wiseman's house?'' she asked.

''I guess it could. Why?''

Shelby hit a key, watched the screen darken and pushed out of her chair. ''Has he turned up yet?''

''Not that I know of,'' Jake said.

''Do I have time to run upstairs and get my walking shoes?''

''Sure. No hurry. Aren't you forgetting something?'' he called after her.

Shelby turned in the door and caught the tablet as he pitched it across the room. ''You're a tease, Jake.''

He crooked a brow and countered, ''Here I thought you had eyes only for your story.''

''You noticed?''

"That you weren't hanging on my every word? Of course I noticed. What man wouldn't?"

He spoke in jest. And still it gave Shelby pause, for until that moment, it hadn't occurred to her that anyone but Patrick would find her preoccupation with her story objectionable. She mulled the thought as she climbed the stairs to freshen up. What good was a forward view if her future became a repeat of the same conflict she had had with Patrick? Hearing the phone ring, Shelby tucked away the thought with her tablet, splashed her face and combed her hair and returned downstairs.

"I thought she left with you," she heard Jake say as she joined him in the living room. "No, she's not here. Sure, I'll send a carton with her if she turns up."

"Who's missing?" Shelby asked.

"Joy. She told her mom she would walk home. Paula thought maybe she could catch her before she left. She's out of eggs." He held the door for Shelby.

The air had cooled. It was fragrant with the neighbor's freshly clipped grass and pine needles. A canopy of old trees shaded the crumbling sidewalk.

"Liberty Flats," murmured Shelby when the silence grew heavy. "Kind of an odd name for rolling prairie, isn't it?"

"I guess it is if you don't know its story," Jake replied. "The township was settled by abolitionist farmers from the east. Along with forty acres of land, each settler got a lot in a little town they called Liberty. Some men in the colony ran a station on the underground railroad. Thus, the name."

Shelby listened as he explained that when the railroad bypassed Liberty a few years before the Civil

War, the tiny village was doomed to return to the prairie.

"A guy by the name of Dan Flats came along and offered to sell the town fathers some land adjacent to the tracks, if they wanted to pull up stakes and relocate Liberty. He quoted a bargain rate with the stipulation that they name the new town for him," Jake continued. "So when the ground was frozen, Liberty loaded their houses and sheds onto ox-driven sleds and moved east three miles. And Liberty Flats was born,"

"Interesting stuff," Shelby said, silently appraising the easy pride he took in his hometown.

"It gets better," Jake continued. "A few years went by, and come to find out Flats didn't have clear title on the land he had sold. The public was put out enough at dapper Dan, they tried to change the town name."

"To what?"

"That was the problem. They couldn't agree. By then, Dan's grown sons had put down roots in town. When it came to a vote, Liberty Flats got seven votes. The rest were split between a dozen other suggestions. So Liberty Flats carried the day," explained Jake. "Dan was pleased enough, he nailed together a little hotel by the railroad tracks, and spent the rest of his life in Liberty Flats, trying to clear himself of any wrongdoing. Claimed he'd been taken in by a slick land agent."

"Was that true?"

"According to Dan's descendants, it is," Jake said. But his grin left room for doubt.

Modern concrete gave way to quaint brick sidewalk. Flower beds dotted green lawns that unfolded toward the street. Jake paused beside a picket fence. "This is it. Wilt Wiseman's place."

Shelby stopped in front of the two-story clapboard of chipping paint and fading glory. The grass needed cutting, the newspapers were piling up and a garbage can at the back corner of the house was overflowing.

Shelby was about to walk on when she heard a clatter. Joy, still clad in her pink dress, darted into view without seeing them. She grabbed the garbage can by one handle and dragged it behind the house.

"Now what do you suppose *she's* up to?" Jake opened the gate, took a beaten path skirting the house and disappeared around the far corner.

Chapter Five

Shelby's nerves leapt as a young man came racing from the far side of the house. He was a dead ringer for the boy she had seen at noon in the alley by Jake's sign building. As she stood watching, he jerked a bicycle out from beneath a bush, pedaled through the open gate, and tore down the street. A moment later, Jake returned with Joy, whining and dragging her feet.

"I suppose you're gonna tell Mom."

"No," said Jake, jaw clenched. "*You* are. If I hadn't come along when I did, you'd have been through that window."

"I was just trying to figure out what happened to Mr. Wiseman," defended Joy. "What if he's lying in there sick or hurt, and nobody checks on him? I keep telling you I have a funny feeling about him."

"I have a funny feeling, too. Says you had some help here," replied Jake. "And I *don't* mean a garbage can for a stepladder."

Joy's gaze skipped over the bush that had only a moment ago concealed a bicycle.

"You want to tell me who talked you into doing something so irresponsible?" Jake pressed.

"Nobody," Joy said, sulking.

"Come on, Joy. Level with me. Was it Dirk?"

"You're not my dad, I don't have to tell you anything," Joy huffed. She swung around with her chin set and stormed away.

"Dirk, or I miss my guess," Jake muttered, watching her flounce down the street.

"You saw him?" Shelby asked.

"After church," Jake said. "He followed us home on his bike."

"He was here a minute ago," Shelby informed Jake. "He tore away while you were in back. Is he prone to trouble?"

"Not that I know of. Though crawling through Mr. Wiseman's kitchen window is a sure invitation for it," Jake added.

"Granted, it was a poor judgment call. But their motives were understandable," Shelby reasoned.

"I should hope," Jake said, relenting a little. He turned back the way they had come.

Shelby started to follow, then stopped and looked back. "What if they're right, Jake? What if Mr. Wiseman *is* inside alone, needing help? We could at least check with the neighbors, couldn't we?" Shelby persisted for peace of mind.

It didn't seem likely to Jake. But to be on the safe side, he checked with the next-door neighbor, who had a key to the Wiseman house. The neighbor, Roxelle, let herself into the house, and came out a moment later to say there was no one inside.

"Mrs. Wiseman works for a genealogical research firm," Roxelle explained. "Sometimes, Mr. Wiseman helps her with the research. Especially when it takes her out of town."

"That must be what happened," Jake agreed.

"I'll have them call Joy when they arrive home," the neighbor promised.

Jake thanked her for her trouble. He and Shelby walked home where Jake showered and changed for their dinner date. They took the interstate to a fifties-style diner at the south edge of Bloomington. Inside, neon, classic car posters and photos of movie stars from that era brightened the walls. Jake emptied his change into a jukebox. He and Shelby poured over a collection of oldies, making selections, and then studied the menu while pop country entertainers crooned the blues.

"Paula did the neon for this place," Jake told Shelby.

"It's very nice," Shelby said. She hesitated a moment. "Forgive my curiosity, but I've been wondering about Joy's father."

"Colton? I take it Joy mentioned the billboard," Jake responded.

"Billboard?" she echoed.

"The Voyager." Belatedly, Jake saw he had jumped to conclusions, that she didn't know about Joy's father after all. "Colton did some modeling for Wind, Water and Sky. It was the beginning of an ad campaign that has since given him nationwide recognition."

"I'm sorry, I'm not following you," Shelby said, struggling to make the connection between a billboard and Joy's father.

"That's Colt," Jake told her.

"The Voyager? The guy in the canoe wearing the red cap? You don't mean it!" cried Shelby.

"One and the same," Jake said, as amazement lighted her eyes.

"The Voyager! I can't believe it! Why, he's a household word, and has been for years. And he's Joy's father! How on earth did he and Paula meet?"

"Colt came to Liberty Flats as a investigative journalist, looking into a train derailing and a nasty chemical spill that hadn't been properly cleaned up," Jake explained.

"A writer, too. I had no idea," Shelby murmured, pleased to learn that there was more to the man than rugged handsomeness. "How long did he live in Liberty Flats?"

"He didn't. He was here just three weeks getting the details for his report and romancing Paula. He returned a few weeks later and they were married. It didn't last long. The day Colt left, Paula was sick in bed in their Chicago flat with what she thought was the flu. By the time she realized it was morning sickness, she had moved back home, and Colt was out of her life for good."

"Why would he have such a change of heart?" Shelby asked, her heart hurting for Paula.

The answer lay on a dark rainy road strewn with premature loss and memories that remained painful even with the passage of time. Reluctant to go there, Jake was relieved when the waitress arrived to take their orders.

When she had gone, he guided the conversation down less treacherous paths, asking Shelby about her former books, the titles, the content, the message. A light came on in her eyes as she spoke of those things. Jake smiled as she confided that she found Joy to be interesting story inspiration.

"Do us a favor, and don't tell her," he quipped. "It'll go straight to her head, and there'll be no living with her."

Shelby smiled and cleared up his misconception, saying, "The book isn't *about* her. By inspiration, I mean Joy freshens in me the angst, the dreams, the pressures of those teen years."

"Oh, that! Terrific! Glad to hear someone's getting some good out of her mood swings. She's giving Paula anxiety attacks."

"And her uncle?"

Jake grinned at her shrewdness. "She's a good kid. Other than your occasional break and entry."

They lingered over coffee and conversation. It was dusk by the time they arrived at Jackson Signs to retrieve Shelby's book bag from the trunk of her demolished car.

"If my insurance agent doesn't come through with that loaner tomorrow, you're welcome to use the Jeep," Jake told Shelby as they climbed out of his vehicle.

"That won't be necessary," Shelby said. "I'll spend the day writing. Or will you be needing your computer?"

"No problem. I have access at both shops," Jake assured her. He paused beneath a vapor light and plucked a crowbar from the toolbox of a crane truck. "How much vacation time do you have?"

"A week," Shelby replied. "But I'll get out of your way just as soon as I get a car."

"You're not in my way. Gram's enjoying having another woman in the house," said Jake.

"She thinks I'm your sister."

"That bothers you?"

"No, of course not. She's very sweet," Shelby amended hastily.

Jake slapped a mosquito and fell silent as they closed the distance to her battered car. An apology hovered on Shelby's tongue. But the moment was lost to the shriek of metal as Jake, crowbar in hand, pried at the stubborn trunk lid.

"I'm sorry, Jake," Shelby said quietly, when he paused to wipe his glistening face and calibrate his progress.

"For what?" His eyes met hers and tinged the dusky light.

Shelby lost her courage in that haze of midnight blue. "I didn't realize it would be such a job."

"It's me. I'm making uphill work of it." He slapped and bloodied another mosquito. "I'll open the shop and get the handyman jack."

Upon his return with the jack, Shelby got a glimpse of his face as he passed beneath the vapor light. *He's forgotten it. Let it go.* She trained a curl behind her ear, and stood by as Jake secured the jack. It didn't take him long to pop open the trunk. Shelby dived past him and scooped up her book bag.

"Safe and sound?" he asked, thinking what a waste it was, those slim arms hugging soulless tapestry and paper.

Shelby checked inside. "Seems to be."

"Good. I'll lock up and we'll get going, before the mosquitoes eat us alive," he stated, and strode away, whistling off-key, his cap askew and the heavy jack slung over his shoulder.

On the ride home, Shelby said no more about leaving. That pleased Jake. The truth was, everything about her pleased him. Her shining curls and hazel eyes. Her mannerisms. The notice she took of the smallest kindness.

While her remark concerning Gram's forgetfulness had caught him off guard, on further reflection, he appreciated her honesty. Some folks pretended not to notice Gram Kate's confusion while other well-meaning friends didn't understand the family effort to keep Gram in her own home.

"A few weeks, and she wouldn't know the difference," a neighbor had said not long ago.

Maybe not. But he would and his sisters would, too.

Wendy turned into the driveway just ahead of them and let Gram Kate out. Gram said her goodbyes. She linked arms with Jake and Shelby and strolled to the house between them. "Let's have some tea and toast," she said.

In no hurry to see the evening end, Jake smiled at Shelby, bidding her to join them. "What's your pleasure, whole wheat or sourdough?" he asked.

"Whole wheat. Point me in the right direction, and I'll help," she offered.

"It's my treat, dear," Gram responded. She padded from the kitchen sink to the stove with the teapot. "How was the picture sho-sho-shoot?"

"We didn't go to the show. But we had a nice dinner," Shelby said.

"This finicky old fussbudget," grumbled Gram

Kate when the burner failed to light. "Where did I put the matches?"

"Gram, you don't need a match." Jake stepped in. "The stove is new, remember? Just turn it to 'light.'"

"The tin, of course." Struggling to open the match tin, Gram missed Jake's demonstration of how to operate the stove. "Empty," she muttered, frustration creeping into her voice.

"It's real simple, Gram Kate. Look. Like this." Jake took the empty tin. He showed her the light indicator on the burner knob and indicated the clicking sound that began when the burner lit. "Adjust the flame and the clicking stops."

"Fuss and nonsense," grumbled Gram. Toast and tea forgotten, she ambled off, muttering to herself.

Jake met Shelby's sympathetic glance. "So much for electric ignition. Matches, she understood."

"But of course," Shelby said. "Where else do you get such instantaneous results?"

"Women." Jake wagged his head and turned up his palms with an engaging grin. "*I'll* make the tea. You man the toaster, and stay away from the matches."

Shelby chuckled and reached into the bread box.

It was a big kitchen, but it closed in nicely as they shared counter space and a simple task. Jake held the door leading out to the summer porch where Gram had settled. Shelby brushed by him, tea tray in hand. The ceiling fan hummed lazily overhead, blending fragrances—dew-drenched flowers, green grass, sweet clover and the apple blossom scent Shelby was wearing.

A yellow tabby begged from the porch steps.

Gram swung the screen door open and let the cat in.
"There, there, Kitty," she soothed the cat's plaintive
meow with a toast crust dipped in cream. When the
treat was gone, Kitty groomed and preened, then
played a game of cat and mouse with a moth.

Shelby took pity and released the moth outdoors.
She refilled Gram's cup and her own cup, too.

"No, thanks." Jake declined, covering the rim of
his cup with his hand.

Shelby wandered to the edge of the porch with her
cup and saucer in hand. Jake admired the pretty silhouette she made. He joined her there, enjoying the
dark air, the shadows and placid sounds of night settling in.

Fireflies danced and a new moon climbed the sky.
Kitty purred from pillar to post, arching her back
against Shelby's shapely ankle, then weaving a path
between Jake's spread feet. He stooped and stroked
the cat's ears, then let her out to prowl the summer
night.

Gram yawned and came to her feet. "You have
school tomorrow, Jill. Ten minu—men you mend,
say good—good…" she sighed and gave up getting
the words out and kissed Shelby's cheek. She kissed
Jake, too, and went inside.

Shelby slipped into the chair Gram had vacated
and brushed a loose thread from her skirt. "Who's
Jill?" she asked quietly.

"My mother."

He glimpsed Shelby waiting, lips parted. When he
offered nothing further, she busied herself clearing
away. The clamor of clattering spoons and cups and
the graceful hands that gathered them revealed a void
in Jake he hadn't had the luxury to think about much

lately. He moved to the porch swing, and patted the slatted seat.

"Let those go, and come sit a while."

Shelby swung around, her smile barely touching down.

"You're supposed to be on vacation," he reminded.

"I know. I think I'll work a while," she said, then grimaced at the inconsistency of her words, and laughed at herself.

Jake planted his feet, stopping the swing in wordless entreaty. She joined him there, her elbow finding rest on the wooden arm. She seemed more relaxed than she had a day ago. Yet on closer accounting, Jake saw that moonglow and cricket cadence hadn't erased the pinched expression from her eyes.

"Here's a penny for your thoughts," he offered.

Shelby touched the coin he fished from his pocket. "I was thinking about the unplanned turns in the line."

"What lines?" asked Jake.

"Life."

Jake turned her hand up. It was soft to the touch, pliant, yet firm. He traced a faint crease. "This one the lifeline?"

Her gaze fell to his hand holding her open palm and suddenly, levity vanished and pliancy too. "That isn't what I meant."

"What, then?" Jake released her hand before she could withdraw it.

She ducked her head. He thought she would duck the question, too. Instead, she murmured, "We were a year planning this weekend."

"So what gives with the guy?" Jake took the opening her words provided.

"His name is Patrick," she said in a hush.

Jake watched her fingers tighten around the supporting swing chain. "Patrick has a hard time making up his mind, does he?"

"Not as a rule," she said in the same careful voice. "He's an attorney and proficient at it. Analytical. Methodical. Nothing escapes him."

"You did."

"That was *his* choice."

"Suppose he does an about-face?" asked Jake.

"He won't. He said it was paramount to adultery."

"He's married?" blurted Jake, startled out of his feigned casual pursuit of her severed relationship.

"No. I am. To my writing, he says." Her attempted levity failed. Fatigue tugged at her eyes, painting shadows.

Jake stretched his arm across the back of the swing. He started to cup her shoulder, to commiserate with a pat and a word, but on further consideration, found his motives suspect, and thought better of it.

"Forgive me, I didn't mean to unload on you," she murmured at his silence.

"Get it out, if it helps."

"To bore you with it?"

"You couldn't if you tried."

"You're sweet," she said.

He could be a lot sweeter. Wanted to be. Her chin quivered, a brave effort at a smile that turned watery. He gripped splintered wood, countermanding the urge to gather her in. The porch lamp illuminated lines and traces beneath misty eyes and a fragile mouth. Moth wings brushed the glass lamp, soft as the breath she expelled.

"We'd been dating for two years before marriage came up. It took us another year to plan the perfect wedding," she confided. "Then a week ago, all that changed. I spent every spare moment returning gifts, calling guests, the florist, the caterer, the bakery. The only thing Patrick canceled was the one thing I was still counting on."

"The cottage at Wildwood?"

Shelby nodded.

"Deliberately?"

"No. Patrick isn't like that," she replied quickly. "It was lack of communication. He didn't know I had decided to go alone."

Her defense of the guy surprised Jake less than the sting it gave him. He fumbled his coin, wrestling with the realization she was just the kind of woman he'd like to have in his corner. The penny bounced to the floor and rolled into a puddle of light.

Shelby stopped it with her foot. "Next time I'm eloping," she said surprising a smile out of him. "No fuss, no bother,"

"That's right, climb right back into the saddle," he encouraged, finding his stride, heart soaring at the possibilities.

"You bet," she said.

Through a divide in the slatted swing, Jake stroked her back with the flat of his thumb. She retreated from his touch, leaning forward ostensibly to pick up the coin. Jake caught his breath, waiting.

"I didn't mean..." she began as she straightened.

"Course not," he said. He jammed the offending

thumb inside a curled fist and commiserated, saying, "Hurts, huh?"

She darted him a wary glance. "You've been there?"

"Not in the same way," he said. "But loss is loss."

"How did you weather it?"

"Not too well. It was my parents."

Jake heard her breath catch. "Both of them?" she asked.

"In a car accident. Paula's husband was driving the car that hit them," he said tonelessly, and saw her hand fly to her throat. "He wasn't seriously hurt. But it was a tough time for everyone."

Appalled at all Jake's family had suffered, and feeling her own troubles slight by comparison, Shelby murmured, "I'm so sorry, Jake."

Her eyes swelled with compassion, and the emotion caught him by the throat. The tightness of the grip got beyond his guard. He averted his gaze. A window closed across the street. A car turned around in the alley. Water dripped from the nearby faucet where the garden hose and the spigot met. He shifted to his feet to shut off the sprinkler. Time fell away and in spirit, he was that grown boy again. Coming home late, dodging the lawn sprinkler, wondering what Gram was doing at their house. He was that fly-apart boy, hearing the words and going to pieces. And Gram was herself again, her faith strong even in her weakest hour. She said of his parents, "'Jesus called in a trumpet voice, Come up here.'"

Later Jake had found those words in his Bible and understood better the tender concern behind them, and the power with which they were spoken. He couldn't verbalize what they had come to mean to him. Or why they were so strongly in mind as he reclaimed his place on the swing.

It was Shelby who moved closer. Her voice was softly plaintive. "Is it just a cliché, time heals?"

"Time doesn't just heal. It moves forward with a will and a purpose."

"On better days?" she said finally.

"On eternity."

Her eyes filled again. Too late, Jake saw that forever was a long time to be disconnected from a man she had loved and lost, not by death but by a change of heart. "It was a quote from something a friend sent to me after the funeral. I didn't understand it at the time," Jake admitted.

"And later?"

"It's the Spirit that gives life. Mom and Dad had already died to themselves years before when they said I do to God." Seeing her confusion, he murmured, "Their confession of faith."

"Oh, *that*," she said and closed her eyes, remembering a time when Patrick had had everything she wanted in a man, *except* faith. It was at Can-Do, a homeless mission where Shelby had talked him into volunteering several hours a week, that he came to know the Lord. In her eyes, that made him complete. But shared faith had not saved their relationship.

"I'm sorry," Jake murmured, his eyes seeming dark in the shadows. "I'm not much good at this."

"Yes, you are. You've helped." So saying, she tucked heart wounds beneath a veneered smile and tilted her chin. "No good sympathizing with myself. Onward and upward, as they say."

But for all her brave intentions, tears escaped and

coursed down her cheek. "Stop that." She mopped her cheek with the back of her hand and flashed a watery smile.

Jake offered his handkerchief.

"Feel better?" he asked, when she had dried her eyes.

"I'm going to, I promise." She returned his handkerchief and reached as if to touch him the way friends will. But at the last moment, her hand drifted back to her lap without making contact. "Thanks for listening. You've been an angel. Offering your home, your family, your hospitality. You're heaven sent," she insisted.

"To drop a crane on your car?"

She dried the last stray tear from her cheek with the back of her hand. "Perhaps I'll get a chance to return the kindness."

"No need. Really," he said and flung arms in the air as if ducking a falling crane.

Her smile jerked at his heart. Caught between laughter and an open flame, he curled his hand around the handkerchief, damp with her tears and got to his feet.

Together, they carried the cups and saucers and remnants of their snack inside. Together, they washed and wiped them dry. Together, they spoke of everyday things. The sign business. Her family. His. And mosquitoes. She rubbed one welt and then another. Jake had a dozen to match.

"There's ointment upstairs in the medicine cabinet that will take the sting away," he told her.

Wishing the cut of severed hearts could be so easily remedied, Shelby thanked him again, bid him good-night, and climbed the stairs.

Family portraits lined the landing walls between closed doors. Previously, she had given them only passing notice. Now, she searched faces and found Jake's parents among them, encircled by Jake's bevy of sisters. Paula, the eldest, glowing with happiness, no clue as to the heartache that lay ahead. And Jake, his hand on his mother's shoulder. Jake hadn't shared his family tragedy to minimize her loss. And yet it did. It dwarfed her childhood pangs, as well. She remembered once, questioning her mother for writing *Homemaker* as her occupation on a grant she was writing for one charity or another.

Confused, she'd said, "But Mommy, you are never home."

"How can I be, as long there are little girls and boys in this world, some no bigger than you, who *have* no home?"

With her mother's life and lap so full of faceless girls and boys, Shelby felt she had been blessed to find a lap in books. That wasn't a bad thing at all. It had given her a love of storytelling, of words, of drama at an early age. As for her parents, even at their busiest, they had always assured her they were only a phone call away. Shelby prepared for bed, then dialed their number. No one was home. She wasn't surprised. Just a little lonely. That too passed as she snuggled up with her pillow and prayed for Jake's losses, and Paula's and Joy's, too, before sharing her hurt and confusion over Patrick with God.

I was so sure he was the one, Lord. The matter was settled in my mind. So settled, that tonight, when Jake touched me, my first response was guilt. Her second was pleasure. That was harder to admit, and even harder to sort out why it was so. Salve for her bruised ego, she decided, and drifted off to sleep.

Chapter Six

The faint fragrance of Shelby's perfume lingered in Jake's office as he sat down to work on business accounts. Shelby had left the computer on screen-saver. The darkened screen lit up at his touch, illuminating double-spaced lines of words.

Jake read several paragraphs before he realized it was Shelby's story. He couldn't read this. Shouldn't. Intriguing, though. Words from her mind, making pictures in his:

> Jack straddled a chair. He nudged his glasses to the bridge of his nose and faced Cheryl across the table. "So what's this all about?"
>
> "I've been working for Mr. Weedman, cutting weeds out of fields," said Cheryl.
>
> Jack couldn't corral his grin. "Weed bustin' Weedman. That name for real?"
>
> "Yeah, it's a hoot. Like Cookin' Jack Cook." But Cheryl wasn't laughing. "The joke's on me. I think Mr. Weedman has skipped town."

"Without paying you?"

Cheryl's bottom lip quivered. "If this is justice, it stinks! I worked hard, and I want my money."

Jack hated scenes. Tears made him queasy. Especially in Cheryl's eyes.

"Track them down, Jack," she pleaded. "Be a piece of cake for you."

Cheryl stopped short, her gaze riveted on a spot over Jack's left shoulder.

Jack knew without turning that Tara had slipped into the room. He could smell her exotic perfume.

Three's a crowd. Oldest conflict since Adam, Eve and the snake. Jake reached for the arrow key and wrestled his conscience. Accidental trespass was one thing. But to keep reading took intrusion to another level. Then again, it was written to be read, and she hadn't exactly made it inaccessible.

Conscience gagged and bound, Jake scrolled to the next chapter and found the viewpoint had shifted. The story was now from Tara's point of view:

Tara stretched a slim manicured hand to Cheryl. "I'm Tara Hilton. I'm here visiting from Chicago. And you're…?"

"Cheryl Williams."

"It's nice to meet you, Cheryl." Tara gripped Cheryl's hand, noting callused palms and ragged, broken nails. "I couldn't help overhearing. How can I help?"

"Like I was telling Jack, no one's seen Wiley Weedman or his wife in two days. And believe me, I've walked my feet off looking.''

Tara noted Cheryl's green T-shirt imprinted with the slogan, Weed Busters! We Take Your Field Through a Cleaning. ''So tell me, how long have you known the Weedmans?''

''Do you mind?'' Jack interrupted. His frown melted away as he turned back to Cheryl. ''We can go in the other room, Cheryl, if you'd rather not discuss this in front of a perfect stranger.''

''I'm not all that perfect,'' Tara interjected mildly.

''You think?'' he muttered.

Tara overlooked his sarcasm, and his invitation to butt out and replied, ''So where do we start?''

''*I'll* start by calling some farmers,'' said Jack, emphasis on the singular. ''Get their make on the guy. Whose fields did you weed?''

''Mr. Blatchford's was the last one we did. I've forgotten the other names, but Dudley will know,'' said Cheryl.

''Who's Dudley?'' asked Tara.

''A guy from school,'' said Cheryl. ''He worked for Weedman, too, until he and Weedman quarreled last week. I couldn't hear what it was about, but I could see their faces. Dudley was hot.''

''What else is new?'' said Jack darkly.

Cheryl shrugged and murmured, ''He's been nice to me. He even let me borrow his truck.''

''You told him you were coming to see me, and he gave you his truck keys?''

''I didn't tell him where I was going,'' Cheryl admitted.

"What is it with you and this Dudley guy?" Tara asked Jack.

But Jack was already out of his chair. "I'll make some calls."

"Dudley and Jack compete for checkered flags," Cheryl confided as Jack's footfalls faded into the next room.

"Checkered flags?" echoed Tara.

"They both race beaters out at the Spoon River Speedway. The hobo division," explained Cheryl. "Dudley bumped Jack and spun him out just short of the victory line last summer. It put him out of contention for the championship. Dudley swears it was an accident. But Jack's been down on him ever since."

"So whose side are you on?"

"I'm not taking sides so long as they both treat me right. Shh!" warned Cheryl. "Here comes Jack."

"Can you describe Mr. Weedman?" Tara asked Cheryl as if there had been no detour in the conversation.

"Medium tall. His hair's turning gray. He's kind of old, fifty, maybe sixty. Oh, and he's got scars on his left hand and he's missing the tip of his ring finger."

"That's Weedman you're describing?" Jack jumped into the conversation.

"You've met him?" asked Tara, swinging her foot.

"No. But I've seen him at the post office. Just didn't have a name for the face." Jack fished his keys from his pocket. "I'm going to run by his place and have a look."

"I'll follow in the truck," said Cheryl.

"I may as well come, too. It beats waiting around for Dad," Tara said, uncrossing her legs.

Jack looked pained as she rose from her chair. But he didn't argue when she followed Cheryl out.

Cheryl climbed into a battered old truck and revved the motor. Tara took one look at the springs erupting from the truck seat, smoothed her designer jeans and called to Jack, "On second thought, I'll ride with you."

Tara climbed into Jack's vintage Bel Air. It was immaculate, the seats so slick, it was hard to keep a grip. It made long work of six short blocks. She asked questions along the way, none of which Jack answered to her satisfaction.

Hot shot, thought Tara. Obviously, it didn't occur to him that she might be of help. He parked behind Cheryl and cut the motor.

Tara climbed out. "Whose van?" she called to Cheryl.

"Mr. Weedman's," Cheryl replied. "But no one's here. I've all but beat the door down, trying to get an answer."

Tara gaped at the two-story house. Paint-bare. Shredded window screens. Leaning porch. Unclipped grass.

The gate was wired shut. Jack vaulted the fence and climbed the rotting porch steps. Tara unwired the gate, picked her way up the rickety steps and waited, hopeful someone would answer Jack's knock.

No one did. Jack tried the door.

"You aren't going in are you?" Cheryl called

to them from the grass.

"I would, but it's locked," Jack said. "I'll have a look around back. You two better wait in the car."

Cheryl strode back to the street. But Tara thrust her hand into her pocketbook. Jack's big baby blues widened behind smudged lenses as she withdrew a pick set.

"What're you doing with that?" he asked.

Tara slipped the pick into the lock, and let her fingers do the talking. She felt the faint click of the tumbler. The knob turned. "After you," she said, with an ushering sweep of her hand.

For the first time since her arrival, Jack paid grudging approval. But Cheryl went to pieces.

"You guys!" she screeched from the street. "Don't go in there, you'll get us in trouble!"

Tara locked glances with Jack.

"I don't think she's up for this, maybe we'd better wait," he said finally.

We? The word glided over Tara like lotion on a sunburn. She slid the pick set back into her pocketbook and went after Cheryl. "It's okay, Cheryl. We'll figure out another way."

A sound from the floor above jolted Jake out of Shelby's story. He lifted his gaze to the ceiling. Shelby's room was directly overhead. He heard springs creak. She was turning in for the night, no inkling he was meddling in her business.

Quickly, Jake closed her file and opened his own. But it took him a while to complete his update. His mind kept toying with Shelby's story. It was apparent what she had meant by Joy offering inspiration. But

Joy's job circumstances were just a framework. The story was about Shelby. Shelby from the inside. She inhabited her words, the narrative, her characters.

Jake wished he had read the story from the beginning. Temptation whispered that it wasn't too late. She couldn't see him. Hear him. She was up there, clueless. And still, he could not. Already, he felt guilty for invading her privacy.

Shelby awoke the next morning to a quiet house. She showered in a bathroom devoid of feminine frills, got shampoo in her eye and reached blindly for a towel. The towel bar was empty. But a crumpled hand towel lay on the old-fashioned marble sink surround beside the soap and razor and shaving cream. She dried her hands and face and rubbed her eye.

It was a long stretch from the shower to an oak cabinet and a stack of thick towels. She dried and draped herself in a dark man-size one, and painted her face while her curling iron heated. Lacey underclothes, bought with a honeymoon in mind, twisted the knife a bit. She slipped into a cotton shirt, khaki walking shorts and her trusty sneakers.

The bathroom now resembled the aftermath of a female invasion. She tucked her lotions and potions out of sight in the oak cabinet, curled her hair, swept up a sprinkling of bath powder, and made a mental note to put the curling iron away once it had cooled.

There was a note waiting for her downstairs on the kitchen table. Jake had left his insurance man's phone number in the event the promised loaner car didn't materialize. He had also dashed down his own cell phone number, should she need to get in touch with him.

There was a postscript directing her to waffle batter and orange juice in the refrigerator. His kind gesture found a grateful target. Likewise, last evening. She hadn't set out to air her hurt over Patrick. In fact, she had deliberately avoided doing so with friends of much longer acquaintance.

But Jake, tempered by his own loss, had been sympathetic without smothering her. He hadn't judged. And he hadn't condemned Patrick. His impartiality had relieved her of a gut defensiveness on Patrick's behalf.

Since the breakup, she had waited for anger to kick in and burn away her loyalty to Patrick. As yet, that hadn't happened. Since coming here and in getting to know Jake, she had caught a glimpse of herself and just how large a part of her life her writing had become, how all invasive it was. As if it had a life of its own.

She had assumed Patrick, ambitious himself, understood. But apparently, he had expected a more attentive soul mate. Someone who was as close as skin. *Someone who understood what it meant for two lives to become one,* he had said the night he pulled the rug from beneath her. For the first time, she was able to glimpse the storm clouds Patrick had foreseen on the horizon of their future as man and wife.

Perhaps it was for the best. She was able to think that, and the world did not crash in on her. Feeling stronger for it, Shelby poured juice and stepped outside while the waffle iron was heating. Jake's garden glittered in the dew. His boot tracks wandered up and down the tidy rows. She ambled through the peaceful garden, taking whimsical pleasure in matching her steps to the prints he had left in the soil.

Sunshine and a satisfied appetite was a nice prelude to the productive morning of writing that followed. Wiley Weedman, sparked by Joy's account of her missing boss, shaped up nicely as a shady character. Shelby took the liberty of borrowing from Jake's account of Dan Flat's alleged chicanery. When coupled with Mrs. Wiseman's genealogical research, it provided plot answers for who did what and why and foreshadowed the unnatural nature of Wiley Weedman's disappearance.

It was a few minutes after twelve when Joy came with a lunch invitation. Shelby went downstairs and helped Paula put the meal together while Joy set the table.

"Still no sign of Mr. Wiseman?" she asked over a tuna salad sandwich and chips.

"I've given up on fieldwork," Joy said. "I'm helping Mom now."

"In the sign shop?" asked Shelby.

"Jake's strong on keeping the business in the family," Paula explained. "I think she's a little young for bookkeeping. But he urged me to give her some pointers and see if she has the knack."

"Adding, subtracting and writing a few checks. What's the big deal? Say! Maybe he fell in the cistern," Joy suggested, changing the subject.

"Who?"

"Mr. Wiseman," Joy said. "There are two in his backyard."

"Where you had no business," countered Paula.

"He could be dead, Mom."

"Oh, don't be silly!" Paula scolded.

Joy slanted Shelby a look from half-lidded eyes.

Her mouth curled into a faint smirk, as puzzling to Shelby as the purple slivers in the tuna salad.

"Purple basil," Paula told her, solving one mystery.

"From Uncle Jake's garden." Joy dampened her finger and drew a path through the potato chip crumbs on her plate. "Do you know that nightshade is fatal?"

"What's nightshade?" asked Shelby.

"A weed. When I was working cutting weeds out of beans, Uncle Jake warned me not to throw any nightshade over fences where livestock might eat it. Suppose it's fatal to people, too?" she asked, and sucked the salt off her fingers.

"Where are your manners?" complained Paula. "Stop licking your fingers."

"Sorry. How do you plot a mystery?" Joy asked Shelby.

"By asking 'what if?'" Shelby answered. "What if he isn't what he appears to be? What if she learns his secret? What if he discovers she knows? What if—"

"Mr. Wiseman is dead of nightshade?" Joy interjected.

"Joy, would you please give it a rest?" Paula said. "Rinse your plate if you're finished."

Joy dumped her dishes into the sink. "I'm out of here."

"Don't leave the yard," Paula warned.

Joy made a face and ambled out with her can of soda.

"She's grounded and I'm suffering. Go figure." Paula pushed her lunch aside and rose with a sigh to put the remaining dishes in the dishwasher.

"Leave those, I'll get them," said Shelby.

When Paula had gone, Shelby filled the sink with hot soapy water. As she washed dishes, she ironed the wrinkles out of the next story scene. Back in Jake's office, the words formed in her mind and trickled from her fingers to the keys like hot fudge over ice cream. By midafternoon, her teen sleuths had stumbled upon the late Mr. Weedman. The scene was a little rough.

Shelby let it breathe and polished what she had written that morning. She worked uninterrupted until Jake and Gram Kate came home. And still the grasping tentacles of her story held her in place. She was giving her revisions a hasty read when Jake knocked on the open door.

"Are you still working?"

"Just finished." Shelby closed her file. "I was thinking—it's about my turn to fix dinner. What do you like?"

"The sounds of that," he said.

Shelby noticed grease smudges on his shirt and trousers and four o'clock shadow darkening his jaw. His hair was tousled with a line of demarcation in chestnut waves where his cap usually rested. She smiled. "Did you have a rough day?"

"A long ride, mostly. We did a job up by Joliet." He leaned a shoulder against the doorjamb and hooked his fingertips in his pocket, adding, "I picked up Gram on the way home. She's in the kitchen, washing tomatoes. How are you with bacon-and-tomato sandwiches?"

"One of my favorites," said Shelby.

"Good. I'll grab a quick shower and come help you keep Gram out of the matches."

They traded smiles. He turned away and back again to ask, "How's the car?"

"The car!" Shelby pressed the heel of her hand to her forehead. "It slipped my mind."

"No one knocked or rang the bell?" asked Jake.

"If they did, I didn't hear them." Shelby crossed to the window and looked out at the white midsize sedan parked beside his Jeep. "Not that that means anything. I warned you, when I write…"

"Comatose, I know." He grinned.

"I'll take it for a spin after supper," Shelby said. "Would you like to come along?"

"Sure. It's black raspberry season. I know a good patch," Jake replied. "A berry pie sounds good, don't you think?"

"Second only to butter bean cake."

Laughter lit Jake's eyes. The ringing phone spared Shelby from admitting that she wasn't a pie baker. She went downstairs to help Gram Kate with dinner preparations.

Over dinner, Jake regaled them with a tale of rescuing a kitten from a tree using his bucket truck.

His story sparked a memory in Shelby. "I called the fire department once to rescue my kittens from the pool house roof." She smiled, remembering. "An ordinary ladder would have done it. But my mother was hostessing a fund-raiser, the housekeeper didn't speak English and I was unwilling to wait. Mom got pretty upset when the fire truck came through the gates. Everyone crowded out into the backyard to see what was burning."

Jake laughed. "You must have been a lively tyke."

"My goodness, yes, she was live…live…oh,"

murmured Gram. She nudged the platter of bacon Jake's way.

"No seconds for me, Gram. I'm saving room for pie."

Gram cocked her head to one side. "Did I make pie?"

"No, Gram. But Shelby and I are going to, once we get the berries picked. You do bake, don't you Shelby?" he asked.

"Only at the beach." Shelby rubbed her cheeks as if coating them in suntan oil.

Jake laughed, secretly appreciative of that fine white skin. "Scratch the pie, we'll go the beach," he said and rose to answer the ringing phone.

Chapter Seven

It was Paula on the phone. The man who dropped the loaner car by had left the keys with her. She had slipped the keys into her pocket, and forgot them until she arrived home.

"We were just talking about taking a drive after dinner," Jake told her. "Ask Joy if she'd mind keeping Gram company for an hour or so. Or is she not allowed out?"

"Hey! I'm a reasonable woman, I'll send her over as soon as we've eaten," Paula said cheerfully.

Joy showed up a short while later with crochet thread for Gram Kate, keys for Shelby and a kiss for her uncle Jake.

"Thanks for cutting me loose, I was going stir crazy," she muttered and rolled her eyes.

"Must be contagious, your mom has a touch of it, too," Jake said.

"You don't care if I use your computer, do you, Uncle Jake?" Joy asked, breezing on through the kitchen. ''Gram? Are you coming? Don't forget your crocheting.''

At Jake's suggestion, Shelby changed clothes for their berry-picking expedition. She came downstairs dressed in a pair of slim-fitting white slacks and a pink-and-white knit T-shirt that gently shaped itself to her contours. Jake pushed away from the porch pillar, enjoying the perfect foil her delicate skin made for the deep-pink trim that edged the scooped neck and cap sleeves of her shirt.

''Do these berries grow anywhere near a soybean field?'' Shelby asked as they crossed the yard to the car.

''Hadn't thought about it. Why?''

''Call it research. Would you mind?''

''Not at all,'' Jake replied. He held the car door for her as she slid behind the wheel, and circled to the passenger's side.

The evening sun flowed through the windshield, warming Shelby's skin as they left the town behind and set out for Wildwood. A rabbit darted across the road a few miles farther along as she slowed for the lane.

''Is the berry patch reserved for Wildwood guests?'' she asked, glancing away from the road to watch the rabbit dart safely into roadside grasses.

''The patch isn't here, we're taking the long way so I can show you a soybean field,'' Jake explained.

''Berries, soybeans. I'm beginning to see that there's a good deal more to Wildwood than meets the eye,'' Shelby said.

''It's a combination working farm and vacation site,'' replied Jake. He reached across the seat, honked the horn and waved to a young man sprawled beneath a tractor.

"That's Rick. He didn't know beans about tinkering when he started coming out here a few years ago. Trace took him under his wing, now there's not a piece of machinery on the place he can't fix. Pull over and we'll ask him about walking through the beans."

Jake rolled down his window, and made introductions. A dark-eyed handsome young man, Rick asked Shelby if she cared to take a hoe along.

"For the weeds?" she countered.

"No, the snakes," he replied.

Shelby shot Jake an alarmed glance.

"He's pulling your leg." Jake chuckled.

Rick conceded it with a grin, waved them on and went back to his tractor repairs.

The ruts Shelby followed per Jake's directions skirted pasture and a cornfield. The dirt trail ended at a body of trees and a creek. Drawn by the tranquil babbling of a tree-lined creek, she climbed out and found her way to the water's edge. Jake retrieved two plastic pails from the back seat of the car. He caught up with her at the creek where she perched on the bank, dangling a stick into the water, knees bent, her feet tucked beneath her.

Peering up at him, she asked, "How deep is the water?"

"Two, maybe three feet," Jake said, seeing her eyes water in the same leaf-dappled sunlight that caught fire in her hair. "There's a footbridge upstream."

Shelby took the berry pail and the hand up Jake offered, but dropped it again once she was on her feet. A campground came into view as they strolled side by side toward a bend in the creek.

"Sounds like the kids are singing for their supper." Jake pointed out a steel building set back in the trees on the other side of the creek.

Shelby stopped to listen to young voices mingling with bird cries and humming insects. A summer camp veteran, the familiar song wafting on the evening air brought back poignant memories of bouts with homesickness. "Church camp?"

Jake nodded. "Kids camps, retreats, family camps, Wildwood has it all."

"And the...cottages?" she faltered, leaving out *honeymoon*.

"Farther along, there in the pines," Jake said, wondering at her thoughts.

Shelby determined not to look should they pass within view of the cottages. Rejection and the memories it tarnished was tough enough without a visual aid of the honeymoon cabin.

The path narrowed, crowded by trees and undergrowth. Shelby fell behind Jake as they crossed the creek on a narrow bridge that brought them to the edge of the pines. So guarded was she against a chance glimpse of the threshold she had not crossed, she dropped her gaze to the path, and in so doing bumped into Jake when he stopped.

"Oops. Sorry," she began, when he turned with a warning finger to his lip, and pointed down the path. The vista opened to a rolling field. Alongside the field grazed two deer.

Shelby watched, transfixed, as the young buck's head came up. The doe lifted her head, too, then bounded after the buck across a pasture and into the woods.

"Beautiful!" Shelby exclaimed, thrilled at the sight.

Jake thought the same of her shining eyes and flushed cheeks. He held back a sapling so as not to let it snap back on her as they resumed walking. "Trace complains they get more than their share of the corn crop. But he wouldn't trade them for money in the bank."

Shelby returned his smile and lengthened her step to walk beside him as they left the woods behind. Planted rows stretched straight and neat and flowed together on the distant horizon. She stooped at the edge of the field and rested on the balls of her feet to pick up a handful of rich black dirt. Murmuring at the moistness of it, she let it sift through her fingers, then scooped again and breathed of its earthy fragrance.

The childlike exploration of ordinary dirt from one wrapped in so womanly a frame quickened Jake's pulse. He shifted his feet. She lifted her face and caught him watching her.

"That your research?" he quipped.

Color rose to her cheeks, heightening her appeal. "Just seeing what it smells like."

"What's the verdict?"

Her mouth tipped at his gentle teasing. "Pretty much the same as city dirt, I guess," she said, and dusted her hands.

There was dirt on the tip of her nose and a curve to her mouth that just begged to be kissed. Jake hunkered down beside her, but on closer examination deemed the impulse reckless. He checked it and plucked a soybean frond from an ankle-high plant. "You left a little research on your nose." He dusted her nose with the bean plant, then grinned and tickled her cheek with it.

The leaf was green velvet against Shelby's skin. His gesture was playful, but distracting just by virtue of her awareness of his fingertips touching her skin. "Soybean?" she asked.

He nodded.

"Soft," she said.

So was her cheek, and the fingers that brushed his as the snippet changed hands. Shelby averted her gaze and in less time than it took to fold the soybean frond into her pocket, was on her feet.

"Ready to go?" Jake asked. He cupped a hand to her elbow and nudged her to the center soil between two rows. It was too narrow for walking side by side. His hand fell away. He stepped over a row of beans and led the way across the field where the fading sun basked a second grove of trees in silvery green light. The berry bushes he had mentioned grew at the edge of the woods.

"This is state property," Jake said. "Keep walking, and you'll run into a dump."

Shelby wrinkled her nose. "Is that what I smell?"

"It's not that kind of dump. It's broken-up road beds and a graveyard of old equipment," said Jake. "There are some grain bins, too. It could be wet corn we smell. Or a dead animal. We'll go the other way. Maybe we can get upwind of it."

They soon came upon a second flush of wild black raspberry bushes. The brambles climbed a steep embankment. Jake left the easy picking to Shelby, and scaled to the top for the less accessible berries.

"Plip, plip, plip, I don't hear yours plipping," she called.

"The bottom of the pail is covered," he said, playing along. "Berries are floating in, not making a sound."

"That, or you're sleeping on the job," she countered. "Ouch! I'm caught on the bush. I should have worn long sleeves. You didn't mention the bushes were full of stickers."

"If you pick as good as you complain, we'll have enough for a pie in no time."

"I've picked them clean, I do believe. See here?"

Jake scanned the bushes and stretched his free hand down to her. "Those are beginner's bushes. Take off the training wheels and hack your way up here with the master berry pickers," he challenged.

"Is there enough to keep both of us picking?" she asked.

"And then some," he claimed.

Berry canes snagged Shelby's T-shirt, slowing progress. She hooked the handle of her pail over her arm and gripped Jake's hand with both of hers. But the bank was steep and slick from recent rain. She lost her footing and toppled into the ditch, squealing.

Jake spilled his bucket of berries, trying to reach her. "Are you okay?"

"Except for my pride and your berries." Flushed and giggling, she tried to get her feet. "I'm stuck! Where's a crane when you need one?"

Jake laughed and gripped her berry-stained hands. He hauled her to her feet, and up the bank before letting go. "You'll have to pick fast to redeem yourself."

"I will, will I?" she countered.

"That's right. A pail of berries before it gets dark."

"Is that enough for a pie?"

"More than," said. "You want make a race of it?"

"What're the stakes?"

"The loser bakes the pie. Deal?"

Reasoning the advantage was hers now that he had spilled his berries, she grinned and cried, "On your mark, set, go!"

Fingers flying, Shelby plucked the sweet ripe berries by the handful. But her pail was only half full when shadows draped the nearby woodlands in shades as deep as the berries.

"Better go," Jake said

"Don't tell me you've filled your pail already!"

"No. But if we don't start back now, we'll be stumbling along in the dark."

Shelby checked the contents of his pail, comparing it to hers. "Close," she said.

Jake grinned and helped her down the embankment. The setting sun was behind them as they crossed the field. When they reached the creek and looked back, it had slipped below the horizon. It sent up rays, gold-leafing the edges of pink-and-lavender clouds.

"Gorgeous," Shelby said, stopping beside Jake to admire the sky. "I love a pretty sunset."

"They're all pretty."

"Even the gray ones?" she asked.

At her smile, he couldn't remember gray. "All of them."

"I needed this," she conceded, as they resumed walking.

"We've had nice rains. Makes the berries plump and sweet," he said, and plopped a handful into his mouth.

"Not the berries. This," she said and stretched her free arm as if to embrace creation itself. "Days get so rushed, it's easy to neglect the simple things."

Understanding came with a smile. Shelby smiled, too. It moved over Jake like a tender glance, that quiet brush of souls that words would only diminish.

They had dawdled long enough that darkness fell en route to the car. "Watch out for the stump there." Familiar with the terrain, Jake made the most of it and caught Shelby's hand under the guise of guiding her safely along.

Her fingers were sticky with berry juice. His were, too. A working hand, strong and scuffed and callused. Solid, like the man. Shelby thought of retrieving her hand, but didn't. Choosing not to examine her reasons too closely she hummed beneath her breath as they ambled the path back to the car. On the ride home, she fell silent, content to watch the thumbnail moon ascend and shoulder the stars about.

"How about a tiebreaker?" asked Jake as he slowed for the road into town.

"A pie breaker?"

He chuckled. "You heard me the first time."

"I write better than I bake," Shelby said mildly.

"I'll introduce you to Gram's fail-proof recipe."

"Not so fast," she protested. "I may not need a recipe. There is a good chance I won this contest."

"Prove it," he countered.

"We'll count them," Shelby said, reaching for her pail.

"Inconclusive. I ate some of mine," claimed Jake.

"Too bad," she said.

Jake laughed. He hit the dimmer switch on the headlights and sang, "She can bake a cherry pie fast as a cat can wink its eye. But she's a young thing and cannot leave her mother."

"Watch it, charming Billy. Pedestrians," Shelby warned, and poured his berries into her pail while he was busy giving his side of the road to two joggers.

Jake stretched an arm along the back of the seat, cuffed her shoulder, and resumed singing, "She can bake a berry pie, fast as a cat can wink its eye. But she's a berry thief and berry thieves barely ever win."

Jake checked on Gram as soon as they arrived home. She had retired for the night. He turned out the light she had left on, and joined Shelby at the kitchen sink.

She looked up from washing the berries. "You mentioned a recipe."

"In here." Jake reached into the cupboard over her head for a cedar box recipe file. "I'll run Joy home and be right back to help," he promised and left her flipping through file cards.

Joy was in Jake's office, glued to the computer screen. She gave a start when he bumped the desk.

"Pry yourself away, and I'll—" Seeing guilt leap to her face, Jake glanced from her face to the screen and back again. "What're you up to now?"

"Nothing," she said and fumbled for the mouse.

Jake caught her wrist before she could clear the screen. "Let's have a look."

"It isn't anything, honest."

"Scoot." Jake waved her out of his chair and away from the keyboard. He scanned a few lines, then bolted out of the chair, scolding, "Joy! You shouldn't be reading this. It's Shelby's story."

"Is it?" Joy paused in the midst of feigned innocence, and narrowed her eyes. "Say, how do *you* know what it is?"

Heat swept up Jake's neck. "Get your stuff together. Your mom will be calling," he replied, dodging her shrewd question.

"She already did," replied Joy. "Twice. I thought you were picking berries."

"We were."

"After dark?"

"Don't change the subject," growled Jake. "That's twice now you've poked your nose into her business."

"Have a cat, why don't you?" Joy flounced out of her chair, pushed out her bottom lip and didn't say a word until Jake stopped the Jeep in front of her house.

"Don't tell on me and I won't tell on you," she said, changing tactics.

Irritated, Jake countered, "Get out before I turn you over my knee."

"We have a deal, then?" she said, so close to gloating, Jake reached as if to make good on his threat.

Joy scrambled out of the Jeep, backed off a yard and drew a finger across her lips. "Mum's the word, partner."

Trapped by his own duplicity, Jake clamped his jaw tight.

Joy flung her backpack over her shoulder and tramped inside. It wasn't good for her, getting away with it. Jake knew that. But he didn't care much for the alternative.

Shelby was in the kitchen, up to her elbows in flour when Jake arrived home. Hearing him come in, she ceased humming "Billy Boy," swung around and flung her arms wide, trying to screen her pie makings on the counter behind her. "Stop! You can't see until it's in the oven."

"Will that be anytime soon?" He glossed over a guilty conscience with friendly banter.

She cast the clock a frowning glance. "At present rate, we'll be having pie for breakfast."

"I'll make the filling," he offered. "You finish the crust, and we'll have hot pie à la mode out in the hammock under the stars."

"I'm having a little trouble," she admitted.

Jake peered through the arch between her outstretched arm and her side. A lumpy wad of dough was caught on the counter between two pieces of waxed paper. He shifted his gaze to her face. She had been eating berries. The evidence at the corner of her mouth distracted him. "Try a little more flour," he said.

"You try. Okay?"

Jake washed his hands, motioned her aside, and peeled away the waxed paper.

Shelby's doleful gaze skipped from her lump of dough to his tactfully held mouth. "Hopeless?" she asked.

"Not at all. It's a fair start."

"That's what I thought," she said, and wrinkled her nose. "Can you fix it?"

Jake divided the dough and returned half to the

bowl. He moistened the counter so the waxed paper wouldn't slip.

"It didn't mention that on the recipe," said Shelby.

"It's a tip from Gram Kate." Jake stepped back and offered her the rolling pin. "Your turn. Get a nice firm grip on the handles. Go on, take it."

Shelby took his place at the counter. The light gleamed on her white neck and red-gold tresses. Jake stepped closer, drawn by curls on cream and her light, sweet scent. She gave the pie dough a nudge with the pin.

"Put some pressure to it," he urged. "That's the way."

"Are you sure you wouldn't like to do this yourself?"

"You'll get the hang of it." Jake stepped behind her and covered her hands on the rolling pin. "Try it like this."

Shelby drew a breath and held it. Jake could feel it, trapped there between them, as surely as the small white hands trapped beneath his. The skin to skin sensation transmitted itself to him like static traveling nerve endings.

"Keep it light, but firm, that's it," he murmured, his voice growing thick as the filling yet to be made. "Now the other way. Make each pass count. Reach out there now and give the paper a turn," he said and moved his hand.

She turned the waxed paper with its half-formed pie crust, then turned herself, too. Caught between him and the counter, she lowered her lashes, unable to meet what she had kindled in his eyes. "I've got it now."

Her subdued manner, the scent of her perfume, and thick-lashed eyes that wouldn't hold Jake's gaze filled his senses. He brushed flour from her cheek with a touch that turned into a caress. But she caught his wrist.

"Don't, Jake," she murmured, before he could cover her berry-stained mouth in kisses.

"You sure?" His voice fell to a corn husk whisper.

"It isn't… It's just that…"

"I'm not pressing you," he said. "I like what I see, that's all."

"But when you say that…" she began.

"You're over thinking this."

"I need some time," she said, heart beating hard.

Jake turned the hand that held his wrist. Matched his palm to hers. Moist and firm, like her mouth telling him no. Easy to look at, hard to hear. He shifted his weight, giving her space. Let go of her hand and the other one, too, and sought words with the right inflection so as to bridge the moment: "Two tablespoons of flour, a pat of butter and sugar to taste. There's a saucepan on the stove. You don't want to cook it, just thicken the berries."

"Jake?"

He looked to find her chewing her lip, anxiety tugging at her eyes and mouth.

"Never mind. I'll make it," he said, letting her off the hook.

"We can still be friends, can't we?" said Shelby.

"I was talking about the pie. I'll make the pie."

Color swept up her ivory neck, staining her cheeks. Her lashes fell, making dusky shadows beneath her eyes. Remorse washed over him. Her words were innocent and well-intentioned. His were duck and cover. Even now, pride had him by the throat. He turned away and ran his finger down the recipe card to keep from saying anything else to be sorry for later.

"I'm not much help here, am I?" she said into the clock-ticking tap-dripping silence. "I think I'll call it a night. If you don't mind finishing it by yourself."

"Sure. Go on," he replied.

"Leave the dishes. I'll clean the kitchen tomorrow," she said before slipping up the stairs and leaving him all by his lonesome.

Chapter Eight

Shelby kicked herself all the way up the stairs. It shouldn't have taken a caress to make her aware of the feelings awakening in Jake. But a relationship gone south and her preoccupation with getting on with life had blinded her to the subtleties of...

Oh, who was she kidding? What subtleties? Jake didn't have to spell it out in neon. His frankness on the heels of that almost-kiss was no more than what she should have anticipated. He'd been silently appraising her with those sky-blue eyes of his almost from the moment they met. His appreciative glances drove back shadows and her battered ego responded in gratitude. And why not? He was an enterprising, good-natured, rugged man's man, his even-keeled personality seasoned with humor and a tenderness for God and family.

Her heart was still rocking; she had come so close to walking into his arms. But it was the rejected part that missed being held and kissed and regarded as unique and worth waiting for. *Wasn't it?* Her hidden self cringed, shrinking from razor sharp reflection. Yet if she couldn't be honest, what was left to distinguish between writing fiction and living it?

Was it time to go home? Before she threw caution to the wind and herself into Jake's arms. Was she that emotionally ragged? She flushed at the thought and tried to wash it away in the shower. At length, she crawled into bed, then out again and to her knees, seeking a sign from God as to what feelings to trust, what to dismiss as tremors and aftershocks, and what to do about Jake.

Jake made short work of the pie and sugared the top crust. But his interest in pie making had fled up the stairs. The arms she had held up to screen her pie from him also held him at bay. Her heart was still living in the past, and his had turned with tenderness for her. If she lived down the street or in the next town, he would bide his time. But she would leave in a few days, and he would know her no better than he knew her right now. *Except through her written words.*

Jake cleaned up the kitchen and made a pot of coffee. He took a cup with him to his study, tucked his conscience into bed, and opened Shelby's file. Starting at the beginning, he took his time, relishing the bits and pieces of Shelby dispersed throughout her characters. His coffee had cooled by the time he reached the additions she had made since last night's reading:

Tara heard a garbage can rattle.

"What was that?" cried Cheryl.

Tara pivoted to see Jack ease around the side

of Weedman's house and out of sight.

"You guys! You're trespassing all over the place!" Cheryl's hoarse whisper trailed after Tara.

"Shh!" Tara pressed into sun-soaked siding. Inched around the house. Made the far corner as a shout rang out. She scanned the backyard, heart in her throat. Tangled grass. Weeds. All of it moving as if by a maverick breeze.

Tara tripped over a bulky tarp. She fell as the canvas moved beneath her. She had fallen on top of Jack!

"My glasses!" Jack's muffled cry brought her scrambling to her feet.

At the same moment, a figure sprang from the moving grass and bolted for the barberry hedge bordering the back alley.

Tara lunged after the fleeing figure and caught a handful of T-shirt. But he outmuscled her and jerked free. She weighed her concern for Jack against the odds of catching his assailant, factored in barbed branches and pricey jeans. She turned back.

"Jack? Are you okay?" Tara cried.

Jack crawled from beneath the crumpled tarp and flung a blind glance toward the hedge. "Where'd he go? Did he get away?"

"I couldn't hold him." Tara eagle-eyed his glasses, scooped them up unbroken and dropped them into his hand. "Who was it?"

"I don't know. Tarp hit me out of nowhere. Had a body behind it. Hit the ground hard. Must have knocked the wind out of me." Jake put on his glasses and staggered to his feet.

"Did you get a look?"

"Male. Five-eleven. Muscular—160 or 170 pounds. Green T-shirt, jeans, a baseball cap." Tara rattled off his assailant's description.

"Dudley," growled Jake. "Figures."

"Where do we find him?" Tara asked, primed to rocket into hot pursuit.

"Ask Cheryl, they're so chummy," Jack growled.

Tara twitched, watching him rein in his emotions. It was a mute and instantaneous exercise interrupted by the hoarse roar of a motor coming to life. "The truck!" she cried.

Jake sped past Tara. She circled the house at his heels as Dudley tore away, his truck tires spitting rocks and burning rubber. Cheryl stood in the avenue, shielding her face and shouting after him.

Jake reread the last few paragraphs again. Three times, Shelby had typed *Jake* instead of Jack. He was intrigued by the mistake, and by the dangled carrot of a love triangle in which hearts were sure to be skinned.

The buttery sweet fragrance of fruit and baking pastry wafted throughout the house. All that remained to be read was bare-boned plot with snatches of dialogue. Stray thoughts and incomplete sentences trailed off into wide gaps between paragraphs yet to be filled in. Jake shut down the computer, returned to the kitchen and took the pie from the oven. But his appetite for sweets had been displaced by a yearning that pie could not remedy. He left it to cool uncut, and went to bed.

* * *

Shelby slept poorly. Singing birds ushered in the dawn. Feeling draggy, she pulled a pillow over her head. But sound carried through the feather pillow, footsteps that caught her ear and made her listen. Certain it was Jake going downstairs, she struggled with the proper way to go about leaving. Should she say goodbye in person? Or leave him a note?

The easy out was cold by any standard, and poor return upon the hospitality she had received. Gambling that Jake would take his time over breakfast, she swung out of bed, grabbed her robe and padded into the bathroom.

The blended scents of soap, shaving cream and a tangy aftershave lotion lingered there. Shelby showered quickly in that haze of masculine scent, and donned a sleeveless dress of pale apricot. The bodice was fitted, the skirt free-flowing and comfortable for travel. She dashed a comb through her curls, tinted her lips, and was on her knees, reaching under the bed for her platform sandals, when Jake's Jeep growled to life in the driveway below. Shelby flung open the window and called to him, but couldn't make herself heard over the Jeep. Abandoning her shoe search, Shelby flew barefoot down the steps, through the house and over the dewy grass.

"Jake!" She waved both arms as he backed into the alley.

Jake glanced around, and hit the brakes. His heart leapt to all sorts of conclusions at the sight of her coming after him. He rolled down the window. "You're up early."

"Yes, I know. Good morn— Ouch! Murder!" she muttered, even as his amiable demeanor quieted her fears over last night's honest exchange.

Jake's mouth twitched at the sight of her mincing across white rock, arms spread, fingers cocked. He opened the driver's door. "Climb in, tenderfoot."

"No thanks, I don't want to keep you," Shelby said, breath coming light and shallow and driven by a heavy pulse. "I just wanted to say—"

"I'm in no hurry. Hop in." Jake slid to one side and patted the remaining portion of bucket seat.

Taking pity on her bare feet, Shelby gripped the steering wheel and swung up beside him. The close fit brought him into sharp focus. The shaving nick on his chin. The associated scents. The strength and tautness of his thigh.

"Careful, you'll fall out on your nose." He draped his left arm over her shoulder, stabilizing her precarious perch.

Hastily prepared speech forgotten, Shelby asked, "How'd the pie turn out?"

"Work of art," he said. "You didn't notice? I'm hurt."

His chuckle resounded at close quarters, evoking an answering smile. "I'll admire it in a minute, I promise." She dropped her gaze, tracing with her eye a raveling thread that hung from the hem of his short-sleeved work shirt and curled against hard biceps. "I didn't want to leave without saying goodbye. And telling you how much I appreciate your hospitality."

His smile died. "You're leaving?"

"It's been three days."

"I thought you had a week."

"I do. But I have a car now. I've imposed long enough." Feeling the ease go out of him, Shelby's heart crowded against her ribs. She lifted her lashes to find his eyes gone somber upon his deeply tanned features. *Like lamps keeping watch over sun-glazed prairie.* The description wrote itself upon the tablet of her heart. Swiftly, she averted her gaze to his forefinger, tracing a dusty crack in the steering wheel.

Madness. She condemned the sudden ache to lock his finger with her own. A trapped fly sounded like a chain saw buzzing against the window glass. She bridged the painful silence. "I need to get my computer fixed and tie up some loose ends before I return to work. I have those manuscripts to read yet. And there's my writing, of course."

"If this is about last night..." he began at length.

"It isn't." Shelby gripped the steering wheel, an anchor as he withdrew his arm. Madness paraded, this time as an impulse to turn her face into that hard arm and hold on tight. Instead, she opened the door and let herself down on the bruising white rock.

"You taking off right away?" he asked.

"Noon or so. It's a three-hour drive."

He nodded. "We do jobs up that way occasionally."

"You do?" Shelby replied. "Then perhaps you'd let me take you out to dinner the next time you're in town."

"I might, if you twisted my arm," he said.

She knew it was an illusion. Yet there it was, that sensation of all else falling away, leaving them showered by blue halo. Twin brackets framed and lifted his mouth as he leaned and offered an arm to twist. She smiled and reached past it for the pen in his pocket.

"Paper?"

He gave her a credit card receipt from the dash-

board, and when she had jotted down her phone
number, traded it for his business card.

"If you ever need a good sign man, give me a
call."

"I will," she murmured.

His grin relieved the heaviness over saying goodbye. She had to pack and change the sheets and e-
mail her story to herself. But all she wanted to do
was look into those eyes looking back at her. Their
fingers brushed as she returned his pen, sending a
pleasant sensation pulsating up her arm.

"I'll call and let you know next time I have a job
in the city. Until then—" he tucked his pen into his
pocket, reached for her fingers and gave them a
squeeze "—take care of yourself."

"You too. I love...I loved being here," she
amended. "In spite of everything."

"You're welcome anytime."

"That's sweet of you. Thank you."

He pressed her hand once more, and let it go.

She watched him drive away, and hugged herself.
Love him? She hardly knew him. Her slipping tongue
was the sign she sought, the billboard spelling out in
urgent letters, Go Home!

Shelby trekked back through the kitchen, and saw
that Jake had tidied it. The coffee in the coffeepot
on the counter was still hot. She poured herself a cup,
and noticed the pie. It was uncut on the counter. Picture perfect. But pies weren't made to be admired for
their beauty.

The pie smirked in its wholeness charging her with
crimes against the pie baker. She had disappointed
him. Stolen his joy. Deprived him of company after

all the trouble of prickly bushes and spilled berries and time spent making and baking.

Shelby threatened the pie with knife, plate and server. It sneered, daring her to help herself. But how could she when Jake had not? She was covering her crimped and crusted accuser in plastic wrap when Jake's sister Christine came for Gram Kate. Gram Kate urged them to have some pie. The dear soul thought she had baked it herself. Shelby declined. But Gram talked Christine into having a piece. She cut a slice for herself, too, then replaced the wrap over the remaining pie and gave it to Christine to take home and share with her family.

Shelby felt badly that Jake's sweet tooth was in for a disappointment. Unable to help, she tried to dismiss it, and padded into his office to e-mail her story home. With time to spare, she reworked yesterday's rough draft. As always, time fell away as the story pulled her in:

"What was he doing here, anyway?" Tara asked as Dudley streaked away, his pickup truck oil-burning a trail of smoke.

"Helping look for Mr. Weedman, I suppose," said Cheryl.

"Some help," muttered Jack.

As Jack popped his knuckles and brooded, Tara explained how Dudley had knocked Jack to the ground and flung the tarp over him.

"I'm sure he didn't mean to hurt you, he probably just wanted to get away unseen," Cheryl said.

"You think?" Jack said.

Cheryl sniffed. Tara looked from one to the

other, but didn't venture a comment.

Jack fished his keys out of his pocket. "No use hanging around here. Come on, let's get going."

Tara slid into the front seat after Cheryl, and closed the passenger's door. "Where to?"

"Blatchford Farms," Jack replied.

"Blatchford? The farm is named for the town?" Tara asked.

"No. The town is named after Mr. Blatchford's great-granddaddy."

"Drop me off at home, would you Jack?" Cheryl spoke up as Jack pulled away from the curb.

"You're not coming with us?" Jack asked.

"Mom's expecting me home to watch the kids. Let me know what you find out."

Jack slowed for a mobile home park at the edge of town. Tara climbed out to let Cheryl out of the car.

"Catch you later," Cheryl said.

A short drive in the country took Jack and Tara past thriving green fields and up a gravel lane. Jack stopped in front of a handsome house with deep porches and tall white columns.

"Nice place," Tara commented, admiring the commanding view of countryside.

"It's on the register of historic homes. Mr. Blatchford's proud of his heritage," Jack told her. "You coming?"

"Wouldn't miss it," Tara said, swinging her door wide.

Jack led the way to the porch where geraniums blossomed in hanging pots, and fans rotated lazily overhead. A little black dog darted out between the feet of the woman who answered the bell.

"Sugar!" cried the housekeeper, hands in her hair. "Catch her before she strikes a rabbit trail and runs off again."

Jack leapt after the dog. "Here Sugar, here Sugar!"

His tone clashed with the sweetness of the name. Tara giggled and trailed them across the yard, singing.

The dog darted straight for the field with no sign of slowing. Jack tore after him, leaping over rows of shin-high beans. Tara's lightheartedness gave way to alarm at the speed with which the dog was outdistancing Jack. "Stop chasing her, you're scaring her," she warned.

Jake stopped. But only because his trailing shoestring tripped him. He sprawled headlong in the dirt. Sugar slowed to a trot, then stopped a short distance away and began digging. Whining. Yelping, front paws showering dirt.

Tara stood by, trying to catch her breath as Jake tied his shoe.

"Okay, I'll go this way and you go thataway," he whispered on the way to his feet.

Tara noticed a rank odor as she crept forward, and wrinkled her nose. "Phew. What is that?"

"I don't know, don't worry about it. Inch up there and grab her."

Tara reached for Sugar's collar, then froze and gaped with unbelieving eyes. Jutting out of the dirt between the dog's paws was a human hand. Scarred. With a missing finger. She shrieked in horror.

Jack bounded to her side, and recoiled, too. All the color drained from his face. "Good gravy, you've found Weedman!"

"How do you..." All at once, Cheryl's remembered description split Tara's drumming ears. The missing finger. She covered her face and didn't look again.

Shelby heard voices in the kitchen and saw that it was noon. Quickly, she reread her story, corrected typos, turning several *Jakes* into *Jacks,* and e-mailed her story to her home computer.

Paula sent Joy with a lunch invitation. With Joy's help, Shelby secured the file so that it was safe to leave on Jake's computer until she arrived home and made a backup.

"Then I'll call you and you can delete it for me, okay?" said Shelby.

"Sure, no problem," Joy agreed. "Guess what? Mrs. Wiseman's car is home. Dirk called and told me."

Chagrined at the realization her story character, Mr. Weedman, was more real to her than Joy's boss, Mr. Wiseman, Shelby said, "I suppose that solves that mystery, then."

"If he's with her, it will."

"You don't know?" asked Shelby.

"Not yet," Joy answered. "When I talked to Dirk, he said none of the crew showed up this morning, so he went home, too. Does Uncle Jake know you're leaving?" She turned from the matter at hand.

"Yes."

"What'd he say? Was he upset?" Joy asked.

"Hardly. What makes you ask?" Shelby returned.

"Aunt Wendy said…oh, never mind," Joy replied. "She's kind of silly sometimes."

Mapped amidst the curiosity of Joy's expression was relief. Shelby didn't quite know what to make of it, so she dismissed it, and thanked Joy for all her help. "If you ever get to Chicago, give me a call and we'll get together."

"Sure, whatever," Joy agreed offhandedly.

Paula was disappointed to learn Shelby was leaving. She had brought a casserole for lunch. Finding it hard to turn her down, Shelby accepted her lunch invitation graciously, and helped make a salad while Paula reheated the casserole in the microwave.

When they had finished eating, Joy poked about, looking for dessert. "I thought you and Uncle Jake were going to make a pie."

Shelby explained about Gram Kate giving the pie away.

"And you didn't say anything?" A snicker escaped Paula. "I can see Jake trying to figure out what became of his pie."

"There's more berries in here," Joy announced. She was standing before the open refrigerator, scanning the shelves for something sweet. "You could make another one."

"If I had time, I could," Shelby said. "But I'd like get on the road."

"Uncle Jake'll live, I guess," Joy concluded. She opened a package of store-bought cookies, and blurted, "Hey, I know! Take 'em to Emmie. The berries, I mean."

"Emmaline Newton. Her uncle owns Newt's Market," Paula explained at Shelby's questioning glance.

"Emmie keeps the pastry counter stocked. She also takes baking orders on the side."

Pleased at the thought of sparing Jake disappointment, Shelby said, "I'll call her, then. Thank you, Joy. That's a great idea."

Shelby phoned the store and made arrangements to drop the berries by the store on her way out of town. Paula trailed her to the car and hugged her goodbye. Joy let a casual wave suffice, then trotted after her mother, coaxing for permission to walk over to the Wiseman's house and collect her pay.

Chapter Nine

Emmaline Newton was a pert, petite young woman in her late twenties. She held up the plastic bag, squinted as she estimated how many berries it contained, then wrinkled her freckled nose. "You're short at least a cup. Two would be closer."

Having put her hand to the plow, Shelby was unwilling to abandon the idea. After all that Jake had done for her, it was a small enough matter to find her way back to the berry patch and pick a few berries for him.

"I'll leave these with you, and be back with more in a little while," she told Emmie, and took the road to Wildwood.

Once there Shelby made the solitary jaunt along the creek, over the bridge and across the field. She stopped at the first berry patch. It was one she and Jake had abandoned the evening before because of the unpleasant odor. The smell was even more overpowering today. But the berries were plump and ripe, and easily accessible.

Shelby unfolded the paper sack Emmie had given her, waded deeper into the berry bushes and tripped over a shoe. The shoe, on second glance, was attached to a foot, the foot to a leg. The leg wasn't moving. Flies swarmed. The body was...

Jake was in the boom truck, on his way to Peoria when he answered his cell phone. It took him a moment to recognize Shelby's broken babbling. When he did, his blood went cold.

"Shelby? Slow down. I can't understand you," he cried.

"He's not moving," she wailed.

"Who isn't moving?"

" I think he's... I know he's..."

"Shelby! Where are you?"

"Where we picked berries. He's dead."

"Dead? Who?"

"I don't know, I don't know. I tripped over...oh, Jake. What if he's been...I don't know...what do I..."

"He didn't hurt you?"

"No! I told you, he's dead!"

"Okay. Calm down, Shelby. Are you calling from your car?"

"Yes," she sobbed. "Near the creek."

"Stay put. I'll call 911 and be there as soon as I can."

"Hurry, Jake. Please hurry."

Heart pounding, ears roaring, Jake took her cell number, called the authorities, then called her back and stayed on the line until the police arrived.

The county sheriff came and then the coroner. The sheriff was accompanied by a female deputy, who stayed in the car with Shelby. Shelby battled for composure as she explained how she had found the body. Even as she spoke, she couldn't stop thinking about the similarity between reality and the story scene she had polished that morning.

What if it was Joy's boss, Mr. Wiseman? Fresh tears burned her eyes. *Not him. Please, God.*

"You say you were here last evening?" The deputy passed her a tissue.

Shelby nodded and dried her eyes. Tears brimmed again as she explained about bypassing the first berry patch and why. There was just no escaping the shock of finding a dead man.

Shelby's relief at Jake's arrival was overwhelming. She burst into fresh tears the moment he opened the car door. "You okay?" he asked, his face rigid with concern.

"What if it's Mr. Wiseman?" she whimpered and clutched his reaching hands with icy fingers.

"They don't know yet?"

"If they do, they haven't told me. But if it is…"

"Wait and see," he soothed. But his eyes, as he helped her from the car, reflected her own half-formed conviction.

"Joy…she tried and tried…we could have…" Shelby couldn't finish.

"Take it easy," Jake murmured. His face blurred before her tear-swollen eyes as he gathered her in. He rocked her in his arms, stroking her back, whispering words of comfort. He smelled of sunshine and soap and life. Unable to stop shaking, she clung to him and wept openly.

"Would it be all right if I took her home?" Jake asked the deputy.

The deputy asked her superior, then granted permission.

Jake drove Shelby's car back to town. Her things were in the back seat. He left them there, kept his arm around her on the way to the house, and put the teakettle on to boil. He dropped a tea bag into a cup and grabbed the kettle before it whistled.

Shelby couldn't get the tea past her swollen throat. But the cup was warm and solid and comforting between her hands.

Jake settled on the living room sofa beside her. "You never did say what you were you doing out there. When I left this morning, you were all set to go home."

"They cut your pie," she said, and explained brokenly about Gram giving the remainder to his sister Christine.

"You were going to make another one?" Surprised, and touched, Jake remarked, "You'd go to all that trouble for me?"

"I wasn't going to bake it. The girl at the store was," Shelby told him. "Emmaline. She said I needed more berries."

"It was a nice thought," Jake said, his voice low and soothing. "I'm sorry it turned out so badly."

She shuddered. Careful not to jostle hands cupping hot tea, Jake put his arm around her.

Fresh tears rose to her eyes. "Jake? I need to know if it's… Who it is and what happened to him?"

"I'll drive back out there and talk to the police," he offered. "Will you be all right here alone?"

Shelby nodded. He came to his feet. Feeling bereft, she set her tea down and reached quickly for his hand. "Thanks, Jake."

He squeezed her slim white fingers, still warm from the cup. "I'll be back as soon as I can. Paula's in the shop, if you need anything."

The news beat Jake back to town. Joy's freckles stood out like knots on her pale face as she burst into the house.

"Oh, Shelby. It's just awful. Mr. Wiseman's dead!"

Joy buried her hands in her face and spilled a broken tale of being on the doorstep of the Wiseman house when the police came and gave Mrs. Wiseman the tragic news.

"I knew it," Joy sobbed. "All along, I just knew something was wrong, that Mr. Wiseman wasn't coming back."

"You'd already spoken to Mrs. Wiseman when the police came?" Shelby asked hesitantly.

"Yes. She said she had tried to call Mr. Wiseman a couple of times while she was away on business. Then she got home and his van was there, but he wasn't." Joy crowded words, one over the other. "When I told her I hadn't seen him in three days, she got really upset. She was inside, dialing the police when they came."

Jake returned as Joy was wrapping up her account. Joy flew into his arms. Retelling the story seemed to help her. Just as she was pulling herself together, Paula came in. Joy turned into her embrace and burst into a fresh storm of tears.

Jake took Shelby to one side, and told her quietly that the police had found a bicycle. Apparently, Mr.

Wiseman had ridden out to the berry patch, left the
bike by a foot path, and died as he was picking berries.

"According to Mrs. Wiseman, he had a heart condition. She wants to be sure, though, and requested
an autopsy," he concluded.

Poor woman. Shelby could only imagine what she
must be going through. A nasty accusation whispered
that without knowing anything of Mr. Wiseman's
true character she had assigned him the role of villain
and had cold-bloodedly written him off at the keyboard. Stricken, she slipped upstairs to the guest
room, pulled a rocking chair to the window and
scanned the room for a book. Any book.

Catching herself at it, Shelby hugged her knees to
her chest and denied herself the comfort of that
makeshift lap she had so often curled into as a child
when her father was away nipping and tucking and
her mother was busy making the city a better place
for those less fortunate. She couldn't escape this. She
had to face it squarely.

Jake grew concerned when an hour had passed and
Shelby hadn't returned downstairs. He knocked at the
guest room door, then let himself in and crossed to
the window where she sat huddled in the rocking
chair. The late-afternoon sun caught fire in her hair
and showered stark light over her tear-ravaged face.

"How's Joy?" she murmured, lowering her face.

"Cried out. Paula took her home. How about
you?" he asked, heart going out to her.

Unable to find words for her remorse, Shelby knotted the damp hanky. Fresh tears pressed for release.

"I can drive you home, if you're not feeling up to it," he offered.

"I don't think so."

"You don't want to go home?"

It wasn't a matter of choice. It was unfinished. How could she pick up and go home now? *As if Mr. Wiseman's life were a story she had bungled and could not finish.*

Shelby hung her throbbing head. Jake hunkered down in front of the rocking chair. He patted her knee and squeezed her hand. His silent sympathy reminded her of Henry, the old gentleman gardener who buried her kitten when she was small.

"Once, Dad took me to get a kitten," Shelby said when the silence grew heavy. "There were two to choose between, and I couldn't decide. Dad was in a hurry, so we took them both."

"What did you name them?" Jake asked, encouraged that her thoughts had momentarily shifted from Mr. Wiseman's demise.

"Kitten names," Shelby replied, for her carelessness had cost one kitten its life even before she had settled on names. "I was supposed to keep them in the backyard. I didn't, and one was hit by a passing car."

"That happens," said Jake.

Mutely, she nodded, all the while remembering her mother's stricken, "I *told* you to keep those kittens in the fence! See what happens when you don't listen?"

They should have listened to Joy. Maybe if they'd listened...if they'd looked, Mr. Wiseman would be in the hospital instead of... Shelby said brokenly, "I'll st-stay until after the funeral."

At Jake's silence, she lifted hot eyelids. "If that's all right with you."

"You're welcome. You know that," Jake told her, wanting her to stay, and yet knowing it would make matters harder on her emotionally. "I just thought you'd made up your mind to go."

"A man died."

"I'm sorry it was you who found him. But Shelby, no one expects you to change your plans for a man you didn't know," he said gravely.

"I wrote about him," she confessed, dabbing at her eyes.

"Used him for inspiration, you mean?"

His words passed right over her head. Her aching eyes swelled again. "In my story...I was so... cavalier."

He hunkered down before the rocking chair and caught her hands in his. "Turn off the wheels for a while," he urged. "Come downstairs. I'll start supper. You can help, if you like."

"I try not to write things that...you know, might have a negative impact on young readers," Shelby continued, following her own dogged train of thought.

"Of course not. That's what I'd expect of you. I knew the moment we met that you had a good heart," he said, little knowing that his kindness only made her feel worse.

"Life is precious. But I devalued it. I did, Jake." She struggled, words catching in her throat. "Last night I asked God for a sign, and today, I find M-Mr. W-i-s-s-e-m-m-an...." Her voice broke.

"What kind of a sign?" he asked.

"...is that?" She anticipated his meaning. "I know. That's what I'm saying."

"No, I mean why were you asking for a sign? About what?" Jake asked.

His calm question logjammed thought waves. She hadn't asked concerning her writing. She had asked what to do about Jake. *And God sent her stumbling over a dead man.*

It washed over her again in a wave of near-physical illness. Reality and her story world had converged. She had lost her internal compass. She didn't know straight up anymore. "You read it, Jake."

"Your story?" he said, surprised.

"Yes, my story."

"Won't it weaken your motivation to..."

"...finish it? It doesn't matter now."

"Why not?" he asked, shifting to his feet as she rose to hers.

"Read it, Jake. Then you'll understand."

Jake accompanied her downstairs. Guilty over earlier trespasses, he stood silent as she brought up her file and scrolled to the last scene.

A muscle twitched in his jaw.

"I'll be in the kitchen," she said and turned away.

"Wait a second, don't go," he urged, and caught her hand to keep her from leaving. She tipped her face. Her red-rimmed eyes were so trusting, he lost his courage to confess and amended, "Let's read it together, okay?"

Fresh tears shimmered. She pressed fingertips to her trembling lips. "I can't, Jake. I can't make myself do it. You read it," she said, and fled, leaving him alone with her story.

Chapter Ten

In the kitchen, Shelby turned idle hands into busy ones, the long-touted panacea for all that ailed. But her strength was riddled with holes through which the darkness crept. She cried to God, and His written word echoed back a familiar promise: "Yea though I walk through the valley of the shadow of death, thou art with me."

She let the verse and the ones that followed flow through her until the rushing quieted and she could hold an ingredient list in mind long enough to retrieve shrimp, mushrooms and fresh vegetables from the refrigerator. Deveining the shrimp, she hugged close the picture of a shepherd comforting a lamb with the touch of his staff. She cleaned the vegetables, capped some mushrooms and was putting rice on to cook when the phone rang.

Jake must have answered, for it didn't ring again. Failing to find a wok, she heated olive oil in a black iron skillet instead. Her stir-fry over rice was almost ready to be served when Jake joined her in the kitchen.

"That was Wendy on the phone," he told her, and crossed to the sink to wash his hands. "She and Homer are going to pick up Gram at Rosewood and take her to dinner and a quilt exhibit downtown before bringing her home."

Shelby passed him a hand towel, and waited. But he offered nothing concerning her story. "Did you read it?" she ventured at length.

"Yes."

"And?" Shelby prompted, anxious for his opinion.

"I like your style."

"That isn't what I meant."

"I know," Jake said. He returned Gram's plate to the cupboard and her cutlery to the drawer. They clanged in the silent kitchen like a tinny piano. "Let's have dinner and then we can talk about it."

"I don't feel much like eating," Shelby admitted, peace seeping away.

"Humor me, then. I don't want to eat alone."

At a loss to deny him, Shelby iced the tea. He poured while she drained rice into a cobalt-blue dish, then seasoned the shrimp and vegetables with fresh herbs.

Jake seated her at one end of the long table and took the corner chair. He caught her cold hand in his. Shelby waited for the blessing. When none was forthcoming, she turned to meet his blue gaze.

"Gram's not here to orchestrate. You take a turn," he urged.

"I don't know if I can," she admitted.

"Sure you can," he said gently. "It'll do your heart good."

Shelby swallowed a painful knot and bowed her head. "Dear Heavenly Father..." The lump grew in her throat. She pressed her lips together, released them and tried again. "Dear Lord..." But the lump swelled and escaped in a sob. "Oh, God, what a dreadful day!"

Self-accusations swamped her again like angry seas. She pushed her plate aside and buried her face in her hands. "I never should have used him in my story."

Jake got up and returned to the table with a tissue. He pressed it into her hand, hunkered down beside her and patted her knee.

"You know what your problem is? You take your work too seriously."

"That isn't it at all!" Shelby cried, stung. "Don't you see? I didn't even know him and I played with his life."

"You played with a pretend character, Mr. Weedman," Jake said with a calmness that left her voice hanging like a shriek. "You didn't intend Mr. Wiseman any malice."

"But he died!"

"Yes he did and I'm sorry. But it isn't as if fact followed fiction. Shelby, it's likely he was dead even before Joy dropped the idea for the story into your head," Jake reasoned.

"You can't know that!"

"Not for sure, not yet anyway," he admitted. "But surely you don't have to wait for autopsy results to see that your story had nothing to do with his death."

"I wished I'd stayed home," she cried. "I never should have come here."

"So why did you?" Jake saw an open door and took it.

"The cabin was all arranged. Things fell apart, but I still…I had writing to do."

"To hide yourself in, don't you mean?" he challenged.

Injured, she defended, "Writing takes solitude. The words don't flow onto the page without some thought and effort."

"I won't venture what it does or doesn't take. All I'm saying is, it shouldn't empty you until there's nothing left for living."

"It doesn't," she said with more heat than intended.

Jake withdrew his hands and turned them palms up. His shoulders rose and fell, too.

"What?" she demanded, though he hadn't spoken.

"I'm beginning to see what your Patrick was up against."

"Patrick?" Startled, she blinked bleary eyes. "What does he have to do with anything?"

"Just about everything, if you loved the guy."

A pulse throbbed in her throat. Heat swept up already flushed cheeks. "That's what you think? That I've taken my hurt over him and used Mr. Wiseman as an excuse to have a good cry?"

"You haven't *used* Mr. Wiseman. You found him. That's your only part in what happened to Mr. Wiseman."

"But Jake, if that were true…"

"It *is* true," Jake said. "A good cry never hurt anyone. Then again, it won't do a lick of good if you turn around and bury yourself so deeply in work, you can't see what's behind the tears.''

"I know you mean well. So I'll just pretend I didn't hear that," Shelby snapped, trying hard not to be offended.

"Maybe you need to hear it. Don't get me wrong, I'm not finding fault," Jake continued hastily. "All I'm saying is it looks to me like Patrick caught you with your armor down and you ducked out. About the time you were ready to go home and take stock, Mr. Wiseman's death triggered all the stuff you buried. You came unstrung and now you can't face going home.''

"That isn't true!" She jumped to her own defense. "I had every intention of going home before I... And I'm *not* unstrung."

"I've got bad news, then. Your face is leaking." He caught a tear on his fingertip and held it up as evidence.

"It could be I was wrong about you," Shelby said, wounded. "I thought you were sweet."

"I am. On you," he admitted.

"Oh, Jake!" she murmured, defensiveness melting as she saw it from his point of view. "I'm sorry."

"Don't be. You're the one with the hole in your heart." Hunkered down beside her chair, Jake tucked a curl behind her ear, traced the tear track and then her bottom lip with the flat of his thumb.

Shelby trapped his hand with both of hers. But it was a poor defense mechanism, for he let her keep it, leaned in and stole a kiss. It sparked heat lightning across the stormy expanse of her heart. Fiercely, she blinked tear-shine, crowded out rational thought and kissed him back. A hard, open-eyed kiss.

Jake tasted anger and hurt and despair and defiance all wrapped up in a pair of tear-salted lips. Undone, he didn't care why she kissed him, just that she did. He drew a ragged breath. "Come here," he said, his voice reduced to a whispered growl.

Wonder of wonders, she did. To her feet and into his arms. Matched him kiss for bottled-up kiss, the hunger of despair. He was searching his soul for the Pause button, when abruptly, she found it of her own accord. Her glistening forehead sagged against his chin.

"What am I doing?" she murmured, "Jake, I don't—"

Certain how the sentence would end, he said against her mouth, "I know. It's all right."

"This isn't fair to you. Forgive me," she whispered.

"Forget it," he murmured, and kissed her again and put the sensation of soft plush lips to memory. "You went to a lot trouble fixing dinner, now it's getting cold." He let her go, rather than to have her pull away on her own. Fighting to stabilize his own emotions, he forced a logic he was far from feeling, and continued, "We'll eat, then I'll take you home."

"I'm staying for the funeral, remember?" she told him.

"There isn't going to be one, Shelby."

She blinked. "There isn't?"

"Just private graveside services. That's the way Mrs. Wiseman wants it," Jake told her.

"But if there's no funeral, where is the closure?"

"For who?" he asked.

The question jerked her up short. What was she out to prove, finding reasons to stay? To whom? And to what end? Cognitive of all Jake could have said and had not, she flushed and murmured, "Point taken. I'll probably thank you later for booting me out."

"I'm not booting," he protested.

"Yes, you are, and you're right to."

"How about a rain check, then?" he asked. "For when you..."

"Bury my baggage?" she said in a voice that turned it into a loaded question.

The ringing doorbell spared Jake a response. He excused himself to answer it. It was just as well. Shelby winced to find her raw edges showing again. She climbed the stairs to splash her face and eyes in cool water and reason with herself. Home wasn't a sentence to dread. She would face down her fears and tears. Let the hurt settle, and when it had, appraise the damage. Surely nothing was broken that God couldn't fix. On that faith-based hope, Shelby collected her composure and returned to find Jake alone in the kitchen. There was a pie on the table. It was even prettier than the one he had made.

"Emmaline?" she asked.

"Now there's a woman who can bake a pie," he said.

Seeing through his banter, Shelby rewarded his effort with a watery smile. "I wonder what she did for berries."

"Used her noggin and opened a can," he replied.

"I'll pay her on my way out of town."

"I took care of it. Get some pie plates. We'll have dessert first. Or has that already been served?"

Shelby colored at his gentle teasing and murmured, "You tell me."

"It has, and pie is poor seconds." He cocked his head, boyishly bold and quipped, "Nudge my memory—where were we?"

"About to eat," said Shelby.

"Oh, that. It's coming back now." He took the chair beside her. Reached for her hand and bowed his head. "We have a long drive ahead of us, and the day's about gone. But thank You for supper, and for the hands that prepared it. For the pie, too, and the thought behind it. Amen."

"Are you relaying information or is that grace?" Shelby asked.

"A little of both."

"I'll put your mind at ease, then." She collected the tattered shreds off her common sense and her pride. "I don't need a driver. I know the way home."

"Good. Then you won't have any trouble finding your way back," he countered.

Shelby looked up from smoothing her napkin. A grave smile lifted one corner of his mouth, punctuating his offer.

Chapter Eleven

Jake reasoned that he hadn't been smitten by Shelby long enough to be overboard. But when she had gone, his heaviness of spirit had her absence all over it. His missed shaded lip signatures on china cups. Dainty footprints in his garden. And fragrances. They had faded from his office, the guest room, and the bathroom closet where the bouquet of bath oils and powders and scented toiletries had lingered the longest. And with that fading away, his loneliness grew.

A week to the day Shelby had returned home, she remembered him with a blooming plant. It was delivered to the Bloomington sign shop by a local florist. He whistled on the ride home, and socked the plant down on the kitchen table where Shelby's thoughtfulness brightened Gram's day, too.

A thank-you card followed by mail the next day. The front of the card depicted a gardener leaning on his hoe, waiting out a summer shower in the doorway of his potting shed. A printed napkin from the Sun-

flower Tearoom fell out of the card as he opened it
to Shelby's longhand.

Dear Jake and Gram Kate,
    Thank you again for your hospitality. I can't
imagine a more congenial place to spend a few
days. Please pass along my greetings to the rest
of your family. It was a pleasure meeting them
and being so warmly accepted. Has Joy had any
word from Mrs. Wiseman? Poor woman. She
has been in my thoughts and prayers, as have
both of you. Should business bring you to the
city, Jake, don't forget my dinner invitation. Or
if that won't work, then how about lunch? There
is a tearoom on Ogden Avenue near my building you might enjoy. They serve their sandwiches on toasted sunweed seed buns. Or is that
sun*flower* seed?

                                          Cordially,
                                          Shelby

Jake chuckled at the sunflower she had scribbled
on the page and traced her signature. The inclusion
of the napkin, the reminder about dinner, and the
invitation to contact her bespoke a forward view and
gave him hope that she had put Patrick behind her.
    Admiring her resilience, Jake looked the card over
more closely, and saw that she had boxed in his name
on the gardener's hat. He tucked the small tearoom
napkin into his wallet, then thumbed through the remaining mail.
    Among the business envelopes was a bid request
from Spot Dry Cleaning, a firm with seven stores in
the Chicago area. One of the stores was on Ogden

Avenue. Jake found it midway between the tearoom and Parnell Publishing where Shelby worked.

With a glut of local work to keep his men busy, the timing wasn't the greatest. And it would mean a week or more away from home, should he get the bid.

Jake weighed the pros and cons briefly, and reached for his calendar. He would have to survey the job before making a bid. It would take a full day. He was looking for one he could free up when Joy burst into his office.

"You'll never guess who I heard from," she cried, her eyes shining like northern lights.

"Dirk?" Jake took a stab in the dark.

"Not on the phone, e-mail! Go on, guess!"

Jake circled a calendar date in red, twisted his mouth to one side and asked, "How about a hint?"

"He has his own Web site. I saw it in a magazine, and sent him an e-mail. But he must not check his mail much, because it took me a long time to hear back," Joy continued.

"You call that a hint?" asked Jake.

"Okay, I'll just tell you. Are you ready for this? Ta-da!" Joy exclaimed with all the grandeur of an unveiling, and thrust an e-mail from Colton under Jake's nose.

Flowers and a bread-and-butter note elicited no response from Liberty Flats. Not that Shelby had expected word. The silence, not to mention the passing days, enabled her to view Mr. Wiseman's death with less trauma and more insight.

She was plotting another book to replace the one

she had left unfinished when Joy e-mailed her, asking if she wanted her to delete her story from Jake's files.

Shelby replied by e-mail that she had already done so.

Joy responded swiftly: "But I thought you wanted me to do it, once you made sure you had received it at home."

Shelby felt no obligation to explain how in one ill-fated moment, the story had become a brick wall she couldn't seem to find passage over, under or through. She closed the subject with a few tactful words and sent her warm regards to the rest of the family.

Once again, days passed with no word. Shelby dug into her work. But her new story, begun with promise, soon fizzled out like a wet firecracker.

Stuck, she buried herself in indexing a cookbook. The associate editor who had begun the indexing was on maternity leave, so it had fallen to Shelby. It was mundane and tedious eye-straining work, her least favorite of jobs. So much so, that when the phone rang one evening as she was pouring over the pages she had brought home from work, she welcomed the interruption. It was a heartbeat past hello when she recognized Patrick's voice. For one unguarded moment, the hurt crowded in.

"I hope I didn't catch you at a bad time," he began.

"Not at all. How have you been?" she said, thinking it pointless to ignore the ashes.

"Fine, thanks. And you?" asked Patrick.

"The same."

"I suppose your writing is keeping you busy," he ventured.

"As always," she agreed, but surprisingly, felt no

desire to offer the particulars as she once would have done.

Patrick cleared his throat and stated the purpose of his call. He had been contacted by Parnell Publishing concerning a potential lawsuit. "Apparently Miss Lockwood doesn't like the cover on her book."

Well aware of the situation, Shelby replied, "She liked it well enough to sign off on it. It's too late to change her mind now."

"I seem to recall an earlier snag—some carelessness in her research, wasn't it?"

"It was a book about traveling in Canada. Very warm and user friendly. But in one instance, some descriptive details were almost a mirror image to those in a Canadian travel brochure," Shelby explained, recovering her ease as it dawned it was business, not personal matters, that had prompted the call.

"As I recall, it was you who caught it," Patrick was saying.

"She knows that," countered Shelby.

"It wouldn't hurt to refresh her memory."

"Apply a little pressure, you mean?"

"It would be a kindness, Shelby," Patrick continued. "She's obviously not thinking this through. If she were, she would be busy writing her next book instead of threatening a suit she can't win. Will you join us for lunch tomorrow?"

"No, thank you, I'd rather not," Shelby replied, shrinking at the thought.

"And here I thought you were a team player," coaxed Patrick.

"I must be, or I wouldn't be taking my work home

with me every night. And with a book of my own to worry about,'' she returned.

''Excuse me, Shelby, but I have an interruption on my hands,'' Patrick said. ''Rethink lunch, and I'll call you back.''

Shelby fidgeted and couldn't get back into her work for second-guessing herself. There had to be a first time of seeing him again. Perhaps after that, it would grow easier to relegate the past to the past, and view him simply as a lawyer Parnell Publishing had retained to handle a legal matter. On the other hand, why should she subject herself to a potentially uncomfortable scene, both in the social and business sense, just to make his job easier? There was something very liberating in her reluctance to do so. It was freeing, too, that the thunder in her ears at the sound of his voice had quickly faded to a distant echo.

Empowered by the realization her heart was on the recovering list, she waited expectantly for him to call back, and when the phone rang, lifted the receiver from the cradle with hard-fought confidence. ''I've thought it over, and the answer's still no,'' she said without preamble.

''Shelby?''

''I've done my part, and I have nothing further to contribute. That's why they contacted you.'' Shelby held her firm line, giving him no chance to squeeze in a word.

''Here I thought it was because I can spell *spot*.''

Confused, Shelby grappled to identify the familiar voice.

''It's Jake,'' he volunteered. ''Did I catch you in the middle of something?''

"Jake! I'm sorry! I was expecting a return call, and I thought—" Shelby caught herself up short. "What do you mean, you can spell *spot?*"

"Spot Dry Cleaning," Jake said. "I'll be in town tomorrow to bid on a job for them."

"*That* Spot!" said Shelby, getting a grip. "They have a store not far from where I work."

"Yes, I know. Are you free for lunch?" Jake asked.

"Yes, and it's my treat," she reminded.

"I got your potted plant. Thanks, that was thoughtful."

"I'm glad you liked it. Is it still blooming?" she asked.

"Most of the petals have faded, but the greenery is nice. Gram is enjoying it, too. About this tearoom—will I be needing a tux?" he quipped.

An image of Jake climbing out of his crane truck dressed in a tuxedo, work boots and a Jackson Signs cap flitted through her mind. She smiled and said, "You'd feel a little out of place, it's casual. Even better, it's within walking distance for me."

"I'm sold. What time?"

"We can beat the rush if we are there by eleven-thirty. Can you make that?" she asked.

"I'll try. You'll be the lady in the sunflower dress?"

"I could be." Looking forward to seeing him again, she twisted the phone cord around her finger and asked, "How have you been?"

"Busy playing catch-up. We had electrical storms and high winds a week ago," he told her.

"I guess that *would* be a boon to the sign industry."

Jake chuckled agreement and went on to ask her if she had replaced her car. She had. Her computer had proved a fatality, as well. Having learned of it through his insurance man, Jake asked if she had had any problems replacing it. Expected call forgotten, Shelby told him all about it. He in turn shared that Joy had received a nice note and a check from Mrs. Wiseman for the hours she had spent weeding fields for Mr. Wiseman.

"That's good, I'm glad to hear it," said Shelby. "She was pleased, I'm sure."

"Oh, yes. She put on her apron in celebration, and was all set to try baking a pie when she got side-tracked."

"What? A butter bean cake recipe?"

"No, the computer. She came across a Web page for Wind, Sky and Water. Being her usual resource-ful self, she got from that to an e-mail address for The Voyager."

"She contacted her father?" gasped Shelby. "Does Paula know?"

"Yes. He called to check out Joy's story."

"What did she tell him?"

"The truth," Jake replied. "Right away, he asked to see Joy."

Clearly, Colton's phone call had caused everyone involved emotional upheaval, Jake included. "Did Paula agree?" she asked.

"Only to think about it. For Joy's sake," he added.

His somber tone was in sharp contrast to the ban-tering tone on which their conversation had begun. Shelby listened, breath caught, as he expressed Paula's concern over Colton having the means to pursue and no doubt win visitation rights, if he so chose. Joy was pressuring Jake to intervene on her behalf and Paula was counting on him to back her up in whatever decision she made. Jake didn't belabor being the man in the middle except to say, tongue in cheek, he was starting to envy Gram in her friction-free world of forgetfulness.

Curious though she was about Colton, Paula and Joy, Shelby didn't want to add to his burden by asking a lot of questions. "How is Gram Kate?"

"Pretty fit, all things considered. We're planning a birthday party for her on the Saturday before Labor Day," he said on a brighter note. "Are you free?"

"Hold on a moment and I'll check." Before Shelby could change to a phone in reach of her calendar, she was signaled by Call Waiting. "Jake? Could I let you know tomorrow? I have another call."

Jake agreed and said goodbye.

It was Patrick, calling back. Shelby felt childish for that momentary lift it gave her to tell him that she had plans for lunch tomorrow and wouldn't be free. Patrick reacted graciously, which wasn't nearly so deflating as it might have been. Repenting of her shallow pride, she prayed for Jake's family. Obviously, what Joy had begun with an e-mail had ramifications she wouldn't know to consider.

Shelby wrapped up the indexing work she had brought home from the office with her, and filled the tub. As she soaked in rose-scented water, her thoughts turned once more to Jake. Looking forward to seeing him, and wanting to look her best, she toweled off, and padded to her closet to lay out clothes for the next day. She deliberated over the yellow pleated dress, then discarded Jake's broad hint as too casual for the office.

The wedding dress was still in the closet, and still in the way. Shelby thumbed past it for a pale-green linen suit and in so doing, realized all that white satin and lace had lost its bite. Behind the suit was a blouse she had bought on sale the previous summer.

It was white silk, with narrow mist-green edging along the button flap. Shelby hung both to one side, and the next morning, found the results pleasing. Lingering in front of the mirror, she ran a comb through her curls and made a mental note to call her stylist.

Jake was on the road before daylight the next morning. He stopped for breakfast midway to the city, and reached the first of seven dry cleaning establishments just as the manager arrived. He measured the existing signs, snapped pictures for documentation, drove to two more locations to repeat the procedure, then made his way back to Ogden Avenue to meet Shelby for lunch.

The tearoom was on the ground floor of a turn-of-the-century building. Bronze gaslight fixtures hung from a high tin ceiling. The gas mantels had been replaced by soft pink bulbs concealed in tulip-shaped stained-glass shades. The tables were covered in antique-white linen and lighted by reproduction Tiffany lamps.

A greeter led him past a wall lined in tea sets to a little built-in nook where Shelby sat looking over typewritten pages. He had almost reached the booth when she lifted her head from her work. Recognition flashed in her eyes, and warmed her whole face.

"Hello, Jake," she said, and folded her glasses

away. "I hope you didn't have trouble finding the place?"

"No. Traffic slowed me down. Sorry I'm late." He slid into the upholstered seat to share the same side of the table, and retrieved a small sack from his shirt pocket. "I found something for you when we stopped for breakfast this morning."

The sack, printed in a floral design, was no bigger than an index card. Shelby reached inside and peeled back tissue paper, revealing a ceramic tea bag holder with yellow petals flaring out from a brown center. "A sunflower. Thank you, Jake."

"Sunweed," he corrected with a grin.

"That's right, I keep forgetting." Shelby scanned his face, searching for telltale signs of weariness and stress. But he appeared relaxed and pleased to see her. She started to ask about Paula, then changed her mind, thinking he would bring up the subject himself if he wanted to talk about it.

"There's a pie pan and a rolling pin to match," Jake said, as she neatly folded the pretty gift sack into her pocketbook. "They were a little bulky. I left them in the truck."

"You'd better take them home to Joy," she said, and wrinkled her nose, admitting, "as a pie baker, I'm a lost cause."

"Here I thought I was a good teacher," he said.

Shelby flushed at his reference to that moment in the kitchen, and welcomed the interruption the waitress provided as she arrived to take their order. She chose cranberry tea for her beverage and when it was served, put her gift to use. Cranberry-tinted tea spread over the ceramic flower.

"A sunflower with pinkeye," observed Jake.

"Is there a physician in the house?" She played along. Following his lead, she kept the conversation general as they waited for their food.

Shelby's spinach salad was more than she needed. She shared it with Jake. In turn, he lobbed off a piece of his sandwich and insisted she try it. The sandwich, smoked ham with a specialty dressing, was tucked between crusty bread and topped in toasted sunflower seeds.

"Very good," she said, smoothing her napkin.

"The salad, too," Jake agreed. "You can take me out anytime."

Shelby smiled and nibbled on a pickle. "Will you be in the city a few days?"

"No. I'll start home as soon as I've checked out the other dry cleaning locations."

"And if you get the bid? When will you be back?" asked Shelby.

"I'm guessing late August," he said.

"Call and let me know, and we'll get together again, if you like."

"I like." Jake smiled, savoring the lushness of her eyes, the hue, the thick fringe of lashes. Just the way he remembered. There was a difference, though. Subtle enough, he kept searching.

"Where's your sunflower dress?" he asked.

"I'm saving it for Gram Kate's birthday party."

"You've cleared your calendar, then?" He watched her over the rim of his coffee cup.

"I have. And I'm looking forward to seeing everyone."

"Have you done something different with your hair?"

A faint blush rose to her cheeks at his lingering

scrutiny. "It's a little long. I've been meaning to make an appointment for a cut."

"It looks nice," he said.

She tucked an errant curl behind her ear, so feminine a gesture. Seemingly of its own volition, his arm draped the seat back behind her. "How's the book coming?"

"The Weed Buster's thing?" She wrinkled her nose but didn't shirk the featherlight touch of his fingers skimming her shoulder. "It isn't."

"What's the problem?" he asked.

"I can't get past the field scene. And I can't take it out. If I do, the plot falls apart," Shelby explained.

"Can't you rewrite the scene?"

"If only I could. But even the thought of trying..." She shrugged and fell short of explaining.

"Oh, go ahead. Bend my ear," he said and leaned closer.

Shelby reached up and patted his ear.

His fingers trapped hers as he cupped the ear she had touched on a whim. "I can't hear you," he said, cradling her hand.

"I don't want to talk about it," she said.

"You'll feel better," he coaxed.

"No, I won't," she said, distracted by his fingers loosely laced with hers. "I told you, when I talk it out, I lose my incentive to—"

"I've already read your story," he reasoned. "So, what's at stake?"

His eyes, so sky-blue earnest, coaxed to light an unvoiced fear that she had lost her first love. Her muse. Her writing. It was a worry she hadn't whispered, not even to God.

She withdrew her hand and settled for half measures, saying, "I've taken the scene apart in my mind more times than I can count. It starts out okay. My characters react strongly. But only for a sentence or so, and then they carry on as if..."

"As if, what?" he prompted when she hesitated.

"As if Mr. Weedman's death doesn't matter beyond giving them a fright."

"And it does."

"Of course it does," she said with quiet conviction. "In their shoes, I was terrified. Sick. It was like someone else reacting from within my skin. I don't know how else to explain it. I still dream about it." Her voice fell. Her lashes swept up in silent inquiry.

"So convey the loss," he said. "You can do it."

When he put it that way, she yearned to rise to the occasion. Because she thought she could succeed where she had thus far failed? Or because she wanted to please him? As with the pie, and even in her care not to speak of Paula's problems, unless he was willing to bring it up himself. What was it about him that made her so eager to accommodate?

The waitress came with strawberries and scones and distracted Shelby from sorting it out. She hadn't ordered dessert. At her wordless glance, Jake shrugged to say he hadn't, either.

"It looks good, but I'm afraid you have the wrong table," Shelby began.

"Compliments of Mr. Delaney. He'd like you to stop by his table when you've finished eating." The waitress indicated a table nearby.

Shelby turned to see Patrick and a striking redhead seated there. Monique Lockwood. Shelby hadn't met her in person. But she recognized the author's profile from the photo on the book jacket, one of several she had submitted throughout the editorial process.

"A work associate," she answered Jake's questioning glance.

He heard the brittle note and drew his own conclusions.

Shelby fumed in silence over the unfair advantage Patrick had taken in knowing her daily patterns, right down to her favorite lunch spot. What did he hope to accomplish? If Miss Lockwood's discontent could have been resolved by Parnell staff, he wouldn't have been called in.

"I'm sorry, I didn't save room," she said to the waitress, waiving dessert.

"Sir?" said the waitress to Jake.

"No, thanks. Do you have our check?"

The waitress tallied their ticket and gave it to Jake. Shelby avoided looking Patrick's way again. But his table was in direct line with the door. She wiped the tea bag holder dry, tucked it into her book bag and excused herself to freshen up.

Jake stood up and let her out. "I'll wait for you up front," he said, and strode for the register, tab in hand.

Shelby ducked into the powder room, made short work with comb and lipstick and let herself out again. As she neared Patrick's table, the waitress served their meal and strode away. Shelby closed the remaining distance, intending to say, Hello-how-are-you-Don't-let-your-food-get-cold-Goodbye. But before she could, Patrick reached for Miss Lockwood's hand. It startled Shelby so, she kept walking.

"Ready?" Jake asked, and held the door for her.

Shaken, she ducked under his arm and into the

noonday sun. Patrick and Monique Lockwood? Had he deceived her? No. Not Patrick. Couldn't be. Lack of wholehearted devotion, he had said. On *her* part, not his. But the possibility—it was like a firecracker going off in her mind.

Shelby unclenched her fists. She felt blood flow into her fingers. Heat radiated off brick walls and from the pavement underfoot. She tipped her head back, gazed through the porthole of tall buildings to God's sky above, emptied a caught breath and realized she was still in one piece. Seeing Patrick with another woman hadn't destroyed her. Even the tremors were quickly settling.

"Careful," warned Jake. His arm shot out to steady her as crumbling sidewalk snagged her high heel.

His hand, strong and scuffed and warm, was a welcome sensation. Shelby drew no comparisons and made no excuses for finding comfort in it. But once he had steadied her, he released her arm and looked back toward the tearoom.

"Did you forget something?" Shelby asked, pausing beside him.

"No. Just wondering about dessert."

"You mean Patrick?"

"*The* Patrick?"

She nodded. A shadow fell over his face and pinched her heart. "I'm sorry. I would have introduced you, but... It's kind of a long story. Do you have time?"

"That's up to you. It's your affair."

The edge to the word seemed premeditated. Shelby tilted her hot face and in so doing caught a glimpse of his hardened jaw. It was wounding, surprisingly so.

"Monique Lockwood has an ax to grind with Parnell Publishing." She found herself explaining. "Patrick is trying to avoid a lawsuit. Apparently he thought that my presence might be of some help."

"He works for Parnell?"

"When they need representation," Shelby said. "That's how we met."

Jake didn't pursue it. Nor did it seem likely that a rush of explanations would soften his demeanor. They passed the remaining block to her building in silence. It was deflating, that silence.

"End of the trail. This is where I work." Shelby pushed the slim strap of her pocketbook higher on her shoulder, then gripped her book bag with both hands, breath caught as she awaited his leave-taking.

"I'll let you get back to your desk," he said. "Thanks for lunch."

"Thank *you*, don't you mean?" Shelby responded, for she had intended it to be her treat before Patrick rocked the boat and rattled her senses.

Jake smiled, faint and formal, his heart all the while twisting. "It was good seeing you again."

"Me, too," she said, purse strap slipping; heart, too, at his toneless and impersonal politeness. "Give Gram Kate my love. Tell Joy hello. Paula, too."

"Will do." Jake lifted his hand and turned away without further mention of being in touch, or reiterating his invitation to Gram Kate's birthday party.

A pungent sense of loss carried her back once again to that day in the potting shed where Henry had come for a shovel to bury her kitten. She remembered his rough earthy hands as he wiped her

tears and sent her inside for a shoe box and something of her own to bury with the kitten. She had
returned with her favorite storybook. Henry, dear old
gentle soul, had held her on his lap and read the story
aloud before tucking it into the box with the kitten.
Carelessness, she learned, came at a cost.

But this carelessness was not hers. It was Patrick's.

Shelby fumbled in her book bag for her keepsake.
She held it aloft and called after Jake as he strode
away, ''Thanks for the sunflower.''

There was a quiet plea in her call. Jake heard it,
but didn't know how it piece it with what had happened in there. *Business?* Maybe. She didn't offer
just where she stood with Patrick now, and he
wouldn't ask. Couldn't, on the basis of their short
acquaintance. But he had as much pride as the next
man, and if it was a game she was playing trying to
make her ex-fiancé jealous, she wasn't the woman
he had taken her to be.

As for Spot Dry Cleaning, he'd gone to the trouble, he might as well follow through and make the
bid. But if the work came his way, that's all it was.
A job, and nothing more.

He climbed into his truck. The rolling pin and pie
plate were in a bag on the seat beside him. Silent
testimony to his weakness for her, a weakness strong
enough to make him crowd out simple logic.

Hadn't he known all along that the responsibilities
he shouldered didn't leave him much liberty to find
someone who could fill that empty place in his life?
That hadn't changed just because his feelings had.
Now, it was more true than ever, what with Colton
hovering like a funnel cloud from a breath-caught
spring sky.

Chapter Twelve

Shelby couldn't get Jake off her mind, nor shake the sinking feeling their relationship had taken a dead end. Thanks to Patrick's little manipulation. *If you didn't know better, you'd think he had done it on purpose.*

Shelby passed the afternoon unfocused and unsettled and arrived home to a ringing phone.

"Hi, Shelby. What happened to you today?" asked Patrick. "I looked up and you were gone."

"You put me in an awkward position, *that's* what happened," said Shelby, temperature rising.

"I'm sorry. When you said you had plans for lunch, I didn't realize it was a date."

"Well, it was. And if I want dessert, I'll order it."

"Of course. Again, I apologize." He cleared his throat. "On a brighter note, Miss Lockwood has changed her mind."

Patrick's hand reaching for Monique's flashed in instant replay. Shelby resisted cross-examining the master of cross-examiners, and said nothing.

"There won't be a lawsuit," Patrick continued. "Shelby? Are you still there?"

"Yes," Shelby said. "I'm just wondering what you said to bring her to her senses."

"It wasn't what I said, it's who I represented."

Shelby assumed he meant Parnell Publishing. "So, she's having second thoughts about burning her bridges?"

"That, too," he said.

"It's a little late. Granted, she's gifted, but who needs the grief?"

"You're still angry."

I'm no longer your concern. Shelby bit her tongue to keep from reminding him.

"I guess I didn't tell you I met Monique several weeks ago," Patrick continued.

Again, she waited him out.

"At Can-Do." He shed her silence like a squeaky clean window sheeting rain. "I didn't realize at the time who she was."

"Monique Lockwood volunteers at Can-Do?"

"No. I said I met her there."

"She's on the board, then?" Shelby sought somewhat impatiently to understand. "Not the staff, surely."

"She's working through some problems."

"What are you saying? Spit it out, would you Patrick?"

"Her marriage failed. Her business, too," Patrick said. "There was no safety net to catch her."

"Monique Lockwood is *homeless?*" Thunderstruck, Shelby cried, "I can't believe it! How could she write a travel book without a corner to call her own?"

"She traveled widely before her divorce and drew from her trip journals."

"Journals?" Shelby echoed.

"And photos. Her journals and albums are just about all she came away with. After the divorce, I mean," said Patrick.

"It boggles the mind."

"Doesn't it? For a few months, she actually lived in her car," Patrick told her.

"She has a car, then?"

"She did, until the insurance and the license tags needed renewing and she didn't have the money. She sold the car, moved into the mission and continued her writing on a computer at the public library," Patrick added. "She wouldn't want her readership to know that, of course."

"Give me a little credit, would you?"

"Could I say something?" Taking her silence for consent, Patrick said, "I know you're hurting, and I'm sorry."

"That isn't fair, Patrick. I'm not hurting, and anyway, it isn't germane. We were discussing Monique," Shelby replied stiffly.

"If it's any consolation, it wasn't cold feet," he spoke over her protest.

Stung, she countered, "If it's any consolation, you were right. I didn't put you first. Today at lunch, it hit me out of the blue—I'd lost my first love."

"Oh, Shelby."

"Not you! My writing!" she cried, at his melting tone.

Silence held the moment. He sighed finally, and said, "Maybe you should check your priorities. Last I heard, God still likes to be first."

Nonplused, she demanded, "What's happened to you?"

"I came to the end of myself. Perhaps you should try it."

"Patrick Delaney! I resent that!"

"I'm wrong? Then maybe we'll run into one another at Can-Do tomorrow night," Patrick suggested.

Shelby tried to recall when she had last volunteered at the mission, and couldn't. It wasn't a deliberate omission. It was just that life over the past couple of years had become a balancing act.

"I can't. I have plans."

"A date?"

"No. I'm working late," Shelby said.

"I see," he drawled.

Loaded words, and he knew it. Shelby ended the call before she lost her grasp on civility. She paced her living room, listing all the reasons she no longer had time to sling hash or sort secondhand clothes at Can-Do. There was the cookbook bearing down on her at Parnell's. Her writing was in collapse. She didn't want to miss Jake, should he call.

Which he didn't, thanks to Patrick.

A week passed with no word. And then another. The wound inflicted by Jake's silence confused her. It's no great loss. You hardly know him, she told herself.

Her writing was no help. Jake's urging had motivated her to revive her attempts on the Weed Busters book. But she continued to hit the same stone wall. One evening, tired of listening for a phone call that wasn't going to come, Shelby locked her apartment and arrived at Can-Do just in time to help with the dishes.

The director, Mr. Weaver came in later that evening as she was hanging up her apron. He thanked her for her help, and commented that they had missed her at Can-Do. Before Shelby could explain her lack of free time, he brought her up to date on a teen program recently undertaken by the mission.

Mr. Weaver asked if she would be willing to help with an outing planned by a supporting church group for a week from Saturday. Not long ago, Shelby would have excused herself by virtue of needing the time to write. Now she agreed readily, partly to disprove Patrick's words about her priorities, partly to avoid confrontation at the keyboard.

Two weeks after submitting his bid on the Chicago job, Jake got word the work was his. He scheduled the work for the last week of August.

Changing the signs required two trucks and three men. Wendy's husband Homer, and another brother-in-law, Gordy, went along with him. Once in Chicago, they got the necessary permits, checked in with the union hall, and made good headway the first day. But the remainder of the week, Jake was faced with delays and complications, one after another.

His men wanted to spend the weekend with their families and return on Monday to complete the job. But Jake talked them into staying one more night and doing the Ogden Avenue location on Saturday. Homer drew his own conclusions.

"You going to give Shelby a jingle?" he asked, as Jake turned the crane truck back toward the motel at dusk on Friday.

"Hadn't planned on it. Why?" Jake asked.

"If you like, I could coach you on the finer points of catching a gal on the rebound," offered Homer.

Goaded, Jake replied, "Make yourself useful and crank that mirror in, would you?"

Homer reached out the passenger's window and adjusted the side mirror. "That better?"

"Can you see yourself in it?" Jake asked. "Tell me—does that look like Dear Abby to you?"

Homer cackled and said no more. He was right, though. There was the rub. Jake couldn't get Shelby off of his mind. A woman crossed his path these days, and all he saw was points of comparison. Shelby came out ahead every time. It wasn't as if he hadn't considered calling her. Truth was, he fought the temptation daily. So far, overcoming had proved a hollow victory.

The next morning, Jake and his men arrived at the Ogden Avenue location early. Using one crane to work out of and the other to lift, they had the old sign down by midmorning.

The proprietor treated them to donuts and coffee. Jake was brushing the powdered sugar off his shirt when his pulse reacted to a familiar figure climbing out of a parked car.

Shelby. It came over him like repetitive motion. Tight chest. Spitfire pulse. Misbehaving limbs wanting to angle her way instead of following his men onto the truck bed to uncrate the new sign.

Her dress was a filmy sea-green thing. The bodice was slim-fitting, the skirt was gored. The breeze filled the skirt, wafting it about her curves and slim calves like delicate sea foam. She circled to the passenger's side, leaned in and plucked something out of the seat.

Jake couldn't tell what, just that it was white and lengthy and covered in plastic. Hands full, she closed the car door with her hip and clipped along half-hidden by whatever it was that encumbered her.

She hadn't cut her hair. Red-gold curls bounced above shoulders that hadn't seen much sunlight. In a city of sun goddesses, she strolled along as creamy-white as the gown in her arms.

Wedding gown. It registered as the distance fell away. She looked so radiant in that shower of sunlight, his heart sank. His gaze went to her left hand. It was hidden in the folds of the wedding dress.

She stepped around the outrigger, set there on the sidewalk. Looked at the truck. Stopped, and for one unguarded moment let a smile blossom.

"Jake! Long time no see!" Shelby exclaimed, awash with spontaneous pleasure at the sight of him.

Her starburst greeting gave rise to all those old feelings. He'd been a fool not to call her. He crimped his hat and asked, "Working Saturdays now?"

"No. I'm running some errands," Shelby said.

"So, he changed his mind again?"

She blinked, and echoed, "Who changed his mind?"

Jake saw her ringless hand, then, and felt as transparent as the plastic covering her gown. "The weather man," he improvised, and shuffled his feet. "Early showers, he predicted. Doesn't look like showers to me, does it you?"

"I won't complain," she said and shrugged her creamy shoulders.

Jake looked over his shoulder. Homer's brother Gordy gawked and grinned. Homer parodied catching a rebound. Jake turned back, neck on fire. He indicated the gown. "So, where you headed with that?"

"The cleaners. My friends tell me it should be treated and packed away," she replied.

"What for?"

"Posterity, I guess," she said with a pretty shrug.

"Seems like a waste."

"Do you have a better idea?"

"Sure do. A better man," he suggested on inspiration.

"You should talk," she countered mildly. "You said you'd call when you came to town. You didn't. Your sign says you're working. You're not."

"What sign?"

"That sign." Her fingers wiggled free of shimmering satin. She pointed to the Men Working sign he had posted along the street.

"I was. Then you came along and distracted me," Jake replied, holding back a grin.

"I'll go, then," she said, and would have, too, except he got between her and Spot Dry Cleaner's front door.

"Have you had breakfast?" he asked.

"Yes," she replied, heart stopping as he blocked her path.

"Lunch, then?"

"It's ten o'clock, Jake. Who eats at ten?" she huffed, pride preventing her from being readily available when he had left her dangling all this time without so much as a word.

"Since when do we eat by the clock? Come on, at least have a cup of coffee with me," he coaxed, determined to make the most of what seemed to him like nothing short of divine intervention.

"I can't. I'm parked in a loading zone."

"How about noon, then?" he pressed.

"I'd like to, Jake," she admitted, yielding a bit. "But I promised I'd chaperone some kids to a Wiffle Ball game. "

"Wiffle Ball?"

"It's all the rave here in the city. They play in bumper cars. With paddles, wickets, whatever you want to call them."

"I'm intrigued," he said, and he was. With her.

A wistfulness softened her face as she reconsidered her day. "Would you like to come along?"

"Sure," Jake replied, feeling like a two-ton boulder had been lifted off him. "If I won't be intruding."

"We could use another chaperon," she said, and gave him the address.

Jake tucked it into his pocket, and reached past her to hold the door. "We'll finish up here, then I'll meet you there."

Her curls brushed his hand as she ducked under his arm. That silky sensation left a sweet ache that stayed with him throughout the morning. The sign was up and working by noon. Homer and Gordy chained down the old sign and left for home.

Jake climbed behind the wheel of the second crane truck, studied the city map a minute, and set off to meet Shelby. It was raining by the time he arrived. But the bumper car court was part of an indoor arcade, complete with video games and a miniature golf course, all under one roof. Judging by the noise, the fun was in full swing. Jake spotted Shelby resting a slender hip against the half wall that enclosed the bumper car court.

His cap, shirt and shoes were rain-spotted. But for the first time in weeks, a sunny front moved in over his heart.

Chapter Thirteen

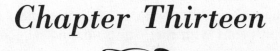

Shelby didn't attend the church supporting the outing. She didn't know any of the kids or the other two chaperons. But all seemed to be enjoying the bumper car sport. Players, divided into teams of five, dodged and bumped and rattled about, trying to keep track of a Whiffle Ball. They used hand-held wickets to steal, to carry, and to pass as well as to score points.

Boisterous cheers chimed with the general clamor of the surrounding arcade. Shelby glanced at her watch for the third time in that many minutes, and turned to see Jake catch her at it. Their eyes met. The din fell away, muffled by the drumming in her ears as he joined her at the wall.

"Am I late?" he asked, reseating his cap.

Shelby's heart responded to the familiar gesture. "Depends on whether you want to watch or play."

"Play, of course. So what's the idea? Bumper car, basketball or baseball?" he asked, turning to watch the kids play.

"A mix, as close as I can tell," she said, and admitted she had never played herself.

"How are we going to compete if we don't know the rules?"

"I'm not," she said. "But don't let that stop you."

"Oh, come on. How hard can it be?" he cajoled. "You can drive, can't you?"

"I haven't collided with any falling cranes lately."

"Don't start with me," he said, and laughed.

Shelby wasn't sure what impulse governed her. But when the opportunity came, she climbed into one of the little cars and complicated the game. It was apparent to all she couldn't catch or throw the Wiffle Ball with any reliability. Twice, she dropped her wicket outside the car and imposed on Jake to retrieve it. But there were advantages to being unskilled. The kids took pity on her, and didn't mix it up with her the way they did with Jake. He was plainly in his element, and quickly developed a rapport with them, whistling in snatches and calling them by name.

"That your best shot, Brady?" hollered Jake, as a skinny curly-haired kid missed his shot.

"Sun was in my eyes," claimed Brady.

"What sun? It's raining out," scoffed Jake.

"So?" said Brady.

Jake chortled and dubbed him Sun-Blind Brady.

Enjoying the status derived from Jake's attention, Brady banged and bumped Jake all over the court. The other kids giggled and shrieked and joined the chase. It didn't take a high-spirited pursuit long to deteriorate into what resembled an all-out demolition derby.

All the chaos reminded Shelby why she preferred word games. She parked her car and joined the other chaperons, looking on as bumper cars converged on Jake from all directions.

"Careful, you'll hurt him!" she cried.

"You heard her—you'll hurt me," chimed Jake. He extracted himself from the melee, clamored out of his car and over the wall, and ducked behind Shelby.

Egged on by his clowning, the kids abandoned their cars and poured over the wall after him. Chaperons seized the moment and announced that it was time to leave. Amidst a chorus of protests and groans, Shelby and Jake helped get the kids lined up. The other chaperons took over, and marched their charges out into the drizzle.

Brady turned en route to the church bus. He looked back at Shelby and Jake standing beneath the portico. "Are you coming with us, Jake?"

"Thanks, Brady, but I've got my truck," Jake called back.

"Follow us, then and you can eat dinner with us."

"Like he wants to eat at the mission," muttered another boy.

Jake glanced at Shelby. He palmed his cap, rubbed the back of his neck and called after the boys, "So, what's on the menu?"

"Hamboogies," said Brady with a toothy grin. "And fries. She can eat with us, too, if she wants."

"Gee, thanks." Shelby deadpanned at his postscript inclusion of her.

Jake grinned and slipped his arm through hers. "Burgers and fries, it is."

Brady's seeking look became a smile. He turned

and climbed the bus steps backward. "I'll save you a place, Mr. Jackson. You riding back with us, ma'am?" he called to Shelby from the top step.

"She better come with me. I may need directions," Jake said quickly.

Brady accepted that as gospel and scrambled into the front seat of the bus.

"What kind of group have we got here, anyway?" Jake asked, as Shelby waved to the lively faces smiling from bus windows.

"Hope Chapel middle graders, plus some kids from Can-Do," she replied.

"Can-Do?"

"It's a homeless mission."

"Kids, living at a mission?"

"With their families," Shelby said, nodding. The drizzle was so fine, it was almost a mist. She ambled at Jake's side, crossing the parking lot to his truck, filling him in on the mission. "Most don't stay long. But, whether it's a day or several weeks, Can-Do provides a safe haven while families work through whatever life crisis put them out of house and home."

"And the outing?"

"A number of churches take turns planning outings. The idea is to give the children a break from burdens kids weren't meant to carry. Having fun with other kids is good medicine," she repeated what Mr. Weaver, the mission director, had told her about the new youth program.

"Tough circumstance for a kid to be in."

"Yes," Shelby agreed. "But they wear it well. I distributed arcade passes at the mission while we were waiting for the church bus to arrive. That's the only way I knew which children did and didn't have homes.''

''It's a good thing you're doing,'' Jake said.

His simple earnest words fell on undeserving ears. Or so Shelby felt, as Jake unlocked his truck and held the door. Had Patrick not hit a nerve over the phone weeks earlier, it was unlikely she would be here now.

''Careful,'' Jake warned, and gripped her elbow to prevent her from slipping on the damp side iron.

Jake read modesty into Shelby's silence. He maneuvered the slick streets. The skies opened up, making visibility difficult for the last several blocks. Jake lost sight of the bus.

''The turnoff is just beyond the sign.'' Shelby directed Jake into Can-Do Mission's fenced-in parking lot.

''No need in both of us getting rained on. I'll pull up to the door and let you out,'' he offered.

''That's okay. Let's wait it out together,'' Shelby suggested, relishing his company.

Jake parked across the lot along the fence. The children disembarked at the mission door. The church bus pulled away in the driving rain.

''I've been thinking about what you said,'' Jake stated, lifting his voice above the clamor of the rain on the cab roof.

''About what?'' Shelby asked.

''Reminding me I hadn't called.''

''It's all right, Jake,'' Shelby murmured, faintly embarrassed by the words that had popped out at their own volition earlier. ''You have a business to run and family counting on you. That's a full plate for anyone.''

Sensing she was gun-shy of probing the real reason, Jake shifted for a better view of her face. Failing to find the answer there, he stretched his arm across the back of the seat. "So you forgive me?"

"Fresh page," she agreed.

It felt so good to be trading smiles again, Jake gave her earlobe a gentle tug. "I've missed you," he said, going out on a limb.

"Me, too," she admitted, heat rising.

Jake moved his arm from the seat to rest lightly across her shoulder and cupped her upper arm with his hand. Her skin was like satin against his scuffed palm. He willed her to tip her face to his and draw closer. But he left the choice to her.

That small courtesy cradled Shelby in the eye of the storm. She lifted her gaze to his. His eyes reflected sky-shine from lightning strobes now tearing the heavens. But their depths were tropical waters, warm and inviting. Her nerves climbed on tiptoes as with his free hand, he traced her ear. His fingertips strew gooseflesh, stroking a path from the curve of her jaw to her chin.

Sudden thunder crashed so loudly, they both jumped. The lights in a tall sign that spelled out the mission name went out and came back on. Shelby arched her neck toward the passenger door, looking through the window and up at the flickering sign. "Got your Men Working sign?"

"Gonna be that tough, just getting a kiss?" Jake rumbled.

She phrased a blushing protest. He drew her face to his and smothered her words with a chuckle still on his lips.

The kiss was tenderly given, both a foretaste and memory stirrer. It transported Shelby back to Gram

Kate's kitchen and fierce kisses that had escalated into a heart storm she had been these past weeks sorting through to no definitive conclusion. And here she was in his arms, his lips plying sweetness, coaxing her to hit the Restart button and play it again Shelby.

There was power in the pause. She used it wisely and opened her eyes. Her hands were between them now, resting lightly on his chest. The tension in her fingers transmitted an unspoken message.

Jake responded accordingly, and let her go. The rain showed no sign of letting up. "Come on," he said, and reached for a summer-weight jacket folded on the seat. "Let's run for it."

Shelby scooted off the seat and out the door after him. Jake held the jacket aloft. She stepped off the running board and ducked beneath it with him. To little avail. The wind laughed at the jacket. They dashed across the lot, jumping shallow puddles. Gusty rain hammered the parking lot and lashed at them as they ran.

Jake held the door. Shelby ducked inside. Her dress was soaked. Her feet slid downhill in her platform sandals, and no mirror in sight. She plucked at her damp skirt and ran her fingers through wet curls.

Brady strode out of the adjoining kitchen. "I wasn't sure you'd come. Dinner won't be ready for an hour or so. I'm going to go tell my mom I'm back. You won't get tired of waiting dinner and leave, will you?" he asked, looking back.

"Of course not," Shelby said. "You go on and check in with your mother. We'll see if Cookie needs some help in the kitchen."

Chapter Fourteen

Cookie smiled at Shelby's introduction, shook Jake's hand in welcome, and gave them each hand towels. When they had dried off, Cookie pointed out a sink full of potatoes waiting to be scrubbed.

Shelby's wet dress had turned to clinging fabric. She tied a bibbed apron over it, and was washing her hands when who should stroll in but Monique Lockwood.

"Monique!" Cookie wheeled away from a stainless steel table that stood like an island in the middle of the kitchen. "I thought you had left us."

"I did," she replied, and fluffed her flaming red hair. "I'm filling in for my friend Patty. He's installing a secondhand computer in my apartment and it's taking him longer than he expected. So here I am. You have recruits, I see," she said, with a glance that encompassed both Shelby and Jake.

Cookie made first-name introductions.

"Come here often?" Monique quipped, with no sign of recognizing Shelby.

"First time for me," Jake said.

"You don't know what you've been missing. How about you?" she turned to Shelby.

"Not as much as I'd like," Shelby replied. Either Patrick had not pointed her out at the tearoom, or she hadn't made an impression.

"Monique is a writer," the cook said, beaming. "Her books will be in bookstores soon."

"I'd do a signing in your kitchen, Cookie. But who could afford it?" Seeing Jake and Shelby trade glances, Monique's grin widened. "Please don't take that disparagingly. This was home for me for a spell and a lifesaver. Then my friend Patty got me back on my feet."

Monique stepped up to the hand sink, and turned on the tap. "That's what I've taken to calling him, Cookie, 'my friend Patty.'"

"Patrick is one of our volunteers," explained the cook.

"Patrick Delaney. He's one of the city's leading attorneys," Monique said, punching the word *leading*. "I didn't know that though, until I ran into him at a lunch joint where it appeared I had been stood up. I assumed he remembered me from the mission and was being a nice guy when he invited me to join him. It was only after we'd ordered that he told me *he's* the lawyer I'd come to meet."

"Patrick's a big help around here, and an asset to our city," Cookie interjected.

"But not such a big shot, he forgets his friends," Monique said.

Shelby angled Jake another sidelong glance. He went on scrubbing spuds, taking no part in the conversation.

Not that Monique left any dead air for anyone else to insert a word edgewise. A loquacious woman in her midthirties, and oblivious to Shelby's identity, she launched into an account of her publishing experience from the acceptance of her book to the phone call in which she had asked for an early advance on royalties.

"You don't know what powerless is, until you're tapped out, no home and no one cares," she told them, sharing her feelings of helplessness at being turned down. "I'd worked harder on that book than I'd worked on anything in my whole life, and I never was any good at the wait-and-see game." Monique went on to relate her squeaky wheel retaliation—the bluff to sue.

"Looking back now, I see that the cover wasn't the problem. I was frustrated and angry and desperate. I kind of lost my grip and vented big time." She rolled repentant brown eyes and added, "Patty reasoned with me, friend to friend. He said that my conduct was unprofessional and a risk to my future as a writer."

"Precise and to the point. That's our Patrick," said the cook.

"Then he gave my hand a squeeze, as if to soften his words." Monique picked up a knife and used it to separate frozen hamburger patties. "He said if I would cease and desist with the cover tempest, he would do his best to persuade my editor to look at my next effort with an unbiased eye."

Shelby ducked her face over the sink, scrubbing the jacket right off a potato. Beside her, Jake broke his silence to ask Monique, "How's that going?"

"It's too soon to tell. I have the book outlined in

my head,'' she said. ''But I've been waiting to settle into my new place before getting it down on paper.''

Monique went on to say how much help she had received from Can-Do and from Patrick in easing back into the mainstream of life.

Cookie slapped oversize baking sheets down on the counter beside the box of frozen burgers Monique was hacking apart. ''Not to change the subject, Monique, but you see the big brute coming across the dining room, there?''

Monique turned and looked through the open serving window, which separated the kitchen from the dining hall. ''You mean Jig-Saw?''

''You're on a first-name basis, then?'' Cookie asked. ''He's been asking for your address.''

''What'd you tell him?'' countered Monique.

''I told him I didn't have it,'' Cookie said.

''Thanks, Cookie. I appreciate your concern,'' Monique told him. ''Have you cleaned the milk cooler lately?''

''Be my guest,'' Cookie replied.

Shelby stepped away from the sink, making room for Monique who trotted off to the dining room with a sponge and a basin of soapy water.

''Shelby, if you'd put these patties on baking trays, I'll get the potatoes ready for the deep fryer,'' Cookie suggested.

Jake helped Cookie put the potatoes through a machine that turned them into fries. Alone at the stainless steel table, Shelby looked up from her appointed task to see the man Cookie had referred to as Jig-Saw limp to the milk cooler. The cooler was a few yards beyond the serving window, giving Shelby a bird's eye view. Jig-Saw was tall and starkly built, with short-clipped hair the color and texture of winter grass gracing a high, proud forehead. He had a strong nose and scar-engraved cheeks and taut jowls. The scars marred what might otherwise have been termed craggy and austere and handsome. His eyes were a piercing gray, intelligent, and deeply set with a wary expression Shelby mentally termed *pity-resistant.* All in all, he was embodiment of the walking wounded, both commanding and unforgettable. He rubbed his left hip, a look of pain dulling his expression as he and Monique talked.

Shelby couldn't hear their words over the noisy electric machine Jake and Cookie were using in the back kitchen. But by all appearances, Monique was at ease with the guy.

Cookie and Jake finished cutting the potatoes and retreated to a deep-fat fryer on the other side of the room. Monique was still working on the milk cooler, and chatting with Jig-Saw.

"Call it research for my next book," Shelby heard her respond.

"An exposé on your ex?" asked Jig-Saw.

"No, nothing so boring as that," Monique said. "It's about a lady and a lawyer who helps her believe she hasn't fallen so hard or so far that God can't give her a hand up."

"Any chance Patrick's turned you into an angel of mercy?" asked the man. "Because if he has, I could use a favor."

"What kind of a favor?"

"A place to stay. I wouldn't ask for myself, but my daughter is wanting to visit me," he said quickly.

"She doesn't know you're homeless?"

"No, and there's no reason to tell her. Provided

you'd cover for me" he added. "It would only be for a day."

"You'd want to make like it was your home, is that what you're saying?" asked Monique.

"If it's all right," he replied.

"Give me a little time to think about it." Monique swung to the serving window and slid her basin of water through it.

Quickly, Shelby averted her glance. "The patties are on the trays. What now?" she called to Cookie.

"Put them in the oven," he instructed, and adjusted the burner on the deep-fat fryer.

Jake had been processing information as well as potatoes. While Shelby hadn't mentioned that Patrick volunteered at the mission, it was reasonable by virtue of their past that they would have interests in common. Further, Monique's tearoom summary had confirmed that Jake's doubts of that day had been unfounded. What had gotten into him, anyway? He should have known Shelby wasn't one to manipulate with her own end in view, even if she did still hold feelings for Patrick. Which she very well might.

But then, he didn't back off from competition when bidding a job. Why would he, where someone as important as Shelby was, was concerned? He crowded out the practical considerations his mind had been repeating by rote all month and strolled over to transfer the trays of burgers to a convection oven and set about testing the waters.

"So what do you think?" he asked, as they slid the last tray into place.

"If it were up to me, I'd grill them," Shelby offered.

"I meant Monique," Jake returned, watching her. "I gather you two never met face-to-face."

"Just that glimpse at the tearoom." Shelby wiped her hands on her apron. "Apparently, she didn't notice us."

"Seems that way," Jake agreed. "So what are the odds on her getting a second chance at Parnell?"

"If it's up to me, she will."

"That's what I figured," Jake said. "You're a good sport, you know it?"

"Not really. I was livid for weeks."

"Change of heart?"

"Hearts will do that," she said and smiled so warmly, Jake allowed himself the liberty of reading into her words.

"It's going to be a little awkward, though, the day we do come face-to-face and she realizes who I am," Shelby continued.

"She'll thank you later for giving her a good story to tell," Jake predicted. "Better yet, she can sell it to your publisher, and you'll all live happily ever after."

"A how-to on how on to live happily ever after," she said with an oblique glance that made him grin. "Sounds like a bestseller to me."

Together, they prepared buns for the burgers, then put out the condiments. By the time the oven buzzer rang, a line had formed at the serving window and wrapped its way around the room.

Brady waited to eat with Jake and Shelby. His mother, Shelby noticed, had nervous hands and a weary, defeated demeanor. She explained that she and Brady had been en route to her brother's home in Iowa when their car broke down. The car held all their earthly treasures, things she was unwilling to leave behind. Her brother had been a week now, making arrangements to come collect them and their meager possessions.

"Go rest, if you want to," Brady told his mother, when she complained of feeling weary. "I'll stay with Jake a while, okay?"

His mother granted permission. Brady led Shelby and Jake to the lounge and brought out a board game. The board was a geography map of the old west. Each player got a share of play loot, a game piece and a handful of cards. There was a feather, too, symbolic of a writing quill. Each time a treaty was made, participating players were to touch the feather.

Shelby slipped off her damp shoes. Noticing, Jake reached down and tickled her toes with the feather. Brady followed suit, and chortled with boyish glee when Shelby squealed.

"Quit, now, or I'll confiscate your feather," she threatened with mock sternness.

Brady giggled and resumed mischievous efforts to tickle her feet.

"Hold it down, would you please?" a deep voice called across the room. "I'm talking long distance."

Shelby, Jake and Brady all swung around to the see the man with the scarred face at the pay phone.

"We're sorry," Shelby said, and touched her finger to her lips.

"Jig-Saw." Brady's voice dropped to a hush as he shrank into his chair.

Jake, who had been sitting with his back to the man, took a second gander and scratched his head. "The name doesn't ring a bell. But there's something familiar about the guy."

"It's not a common face. Poor man," murmured Shelby.

"It isn't his face, it's his voice." Jake's brow pleated. "Can't quite place it, though."

Shelby watched out of the corner of her eye as the man hung up the phone. "He looks lonely. Why don't you ask him if he'd like to join us, Brady?"

Brady hesitated, his expression uncertain.

"Sit tight, son. I'll ask." Jake shifted to his feet, and angled across the room.

Jig-Saw looked up from folding a slip of paper into his pocket. Recognition flashed in those ash-colored eyes, confirming Jake's suspicion that he should know him.

"Have we met?" Jake asked.

The man drew his hand across his face and wheeled away before Jake could thrust out his hand. Jake watched him limp away. But it wasn't the limp, it was those odd-colored eyes that fell into place. *Colton!* It struck Jake like a fully loaded eighteen wheeler.

"What was that all about?" Shelby murmured, looking from Jake to the door that had shut after Colton.

Even now, Jake's certainty was fading. Why would an icon in the advertising world be getting his meals at a homeless mission? Doubt crowding in, Jake kept his private thoughts private, and said, "Guess he doesn't want to join us. Let's finish our game, shall we?"

Shelby wasn't swallowing Jake's easy dismissal of Jig-Saw's brush-off. Something about the man was nagging at him. She could see it working on him. His sudden inattentiveness gave it away, too. His gaze kept returning to the door through which Jig-Saw had disappeared.

Chapter Fifteen

Jake and Shelby played several games with Brady before his mother came to collect him. Before leaving the mission, Jake excused himself for a word alone with the mission director. Shelby ducked into the ladies' room and tamed unruly curls. Jake and Mr. Weaver had emerged from the director's office by the time she reached the foyer.

"Tell Brady and his mom it's to help them get a fresh start in Iowa. No need in saying who," he added, shaking hands with Mr. Weaver.

"I'd like to keep in touch." Shelby retrieved a pad and pencil from her pocketbook and took down Brady's uncle's address in Iowa.

"He'll appreciate hearing from you both," Mr. Weaver said.

Shelby entrusted to Mr. Weaver a contribution toward Brady and his mother's travel expenses. He promised to pass it along, and bid them good evening.

Jake held the door for Shelby. She preceded him

out beneath clearing skies and asked on caught
breath, "What did Mr. Weaver say concerning Jig-
Saw?"

Jake was still reeling from the shock of recognizing Colt and the realization of how far and how fast
a man could fall. Uncertain how to tell her except
straight out, he stopped in the middle of the parking
lot.

"What is it?" Shelby asked, reaching for his hand.

"Colton." Jake pointed to the high-rise sign
across the way.

Shelby glanced at The Voyager paddling his canoe
along the infamous billboard and darted after Jake.
Confused, she said, "What about it?"

"That was him. Jig-Saw."

"*That* Colton? The Voyager? Joy's *father?* You
don't mean it!" she gasped.

"Afraid so." Jake reseated his cap. "As far as Mr.
Weaver knows, Jig-Saw is just another hard-luck
story. He had a bad accident some time ago and no
place to go when he was released from the hospital."

"But how does a guy pulling down that kind of
money end up in a homeless shelter?" cried Shelby.

"I don't know, and I don't like the scenarios that
leap to mind." Jake waited for her while she
searched her purse for her car keys. "Makes me all
the more uneasy about Joy. Funny he'd have a computer, but no home."

"He's planning on Joy coming to see him. I overheard him say so to Monique as she was cleaning
the milk cooler."

Jake listened intently as Shelby related to the best
of her ability the part of the conversation that she
had heard.

"Paula isn't going to agree to that," he said with certainty

"But he *is* Joy's father," said Shelby.

"And for that, he deserves consideration?" he countered.

"I have no idea. You're the one who has been there for them, I know that," Shelby said quickly.

"I'm sorry, I didn't mean to bark at you. I'm still having trouble believing it was him. And yet, I know it was." Jake unlocked her car door, and swung it wide, saying, "Let's just forget it for now, all right?"

Shelby tried not to feel hurt by the barrier he had dropped. It was obvious his encounter with Joy's father had him kicking the ends out of coffins on long-buried feelings. She wished, as she slid behind the wheel, that she had a deeper history with him, the kind that would have equipped her to be of some help.

True to his intention of shelving the whole business, Jake reminded her of the blues festival unfolding at Grant Park.

"It was just a thought, Jake. We don't have to go if you're not in the mood," Shelby said quietly.

"I don't know what to make of the information is all," he said touching once more on Colton.

"Stunned?" she said, with a sympathetic brush of hands.

"Something like that," he admitted, and squeezed her hand, finding healing in her touch. "I'll run my truck back to the motel lot where it'll be secure. Take me a few minutes to shower and change."

"You want me to pick you up there?" Shelby asked.

"We'd have to find a place to park. That'll be a real headache. How about I grab a cab and pick you up. How much time do you need?"

Wrinkles had dried into Shelby's dress. Her shoes were still damp. A soak to ease muscles growing stiff from too many bumps in the bumper car would do no harm, either. Measuring how much daylight remained of the long summer evening, she gave Jake her address and promised to be ready in forty minutes.

The fragrant soak was a short one. Shelby dried and styled her hair, and donned an ankle-length crinkle-pleated skirt. She buttoned and tucked in a crisp cotton blouse with a scooped neckline and loose sleeves that billowed to her elbows. Rolling the long edge of a paisley shawl, she tied it at her waist and turned the knot to the back. The gaily fringed swatch of linen accessorized the skirt nicely, as did hoop earrings and an antique locket. With two minutes to spare, Shelby spritzed her throat with juniper breeze body splash, slipped into her favorite platform sandals, and was waiting when Jake arrived.

He was clad in khakis and a blue shirt that drew Shelby's attention to his eyes the moment he swung open the cab door.

"Want a lift, pretty lady?" he said, and let go a whistle.

Pulse quickening at the open admiration in his eyes, Shelby laughed and countered, "My mama said don't take rides with strangers."

"Then climb on in here and we'll get better acquainted," he quipped, and tucked her in beside him. "Grant Park," he told the cabby.

The sun was setting as they climbed out of the cab

just a block from the heart of the festivities. There was a noisy glazed-eye quality about a city that Jake usually found wearing at the end of a day. But tonight, surrounded by music and the cacophony of voices, the cloud threatening the evening wasn't so much the wall of humanity closing in as concern over people Jake loved standing in hurt's way. He warred it stubbornly with a glib tongue and fluent flirtation that fooled Shelby not in the least. Rather it evoked in her both tenderness and a willingness to let the little actress out of the box if it gave him reprieve from the impending abrasions closing in on his family. So when he compared her skirt to peacock plumage, she spread it like a tail fan and curtsied just to make him smile. They wandered hand in hand until they found a patch of real estate large enough to settle.

"The ground's a little damp," Jake said, testing it. "We should have brought a blanket."

"Fret not," Shelby told him. She untied her shawl from her waist and spread it on the ground.

Jake awarded her ingenuity with an approving grin. "Always prepared. The hallmark of a true scout."

"Peacock troop, reporting for duty," Shelby replied, playing along, and laughed when he saluted.

Jake sat on the shawl beside her, ankles crossed, and waited until she had tucked her feet beneath the folds of her flowing skirt to stretch out on his back and rest his head in her lap.

"Make yourself comfortable," she drawled.

Unscathed by the tongue-in-cheek tip of her mouth, Jake distracted her with the music, urging, "Listen. Tugs at your eyelids, doesn't it?"

"If you say so," she acquiesced on a dry note, and pushed his cap brim down over his face. "Sweet dreams, Sign Man."

Jake grinned and hooked his cap over one knee, and found her face in the dusky twilight. The sky was beyond reach, the stars still in hiding. But a light shone from her eyes that he had not seen before. There were hidden depths there that bespoke endurance. The kind that provided a center, a hearth, a home fire, a buffer against wedges that sought to prevail. The peace that transcended understanding exposed his noisy front for what it was, and quieted him. Oblivious to the sea of humanity surrounding them, he savored the sensation of her hand light on his chest, keeping the beat of the music. He closed his eyes and didn't open them again until the dampness of the rain-soaked ground seeped through their cloth island. He felt her shiver.

"Cold?" he asked.

"Not bad." She crossed her arms, chafing them with her small hands.

Jake sat up and offered himself as a resting post. Shelby turned her knees to one side, and settled back against his chest. As an afterthought, she spread a swatch of skirt over his lap.

Jake smiled at her notion that the flimsy bit of crinkled pleats offered warmth.

"Sing," she said, as his arms closed around her.

"She can bake a cherry pie, fast as a cat can wink its eye," Jake sang, making music in her ear.

She curved her white neck, looking up at him. "Feeling better, Billy Boy?"

Acres of care fell away at that tender glance.

"Starting to," he said, and tucked a curl behind her ear. "You going to take me to church tomorrow?"

"You're staying then? I thought you might have changed your mind."

Because of Colton. She didn't say it. But he knew what she meant. "I'd just have to turn around and come back Monday morning," he reasoned.

"How flattering," she said. "There for a moment, I hoped my company had a little something to do with it."

"More than a little," he admitted and kissed her arching neck.

"Jake?" she began, emboldened by his closeness and the heat he was spreading with his kisses.

"Hmm?"

"I can't get Colton off my mind," she admitted as he rested his chin in her hair. "May I ask—was it because of the accident that Paula divorced him?"

"She didn't," Jake said.

Shelby turned in his arms to meet his eyes. "They're still married?"

"Technically, yes."

"But she hasn't seen or heard from him in all these years?"

"No," Jake replied, stroking the back of her hand with his thumb. "Why? What's on your mind?"

"It's none of my business, but I'm just trying to understand why Paula never told Colton about Joy."

In looking back, it was difficult for Jake to say at what point Paula made that decision. "She was pretty devastated by the accident. We all were, of course. But Paula even more so, partly because of her strong-willed battle to marry Colt in the first place," Jake said, remembering out loud.

Reaching back over the years, he recalled Paula, fresh out of high school, quarreling for parental blessing on her decision to forego college and marry Colt. The arguments had grown pretty heated, his parents deeply concerned that Paula was too young, too inexperienced and too in love to make a clear-headed decision. Jake shared as much with Shelby, concluding, "Once they were married, Mom and Dad accepted it. But it was awfully hard on Paula when the three people she loved most in the world collided on that dark two-lane road."

"She wasn't in the car with Colt?"

"No. He had just dropped her off to visit Gram."

"And still, she was a casualty," murmured Shelby, deeply saddened. Thinking of Colton, so scarred and broken, she asked, "How upset is Paula going to be to realize that Colt isn't all that he seems?"

"She found that out years ago," Jake replied in an emotionless voice that made Shelby wince.

Shifting in his arms, she asked softly, "What about you? Do *you* blame Colt for your parents' death?"

"No," Jake said. "I blame him for not being there to hold Paula when she cried."

Shelby's eyes drew tears at his tender-tough reply. It told her far more than she had asked, about Paula and Colton, and about Jake, too. He would never forsake her that way. The thought startled her, for it revealed the depth of her feelings for him. Quite un-seen, he had been sinking roots into her heart all these weeks, even in separation. Marveling over it, she mused, "You're a pretty special guy, Jake."

"Could I get that in print?" he said.

Smiling, she reached up and patted his cheek. He hadn't shaved since morning. Razor stubble chafed her skin as he kissed her throat. His lips soothed what his skin had roughed. Shooting stars spiraled like pinwheels, showering sparks to far reaches. Shelby lifted her shoulder. He kissed that barrier, too, and kept on kissing her. The flame burned higher until finally, she created some breathing room.

He sighed knowingly, and asked her about her book.

"It's sweet of you to ask. But let's not go there," she said.

Jake contented himself holding her hand until the festival broke up at midnight. They practiced good-night kisses on the ride back to her building, and in the elevator ride up to her apartment, and had them perfected by the time they reached her door.

"The meter's running," she reminded, as Jake lingered.

"That what you call it?" Jake kissed her throbbing temple.

"The *cab* meter."

"Oh, that," he said, and silenced her soft laughter with another kiss. "I'll call you, okay?"

"Where have I heard those words?" she teased.

"I promise," he said, and kissed her one last time.

Shelby hadn't long to wait. Jake called her from his motel room as soon as he returned, just to say good-night.

"Did you call Paula?" she asked.

"No," he said. "It's late. It'd only keep her up, worrying."

Shelby heard the weariness in his voice, and asked

no more questions. I love you, Jake, she thought, and wished for the opening to say it out loud.

The next morning, Shelby took Jake to her parents' home church only to learn her folks were out of town. Afterward, they lunched at a neighborhood restaurant, then strolled Navy Pier, soaking up sun on the boardwalk and watching people wandering in and out of the shops. They bought seed from a vending machine and fed the gulls, then caught a water taxi to Shedd Aquarium. It was one of Shelby's favorite places. She enjoyed sharing it with Jake. He didn't mention Colton all day. Respecting his bid to avoid the subject, she didn't bring it up, either.

Jake bought posies from a corner cart on the way to the restaurant they had chosen for dinner. Excellent food, fresh flowers, candlelight and music made for a lovely intimate dinner. Afterward, at Jake's invitation, Shelby stepped out onto the dance floor and into his arms.

Jake drew her closer. They danced out the slow number and another that followed before he broke the comfortable silence and mentioned her book.

"What book?" she bid for another subject.

He said, "Forget it, then, if you don't want to talk about it. It's not getting me anywhere, asking."

"Where is it you want to be?"

"Right here's nice," he said, and cradled her cheek with the hollow of his hand.

"For me, too."

"God was surely smiling when I bumped into you yesterday."

"Yesterday? Let's see." She fit a finger to a dimpled cheek and sucked her bottom lip, thinking.

"Would that be the day you said I needed a better man?"

He chuckled and admitted, "That was before I knew that Patrick walks on water."

"Kind of stunned me, too," Shelby said, her playfulness receding. "He hasn't always. At first I dragged him to the mission kicking and screaming. He had to have changed right before my eyes. But I didn't see it. I was too busy."

"With your job?"

"And my writing."

"Regrets?" he asked softly.

"About Patrick? No," she said without hesitation. "I admire him for his goodness. But I've moved on."

Jake held her close and didn't ask if she loved Patrick. She didn't. Not with the love from which lovers were carved. She saw that clearly from Jake's embrace. Wanting him to know it, too, so that they could be finished with this conversation forever, she said, "Patrick told me when he broke it off that he needed someone who loved him enough to put everything into the marriage, and not hold anything back."

"Including your writing?"

She nodded. "I guess he saw I was afraid of losing it, and my identity, too. He took exception, saying there was no fear in love. He was right, of course. I see that now."

"New glasses?" Jake asked with a tender smile.

She laced her fingers with his as they danced, kissed the back of his hand and murmured, "No. A new man."

A wild relief swept over him. He pocketed her into

deep shadows, whispering her name and endearments between soft kisses. She slipped her arms around his waist, tunneling between shirt and jacket. The kiss deepened, expelling forever the ghosts of kisses past.

Later, when Jake saw her home, Shelby didn't invite him to linger. Aloud, she reasoned that they both had to work in a few hours. Jake intended to finish the last dry cleaning store by noon tomorrow. Then he would go home. She wouldn't see him again until Gram Kate's birthday party the following Saturday.

Shelby dreaded the separation. At the same time, the stardust needed a chance to settle. Nothing in her past had prepared her for love that came out of broken dreams and all but consumed her. Yet there it was, pure light, radiating hope and inexpressible joy with her every thought of him.

Jake met Shelby for breakfast the next morning. They wouldn't be able to say their goodbyes later, as Shelby had a lunch meeting, and a crowded afternoon. So they lingered long over coffee gone cold, went over their plans for the following weekend and added to the heat of the morning with one last embrace before going their separate ways.

Then Jake finished his job, and left the city behind, already counting the days until they would be together again.

Chapter Sixteen

Paula and Joy had stayed at the house and looked after Gram while Jake was gone. They were eating dinner when he walked in.

Gram Kate beamed and stretched out her hands to him. "Jake! How nice of you to drop by. Have a bite with us, won't you?"

"Did you finish the job?" asked Paula.

"Wrapped it up a little after lunch," he said. "What's this—new potatoes?"

"Fresh out of the garden. The green beans, too," Paula said. "Joy picked them."

"Good for you, sport. Did you keep the weeds pulled, too?" Jake asked from the sink.

"Uh-huh. You owe me big time." Joy had her back to him and her finger in a magazine. She swung around in her chair. "Did you see Shelby while you were in Chicago?"

"Yes. She's coming Saturday for the birthday party," he said.

"Is it your birthday, dear?" Gram Kate spoke up. "Remind me to bake a ca-ca—"

"It's *your* birthday, not his," Joy interjected.

"Saturday, Gram. The whole town is coming," Paula said.

"Aunt Wendy must be right about you, Uncle Jake. She said you had it bad," Joy drawled, arching Jake a glance.

Jake draped the damp hand towel over her shoulder and tugged her braid in passing.

Joy turned calculating eyes from her open magazine, where her father was featured in a full-page ad, to Jake and asked, "Are you going to marry her and move to Chicago?"

"Chicago?" Jake echoed.

"Sure. That's were Shelby works, isn't it? I'm looking on the bright side—if you move to Chicago, it'd give me a chance to know Dad," Joy explained, "which I could anyway, if Mom would quit treating me like a baby. I'm old enough make up mind about him, don't you think, Uncle Jake?"

Jake dodged the question, asking, "So what do I owe you for weeding my garden?"

Joy darted her mother a defiant glance. "Buy me a bus ticket and we'll call it even."

"Don't be ridiculous, you're not going anywhere," Paula snapped. "Sit up straight, would you please? And put that magazine down while you eat."

"I'm finished," Joy said. She bolted from her chair, magazine in hand, flounced out through the porch and slammed the screen door behind her.

"She's going to break hearts someday," Gram Kate mused.

"Sounds to me like it's her mother's will she's set

on breaking," Jake observed. He squeezed Paula's shoulder in passing and added, "But hang tough, you're still the boss, sis."

"So why am I finding it so hard to follow my intuition and flat out refuse to even consider letting her see him?" Paula muttered, rubbing her temples.

"Because you're afraid you'll ignite a fight you can't win," Jake said, as gently as he knew how. "The good news is, you're worrying needlessly. Colt doesn't have the wherewithal to fight."

Paula spared him a dry glance and replied, "No more than you're average kazillionaire."

"Less. A good deal less. Seriously," said Jake.

"What are you saying?"

"I bumped into Colton while I was in Chicago," Jake told her. "At a homeless shelter."

"A homeless shelter?" Paula's hand flew to her throat.

Gram jumped out of her chair. "How much do they need? Where's the cookie jar? I'll send them some muh—muh—matches."

"Hush, Gram, I can't think." Paula's voice, sharp with shock, fell in contrition. "I'm sorry, Gram. I'm sorry." She circled the table and hugged Gram's neck.

"There, there, dear. I lose things, too." Gram patted Paula's hand absently. She left the table, taking the salt and pepper shakers to the sink and her empty plate to the living room.

Jake saw Paula's face contort at the strain of converging anguish. He shifted her empty chair out from the table in wordless invitation. She circled back to it, but didn't sit down. "I can't believe it. Are you sure it was him, Jake?"

"No mistake about it, it was Colton, all right,"
Jake said.

"You spoke to him?"

"He didn't give me the chance. He didn't want to
be recognized."

"Well of course you'd recognize him," said
Paula, frowning. "Half the planet knows that face."

"Not anymore. He's been in an accident. He's
pretty scarred up," Jake told her.

Paula's color fled. She felt behind her for her chair,
dropped and sat emotionless as he repeated what had
transpired.

"Colton always did spend freely." Paula mar-
shaled table crumbs with a trembling hand. "Joy is
my life," she said, tears rising. "I can't entrust her
to him when I don't even know if he's capable of
basic parenting."

"Tell him so."

Paula shuddered and dropped her face in her
hands, wiping away tears. "I don't owe him a reason.
I'll just say no. Let him read whatever he wants into
it."

Jake had no quarrel with that. The accident that
had occurred all those years ago was just that—an
accident. As he had told Shelby, he didn't blame him
for the tragic consequences. However, Colt was responsible for the careless choices he had since made,
and the far-reaching consequences touching Joy and
Paula still today.

After dinner, Jake closed himself in his office. He
wished the work week was gone and Shelby was here
with him. Her presence was a buffer between him
and the uncertainty of this business with Colton. Her
touch and the light in her eyes covered his doubts

about her ex-fiancé, his own crowded life and the isolating miles. Needing to hear her voice, Jake picked up the phone and dialed.

Shelby had had a full day and was late arriving home. The phone was ringing when she walked in.

"Miss you." Jake's voice warmed her ear.

"Me, too," she said. "How was your drive home?"

"Uneventful. Got a little rough at dinner, though," he said, and told her about it.

"What'd Joy say when you related her father's circumstances?" Shelby asked.

"She had left the table by then. Paula said if Colt wants Joy to know his circumstances, he'll tell her himself."

Shelby sympathized with Paula's difficult position before the conversation moved ahead.

"I phoned the mission this afternoon. Brady's uncle arrived yesterday. They left for Iowa this morning," she said by and by. "I was working on a card when you called. There's room for a line from you if you like," she said, after sharing what she had written.

Jake sent along his greetings, then promised to call again.

They spoke each night that followed. Jake was watching the weather with Gram's birthday party in view when Shelby phoned him on Thursday.

"The girls have a garden party in mind. Hope it doesn't rain," he told her. "You might want to bring—"

"My sunflower dress?" she interjected.

"You're pretty sunny in that. May hold back the

rain," he agreed, and chuckled. "But I was thinking more along the lines of that dress you dropped by the cleaners."

"A little formal, wouldn't you say?"

"Depends on how you look at it," countered Jake, emboldened by the smile in her voice. "Of course you'd have to get here tomorrow afternoon before the courthouse closes so we can get a marriage license."

"Very cute, Jake."

"So you're sticking to Plan E then?"

"*E?*" she echoed.

"Elopement."

"I did say that, didn't I?"

"In your own bittersweet words."

Smiling, Shelby twined the phone cord around her finger, cautioning, "Keep it up, and I may call your bluff."

"It's no bluff," he said. "I've got the preacher's number jotted down right here. 1-555-1212."

"That's directory assistance, Jake."

"I could use some assistance." He made the most of his joke. "Hello, Operator? Something wrong here. I've been put on hold."

Shelby sensed serious intent beneath Jake's levity. *There is no fear in love.* In his arms, that was so. But the miles separating them left a crack through which slipped the issue that had come between her and Patrick. She shied from thinking history could repeat itself. Jake would never forsake the woman he loved. Knowing it as surely as she knew anything, Shelby said, "You're so very patient. That's what I love about you, Jake."

"Love?" he echoed.

"Is that what you heard? Must have slipped," she said, and laughed softly. "I'll see you Saturday, Billy Boy."

Encouraged at how well she'd nibbled his test bait, Jake went out to the shop and made preparations for a sign. He had made a lot of signs over the years. But his heart was in this one. He ran a pattern off on his computer, spread it on Paula's workbench and spread a piece of screen wire over it. Then he heated clear glass tubes and bent them into shape to match the pattern.

The next day Jake found a discarded neon window sign in the boneyard at the Bloomington shop. The frame and transformers would work for his new sign. He stripped away the glass spelling out the café's name and the words *Open* and *Closed* and took the frame home with him. After dinner, Jake mounted the new glass, attached three transformers and wired the transformer leads to the glass electrodes.

Joy came sidling into the neon workshop as he was testing out the sign.

"What's that for?" she asked as the message, Marry Me? lit up.

"What do you think?" he replied.

She rolled her eyes and dismissed the sign with a sniff. "I got a blue ribbon on my cake at the fair last week," she told him.

"Then all that practice paid off. Well done," Jake said.

"Dirk asked me to ride the rides. But I wouldn't, 'cause I caught him on the Ferris wheel with this orange-haired twerp who belongs to his 4-H club."

"Plenty of time and plenty of Dirks out there," Jake soothed.

"Who cares? He's a know-nothing turkey, anyway. He acts like Dad's a sissy or something. Because of the billboard, I mean. Like modeling is just for girls. But I say Dad's free to make a living however he wants, don't you think?"

"It's his choice, his life," Jake said. "It's no different with you and me, blondie. Every day we make choices we have to live by."

"You, maybe. But Mom makes all of mine," she complained.

"She's just trying to teach how to choose for yourself."

"What's wrong with wanting to see Dad?"

"That's not my call," Jake replied, getting out of the middle.

"You always say that," Joy complained. "Makes me want to scream."

"I'll try to remember that, when I have kids of my own."

Met with a cold stare, Jake's grin felt out of place. He tried to redirect Joy's attention to the choices spelled out in neon. "Pull a chain," he prompted.

Joy chose without hesitation and smirked as the word *No* lit up.

"You can sweep up for me, if you want." Jake overlooked her petulance.

"Better not. Wouldn't want to get in your way," she said, and let the door slam on her way out.

Jake cleaned up the shop, took the sign inside and went to bed, debating presentation. With extended family and a good part of Liberty Flats coming for

Gram's birthday, it was going to be a job, finding the right time and place.

The answer came in the night. The next morning, Jake strung a cord through the attic to the catwalk atop the house, and plugged in the neon sign. He pulled the chain, testing the only answer he wanted to hear.

Neon flashed affirmatively to the vivid red question, Marry Me? Satisfied, Jake went downstairs and made coffee. Gram was still in bed, so he took his cup back up on the catwalk. Eager as a kid awaiting Christmas morning, he watched the street until he ran out of coffee and returned to the kitchen.

Gram was puttering around in her housecoat, sifting through drawers. When Jake questioned her, she couldn't remember what she was looking for.

He settled her at the table with coffee and cream, and had breakfast on the table by the time Shelby arrived. Pink suit, short skirt, white tights hugging slim shapely legs. Curls shining and her face alight, too. Jake registered this and much more in the heartbeat it took him to unhook the screen.

"Hi. I got an early start," she said, a little piece of heaven walking into his arms, with cloud-soft hair and skin and full moist lips smiling at him. "Did you save me any coffee?"

"We'll get to that," Jake said. He kissed her and would have taken her up to the catwalk then and there except Gram was on her feet, trying to put the electric pot on the burner.

Shelby slipped out of Jake's embrace and renewed acquaintance with Gram Kate. Gram Kate mistook her for Paula, and then Wendy. After breakfast, Gram told her, "I'll wash the dishes, Jill. You're going to miss your ride. Here they are now."

It was Paula, letting herself in. Joy scuffed along at her heels. Dressed in a black T-shirt, black jeans and a demeanor to match, she brushed past Shelby without speaking.

"Joy?" prompted Paula. "Aren't you going to say hello?"

"Hi," Joy muttered with a half-hearted wave. "Where's the Christmas lights, Uncle Jake? I'm going to string the white twinkly ones over the rose arbor. Help me, okay?"

"In a little while," Jake promised. "I hear a car."

Joy sauntered to the window. "Uncle Hershel and Aunt Marge," she said, with a spark of animation. "Uncle Hershel brought his fiddle."

"Gram's sister and her husband," Jake told Shelby. "Marge brings three-bean salad to all the family shindigs, and Hershel brings music."

"Oh, dear. I didn't...did you? Change the sheets in the guest room, would you, Wendy?" Gram said to Shelby.

"I changed them yesterday, Gram," Paula said. She winged Shelby a quick glance. "You don't mind staying at my house, do you?"

"Whatever is convenient," Shelby replied.

"You can have my room, I'll sack out here on the sofa," Joy offered. "Uncle Jake doesn't care, do you Uncle Jake?"

"Suit yourself," Jake said. He caught Shelby's hand in his. "Come along and I'll introduce you."

Uncle Hershel was a portly, red-faced, amiable man. He beamed at Shelby. "Pleased to meet you."

"You must be the little author. How nice to make

your acquaintance, dear.'' A thin, thistle-haired woman with Gram Kate's eyes, and a covered dish in hand, Marge smiled brightly. "Three-bean salad. The dish is a little drippy, it has been in the ice chest.''

"Why don't I get your luggage?" Jake offered.

"While I poke this in the fridge,'' Marge agreed, nodding. "Come along, Hershel and we'll jog Kate's memory.'' She strode up the path to the house arm in arm with her husband.

Two more cars had pulled in as Shelby was trailing Jake with luggage. Within minutes, the whole place churned with Jacksons, their mates and their offspring. All of them were loaded down with food and presents and potted plants and plans to dress the yard in party garments.

The men rolled up their sleeves and drove stakes on the lawn to pitch a striped canopy in case of rain. The women had a penchant for organized chaos that delivered surprising results. Shortly before noon, Jake finished setting up chairs and tables beneath the canopy, and joined Shelby in the porch swing.

"It looks like a garden magazine centerfold.'' Shelby indicated with a sweep of her hand the transformation achieved by creative lighting and multiple seating arrangements, potted plants and a trickling fountain. "Your sisters should go into business.''

Jake rubbed a smudge of flower pollen off her chin. "You did your share of arranging flowerpots.''

She smiled. "Just stopping to smell the roses.''

"The roses have seen more of you than I have,'' he complained, and pulled her to her feet. "Paula's got a ham in the oven she'd like someone to fetch. I think we can handle that, don't you?''

"Certainly," Shelby said. Enticed by the twinkle in his eye and his hand pressed to the small of her back, she led the way down the porch steps, all too eager for a moment alone with him.

Chapter Seventeen

Jake's Jeep was blocked by family vehicles. Shelby gave him her car keys. They drove across town to Paula's house. Jake took her suitcase from the trunk and led the way inside. Shelby took the ham out of the oven while Jake carried her luggage back to Joy's bedroom.

"What do you know. Dessert!" he called to her on his way back through the living room.

Shelby declined his offer to share the candy bar he had found in Joy's room. "I'm saving my appetite for Aunt Marge's three-bean salad," she claimed.

"I hate eating alone," Jake protested, and patted the sofa in invitation.

Shelby joined him there. At his coaxing, she shared the half-melted chocolate bar with him, and melted herself when he traced the gold chain on her neck. A shower of phantom sparks radiated from his touch.

"Any pictures inside?" He fingered the antique locket that hung in the hallow of her throat.

"I've been saving that for someone special," she said.

He brought his other hand to the locket, seeking the catch. The concentrated effort put lines in his brow and goose bumps on her skin. Her fingers brushed his as she opened the locket. He murmured at the absence of a picture inside, and was gathering her into his arms when the phone rang. It was Joy.

"Uncle Jake? Mom's waiting to slice the ham. What're you guys doing, anyway?"

"We're on our way." Jake hung up the phone, and sighed. "Duty calls. Shall we go?"

"I thought I'd freshen up first."

"You're fresh enough for me," he teased. "But give me a call, and I'll come pick you up when you're ready."

When Jake had gone, Shelby showered and shook the folds from her sunflower dress. She had shopped for a wide-brimmed hat just for the occasion. It was lavishly adorned with flowers and yellow ribbon, a perfect compliment to the dress.

As was Jake's tie, when he arrived, his shirt starched, his trousers crisply pleated and his shoes polished to a picture-glass shine.

"Did I mention sunflowers become you?" he said of her dress.

"This old thing?" She flashed a coy smile and fluttered her lashes.

"You're radiant. I mean it," he said, and kissed her cheek.

"And speaking of vivid..." Shelby laughed and trailed her fingers over the screen-painted greenery vining up the yellow tie. "Looks like something from *Jack and the Beanstalk.*"

"That's where impulse shopping will get you." He feigned injured feelings. "I can change it if you think it's too much."

"Don't you dare. A little smoothing is all that it needs."

"Smooching?" He pretended to misunderstand.

"Smoothing." She enunciated it clearly, and laughed. "I move the mutual admiration society adjourn for the birthday party before we succumb to our own devices. Do I hear a second?"

"I second the motion." Jake laughed and kissed the hands that straightened his tie. He folded one neatly over his arm and covered it with his hand. "Before they start without us."

They arrived to such a crowd, it was unlikely they would have been missed by anyone other than Joy. The house, the yard and the canvas canopy overflowed with guests, a token of the affection in which Gram Kate was held by both family and community.

The guests served themselves from the endless buffet spread in the kitchen. They ate their fill at tables and lawn chairs and garden benches scattered throughout the yard. Gram received such a mountain of presents, the grandchildren had to peel off the wrappings when her attention strayed from the task.

Afterward, Paula asked Shelby to help serve the cake and punch. They had prepared a beautiful table set beneath the striped canopy. A festoon of ribbons and paper flowers adorned the lacy tablecloth. Emmaline from Newt's Market had baked a huge sheet cake. The icing spelled out a birthday greeting in colors to match the rainbow sherbet that floated atop the punch.

"We'll serve the cake if you two want to man the punch bowl," Paula said to Shelby and Wendy.

"Here. You dip, I'll pass you the cups." Wendy gave Shelby the silver ladle and a crystal cup.

Joy crowded between Shelby and her mother, matches in hand. "I get to light the candles."

Gram beamed as Uncle Hershel brought out his violin. Friends and family closed in and sang the birthday song. When the last notes faded, Gram blew out the candles. But before they could be plucked from the cake, she picked up the abandoned matches and began relighting the candles.

"Gram! You blew them out once," reminded Joy.

Confused, Gram Kate paused with the lighted match in hand. "Hot, hot." She tried to shake it out, but dropped it instead into one of the paper flowers. The tissue paper went up in flames.

A collective gasp rose from the party goers. Jake bounded forward and eased Gram out of harm's way. Shelby, at ground zero, tossed a cup of punch on the flames. The ribbon connecting the garland of paper flowers smoldered. Intent on preventing the flames from spreading over the table Shelby grabbed another cup. She dipped and tossed and dipped and tossed until Joy screeched, "That's enough! It's out!"

Shelby blanched to see sherbet dripping off Gram Kate's dress. It was trickling down Jake's pant leg, too and the party garments of half a dozen guests.

Cheeks hot, Shelby hurried around the table and in a flurry of apologies, dabbed at Uncle Hershel's tie with her scented lace-trimmed hanky.

"Forget it! We'll wash." He brushed aside her concern as if flames and punch flew at all the Jackson parties.

Smothered snickers and giggles caught a draft that carried the sherbet-splattered guests along. Most chortled even as they sponged their clothes. Emmaline wrinkled her cute snub nose and promised Jake, "I'll send you my dry cleaning tab."

"You shouldn't have left the matches where she could get them," Paula scolded Joy.

"At least I didn't throw punch on everybody," Joy huffed.

Paula poked the matches into her apron pocket, and propelled Joy toward the house. "Run get a fresh tablecloth. Come on girls, let's clean up this mess. All's well that ends well."

Shelby wasn't sure it had. She caught her lip, watching as Joy stormed to the house like a bull with her head down.

At Shelby's side, Wendy soothed, "Pay no attention to Joy. She has her nose out of joint is all."

"What's wrong?" murmured Shelby.

Paula shot Wendy a warning glance. "Would you wash out the punch bowl and make some fresh punch, please, Wendy?"

"I apologize for Joy," Paula said, when Wendy had gone. "She's a little old to be reacting this way. But then, Jake is like a father to her."

"Reacting?" Shelby echoed. "To what?"

"You haven't been up to the catwalk yet?"

Shelby tipped her head back, and eyed the decorative wrought-iron railing atop the house. "I didn't realize it was accessible. Why? What's up there?"

"I'm sorry. I seem to have spoken out of turn." Paula's mouth tipped in an enigmatic smile.

Jake's sisters closed ranks and filled the air with chatter. Mystified by the whole lot of them, and feeling like the odd man out, Shelby lent her efforts to cleaning up the mess she had made of the table and gave up trying to understand Jacksons.

Jake put Joy in charge of helping Gram change her dress. He donned a fresh pair of trousers, and found Shelby at the punch bowl again. A line had formed. She was filling cups as fast as Wendy could hand them off.

He slipped up behind her and tugged at her hat. "Now you're getting the hang of it."

Shelby's color rose as she turned and angled him a brave smile.

"Mom says take Gram and Aunt Marge some cake and punch," Joy said as she proceeded to help herself from the serving side of the table. "You can come sit with us if you want, Uncle Jake."

"You go ahead, I'll wait for Shelby," Jake replied.

"I need help carrying the punch," entreated Joy, three plates of cake in hand.

Jake dropped something between a sigh and kiss on the nape of Shelby's neck, then followed Joy to the rose arbor where Gram and her sister were sitting. He distributed the cups of punch and chatted a moment before joining Uncle Hershel on the porch.

"Say, Jake, but doesn't that little gal of yours have a good arm on her?" greeted Uncle Hershel.

Jake grinned and flicked the spot on Hershel's tie. "Now to fine-tune her aim."

"Setting her sights on you, you mean?" Hershel cackled. "I kind of wondered myself if she knew the whole business."

"The business has never been better," Jake said.

"I'm not talking about the sign business, boy. I'm talking about Kate. She's slipped considerably in the past few months. "

Jake tried to change the subject. But Uncle Hershel, having none of it, set his plate and cup aside, and leaned forward, forearms resting on his knees. "You got a right to a life of your own, son. Kate'd be the first to tell you so if she was up to par."

"I appreciate your concern, Uncle Hershel, but—"

"Hear me out, son," Hershel wagged an open hand before Jake's face, forestalling interruption. "There's some mighty nice retirement apartments these days, some with assisted living. Marge and I have been looking into it ourselves. No point in holding out so long we become a burden to others, you see what I mean?"

"Gram Kate isn't a burden," Jake said.

Hershel patted him on the shoulder. "That's a nice sentiment, boy. But if you're serious about that pretty little gal, then you need to take her into consideration, too."

The endless commotion, playing host and holding his tongue in the face of well-intentioned advice ground away at Jake. He counted the hours until he could steal away with Shelby, light the question and settle the matter once and for all. "Can I get you some more punch, Uncle Hershel?" Jake offered. "Another piece of cake, maybe?"

"No thanks, Jake. I'm watching my figure. But you go ahead. And don't forget what I told you, now, you hear?"

Chapter Eighteen

Shelby eased back into her pinching shoes as Jake sidled up at the tail end of the refreshment line.

"Save any punch for me?"

The smile lighting his face was refreshment to Shelby. "That, and the biggest piece of cake I could find." She peeled back the napkin covering the plate she had set aside for him.

Jake grinned. "Well done. I heard a rumor there was an unoccupied patch of grass and a nice shade tree around front. Interested?"

"Very," she said, and took the arm he offered.

Jake strolled her past a cluster of children playing dodge ball on the front lawn. Joy turned from her companions, and tossed the ball.

"Think fast, Uncle Jake!"

Jake blocked it with his foot, passed Shelby the cups of punch, and flung the ball back into the circle of children. They giggled and scattered so as not to be tagged by the ball.

"Missed me!" chanted Joy.

Jake tugged her plaited braid in passing, and led the way to the widespread maple tree. A massive old tree, it was set apart from the house and front lawn by low shrubs and a brick path that widened into an inviting paved outdoor living space leading up to the front portico. The trunk of the tree served as a back rest and partially screened them from the children's game and wild tosses of the ball.

"I was thinking that after dinner we could go up on the catwalk and watch the sunset," Jake suggested.

Intrigued, Shelby tucked her feet beneath the fan of her skirt and asked, "What is it with the catwalk? Paula mentioned it too."

"She did, did she?" He tantalized her with a enigmatic grin and shared the double-size wedge of cake. "By the way, how are you at ladders?"

"That depends. Is it attached to one of your crane trucks?"

Jake chuckled. "I'm never going to live that down, am I?"

Shelby smiled and brushed crumbs from her lap. Jake reached for her hand. Together, they watched a boy pedal up the street on his bicycle. He pulled up on the handlebars, rode a wheelie for a half a block, then turned and paraded past again.

"Is that who I think it is?" asked Shelby.

"Dirk?" Jake grinned and nodded. "Word is he's sweet on a girl in his 4-H club."

"Perhaps he's having second thoughts," Shelby said.

"For all the good it will do him. Joy isn't much at second chances."

"I don't know about that. She wants to see Colton, doesn't she?" Shelby reasoned.

"That's different," Jake said. "She's curious, naturally."

Before Shelby could invite him to elaborate, the children's game ball splashed through the bird bath, bounced over the bricks and came rolling under the maple tree. Joy meandered over to retrieve it.

Jake changed the subject accordingly. "I've been thinking about your problem book this past week and the question comes to mind—who murdered Mr. Weedman?"

"You think he was murdered?"

"Are you saying he wasn't?"

Shelby settled her punch cup on the empty cake plate. "First, tell me who you find suspicious."

"Old man Blatchford, for starters. The body was found in his field."

"He's rather feeble as suspects go," Shelby said.

"Exactly! Frailty deflects suspicion." Thoughts engaged, Jake watched idly as Joy dried the ball in the grass and studiously ignored the bicycling boy wonder, who was making another pass up the street. "Then there's the tough guy on the bean crew—what's his name?"

"Dudley?"

"Right, Dudley. Had a row with Weedman, as I recall. Which could make him either a rogue, or a diamond in the rough."

"You've given this some thought, I see."

"But of course," Jake said. "If you have a problem, I have a problem."

"What a nice sentiment," Shelby murmured.

Taking that to mean she was open to advice, Jake

said, "If you're still stuck, you could write the last chapter and work backward. By the way, does Weedman have any life insurance? If so, his wife would make a good suspect."

"Write backward?" She dismissed the idea with a smile that broadened as she asked, "And how in the world can you suspect his wife? She hasn't even appeared on the page."

"That in itself is suspicious," Jake said. "I propose we collaborate."

"Why? Who do you have in mind for a villain?"

"I'll leave that up to you. But I'm more than willing to help you narrow down that love triangle thing."

Shelby wagged her head at his leading grin. "I should have seen that one coming."

"So now *I'm* on the suspect list?" Jake feigned injury.

"Jack's the hero, Uncle Jake. He couldn't have done it,"

Shelby looked to find Joy standing a few yards away with the ball tucked under her arm. "Who said anything about Jack?"

"Jake, Jack. What's the difference?" Joy said.

"Wait a second, wait a second!" objected Shelby, the conversation gone suddenly awry. "Joy, how did you know about Jack?"

Joy cut her eyes from Dirk, who was pedaling away, arms folded across his chest, to Jake. She blanched and darted away without answering.

"You told her?" Shelby leaned away from Jake, the better to see his face. Once, she had seen a stray pup get that same look as the dog catcher's net closed over him. "Jake?"

His jaw twitched. But he didn't affirm or deny it. Or try to stop her as she slipped into her shoes, and crossed the yard to where Joy was watching her cousins from the sidelines.

"Joy?" Shelby said quietly.

Joy pivoted. Her freckled cheeks turned pink. "Okay, so I snooped. Big deal."

Had she misread him, then? Confused, Shelby glanced from Joy to Jake, coming to join them.

"If you didn't want it read, you should have secured your file." Joy took the offensive. "A first-grader could have opened it."

"Joy! Are you saying that I think your saying?" Paula asked, overhearing from the nearby portico. "Did you read Shelby's story without her permission?"

"I was just curious," Joy whispered, her meek tone at odds with the mutiny flagging her cheeks, as her mother joined them.

"You did, then? Joy Blake, if it's not one thing, it's another. What am I going to do with you?" Paula huffed in exasperation.

"As it turns out, it's looking as if I won't finish it anyway, Paula," Shelby said quietly, hoping to relieve Paula's embarrassment and Joy's growing resentment against her.

"Thanks, Shelby. But Joy's conduct is the issue," Paula said.

"What about Uncle Jake? He read it, too. Didn't you, Uncle Jake?"

Shelby was about to explain that she had asked Jake to read her story. But the contrition in his blue eyes stopped her cold.

"Go on, tell her Uncle Jake!"

"That's enough, Joy," Paula rebuked, and pointed

Joy toward the house. She spoke to the remaining children. They scooped up their ball and with a collective backward glance, trotted around to the other side of the house.

Jake's gaze shifted from Shelby to Paula hurrying after Joy. He shoved his hands into his pockets and offered no defense. A moment ago, the air had writhed with words. Now it was so quiet, Shelby heard the breeze purring high in the trees. Eons passed as she waited for Jake to explain.

"Mad?" he asked finally.

"Then you did read it? Before I asked you to?" said Shelby, heart constricting.

He nodded.

"Why didn't you say so?"

Jake squinted out of one eye and rubbed the back of his neck. "I wanted to. But you were pretty upset over Mr. Wiseman at the time."

"And in the time since?" she asked.

"Didn't figure you'd find out," he admitted.

"Jake!"

"I'm just being honest."

"Now *that's* rich."

Jake reached to stop her from flight. Shelby stiffened her arm beneath his hand. "It was on the screen when I turned on the computer," he said and let his hand fall away. "I started reading before I realized what it was. I should have stopped, but I'd swallowed the hook, so to speak."

"I told you I had a problem with people reading my stuff before it was finished. I was very clear about that, Jake."

"I know."

"But you did it anyway?" She paused, waiting.

When he offered nothing, her hurt gave rise to frustration and anger. "Is it any wonder I haven't written anything worth reading since leaving this place?"

"Now wait a second," Jake objected. "You're surely not blaming that on me?"

"What if I am?" she said, and tilted her chin.

"Your writing wasn't going well when you arrived," he reminded.

"I soon found my stride."

"And without blaming Patrick. Imagine that."

Stung, she retorted, "Patrick never hacked into my work."

"And for that lack of interest, you commend him?"

"It wasn't a lack of interest, it was respect for what I do."

"Oh, that's right. I forgot. Impeccable Patrick."

"So now you're jealous?"

"Should I be?" he countered, then looked past her, distracted by approaching guests.

Shelby turned as Emmaline, the cake baker, strolled across the grass between her uncle and Liberty Flat's mayor. Jake cupped his ear to some smiling remark Emmaline was calling to him. To Shelby he said, "Could we finish this later?"

It wasn't a question. The party was breaking up. He strode to meet his approaching guests, and with a rejoinder for Emmaline, resumed his role as host. Shelby left him to his goodbying, climbed the portico steps and went inside.

The foyer was empty, but voices resounded from the back of the house. Feeling adrift on uncertain seas with her eyes awash with tears, she paused at the foot of the main staircase and slipped out of her

shoes. A snatch of conversation carried to her from
the kitchen:

"If you're worried Jake's feelings toward you will
change because he's met someone he cares for—"

"I'm not worried. And I'm not jealous, okay,
Mom?" echoed Joy's caustic retort.

"You liked her at first. If you would give her a
chance, I'm sure you could like her again."

"Like you and Dad?"

Oppressed by the weight of baggage before her
time, Shelby crept up the stairs on soundless feet.
Small children played on the second-floor landing.
She stepped over their building blocks into the bathroom and sat down on the edge of the tub, elbows
on her knees, hands cupping her chin. But the urge
to cry had passed. Her ears had trapped Paula's
words to Joy. Jake *did* care. She cared, too. So much,
she had temporarily ceased to anguish over her creative blockage. Until Jake ran slipshod over the
wound and the blood-letting began.

A gentle rap on the door brought Shelby's heart
to her throat. "Who is it?"

"Jimmy. I got to go," a small voice replied from
the other side of the door.

Shelby surrendered her hiding place to Jake's little
nephew. She cast about for a quiet spot in which to
sort conflicting feelings. Jake's door stood open. But
it was the last place she cared to be found should he
come looking. Likewise, the guest room, littered with
luggage and Uncle Hershel's fiddle case was out of
bounds. A third door revealed steep and narrow
stairs.

Shelby flipped on the light and climbed to the attic. Sunshine poured from an open trapdoor in the

attic ceiling. It lit her way past trunks and boxes and cast-off furnishings to a five-step fold-down ladder leading up the catwalk. She hesitated a moment, then climbed it to find a small patch of unadorned roof. There was no furniture, nothing on which to perch and nothing spectacular about the view—just tree-tops, the street and neighboring homes. Shelby was about to return the way she had come when a neon sign hanging from the wrought-iron railing caught her eye. Modest in size, it wasn't lighted. But on closer inspection, the message was perfectly legible. Jake's intentions, too. He wasn't joking with that implied, over-the-phone proposal. He *did* want to marry her. Tears stung her nose and filled her eyes. "Oh, Jake," she whispered, and ran her hands over the glass letters, in equal parts of joy and trepidation.

Chapter Nineteen

It was the quarrel in the yard, and the fuse that had ignited it that filled Shelby with misgivings. Had she not been so plain about keeping her unpublished work private, she could write Jake's trespass off as live and learn.

Maybe she should anyway. Jake hadn't known her then as he knew her now, Shelby tried to reason away doubt. They would talk. Lord willing, he would see that just as she would not presume to tell him how to do his job, she couldn't let him hamper hers by disregarding her established methods. So thinking, Shelby ignored the clamor of her first love, that jealous muse that shouted, *He'll destroy your writing. Just wait and see! The first time it gets in the way of what he wants, he'll expect you to give it up for him. He's just like Patrick.*

He isn't *anything* like Patrick, she thought wordlessly, and retraced her steps to the landing.

The tots had angled a storybook on the top step, and were using it as a ramp to slide their building blocks down the stairs. Concerned over the hazard the blocks presented to Gram and others using the stairs, Shelby resisted the urge to seek out Jake for bridge-mending.

"What a lovely book. Who wants to hear the story?" she said, and gently coerced the children into picking up their blocks.

Jake thanked the community one by one for coming to share the day with Gram Kate. Each hand he shook and each goodbye seemed like a stone on a rising wall that was blocking his way to Shelby. At long last, with only family remaining, he let himself into the kitchen where the women were transferring party leftovers from the refrigerator to the dinner table.

When Shelby turned with a dish of fresh fruit in her hands, Jake was there to take it. There was a searching light in the hazel eyes that darted to meet his gaze. Or was it discomfort over their quarrel? Uncertain, Jake murmured, "Still mad at me?"

"I don't want to be," she replied in quiet tones designed to keep it between them.

"I'm sorry."

But before he could say anything else, Paula brushed past, moving dishes and tableware.

"Have you seen Gram's glasses, Jake? She's misplaced them again."

Jake scoured the kitchen, the porch and the yard before Joy found the glasses in Gram's pocketbook. It was that kind of evening, and dark before he had a chance to be alone with Shelby.

"Sun's set. But it's a starry night, and worth seeing," he said, on the way upstairs.

"Where you going?" Joy called after them.

"Catwalk," Jake replied.

He smiled at Shelby. "Stairs are steep. Watch your step." He switched on the light and took her hand.

Midway to the attic, Shelby paused.

Jake stopped a step ahead and turned back. The naked overhead bulb cast him in garish light. *As did his deed.* Shelby couldn't just sweep it under so as to get on to the rooftop and horizons that beckoned with promises of having and holding and being held forever after with a man who would never let her cry in the dark alone. Struggling, she said, "Could we clear the air?"

"Now?" he asked.

"I'd like to." Shelby sought flame-retardant words so as to get to the heart of the matter without igniting sparks that could so easily burn their bridges. "I shouldn't have said what I did about Patrick this afternoon," she began.

"That I'm jealous?" said Jake. "I'm not."

"There's no reason for you to be," she said earnestly. "I was upset."

"I noticed. What is this love-hate thing you've got going?"

"I don't love him, Jake." Determined to have it said without being sidetracked from the real issue, Shelby admitted, "Not in the way that you mean. I can't hate him, either."

"I thought we'd finished with Patrick, I was talking about your writing."

"You were?" Relieved, she said, "That's good. Because that's what I want to talk about, too. When it comes to writing, I'm compelled. Books have always been my sanctuary."

"I was kind of hoping I could be that."

"My sanctuary?" she said in wonder.

"Your sanctuary." His voice was like a corn husk touched by early frost. His hands spanned her waist. The soft gleam in his eye pleaded be done with words.

Shelby rested her hands on his shoulders, a half measure between holding and being held. She teetered on the steps, relishing bone, sinew and muscle gathered beneath flesh-warmed cotton. Books weren't just her sanctuary, they had also become her solace. But Jake's fingers, tucking a curl behind her ear, caressing her cheek, obliterated the appeal of black type on crisp white pages.

She longed to tell him how storybooks had become both lap and latch string. But he had lost parents and seen his sister's marriage crumble in one fell swoop. His losses belittled her petty scrapes, for her parents were both well and well-intentioned and she had no siblings casting their cares on her. She said instead, "I respect the gift and I need you to respect it, too."

"I will. So long as it doesn't use you up until there's nothing left."

"For you?" she said, feeling her muse stir, hackles rising.

"Is that so selfish?" he countered. "I can tell you right now, if sign work ever gets to be the struggle for me that writing is for you, I'll give it up."

"It isn't in me to quit," she asserted, bidding his understanding. "Anyway, when a book is finished, it isn't the struggle I remember."

"Are you going to be able to finish this one?" Jake asked.

"I don't know," she admitted. "It was careless of me not to have safeguarded my work. But on your behalf, and Joy's, too, it was unfair of me to imply that your previewing in some way prevented me from moving ahead with the story."

"We'll do some more brainstorming, maybe we can jury-rig it," he said.

"It isn't as simple as a toggle switch gone awry," Shelby objected.

"So what do you suggest?" he asked.

"For starters, stay away from my works in progress and I'll stay out of your shop." She put it as simply and as nicely as she knew how.

"Not so fast," he objected and covered her hands to keep them from falling away from him. "You're welcome in my shop anytime."

"Jake, don't make this more difficult than it has to be. You know what I'm saying."

"Sanctified. Set apart. No Jake allowed?"

"It safeguards the process," she reasoned. "Then, if I hit a brick wall, I know it isn't because I ignored what works. That's not unreasonable, is it?"

"No, not in theory," he replied. "Come on up on the roof. I want to show you something."

"As soon as we settle this."

"I thought we just did," he said.

"Then you understand that I need some privacy while I'm working?"

"For how long?" he asked.

"However long it takes to grow words into something ready for publication."

"At which point you share it with how many million readers?" he asked.

"Tens of millions would be a dream come true,"
she said.

Jake saw her color deepen, and knew he'd caught
her fantasizing. It frustrated him that she could bare
her soul to readers and be so reluctant to let him in.
He was thinking how to ask why that was so when
Joy called to him from the landing. She had the portable phone in one hand and covered the receiver
with the other.

"It's for you, Uncle Jake. I think it's important.
Whoever it is, she's asking about Dad."

Defeated, Jake sighed. "Do you mind, Shelby?"

"No, go ahead."

Jake glanced back to see Shelby sit down on the
steps and hug her knees. Something in her eyes and
the downward sweep of her lashes brought a knot to
his throat. If not for Joy and the call to which he was
now obligated, he would forego ambiance, starlight
and neon and propose on the spot before the Jackson
clan started looking like a pill she couldn't swallow.
"As soon as I'm done here, we'll finish this uninterrupted, okay?"

"Okay," she agreed, with a tentative smile that
squeezed his heart even as he turned away to take
the call.

"Jake Jackson speaking. I'm sorry, I can't hear
you. Hold on, and I'll try an extension."

"Battery must be low." Jake started down the
stairs, glanced back and held up a finger to indicate
he'd return in a moment.

Hedged in by the proposal waiting above, Shelby's
misgivings gave doubts a leg up and over the hastily
constructed white picket fence about her heart. She
loved him. And he loved her. Yet he had said in

essence that he would quit rather than struggle
through when the joy went out of his work. Would
his attitude hinder his tolerance toward her writing
when she hit stubborn patches? Did that explain this
crowdedness? This press of doubt? Jake's work was
straightforward and logical. He would not forever ac-
quiesce to the demands of her muse, demands which
defied logic and challenged explanation.

"So, what'd you tell him?" Joy broke the silence.

Shelby started. Sifting her thoughts, she had forgotten Joy there at the foot of the attic steps. "Tell
him?" she echoed. "About what?"

A shrewd expression stole over Joy's face. "Never
mind. I smell popcorn. You coming down?"

Shrinking from doubts exposed beneath the dim
light of the staircase, Shelby came to her feet and
followed Joy downstairs. The front door stood open.
A clear invitation. Her hat was there on the deacon's
bench just inside the door.

"Where you going?" asked Joy.

"It's been a long day. When Jake gets off the
phone, tell him I've gone, would you please?"

"Okay, sure. Mom'll be along soon as she gets
Gram to bed. There's a key under the mat, if the
door's locked," Joy said.

Shelby didn't correct her assumption that she
meant to stay the night at Joy's home. Until she
could lay her fears to rest and say in all confidence
that she could and would and very much wanted to
be Jake's wife, she was less than Jake needed her to
be. It wasn't fair to let him show his heart only to
be put on hold while she made up her mind which
she wanted most: her writing, or Jake. In essence,
that's what he was asking—the right to be the only

one left standing. *If it came to that.* And who knew better than she just how easily it could?

Jake took the call in his study.

"Mr. Jackson? This is Monique Lockwood. We met at the mission last weekend. Mr. Weaver gave me your number. He said you had asked about Jig-Saw. You *do* know Jig-Saw?"

"Yes, I know him. But I'm not sure I can help you."

"I can understand how you might be reluctant to pass along information to a stranger," Monique said at his guardedness. "But I'd appreciate it if you would hear me out."

"Very well," Jake replied.

"Jig-Saw would like to see his daughter, now that he's more fully recovered."

"Recovered?" Jake echoed, sifting her voice for clues.

"From his accident. I assumed you knew about that."

"Very little," Jake admitted.

"The bottom line is, he's jobless and penniless and trying hard to get back on his feet. In the meantime, he would like to use my apartment as home base. Just for a day, long enough to have a nice visit with his daughter."

She paused. Jake volunteered nothing.

"In your opinion, would I be safe in letting him stay?" she continued.

"You're asking me if he's dangerous?" Jake queried.

"Exactly."

"If you don't know him any better than that, why

would you consider opening your home to him?''
Jake wondered, mystified.

''I've been in desperate need myself, and received
help with no motives beyond simple kindness. You
understand?''

''I'm trying to,'' Jake said. Picking words carefully, he offered, ''The guy I knew wouldn't be a
risk to your property or your safety. But it was years
ago that I thought I knew him.''

''May I ask what your relationship to him was in
the past?''

Jake turned as Joy let herself into his office. ''I'm
not free to say.''

''All right. I think I understand. Thank you for
your time.''

Joy glanced at the Caller ID as Jake was hanging
up the phone. ''Who is she?'' she asked.

''Someone wanting to know about your dad,''
Jake replied.

''I *know* that much. Did you tell her that him and
Mom are still married?'' Joy asked.

Hope was a stubborn thing in the heart of a child.
It seemed cruel to uproot it. Jake said, ''All she
wanted was a character reference.''

''So that's it.'' Joy reached for a stickie note and
a pen. ''Shelby went home.''

''Home?'' Distracted from pursuing her note taking, Jake asked, ''What for?''

''Long day is all she said. I told her where we
hide the door key.''

Jake was almost to the corridor when Joy asked,
''What'd she think of your sign?''

Pained, he turned back. ''Let me guess—you
showed her?''

"Not on your life. She took herself up."

"You saw her go?"

"No. But Jimmy and the others did. Earlier. They were playing on the landing."

"You're sure about this?"

Joy nodded. "Kind of nervy of her, huh? Poking around after making such a big deal over us reading her story."

"How long ago did she leave?" Jake asked.

"Five minutes, thereabouts."

Jake crossed to the desk and dialed Paula's house. It rang unanswered. "What else did she say?" Jake queried, hanging up as Paula's answering machine clicked on.

"Nothing. Where're you going?"

"Your house."

"What for?"

"I'm going to marry that woman, that's what for."

Jake left Joy so that he could take down the number from caller ID and drove over to Paula's. Shelby's car wasn't there.

Jake circled the village until his sinking heart could no longer avoid the truth. Shelby had left Liberty Flats. Working through to the inevitable conclusion, he thought about taking the interstate north and going after her. But why drive like a madman just to hear what her absence said so clearly?

Jake returned home but couldn't bring himself to go inside. He sat on the porch a foot from where Uncle Hershel had plied him with advice. If it wasn't so gut-wrenching, it would be poetic. Not the part he had heard. Rather, the part about taking Shelby into consideration. Even Joy had assumed he would. A week ago, when she had asked if he would be moving to Chicago, he had chuckled. His roots were here. He had obligations he couldn't and had no wish to abandon.

It was that which kept Jake on the porch in stubborn resistance to his heart's entreaty until the deep night dampness finally drove him inside. Concern couldn't be shut off like a tap just because hope had dwindled to one thin drip. It was a long drive home, and she was tired. Jake phoned and left a message asking her to call him when she arrived so he wouldn't worry. From there, it was a waiting game. He propped his feet on his desk and leaned back in his chair.

It was daylight when Jake awoke to the ringing phone. Heart slamming, he was wide awake in an instant. But it was Paula calling to remind Joy that the youth group were serving pancakes before Sunday school.

"I'll tell her," Jake promised.

The sofa was empty. Joy had left a note, saying she had left for the youth group pancake breakfast fund-raiser. Gram, Uncle Hershel and Aunt Marge were dressed for church, drinking coffee as they waited for the appointed pancake hour.

Jake climbed the stairs and showered and shaved. The mirror was a steamy prism multiplying endless years of showering and shaving to meet a day like the last one. Because the woman who prided herself on not being a quitter had stolen his future on the way out the door.

But there was a door in. Jake took it on his knees, and rose with a clearer idea of stones left unturned. Yes, he and Shelby were worlds apart in some ways. Yes, there would always be conflicts. But he wasn't

Colt, and she wasn't Paula. They weren't quitters.
They shared a center. That center was more than
love, it was God Himself.

Hope restored, Jake retrieved his sign from the
roof and put it in the back of the Jeep. A few miles
past Bloomington, he reached for his cell phone only
to realize he had left it in one of the work trucks.
Uncle Hershel and Aunt Marge would be leaving after lunch, and someone needed to be at the house
with Gram. Unwilling to turn back for the phone,
Jake reasoned he could call home from Shelby's. His
family would all be in church by now, anyway.

Chapter Twenty

Shelby crawled out of bed and into the shower. Steamy water and scented gel soap did little to ease her inner pain. *If sign work ever gets to be the struggle for me that writing is for you, I'll give it up.* Jake's words played in her head like a runner jogging in place, trampling dreams underfoot.

How could she give up writing? It was like asking a bird not to fly. Shelby shut off the water tap, toweled off and slipped into a soft pink robe. She then checked her phone messages. Jake's voice on her machine broke the silence of her apartment and brought a wave of pain that was both emotional and physical. She played the message a second time.

"It's a long drive to make twice in one day. Call and let me know you're home safely."

He would want to know why she had left without a word. What was she supposed to tell him? The truth, scolded her muse. Tell him the truth! There isn't room for him.

She reached for the phone, and had second

thoughts. Maybe a fax? No, that was worse than ignoring the message altogether. Her pulse pounded as
she dialed. Jake's machine picked up. She hung up
without leaving a message, thought a moment how
to word what needed saying, and redialed only to
lose courage again.

"This is all your fault," Shelby muttered to the
short shelf of teen novels displayed on the wall over
the living room nook where she did her writing.
"You're supposed to inspire me, not sabotage my
life. Look at me! I'm talking to books."

Pitiful!

Before she could follow through with her intent to
call, someone knocked at her door. Heart in her
throat, she rose on tiptoes, looked through the peep-
hole and gaped with wondering eyes. "Joy!" She
gasped and slid the dead bolt free.

"I'm alone," said Joy, wise to Shelby's darting
glance down the empty corridor.

"How did you get here?" blurted Shelby.

"Uncle Jake had a service job."

"On Sunday?"

"It was an emergency. You said drop by if I got
to Chicago. So here I am," she said with a vagrant
grin.

Reeling with misgivings, Shelby framed and discarded half a dozen questions in the time it took Joy
to step inside and drop her overnight bag in the entry
foyer. "Call your mother, and let her know you arrived safely," she said, and closed the door.

Joy tugged at her rumpled sweatshirt and tilted one
shoulder. "She's probably already left for church."

"Try her anyway," Shelby said. "Have you
eaten?"

"Not yet."

"I'll fix you some breakfast while you're on the phone."

"Okay. Can I use your bathroom?" Joy asked.

"Yes, of course. Through the living room and to your left."

"I like my eggs hard." Joy picked up the portable phone on her way by.

Cheeky little thing, of course she did.

Shelby waited until the bathroom door closed, then returned to the foyer to look inside the canvas bag. She found a round-trip bus ticket from Bloomington to Chicago, with the return ticket still to be redeemed. How had Joy had traveled the twenty miles between Liberty Flats and Bloomington? Anyone's guess. Hearing Joy on the phone, Shelby replaced the ticket, trekked into the kitchen and quietly picked up the extension.

"Okay, Mom. Yeah, Uncle Jake dropped me off." Joy carried on a one-sided conversation. "She's fixing breakfast for me now. But I'll tell her you said hello. Love you, too. Bye."

Shelby had eggs, toast, cereal and juice waiting by the time Joy joined her in the kitchen.

"Mom says hi. What happened to you last night?" Joy shoveled in eggs and chewed and sipped her juice, looking vaguely discomfited. "It wasn't anything I said made you go, was it?" she asked finally.

"My coming home had nothing to do with you."

"That's good. 'Cause last night, Uncle Jake was all set to blame me."

"And this morning?"

"I don't know, I left before he got—" Joy

blinked. Had she slapped her hand over her gaping mouth, it couldn't have been more telling.

"That's what I thought," Shelby said, a dull pounding at her temples. "You want to tell me what you're really doing here?"

Joy's chin came up. Her shoulders, too. "Okay, so I came to see my dad."

"He's expecting you?" Shelby asked, struggling to remain calm.

"No. Not yet. But a friend of his knows I'm here. She's trying to get in touch with him and let him know I'm here. I wouldn't have bothered you, but I don't know anyone else in Chicago."

Shelby remembered Jig-Saw's request of Monique at Can-Do and thanked God that Joy had trusted her enough to seek her out rather than kill time on her own on the streets of Chicago. "This friend—she's going to call you here?"

Joy nodded.

Shelby sipped her coffee and traced the cup rim with her finger. "Let me see if I have this right— you're letting go of your mother and Jake and Gram Kate and the rest of your family to make room for your father?" she queried, trying her hand at psychology.

"Well, no. I'm taking the bus back tomorrow."

"What if they don't want you back? What if they say, you made your choice, live with it?"

Joy looked at her as if she had the brain power of a staple. "Yeah, right. Like they're really going to do that."

"Call and let them know you're safe."

"I called."

"No, you didn't. I listened. That was a dial tone you were talking to."

Joy's eyes glittered. "You're a sneak."

"That's right. We're both sneaks. Now, do you want to call home, or shall I do it for you?"

"Oh, all right. So it was a bad idea. Forget the whole thing. Dad can come see me in Liberty Flats. Mom will just *love* that," she said, rolling her eyes.

Shelby ignored her theatrics and crossed to the wall phone. "What's your home number? I'll punch it in for you," she said, and passed Joy the receiver.

Paula's shout of mingled relief and distress was loud enough to be heard without the phone. "Joy? Thank God! Where are you? I've been worried sick."

Joy set her jaw, insisting that she wanted to see her dad. Whatever Paula's response, Joy received it with undisguised impatience "Okay, Mom. I heard you the first time," she said and passed the phone to Shelby. "She wants to talk to you."

"Shelby? I'm coming for her," Paula said, her voice high and tight.

"I can put her on a bus, train or plane, and save you the trip," Shelby offered.

"No, no. I'll come," Paula cried. "I'm sorry to put you in the middle of this. But just don't let her leave, okay?"

Shelby promised. She poured herself a second cup of coffee and had no more than sat down, when the phone rang again.

"I'll get it." Joy nearly knocked over her chair, in her rush to answer it. "Yeah, it's me, Joy. Can I talk to him? Oh." Joy's face fell. "Well, okay. Thanks, anyway."

"Let me talk," Shelby offered, reaching for the receiver.

"Too late," Joy said, hanging up the phone. "That was Dad's friend. Dad can't make it today."

Shelby saw her slump in disappointment, and still, she wasn't entirely sure Joy was telling her the truth. Reluctant to leave her unattended for the short time it would take to throw on some clothes, Shelby winged silent petitions to God as she washed and dried the dishes. Joy watched the clock.

"You're welcome to turn on the television," Shelby said.

"No, thanks."

"How about a book?"

"I'm fine."

Shelby offered another diversionary idea or two, then gave up. Joy drummed her fingers on the table-top. With the morning stretching endlessly before her, Shelby resorted to the panacea for whatever ailed and sat down at her laptop.

On impulse, she tried Jake's idea about writing the ending. That, at least, was firmly set in her mind. Fingers poised over the keys, she opened the tap and let her thoughts flow.

The rest of Tara and Jack's day passed in a blur. Their statement at the police station. The piecing together of details. And finally, after dinner, a little time to themselves. They left Jack's house behind and walked toward the music and the lights on the square downtown where Blatchford's street festival was in full swing.

"You want to ride some rides?" Jack asked, as they neared the Ferris wheel with its flashing lights.

"Sure," said Tara.

"Come on, and we'll get some tickets."

Jack caught Tara's hand in his and whistled off-key as they strolled along.

"Jack and Tara? That's how this turns out? Bummer!" Joy complained, reading over Shelby's shoulder. "I thought he liked Cheryl."

"He did. But it didn't work," Shelby said.

"Why not?"

"Because they aren't right for one another. So he had a change of heart."

Feeling hopeful now that words were finally flowing, Shelby relegated Joy's voice to background noise and scrolled back to the scene where Tara and Jack discovered Mr. Weedman's body.

She worked doggedly, adding then deleting words and dialogue and paragraphs until the whole screen was a mess. She sat back in the chair, defeated once again.

"Looks to me like you're stuck in the field with a dead body and getting nowhere fast," Joy crowed.

"That's about the size of it." Shelby sighed. "The kids should be shocked and scared and feel the loss."

"Like when I heard about Mr. Wiseman," Joy said, nodding.

Shelby turned back to the screen. "I can get the shocked and scared part, it's the loss that eludes me. I was hoping it would go easier, now that I have the ending down. But I still can't get it right."

"Want me to give it a go?" Joy offered.

Shelby didn't expect her to be of much help. But at this point, she was amenable to anything that would shed light on what was missing. "Be my guest," she said, and gave up the chair.

Joy's hands fell over the keyboard and hovered a moment. At length she typed: "It was like the day I found out my dad didn't know about me. I was dead to him. But this guy was *dead* dead. I cried."

The switch to first person jarred Shelby. The voice was not hers. But the emotion was so real, her story world fell away, leaving only Joy, cherished by her mother, awash with family, and still needy. It was almost as if she had stepped into Joy's head and was seeing her neediness from the inside.

A neediness Jake wasn't meant to fill. Jig-Saw himself couldn't, though as the missing piece, he distracted Joy from letting God's love fill the void. *But who was she to tell Joy?* Shelby read it over again, this time with the heat of repentance behind her eyes.

Somewhere in the neighborhood, church bells rang. Shelby moved to the window of her corner apartment and found a steeple on the horizon. "He does not dwell in temples built by hands." Snatches of remembered verse fell to mind. "In him we live and move and have our being."

How could she have relegated her first love to second place? It wasn't books, it was God! He was the lap in the story when she was a child. He was the flame when her muse burned the brightest. It was so blessedly simple. How could she have been so mistaken? And at what price?

"What's the matter?"

Shelby glanced around to find Joy watching from the desk chair. "It's good, what you wrote."

"Really?" Joy couldn't hide her pleasure. "Must have got it from Dad."

Shelby remembered Jake telling her Colton had been a young journalist in pursuit of a story when he first met Paula. Shelby wiped her eyes before turning to face Joy. "Maybe you should finish it."

"Huh?"

"The story," Shelby said, the idea gaining strength. "Would you like to finish it?"

"How? You wrote it. It's yours."

"It doesn't have to be. I could give it to you."

Joy shift uneasily. "Just like that?"

"You inspired it. I've beat myself up trying to finish it to no avail." *And in the process neglected a greater love.* Fresh tears stung Shelby's eyes. "Play with it, see what you think."

Joy turned back to the computer screen.

Oh, God. Forgive me! I'm just a little child. But I'm Your *little child. Tell me it isn't too late!* The joyous peal of bells swelled as if carrying her prayer along.

The paperboy was whistling his way down the corridor just beyond the front door. Shelby heard him trade greetings with someone as the newspaper thudded against the door.

With Joy engrossed at the computer, Shelby retrieved the paper from the hallway. She was about to close the door when an out-of-place red glare at the end of the hall caught her eye. There was a table of potted plants next to the elevator. Above it hung a neon question: Marry Me? Jake was hunkered down, his back to her, picking up sign-hanging tools.

Dust motes danced over his head in a shaft of sunlight from the eastern window. A mountain moved off Shelby's heart and slipped past the tears in her throat. She was about to duck inside and trade her robe for something more suitable when Jake came to his feet and stepped into the open elevator.

"Jake! Wait!" she cried, dismayed to see him leaving.

Jake scanned the panel for the door control button. Shelby was taking no chances. She plowed through the closing gap into the elevator. "Where are you going?"

"Down," he said.

"Without a word?" Shelby cried, arms crossed, hugging her waist.

"I was coming right—" he began. Then he caught himself, and said, "I've had my word. It was lit up in red, in case you missed it."

"I didn't miss it. You didn't give me a chance to answer."

"Me? What about you? You took off last night before I could ask."

"You're right. I'm sorry. I was so confused." Trembling, she leaned against the wall as the elevator took them down.

"Joy said you'd seen the sign. So when you left, I figured that was your answer." Jake nudged his cap back and shifted his feet. "I had a little talk with myself, and decided maybe that as package deals go, we Jacksons are high maintenance. But there's no reason I couldn't move part of the sign business here to Chicago. We could keep your apartment, take our turn with Gram in Liberty Flats and stay here the rest of the time. I haven't talked to my sisters about it yet, but they've always done their part." The elevator stopped. The door opened. Their fingers brushed as they reached at the same moment to hit the "3" button.

"You thought I left because I didn't want to share your family?" she said, slowly taking it in, as the elevator reversed its course.

"That wasn't it?"

"No, of course not! Jake, I had no idea you thought that."

"What is it, then? You just don't want to marry me?"

"That isn't it at all." Shelby's eye drew tears. She fought them back. "I thought I had to make a choice."

She was captivating, wrapped in a deep flush and a fuzzy robe. It was a sight he could drink in for a lifetime of mornings. And nights, too. He tensed, waiting for the picture to cloud. But she didn't mention Gram Kate, Joy, Paula or any of his clamoring clan. Instead, she spoke of worrying that anything that got in the way of her writing would get in the way of her wholeness.

"And you thought *I* was in the way?" He finally caught her drift.

"Yes," she admitted. "But I had it backward. My writing was getting in the way of living. I don't want to lose you, Jake. You're so precious to me," she said earnestly.

A wave of tenderness swept over him at the glimpse of her exposed heart. He cupped her ears and tipped her face. "Is that a yes?"

Even her toes were tinted pink. They wiggled fetchingly as she closed the remaining step and leaned in to kiss a smile to his face.

The elevator whispered to a stop, cutting short their reconciliation. Jake nudged her ahead with a hand on the small of her back. She paused to pull the Yes chain on the neon sign, then turned with a seeking light in her hazel eyes.

"Now you're talking." Jake swept her off her feet and carried her down the hallway.

"Practice run," he said, and laughed when she protested.

But once inside the door, Jake saw she had company and set her down in a hurry. "Joy!"

"Hi, Uncle Jake. Mom send you?"

"What're you doing here?"

"Writing," Joy said. She threw a glance over her shoulder. "Say, I've been meaning to ask—is nightshade fatal to people, too?"

Shelby excused herself, ducked into her bedroom to dress, and left them to sort it out. When she returned, Joy had dragged herself away from the computer and was chewing her nails down to the quick. Jake was on the phone with Paula en route to Chicago. He told her she could turn back, that Joy could return home with him.

Shelby decided a little makeup would do no harm. She ducked into her bedroom and didn't come out until she heard the door slam.

Jake nudged his cap back as she slipped out again. He leaned against the closed door, ankles crossed, watching her approach. Her heart turned at the tender devotion on his face.

"Joy's checking out the sign," he said, and reached for her hand.

"She hasn't given up the idea of seeing her father, Jake," Shelby warned, clutching his fingers.

"Relax, she's on good behavior. Paula's reconsidered," he said, and sandwiched her hand between his.

"She's going to let Joy visit Colton?" asked Shelby.

"Paula wants to size him up first. If he doesn't run afoul of her maternal instincts, it could be a new beginning. For Joy and Colt, anyway," Jake amended. He kissed her, and traced with his fingertip the lips he had warmed. "Speaking of new beginnings, I've been thinking about your story world."

"What about it?" she asked.

"I'll leave it to you, and be the happiest guy around, just as long as there is always room for me in your real world."

"It would be empty space without you, Billy Boy."

A light leapt behind his bottle-blue eyes. "Keep that up, and you'll have to learn to use that rolling pin," he warned.

"For what?" she asked with an innocent tilt of her face.

Jake spelled it out in kisses that deepened until the world fell away leaving only the two of them. Shelby's heart sang in anticipation of that celebrated day when their lives would be truly one. It raised such a clamor, she didn't hear Joy return until she cleared her throat noisily.

"Don't mind me," Joy said, rolling her eyes.

"We're trying not to," Jake said. He pressed a kiss to the palm of Shelby's hand before letting her go.

Shelby stored away the sensation in the treasure trove where the richest of ideas germinated. As she did so, the love God had given her for Jake dispelled every concern over her future as a writer. Whatever she gave, he gave back to her, multiplied in emotions so lavish in detail, it would take her a lifetime to get it all down.

''I love you, Jake. I'll be in the kitchen,'' she whispered, and slipped off to hide the rolling pin.

Epilogue

Shelby awoke ahead of her alarm. She slipped out of bed and threw the drapes wide. A marry-me sunrise pinked the sky and polished the lake. Kneeling, she thanked God for this, her wedding day. For the story proposal that had been accepted by her publisher. For May flowers blooming on the shores of Lake Michigan where she and Jake were to be wed. And most of all, for Jake.

She soaked in a scented bath, then dressed in a jade-colored sheath and stole a moment to thumb through her pile of greeting cards.

There was one from Monique, who had moved out of state last fall, and another from Patrick who wrote that he was leaving his law practice to attend seminary. There was a card from Joy as well, one she had made on her computer. In it, she wrote that her father was going to help her with the Weed Buster book, but that they hadn't made much progress yet, as they were doing their cowriting by e-mail. Same old Joy, Shelby thought with a faint smile. Paula gave an inch, granting Colton biweekly visitation rights, and Joy wanted a mile, begging her to let her father come for the summer, now that he was well again and gainfully employed.

The doorbell stirred Shelby from her musings. It was her parents with the pastor in tow. Her mother helped Shelby arrange her hair in a tumble of loose curls and a simple garland of May flowers.

"It looks as if she's going through with it this time," her father remarked to the minister when Shelby emerged from the bedroom.

"At long last, your chance to give me away," she said, and pinned a carnation to his lapel.

"Look at her glow!" her mother said to her father.

"I'd glow, too, if I could quit my job and move to the country," replied her father.

"I haven't quit writing. And Liberty Flats isn't country living, it's a village," Shelby said. Her notice, given at Parnell Publishing two weeks earlier, had been met with kind wishes for her future as a full-time wife and a part-time novelist.

The phone rang. Her mother answered it. "Hello, Jake. Yes, she's right here."

Shelby took the portable phone.

"Hi, honey," Jake's voice stroked her ear. "Look out your east window."

Shelby took the phone to her bedroom, glimpsed a man looking back at her through her third-story window and let out a yelp.

"Ouch!" Jake, just outside her window, held the phone away and wiggled his finger in his ear.

"You scared the wits out of me!" Recovering, Shelby put the phone down to open the window. Jake was standing on the platform at the top of the ladder extending from one of the company trucks parked in the lot below. "Is that our honeymoon transportation?" she asked.

"The Jeep had a flat," he teased, and leaned through the open window for a kiss.

"Please please climb in here," pleaded Shelby, gripping the lapels of his tuxedo. "You'll give me a heart attack on my wedding day."

"Speaking of hearts, I seem to recall yours was secretly set on elopement," Jake said, coming through the window. "A ladder is a nice concession."

"You surely don't plan to take me down that ladder!" she cried.

"What? You don't trust me?"

Relishing the love in those summer-sky eyes, Shelby came to terms accordingly. She let the repressed actress out of the box, saying, "Very well, then. But if we're going to put on a show, I'll have to change into satin and lace."

He crooked an eyebrow. "You don't mean the wedding dress?"

"Isn't that why I kept it—for a better man?"

Jake laughed and kissed her and let her go. She rubbed away the painted lips she had left on his mouth, and pointed him toward the living room to usher her father and Pastor Fuller downstairs while her mother helped her change into the wedding dress.

Twenty minutes later, Shelby was tucked firmly in Jake's arms on the small platform at the top of the ladder. She clutched his arm, her long white skirts and her bouquet of sunflowers. With a radiant smile, she tilted her face to the lakeshore breeze. It rearranged her curls and set her skirts to rustling.

"You're drawing a crowd in that dress," Jake said.

Shelby stole a kiss for courage and looked down. Her eyes welled up at the sight of their loved ones intermingled below, smiling and waving, celebrating this long-awaited day.

On cue from below, Jake manned the controls. "Love me?" he asked in a tender voice.

"Forever," she promised and kissed him all the way to the ground.

*   *   *   *   *

Dear Reader,

When I was a little girl practicing piano and missing more notes than I hit, my father would call out, "Would you play 'Long, Long Ago and Far, Far Away'?" At the time, his humor was lost on me. Now as a writer I smile over the irony that I should so often inhabit Storyland, that set-apart place that is often "Long, Long Ago" and always "Far, Far Away."

It opened to me first in daydreams and childhood games of "dress up" and "pretend." Now, as a writer, I find that the God-given link between daydreaming and plotting a story is very clear to me. Thanks to Him and to readers, I have license to daydream! Which makes Shelby's world familiar territory. Like her, I spend my days shifting from reality to fiction and back again. It's a dance, and I'm not all that graceful. But I *am* grateful to family and friends who overlook my absenteeism and wait for me to catch the next thought-wave home. For as much as I enjoy creating story worlds, home is my most cherished place this side of heaven, as I'm sure is true for you, too.

Susan Kirby

Father Most Blessed
Marta Perry

Books by Marta Perry

Love Inspired

A Father's Promise #41
Since You've Been Gone #75
*Desperately Seeking Daddy #91
*The Doctor Next Door #104
*Father Most Blessed #128

*Hometown Heroes

MARTA PERRY

wanted to be a writer from the moment she encountered Nancy Drew, at about age eight. She didn't see publication of her stories until many years later, when she began writing children's fiction for Sunday school papers while she was a church educational director. Although now retired from that position in order to write full-time, she continues to play an active part in her church and loves teaching a class of lively fifth- and sixth-grade Sunday school students.

Marta lives in rural Pennsylvania with her husband of thirty-seven years and has three grown children. She loves to hear from readers and enjoys responding. She can be reached c/o Steeple Hill Books, 300 East 42nd Street, New York, NY 10017.

Father Most Blessed
Marta Perry

Love Inspired®

Published by Steeple Hill Books™

STEEPLE HILL BOOKS

2 in 1 ISBN 0-7394-1782-7

FATHER MOST BLESSED

Printed in U.S.A.

For it is by grace you have been saved, through faith, and this not from yourselves: it is the gift of God—not by works, so that no one can boast.

—*Ephesians* 2:8-9

This story is dedicated with love and gratitude to the siblings and spouses who add so much richness to our lives: Pat and Ed, Bill and Molly, Herb and Barb, Gary and Arddy, and Chris. And, as always, to Brian.

Chapter One

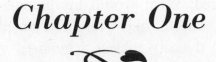

A man who lived in a twenty-room house ought to be able to have silence when he wanted it. Alex Caine tossed his pen on the library desk and stalked to the center hallway of the Italianate mansion that had been home to the Caine family for three generations. The noise that had disrupted his work on a crucial business deal came from beyond the swinging door to the servants' area.

Frowning, he headed toward the sound, his footsteps sharp on the marble floor, and pushed through the door to the rear of the house. He'd told his ailing housekeeper to rest this afternoon, so there should have been no sound at all to disturb his concentration. But Maida Hansen, having taken care of him since the day his mother died when he was six, tended to ignore any orders she didn't want to follow.

Well, in this case she was going to listen. If he didn't find the right words for this delicate negotiation, Caine Industries might not survive for another generation. There might be no company at all to leave to his son.

He winced. What would his grandfather or his father have said to that? They'd assumed they were founding a dynasty to last a hundred years. They wouldn't look kindly on the man who presided over its demise.

The noise came from the pantry, down the hall from the kitchen. He seized the doorknob and yanked.

The figure balanced precariously on the step stool wasn't Maida. Maida had never in her life worn blue jeans or a sweatshirt proclaiming her World's Greatest Teacher. His heart stopped, and he looked at the woman he had thought he'd never see again.

''What's going on?''

She spun at the sound of his voice, wobbled and overbalanced. Her arms waved wildly to regain control, but it was too late. The step stool toppled, sending her flying toward him. Pans clattered to the floor. In an instant his arms had closed around Paula Hansen.

The breath went out of him. Carefully he set her on her feet and stepped back, clamping down on the treacherous rush of feelings. Paula—here in his house again, looking up at him with what might have been embarrassment in her sea-green eyes.

With an effort he schooled his face to polite concern and found his voice. "Paula. I didn't expect to find you here. Maida didn't tell me you were coming."

Maida's time outside her duties was her own, and she was perfectly free to have her niece stay at the housekeeper's cottage whenever she wanted to. But in the almost two years since the plane crash, since what had happened between them, Paula hadn't returned to Bedford Creek.

"She didn't tell you?" Surprise filled Paula's expressive face. She tried to mask it, turning away to right the step stool.

"No, she didn't." If he'd known Paula was on the estate, he wouldn't have betrayed shock at the sight of her. In fact, he'd probably have found a way to avoid seeing her at all.

"But I thought she…" Paula stopped, seeming to edit whatever she'd been about to say. "My school just got out for the summer yesterday, so I'm on vacation now." Again she stopped, and again he had the sense of things left unsaid.

She'd been on vacation two years ago, when she'd come to Pennsylvania to spend the summer taking care of his son. It had seemed the perfect solution. He had needed someone reliable to care for Jason until kindergarten started in the fall. His housekeeper's niece needed a summer job. Neither of them had anticipated anything else.

The June sunlight, slanting through the small panes of the pantry window, burnished the honey blond of her hair. Her hair was shorter now than the last time he'd seen her, and it fell in unruly curls around her face. Her green eyes still reflected glints of gold, and that vulnerable mouth and stubborn chin hadn't changed.

Tension jagged along his nerves as images of the last time he'd seen her invaded his mind—lightning splitting the sky outside the small plane; the brief hope the pilot would manage to land, shattered when the plane cartwheeled and flames rushed toward him; Paula, several rows ahead, trapped in a mass of twisted metal. If an unexpected business trip hadn't put him on the daily commuter flight the same day that Paula was leaving to go home, what might have happened? Would someone have pulled her from the jammed seat to safety?

"Is something wrong?" She pulled her sweatshirt sleeves down, frowning. "You don't mind that I'm here, do you?"

"Of course not. I'm just surprised." He tried for a coolness he didn't feel. "It didn't bother you, flying back into Bedford Creek again?"

"No." She shook her head, then smiled ruefully.

"I suppose it might have, if I'd tried to do it. I drove up from Baltimore."

Her admission of vulnerability startled him. The Paula he remembered had been proud of her self-reliance and determined not to accept help from anyone. Even after the accident, when he'd awakened in the hospital and learned her family had taken her home to Baltimore for medical care, his offer of financial help had been quickly refused.

"Driving instead of flying sounds reasonable to me," he said. "I don't enjoy getting on a plane now, either."

His own admission shocked him even more. Alexander Caine didn't admit weakness, not to anyone. His father had trained that out of him when he was about his own son's age.

"I haven't been on a plane since..." Paula's gaze flickered away from the scar that accented Alex's cheekbone.

His mouth stiffened, and he read the reaction he should have gotten used to by now. "The plane crash," he finished for her, his tone dry. "You can say the words, you know." He didn't need or want her pity.

"The drive up wasn't bad—just long." She seemed determined to ignore his reference to the crash. She stared at the rows of shelves with their seldom-used dishes as if she really didn't see them. Then her gaze shifted to him. "As I said, I'm on vacation, so I was free to come when Aunt Maida needed me.'' Her expression turned challenging. ''You have noticed she's in pain lately, haven't you?''

He stiffened at the implication of neglect in her pointed question. Of course he felt responsible for the woman who'd cared for his family all these years. But it wasn't Paula Hansen's place to question him.

''I've asked her repeatedly about her health,'' he said. ''She keeps insisting she's fine.''

She lifted her eyebrows, her gaze turning skeptical. Paula's face had always shown her emotions so clearly. A picture flashed into his mind of her lips close to his, her eyes soft.

No. He pushed the errant thought away. *Don't go there.*

''Aunt Maida always insists she's fine. But you must have noticed something.''

''She's been tired and limping more lately.'' He reached behind him for the door, hoping he didn't sound defensive. He was wasting time in this futile discussion—time he didn't have to spare. ''I told her to take it easy this afternoon. She does too much.'' He glanced at the pans scattered on the worn linoleum. ''Instead, she seems to have enlisted you as assistant housekeeper.''

Her chin came up at that, as if it were an insult. ''I'm glad to help my aunt.''

The last time she'd been here, it had been for her brief job as Jason's nanny. Alex tried again to ignore the flood of memories of that time: the laughter and warmth she'd brought to this house, her face turned toward his in the moonlight, the moment he'd forgotten himself and kissed her—

Enough. He'd gotten through the remainder of her stay in Bedford Creek by pretending that kiss had never happened. Paula was probably as eager as he was to avoid the subject.

"I've already told Maida to rest more," he said. "She won't listen."

"It isn't just rest she needs." She stared at him, a question in her green eyes. "You really don't know, do you?"

"Know what?" He couldn't erase the irritation from his tone. "What are you driving at, Paula? I don't have time for guessing games."

Her eyes flashed. "She can't put it off any longer. Aunt Maida has to have hip replacement surgery."

Surgery. The implications staggered him. Maida, the rock on which his home life depended, needed surgery. He fought past a wave of guilt that he hadn't guessed what was going on.

"No, I didn't know." He returned Paula's frown. "I wish Maida *had* told me, but if she didn't want to, that was her right."

"She didn't tell you because she didn't want you to worry."

Paula clearly didn't consider protecting him from worry a priority. Antagonism battled the attraction he felt just looking at her. Maybe it was a good thing she annoyed him so much. It reminded him not to let that attraction get out of control, as it had once before.

"That's ridiculous," he said shortly. "If she needs the operation now, she has to have it. There's no question of that."

Even as he frowned at Paula, his mind raced from one responsibility to another—his son, the factory, the business deal that might save them. His stomach clenched at the thought of the Swiss firm's representative, due to visit any day now. He'd expect to be entertained in Alex's home. How could Alex swing that without Maida's calm, efficient management?

"My aunt knows this is a bad time for you. That's probably why she hasn't told you."

He sensed Paula's disapproval, although whether it was directed at him or her aunt, he didn't know. "I'll manage," he said curtly. "I'll have to find someone to fill in for her, that's all."

He knew when he said it how futile a hope that was. An isolated mountain village didn't boast an army of trained domestics ready for hiring. He'd be lucky to find anyone at all in the middle of the tourist season.

"It won't be easy to hire someone, will it?" She seemed to read his thoughts.

"No. I'm afraid Maida has spoiled us." He should have known things couldn't run so smoothly forever.

"Aunt Maida thinks she has a solution, if you'll go along with it."

He realized Paula was carefully not looking at him, and that fact sent up a red flag of warning. "What is it?"

Paula took a deep breath and fixed him with a look that was half embarrassed, half defiant. "She wants you to hire me as her replacement."

For a long moment he could only stare at her. Paula—back in his house, cooking his meals, looking after his son. Given what had happened between them the last time she worked for him, he couldn't believe she'd be willing to try it again.

One thing he could believe, though. Having Paula Hansen in his house again wouldn't just be embarrassing. Having her there, seeing her every day, no matter how desperately he needed help— that would be downright insane.

The expression on Alex's lean, aristocratic face showed Paula only too well exactly what he thought of her aunt's idea. Why on earth hadn't Aunt Maida

told him before Paula arrived? Maida knew this situation would be difficult. She'd said she'd prepare
the way. Instead, she'd brought Paula here without
saying a word to Alex about it.

Of course, Aunt Maida couldn't have known her
niece would go weak-kneed at the sight of Alex
Caine.

"I see." Alex's tone was coolly noncommittal,
and the polite, well-bred mask he habitually wore
slid into place.

It was too late. Naturally he wouldn't come right
out and tell her he didn't want her in his house
again. But she'd seen his swift, unguarded reaction.
Her heart sank. She should have known he wouldn't
agree to this.

"Where is Maida? We need to talk about this."

"She's not here." She took a deep breath and
prepared for an explosion. *Oh, Aunt Maida. Why
didn't you tell him?* "She's already checked into
the hospital in Henderson."

He started to speak, then clamped his mouth
closed. Maybe he was counting to ten. She could
only hope it worked.

"She's scheduled for surgery tomorrow." She
might as well get it all out. If he intended to ex-
plode, he'd just have to do it once. "I guess she
thought I could help out here, at least until you
make a decision about replacing her."

"You said she didn't want to worry me. Did she

think this wasn't worrying—going to the hospital and leaving you to break the news?''

The fine lines around Alex's dark eyes seemed to deepen. She longed to smooth them away with her fingertips. The urge, so strong her skin tingled, shocked her. She couldn't think that, couldn't feel it.

She didn't have a good answer to his question. ''I thought she planned to tell you. When we talked on the phone last week, she said she would.''

Maida had sounded so desperate. *''I need you, Paula. Jason needs you. That child is hurting, and you might be the only one who can help him.''* Maida must not have wanted to risk telling Alex, and his finding some other solution to her absence. She could only pray Maida was right.

''Why didn't you tell me, then?''

Alex's intense, dark stare seemed to pierce right through her, finding the vulnerabilities she longed to hide. She took a deep breath, trying to quell jittery nerves. She'd known it would be difficult to come back here. She just hadn't anticipated *how* difficult. If Aunt Maida knew how hard this was for her—

No, she couldn't let Maida know that. She'd agreed to do this thing, and she had to do it.

''I am telling you. I mean, now you know, don't you?'' She clenched her hands together, hoping he didn't realize how much of her attitude was bravado. "Look, all I know is that she said she'd tell you. I thought it was all arranged. That's why I'm here—" she gestured toward the scattered pots "—trying to fix dinner for you and Jason."

Alex looked if it was the worst idea he'd ever heard. If he sent her packing, she'd never have a chance to make up for the mistakes she'd made the last time she was here.

"I can cook, you know," she assured him. "I learned from the best." Maida had insisted on giving her cooking lessons every time Paula came to visit.

"Of course you're going to get an education and have a profession," Maida would say. *"But it never does any harm to know how to cook."*

He looked at her skeptically, and her doubts rose. Why was this so difficult?

Lord, if this really is the right thing to do, please let me know it.

"Dinner tonight isn't important." His voice was clipped. "I'll take Jason out for a hamburger—he always welcomes that. As for the rest of it, I'll make a decision later. You can go to the hospital to see Maida. Tell her I'll be there tomorrow."

She nodded, trying not to react to his tone. As heir to the Caine family fortune, he'd probably been born with the commanding manner that assumed compliance with his orders. The quality never failed to irritate Paula, but Alex had a right to make his own decisions about his staff. And if she did work for him, he'd also have a perfect right to give her orders and expect obedience.

Seeming to consider the matter settled, Alex turned toward the front of the house.

She wanted to let him go, because his disturbing presence upset her equilibrium and made her silly heart flutter. But she couldn't. There was too much yet to be settled. She had to convince him that she was the right person for this job.

She caught up with him at the swinging door marking the boundary between the family's part of the mansion and the servants' section.

"Alex—" She put her hand on his arm to stop him, and was instantly sorry. Through the silky broadcloth of his shirt, his skin warmed to her touch. He wore the dress shirt and tie that was part of his usual attire, but the sleeves were turned back at the wrists, exposing a gold watchband that gleamed against his skin.

She pulled her gaze from his hands, fighting for balance, and focused on his face, instead. It didn't help. He bore lines he hadn't two years ago, and the narrow scar that crossed his cheekbone added an attractively dangerous look to his even, classic features.

She snatched her hand away. "I mean, Mr. Caine." She felt her cheeks flushing. Observing the proprieties might help keep things businesslike between them. It might prevent a recurrence of what happened two years ago.

He stopped, looking down at her, his dark eyes unreadable beneath winged brows. Then he shook his head.

"You've been calling me Alex since the first time you came here. You were only about Jason's age."

She nodded, deflected by memories of the past. At least Alex seemed able to put his antagonism aside for the moment and remember a more peaceful time. That had to be a good sign.

"I was eight. And homesick as could be. You showed me where the children's books were in the library and told me to help myself."

She'd been awestruck when Alex Caine, only child of the town's richest man and the prince in the Caine castle, had made the effort to be kind to her. She'd felt like Cinderella when he'd led her into the elegant room lined with books and shown her the window seat next to the fireplace where she could curl up and read. Not that she'd ever done it when there was a chance his formidable father might find her.

"So we're old friends." The smile that came too rarely lit his lean face, causing an uncomfortable flutter somewhere in the vicinity of her heart. "Alex will do."

"Alex," she repeated, trying not to linger on his

name. "You know how stubborn Aunt Maida can be. I'm sure she was just doing what she thought would cause the least trouble. If she could have delayed the surgery, she would have, but the doctor insisted."

She wanted to say the words that would convince him to let her stay, but she couldn't find them. Instead, she swung back to her worries about Maida.

"She told me Dr. Overton retired. Someone else took over his practice."

"You can have confidence in Brett Elliot," he said promptly, apparently reading her concern. "He's an excellent doctor, and I'm sure he's recommended the best surgeon." A hint of a smile touched his lips again. "And I'm not saying that because Brett's an old friend."

She suddenly saw herself as a child, peering from the housekeeper's cottage toward the swimming pool. A teenage Alex entertained two other boys: Mitch Donovan and Brett Elliot, his closest friends.

"Aunt Maida seems to trust him. That's the important thing."

He nodded, hand on the door. She could sense the impatience in him, as if he wanted to be elsewhere, as if only his deeply ingrained politeness kept him standing there.

She probably should let this go, but she couldn't. She took a breath. "I know Aunt Maida's suggestion has put you on the spot. But it really would ease her mind if she knew I was staying.''

She knew instantly she'd pressed too hard. He seemed to withdraw, putting distance between them even though he hadn't moved. His face set in bleak lines.

Alex had never looked that way when she was growing up. He'd always been surrounded by a golden aura nothing could diminish. But that had been before his wife left, before he'd spent too many weeks in that hospital himself.

''Let's get the immediate situation taken care of first,'' he said. ''You settle Maida at the hospital. If she needs anything, she just has to ask.''

''I know that. I'm sure Maida does, too.'' She tried to deny a wave of resentment that he could so easily grant any wish of her aunt's, while she couldn't.

He clasped her hand, sending a surge of warmth along her skin and stealing her breath. Then he dropped it as abruptly as if he'd felt that heat.

''Maida will be glad to have you with her for the operation. I know how much she enjoyed it when you worked here.''

He almost seemed to stumble over the words, as if he found this situation as awkward as she did. It surprised her. Smooth, sophisticated Alex had never been at a loss for the right phrase. That ability was something else the upper crust seemed to be born with.

All the things she didn't want to say about the time she worked in the Caine mansion skittered through her mind. Still, it wouldn't hurt to remind him that his son already knew her. "I appreciated the chance to take care of Jason. How is he?"

"Fine." His face seemed to stiffen again. "Looking forward to summer vacation after the rigors of second grade."

She had the sense of something suppressed, something he didn't want to say about his son, and thought again of Aunt Maida's worries about the boy.

"He used to be such a happy child. But his mother went away, and then Alex was in the accident and in the hospital all those weeks. Jason's changed. He's all curled up inside himself, and I don't know how to help him."

"I'm looking forward to seeing him." She tried to keep the words casual. "Does he really want a fast-food burger, or did you just make that up?"

"Believe it or not, he does. Maida and I try to educate his palate, but he's very much a seven-year-old in his tastes." The skin at the corners of his eyes crinkled. "I think you gave him his first trip to get fast food when you took care of him, didn't you?"

"I'm afraid so." She remembered it as if it were

yesterday. Jason's excitement at ordering from the counter, the awed look on his face as he sat across from her in the booth. The feelings that welled up at how much he resembled his father. That emotion struck her again, as strong as if someone had hit her.

Lord, what's happening to me? I thought I was over this.

Alex's dark, intent gaze penetrated the barrier she'd so carefully erected to shield her errant emotions. "What is it? What's wrong?"

"Nothing." She looked up and summoned a smile that felt tight on her lips. "Everything's okay."

She'd like to convince him. She'd like to convince herself. Alex couldn't know that, thanks to the accident, for nearly two years she hadn't been able to remember the crash or the months that had preceded it.

He didn't know that the memories of the time she'd spent in this house had fallen out of the hidden recesses of her mind a week ago, as fresh and as emotional as if they'd happened yesterday.

And prominent among them was the fact that the last time she was here, she'd fallen in love with Alex Caine.

Chapter Two

"Dad, is Maida going to come back?"

The forlorn note in his son's voice touched Alex's heart. What did Jason fear? That Maida had gone away and would never come back, like his mother?

Careful, careful. "What makes you think she won't come back?"

Alex glanced across the front seat of the car. Jason, who'd seemed happy enough at the restaurant, now sat clutching the plastic action figure that had come with his meal.

He frowned down at the figure, then looked up, his small face tightening into the mask that frustrated Alex as much as it did Jason's teachers.

Where has he gone, Lord? Where is the sunny little boy Jason used to be?

He felt almost embarrassed at the involuntary prayer, and his hands tightened on the wheel with determination. He was all Jason had, and he wouldn't let him down.

His son shouldn't have to worry, about Maida or anything else. Naturally he'd had to tell Jason something to explain Maida's absence, but he'd said as little as possible.

"She's just tired," he said now, trying to sound cheerful. "She needs to rest more. It's nothing you have to be concerned about. She'll be back before you know it, and everything will be fine."

They passed twin stone pillars and swung into the driveway. Paula, still wearing the jeans and sweatshirt that seemed to be her uniform, was bending over the trunk of a disreputable old car in his garage. She looked up at their approach, and he pulled into the bay next to her. When he got out, she was already explaining.

"I hope this is okay. Aunt Maida said you wouldn't mind if I parked my car here." She glanced down the row of empty bays, a question in her eyes.

"No problem. I got rid of the other cars after my father died."

Nobody needed five cars. His father had insisted on trying to relive the old days, when a full-time chauffeur had taken loving care of a fleet of vehicles, a full-time gardener tended the roses, and

Maida supervised a staff of three indoors. Now they made do with a cleaning company and a lawn service, with Maida watching Jason when he wasn't in school.

He waited for Paula to make some comment, but her attention was fixed on the small figure coming around the car.

"Jason, hi. It's good to see you again."

Jason nodded warily, always seeming on guard with strangers. Not that Paula was exactly a stranger, but at his age, two years was a long time.

"Hey, you got the green Raider." She touched the action figure Jason held. "Good going. He's the best, isn't he?"

His son's protective stance relaxed a little. "One of the guys in my class says the orange one's better, but I like the green one. He can do cool stuff."

"He sure can. Did you see the story where he rescued the princess?"

"Yeah. And when he set all the horses free. That was neat." Jason's face grew animated as he talked about the latest adventure of his action hero.

How had Paula gotten past his son's defenses so quickly? Alex felt something that might have been envy, then dismissed it. She was a teacher—she should be good with children.

Paula pulled a duffel bag from the trunk, and Alex reached out to take it from her. It was heavier than it looked, and for a moment their hands entangled.

"Rocks?" he enquired, lifting an eyebrow.

"Books." She made an abortive movement, as if to take the bag back, then seemed to think better of it. "I never go anywhere without them."

He glanced into the car's trunk. One cardboard carton overflowed with construction paper, and a plastic Halloween pumpkin poked improbably from another. "It looks as if you've brought everything you own."

He meant the comment lightly, but a shadow crossed her face. It told him more clearly than words that how long she stayed depended on him. She shrugged, turning to pull out another bag.

"Most of this stuff is from my classroom. I loaded it up the last day and didn't take the time to unload before I left to come here."

"I'll carry that one." Jason reached for the small bag.

"Thanks, Jason." She smiled, surrendering it to him, then hefted a box out and slammed the trunk. "I think that's it." She glanced at Alex. "If you're sure it's okay for me to leave the car here?"

"It's fine," he said firmly. He'd rather see that poor excuse for a car hidden behind garage doors than parked in his drive. Lifting the duffel bag, he led the way around down the walk toward the rear of the house.

The setting sun turned the swimming pool's surface to gold as they neared the flagstone patio. He hadn't done the water exercises for his injured leg today, and it took an effort to walk evenly carrying the heavy bag. He'd already seen Paula's expression at the scar on his face. He didn't want to see more pity if she caught him limping.

What did she really think about this idea of Maida's? Had it made her remember what happened between them the last time she was here?

One kiss, that was all. It was ridiculous to worry about the effect of one kiss. Of course he shouldn't have done it. She'd been working in his house, and that alone made her out of bounds to him.

Even if that hadn't been the case, he'd learned something when his wife's death, so soon after she'd left him, had made patching up their failing marriage impossible. Even if Karin had survived, even if she'd come back to the small-town life she detested, he'd known then that finding the love of a lifetime was an illusion. Reality was raising his son properly and maintaining the business this whole town relied on. He didn't intend to chase any more romantic rainbows.

So what was he doing watching Paula's smooth, easy stride, eyeing the swing of blond hair against her shoulder when she looked down to smile at Jason? He should have better sense.

She paused at the pool, bending to dip her fingers

in the water. "Nice. I'll bet you're in the pool all the time, now that school's out."

Jason shrugged. "Mostly my dad uses it. To make his leg better."

Alex braced himself for the look of pity, but she just nodded.

"Good idea."

"If you'd like to use the pool while you're here, please do." He disliked the stilted tone of his voice. Paula's presence had thrown him off balance. She was part of an embarrassing incident in his past, and she was also a reminder of the plane crash.

But she'd probably long since forgotten about that kiss. As for the accident, that was something every survivor had to deal with in his own way.

"Thanks." She stood. "I don't know if I'll be here that long."

Her words challenged him, but he wouldn't be drawn in. He'd ignore that particular problem for the moment. Jason had gotten several strides ahead, leaving them side by side. As they headed for the housekeeper's cottage, Alex lowered his voice. "How did Maida seem when you visited her? I hope she's not too worried about the surgery. Or about not having told me. She needs to concentrate on getting well, rather than worrying about us."

She hesitated, frown lines creasing her forehead. "She seems to trust the doctor to put things right. We didn't talk long."

"That sounds a bit evasive."

She shot him an annoyed look. "Don't you think it would be more polite not to say so?"

He'd forgotten that directness of hers. It made him smile—when it wasn't irritating him. "I'm worried about Maida, too. Remember?"

"Are you?"

"Yes." All right, now he was annoyed. Maybe that was a safer way to feel with Paula, anyway. "Believe it or not, you're not the only one who cares about her."

Her clear green eyes seemed to weigh his sincerity. Then she nodded with a kind of cautious acceptance. "The surgeon says she should come through the operation with flying colors, and then Brett will supervise her rehabilitation. That'll take time, and he wouldn't guess how long until she can come home."

He glanced at his son. "I haven't mentioned the surgery to Jason. I just said Maida needed a rest. The less he knows, the better."

She frowned as if disagreeing, but didn't argue. She moved toward his son. "Just put that on the porch, Jason. I'll take it in later."

She dropped her bags and sat down on the step, then patted the spot next to her. "Have a seat and tell me what's been going on. I haven't seen you for a long time."

Jason sat cautiously, seeming ready to dart away at a moment's notice.

Had Alex been that shy when he was Jason's age? He thought not, but then his father had always insisted on the social graces, no matter what he actually felt. Maybe, if his mother had lived, things would have been different. He stood stiffly, not comfortable with sitting down next to them, not willing to walk away, either.

"Bet you're glad school's out for the summer," Paula said. "I know my kids were."

Jason glanced up at her. "You have kids?"

"My students," she corrected herself. "I teach kindergarten. My school finished up yesterday, and everyone celebrated. Did you have a party the last day?"

Jason nodded. "We played games. And Maida made cupcakes for me to take."

Alex hadn't known that, but, of course, it was the sort of thing Maida would do. He shifted uncomfortably, trying to ease the pain in his leg. With the crucial business deal pending, he'd had trouble keeping up with anything else lately, including second-grade parties. He should go in and get back to work, but still he lingered, watching Paula with his son.

"I'll bet the kids liked those," she said. "Maida makes the best cupcakes."

Jason nodded, glancing down at the step he was

scuffing with the toe of his shoe. Then he looked up at Paula. "Did you come here to teach me?"

"Teach you?" she echoed. "Why would I do that? School's out for the summer."

Jason shrugged, not looking at either of them. "My dad thinks I should do better in school."

Shock took Alex's breath away for a moment. Then he found his voice. "Jason, I don't think that at all. And it's not something we should talk about to Paula, anyway."

Paula ignored him, all her attention focused on Jason. Her hand rested lightly on his son's shoulder. "Hey, second grade is tough for lots of people. I remember how hard it was when I had to start writing instead of printing. My teacher said my cursive looked like chicken scratches."

"Honest?" Jason darted a glance at her.

"Honest." She smiled at him. "You can ask Aunt Maida if you don't believe me. She probably remembers when I used to try to write letters to her. Sometimes she'd call me to find out what I'd said."

She'd managed to wipe the tension from Jason's face with a few words. Alex didn't know whether to be pleased or jealous that she'd formed such instant rapport with his son. Paula seemed to have a talent for inspiring mixed feelings in him.

Her blond hair swung across her cheek as she leaned toward Jason, saying something. The impulse to reach out and brush it back was so strong that his hand actually started to move before common sense took over.

Mixed feelings, indeed. The predominant feeling he had toward Paula Hansen wasn't mixed at all. It was one he'd better ignore, for both their sakes.

Paula stood on the tiny porch of the housekeeper's cottage the next morning, looking across the expansive grounds that glistened from last night's shower. The sun, having made it over the steep mountains surrounding Bedford Creek, slanted toward the birch tree at the end of the pool, turning its wet leaves to silver. The only sound that pierced the stillness was the persistent call of a bobwhite.

The stillness had made this secluded village seem like a haven to her when she was a child. She'd arrived in the Pennsylvania mountains from Baltimore, leaving behind the crowded row house echoing with the noise her brothers made. Four brothers—all of them older, all of them thinking they had the right to boss her around. Her childhood had sometimes seemed like one long battle—for privacy, for space, for the freedom to be who she was.

Here she'd stepped into a different world—one with nature on the doorstep, one filled with order and quiet. She couldn't possibly imagine the Caine mansion putting up with a loud game of keep-away in its center hall. It would have ejected the intruders forcibly.

Paula glanced toward the back of the mansion, wondering how much Alex had changed it since his father's death. The room on the end was the solarium. She remembered it filled with plants, but Alex had apparently converted it to a workout room. She could see the equipment through the floor-to-ceiling windows.

Next came the kitchen, with its smaller windows overlooking the pool. She should be there right now, fixing breakfast for Alex and Jason, but Alex had made it very clear he didn't want that.

Aunt Maida wasn't going to be happy. The last thing she'd said the night before had been to fix breakfast. Paula's protests—that Alex had told her not to, that Alex hadn't agreed to let her stay yet— had fallen on deaf ears.

Maida's stubborn streak was legendary in the Hansen family. Paula's father was the same, and any battle between Maida and him was a clash of wills. She vividly remembered the war over Maida's determination that Paula go to college. If not for Maida, Paula might have given up, accepting her father's dictum that girls got marriage certificates, not degrees. Her dream of a profession might have remained a dream.

But Maida wouldn't allow that. She'd pushed, encouraged, demanded. Paula had worked two jobs for most of the four years of college, but she'd made it through, thanks to Aunt Maida.

She leaned against the porch rail, watching a pair of wrens twittering in the thick yew hedge that stretched from the housekeeper's cottage toward the garage. If only she could find a way to help her aunt, to help Jason, without being a servant in Alex Caine's house.

She and Jason had played on the flagstone patio when she was his nanny. They'd sat in the gazebo with a storybook, and he'd leaned against her confidently, his small head burrowed against her arm. She remembered, so well, the vulnerable curve of his neck, the little-boy smell of him. He'd look up at her, his dark eyes so like his father's, sure he could trust her, sure she'd be there for him. And then she'd gone away.

What am I supposed to do, Lord? If Alex said no, would she be upset or would she be relieved? Only the guilt she felt over Jason kept her from running in the opposite direction rather than face Alex Caine every day and remember how he'd kissed her and then turned away, embarrassed.

Infatuation, she told herself sternly. It was infatuation, nothing more. She would stop imagining it was love.

She remembered, only too clearly, standing in the moonlight looking up at him, her feelings surely written on her face. Then recognition swept over her. Alex regretted that kiss. He probably thought she'd invited it. Humiliation flooded her, as harsh and scalding as acid.

She'd mumbled some excuse and run back to Aunt Maida's cottage. And a few days later, when she'd realized the feelings weren't going to fade, she'd made another excuse and left her job several weeks earlier than she'd intended, prepared to scurry back to Baltimore.

The flow of memories slowed, sputtering to a painful halt. Her last clear recollection was of Alex lifting her suitcase into the limo next to his own, saying he had to take the commuter flight out that day, too. Then—nothing. She'd eventually regained the rest of her memories, but the actual take-off and crash remained hidden, perhaps gone forever.

When she'd recovered enough to ask questions, her parents had simply said she'd been on her way home from her summer job. If she'd remembered then, would she have done anything differently? She wasn't sure. The failure had lain hidden in her mind.

Now, according to Aunt Maida, anyway, God was giving her a chance to make up for whatever mistakes she'd made then. Unlike most of the people Paula knew, Aunt Maida never hesitated to bring God into every decision.

Whether Maida was right about God's will, Paula didn't know. But her aunt was right about one thing—Jason had changed. Paula pictured his wary expression, the way he hunched his shoulders. The happy child he'd been once had vanished.

Of course, he was old enough now to understand a little more about his mother's leaving. That traumatic event, followed so soon by the plane crash that injured his father, was enough to cause problems for any child. And he must know that his mother wouldn't be coming back. Maida had told her the details that hadn't appeared in Karin's brief obituary—the wild party, the drunken driver. Paula frowned, thinking of students who'd struggled with similar losses.

A flicker of movement beyond the yew hedge caught her eye. Between the glossy dark leaves, she glimpsed a bright yellow shirt. She'd thought Jason was at breakfast with his father. What was he doing?

She rounded the corner of the cottage and spotted the child. The greeting she'd been about to call out died on her lips. All her teacher instincts went on alert. She might not know Jason well any longer, but she knew what a kid up to something looked like. Jason bent over something on the ground, his body shielding it from her view.

She moved quietly across the grass. ''Jason? What's up?''

He jerked around at her voice, dropping the object he held. The crumpled paper lit with a sudden spark, a flame shooting up.

She winced back, heart pounding, stomach contracting. *Run!* a voice screamed in her head. *Run!*

She took a breath, then another. She didn't need to run. Nothing would hurt her. *It's all right.* She repeated the comforting words over in her mind. It was all right.

Except that it wasn't. Quite aside from the terror of fire that had plagued her since the accident, what was Jason doing playing with matches? Another thought jolted her. Was this connected with his father's narrow escape from a fiery death?

Carefully she stepped on the spark that remained, grinding it into the still-wet grass. The scent of burning lingered in the air, sickening her.

She looked at Jason, and he took a quick step back. "Where'd you get the matches, Jason?"

His lower lip came out. "I don't know what you're talking about. I don't have any matches."

"Sure you do." She held out her hand. "Give them to me."

Maybe it was the calm, authoritative "teacher" voice. Jason dug into his jeans' pocket, pulled out the matchbook and dropped it into her hand.

She closed her fingers firmly around it. She wouldn't let them tremble. "Where did you get this?"

For a moment she thought he wouldn't answer.

He glared at her, dark eyes defiant. Then he shrugged. "My dad's desk. Are you gonna tell him?"

"I think someone should, don't you?" It would hardly be surprising if Jason's unresolved feelings about his father's accident had led to a fascination with fire. Not surprising, but dangerous.

"No!" His anger flared so suddenly that it caught her by surprise. His small fists clenched. "Leave me alone."

"Jason…" She reached toward him, impelled by the need to comfort him, but he dodged away from her.

"Go away!" He nearly shouted the words. "Just go away!" He turned and ran toward the house.

She discovered she was shaking and wrapped her arms around herself. Jason had made his feelings clear. His was definitely a vote for her to leave.

Alex put the weights back on their rack and stretched, gently flexing his injured knee. Brett Elliot, one of his oldest friends as well as his doctor, would personally supervise his workouts if he thought Alex was skipping them. And Brett was right; Alex had to admit it. The exercise therapy had brought him miles from where he'd been after the accident.

He toweled off, then picked up his juice bottle and stepped through the French doors to the flagstones surrounding the pool. The water looked tempting with the hot June sunshine bouncing from its surface, but he had another goal in mind at the moment. Jason was off on some game of his own. It was time Alex talked to Paula. He had to find some graceful way to get them both out of this difficult situation, in spite of the fact that he hadn't yet found someone else to replace Maida.

His timing seemed perfect. Paula was coming around the pool toward the house, dressed a bit formally for her. Instead of her usual jeans, she wore neat tan slacks and a bright coral top—probably a concession for a trip to the hospital. She briefly checked her swift stride when she saw him, and then she came toward him.

"Good morning." He tossed the towel over his shoulder and set his juice bottle on the patio table. *Business,* he reminded himself. "I hoped I'd have a chance to see you this morning."

Paula rubbed her arms, as if she were cold in spite of the June sunshine. "Aren't you going to the factory today?"

"Not until later," he said. "I'll work at home for a while, then stop by the hospital to see how Maida's doing." He hesitated, looking for words, but since Paula was so direct herself, she should appreciate the same from him. "We should get a few things settled."

For just an instant Paula's eyes were puzzled, as

if she'd been thinking about something else entirely. Then she gave him a wary look and took a step back.

"I have to leave for the hospital." She glanced at her watch. "I want to be there when Aunt Maida wakes up from the operation."

"This will take just a few minutes. We've got to discuss this idea of Maida's." He knew he sounded inflexible, but he didn't want to put this off. The longer he waited, the more difficult it would be.

He pulled out a deck chair for her. Looking reluctant, she sat down. He settled in the seat next to her and instantly regretted his choice. They were facing the gazebo at the end of the pool. They shouldn't be having this conversation in view of the spot where he'd kissed her.

But it was too late now, and maybe it was just as well. That embarrassing episode should make her as reluctant as he was to pursue Maida's scheme. He'd give her an easy way out of this dilemma, that was all. And she'd be ready to leave.

Paula tugged at the sleeves of her knit top. Apparently she did that whenever she was nervous, as if she were protecting herself. He tried not to notice how the coral sweater brought out the warm, peachy color in her cheeks, or how the fine gold chain she wore glinted against her skin.

Stick to business, he ordered himself. That was a good way to think of it. This was just like any business negotiation, and they both needed to go away from it feeling they'd gained something.

"Be honest with me, Paula. You don't really want to work here this summer, do you?"

She glanced up at him, a startled expression in her eyes. "What makes you say that?"

To his surprise, he couldn't quite get the real reason out. *Because the last time you were here, I kissed you and created an awkward situation for both of us. Because in spite of that, I still find you too attractive for my own peace of mind.*

No, he didn't want to say any of that. He tried a different tack.

"You probably had a teaching job of some sort lined up for the summer, didn't you?"

She shook her head, a rueful smile touching her lips. "There's not much teaching available in the summer. I was signed up with a temp agency for office work."

"Office work?" He couldn't stop the surprise in his voice, and realized instantly how condescending it sounded. "Why? I mean, couldn't you find anything else?"

Her expression suggested he didn't have a clue as to how the real world worked. "Kindergarten teachers aren't exactly on corporate headhunters' wish lists, you know."

"But aren't there courses you want to take in the summer?" He didn't know why the thought of

Paula taking temporary work to make ends meet bothered him so much. His reaction was totally irrational.

"I can't afford to take classes." She said it slowly and distinctly, as if they spoke different languages. "I have college loans to pay off."

Belatedly he reminded himself he was supposed to be dissuading her from working for him. "Even so, I can't imagine that you'd want to come here to cook and take care of Jason, instead."

He saw immediately that he'd said the wrong thing. In fact, he'd probably said a lot of wrong things. Paula had that effect on him.

She stiffened, and anger flared in her face. "Cooking is honest work. There's nothing to be ashamed of in what my aunt does," she snapped, and she gripped the arms of the deck chair as if about to launch herself out of it.

"No, of course not." He seemed to be going even farther in the wrong direction. "I didn't mean to imply that."

She stood, anger coming off her in waves. "I really have to leave for the hospital now, Alex. I've told my aunt I'm willing to fill in for her here as long as necessary, but, of course, you may have other plans. Either way, it's up to you."

She spun on her heel before he could find words to stop her. He watched her stalk toward the garage, head high.

Great. That was certainly the clumsiest negotiation he'd ever attempted. If he did that poorly in the business deal, the plant would be closed within a month.

Paula had thrown the decision right back into his lap, and she'd certainly made her position clear. If he didn't want her here, he'd have to be the one to say it. Unfortunately, where Paula was concerned, he really wasn't sure what he wanted.

Chapter Three

Alex hadn't hired her, and maybe he wouldn't. But she couldn't just let things go. Paula pulled into the garage late that afternoon, aware of how pitiful her junker looked in the cavernous building. Aunt Maida was still groggy from the successful surgery, but she'd soon be well enough to demand a report. Paula had to be able to reassure her.

She walked quickly to the back door of the mansion. A small bicycle leaned against the laundry room door, reminding her of Jason and the matches. She should have told Alex, but their conversation had veered off in another direction entirely, and she hadn't found the words. Maybe she still hadn't.

Even the geranium on the kitchen window sill seemed to droop in Maida's absence. Breakfast dishes, stacked in the sink, made it clear that when

Alex said he'd fix breakfast for himself and Jason, he hadn't considered cleaning up. She turned the water on. It wasn't her job. Alex hadn't hired her. But Maida's kitchen had always been spotless, and she couldn't leave it this way.

This was for Maida, she told herself, plunging her hands into hot, sudsy water. Not for Alex.

She'd been angry at Alex's implications about the housekeeper position, but she'd been just as guilty of thinking Maida's job less important than her own. Now it was the job she needed and wanted to fill—if only she could erase the memory of Alex's kiss.

Enough. She concentrated on rubbing each piece of the sterling flatware. She'd come here to make up for the past by helping Jason through this diffi- cult time. That was all.

She heard the door swing behind her and turned. Jason stood staring at her. For a moment he didn't move. Then he came toward her slowly. He stopped a few feet away.

"I came to say I'm sorry."

"Are you, Jason?" Was it regret or good man- ners that brought him here? Maybe it didn't really matter. At least he was talking. That was better than silence.

"I shouldn't have yelled at you." A quiver of apprehension crossed his face. "Did you tell my dad?"

"No." She pulled out a chair at the pine kitchen table. "I think Maida has some lemonade in the refrigerator. Want a glass?"

He nodded a little stiffly. "That would be nice."

He was like his father, in manner as well as in looks, she thought as she poured two glasses of lemonade. Same dark hair and eyes, same well-defined bone structure, same strict courtesy.

He didn't have the stiff upper lip to his father's degree of perfection, though. He watched her apprehensively as she sat down across from him.

"I don't want to tell him." The words surprised her. Surely she should—but if she did, she'd never get beyond the barrier Jason seemed to have erected against the world. "I think *you* should, though. It's pretty serious stuff. You could have gotten hurt."

"I won't do it again." Dark eyes pleaded with her. "Promise you won't say anything. I won't do it again, honest."

She studied his expression. Even at seven or eight, a lot of kids had figured out how to tell adults what they wanted to hear, instead of the truth. But Jason seemed genuinely dismayed at the result of his actions.

She took a deep breath. *Let me make the right decision. Please.*

"Okay, Jason. If you promise you won't do it again, I promise I won't tell."

His relieved smile was the first one she'd seen

from him. *Like his father,* she thought again. A smile that rare made you want to forgive anything, just to see it.

Jason didn't seem to have inherited any qualities from his mother. Did he miss her and wonder why she'd disappeared? Maybe by now he'd made peace with his loss.

She watched as he gulped the lemonade. Guilt seemed to have made him thirsty. Finally he set the glass down, looking at it, not at her.

"Is Maida really going to come back?"

The question startled her. "Sure she is. Why do you think she wouldn't?"

"I heard Daddy talking." He fixed her with an intent gaze. "He told me she just needed to rest a while, but I heard him tell somebody on the phone that she was in the hospital. Is she going to stay there?"

Never lie to a child; that was one of her bedrock beliefs as a teacher. If something was going to hurt, going to be unpleasant, a child had the same right as an adult to prepare for it.

"Only for a little while," she said carefully, re-membering Alex's determination to shield his son. "She had to go into the hospital to have her hip fixed."

His face clouded. "I don't want her to stay there. Can't Dr. Brett just give her some medicine?"

The bereft tone touched her. "I know you don't

want her to be away, but medicine won't fix what's wrong. She had to have an operation, and they gave her a brand-new joint. Now she has to stay at the hospital and do exercises until she's better.''

"Like my dad does for his leg?''

"Sort of like that.'' She seemed to see Alex again in the workout clothes he'd worn that morning, and her mouth went dry. "Then when she's well, she'll be able to come back.''

His gaze met hers, and she read a challenge in it. "You didn't come back. Not for a long time.''

It was like a blow to the heart. Jason was talking about when she'd been his nanny. Maybe, underneath the words, he was thinking about his mother, too.

She longed to put her hand over his where it lay on the table, but he was such a prickly child that she was afraid of making him withdraw. She prayed for the right words.

"I want you to listen, Jason, because I'm telling you the truth. Maida loves you. If she could have skipped the operation to stay with you, she would have. She's going to come back, and in the meantime, you'll be okay.''

"Are you going to stay?'' His lips trembled. "Are you? I know I said I wanted you to go away, but I didn't mean it. I want you to stay.''

Guilt gripped her throat in a vise so tight she couldn't speak. She'd asked God to show her what

to do. Was this His answer, in the voice of a troubled little boy?

She cleared her throat. "I'm not sure, Jason. But
I'm going to talk to your daddy about it."

"When?" Urgency filled his voice. "When?"

Somehow, whatever it took, she had to convince
Alex to let her stay. She stood. "Right now."

Alex had been trying to concentrate on work for
the past half-hour, but all he could think about was
how he'd manage the coming weeks. His business,
his family, his home were too intertwined to separate.

He didn't have any illusions that it would be easy
to replace Maida. First of all, no one *could* really
replace her. She was the closest thing to a mother
Jason had.

Tension radiated down his spine. Jason had had
enough losses in his young life. It was up to his
father to protect him from any more.

It was also up to his father to provide for his
future. If this deal with Dieter Industries didn't go
through, and soon, the Caine company would be on
the verge of collapse. Their hand-crafted furniture
would go the way of the lumber mills founded by
his great-grandfather. Probably not even his private
fortune could save it. Several hundred people would
be out of work, thanks to Caine Industries's failure.

He didn't have the luxury of time. Dieter was

sending someone over within weeks. Alex had to be ready, or they all lost.

He glanced up at the portrait of his father that hung over the library's tile fireplace. Jonathan Caine stared sternly from the heavy gold frame, as if he mentally weighed and measured everyone he saw and found them wanting. He would no more understand the firm's current crisis than he'd be able to admit that his mistakes had led to it.

His father's stroke and death, coming when he heard the news of the crash, had seemed the knock-out blow. But Alex had found out, once he took over, just how badly off the company was. And he'd realized there were still blows to come. He'd spent the past two years trying to solve the company's problems, and he still didn't know if he could succeed.

This was getting him nowhere. Alex walked to the floor-length window and looked down at the town—his town. He knew every inch of its steep narrow streets, folded into the cleft of the mountains. Sometimes he thought he knew every soul in town.

Caines had taken care of Bedford Creek since the first Caine, a railroad baron, had built his mansion on the hill in the decade after the Civil War. Bedford Creek had two economic bases: its scenic beauty and Caine Industries. If the corporation went under, how would the town survive? How would he?

The rap on the door was tentative. Then it came again, stronger this time. He crossed the room with impatient steps and opened the door.

"Paula." That jolt to his solar plexus each time he saw her ought to be getting familiar by now. "I'm sorry, but this isn't a good time."

"This is important."

What was one more disruption to his day? He wasn't getting anything accomplished, anyway. He stepped back, gesturing her in.

"Is something wrong?"

She swung to face him. "Have you made a decision about hiring someone to replace my aunt?"

He motioned to a chair, but she shook her head, planting herself in the center of the oriental carpet and looking at him.

"Not yet," he admitted. "Summer is tourist season in Bedford Creek. Everyone who wants a job is probably already working."

He couldn't deny the fact that Maida had been right about one thing. Paula could be the answer to his problems. But the uncomfortable ending to her previous stay, his own mixed feelings for her, made that impossible. He couldn't seem to get past that.

"You have to have someone Jason can get along with." She hesitated. "I couldn't help thinking that he's changed."

He stiffened. "My son is fine." *Fine,* he repeated silently.

"He seems to believe you're disappointed in his school work."

Her clear, candid gaze bored into him. "He misunderstood," he said shortly. "Jason is very bright." He glared at her, daring her to disagree.

"Yes, of course he is. But that doesn't mean school is easy for him."

"Paula, I don't want to discuss my son with you. Jason is fine. Now, is there anything else?"

She looked at him for what felt like a long moment, and he couldn't tell what was going on behind her usually expressive face. Then her eyes flickered.

"Just one thing. You should hire me to fill in until Maida is well again."

Paula's heart pounded in her ears. She hadn't intended to blurt it out like that. She'd thought she'd lead up to it, present her arguments rationally. Unfortunately, she didn't seem able to think in any sensible manner when she was around Alex.

That in itself was a good reason to run the other direction. *"You didn't come back, not for a long time."* Jason's plaintive voice echoed in her mind. No, she couldn't let him down. He needed someone, and she was the one he wanted right now.

Alex wasn't answering, and that fact jacked up

her tension level. He was probably trying to find a polite way to tell her he'd rather hire anyone else but her.

He walked to the other side of the long library table he used as a desk. It was littered with papers, and supported an elaborate computer system. Maybe he wanted to put some space between them, or maybe he was emphasizing the fact that this was his office, his house, his decision.

But there, beyond him, was the window seat where she'd curled up as a child. There, on the lowest shelf, were the storybooks she'd read. She had a place here, too.

He looked at her, a frown sending three vertical lines between his dark brows. "Are you sure this is something you want to do?"

She took a breath. At least he hadn't started with "no." Maybe he was willing to consider it. "Jason knows me, and Aunt Maida would feel better. I'm sure she'd call me five times a day from the hospital if the doctor would let her, just to be sure everything is all right."

"That's not what I asked." His gaze probed beneath the surface. "How do you feel about it, Paula?"

How did she feel about it? Mixed emotions—that was probably the best way to describe it. But Alex didn't need to know that. "I want the job. I think I can do it, although I don't have much experience.'' She remembered Aunt Maida's concerns, and plunged on. ''I know you have some important entertaining coming up in the next month. If you're worried about that...''

What could she say? She couldn't claim expertise she didn't have. She'd never put on a fancy party in her life, and she didn't think her usual brand of entertaining was what Alex was used to. He'd probably never ordered in pizza for guests.

''I'm not.'' He glanced toward the portrait above the mantel, then away. ''It's important, of course, but I'll hire a caterer for that, in any event. Maida's job would be to oversee the staff.''

It sounded like a breeze compared to the elaborate cooking she'd been imagining. If someone else was doing the work, she ought to be able to manage a simple dinner party. ''I think I could do that.''

His gaze assessed her, and she stiffened. Maybe she hadn't lived all her life in a mansion, but she was smart enough to work her way through college. How hard could this be in comparison?

''Actually, that's not my concern at the moment.'' He looked impossibly remote, as if he viewed her through the wrong end of a telescope. ''I want to know how you feel about working for me again, after what happened the last time you were here.''

It was like a blow to the stomach, rocking her back on her heels. She hadn't dreamed he'd refer to it, had assumed he'd ignore what he probably saw as an unpleasant episode. Or that he'd forgotten it.

"That's all in the past," she said with as much firmness as she could manage. "You apologized. You said we'd pretend it never happened." He'd done a very good job of that, as she knew only too well. The humiliation she'd felt when he'd said those words brought a stinging wave of color to her cheeks. "Why are you bringing it up now?"

"Because I don't want it hanging between us," he said. "I don't want you to spend your time here worrying that I'll make the same mistake again."

A mistake, that's what it was to him. A moment of weakness when the moonlight had tricked him into a brief, romantic gesture he later regretted. Well, he was never going to know it meant any more than that to her.

"Please, forget about it." She forced herself to keep her voice steady and unconcerned. "I already have."

She had, of course. For nearly two years she'd forgotten it entirely. Maybe she'd have been better off if she'd never remembered. But just a week ago, the memory had popped out from behind the locked door in her mind. The doctors couldn't explain why. They'd said she could remember any time, or never.

She swallowed hard. What else might be hiding

there? She still didn't remember anything about those moments when the plane went down. Would she suddenly find herself reliving every painful second of the crash?

"Good." He was briskly businesslike. "In that case, we can start with a clean slate between us. If you're really willing to take on this position, it seems to be the best solution for everyone."

She tried to smile. *Position* was a fancy word for it. She was about to become an employee in his house. And she'd have to do it without ever letting him know how she felt about him.

"The best solution for everyone," she echoed. "We couldn't ask for better than that."

She had to find a way to keep her relationship with Alex businesslike—pleasant, but businesslike. She was just another employee to him, and as far as she was concerned, this was just another job. It was no different than if she'd been filing paperwork in someone's office.

Well, maybe a little different. If she were filing papers, she wouldn't be working for someone who tied her heart in knots.

Chapter Four

Paula put the carafe of coffee on a tray and glanced at the schedule Maida had taped to the kitchen cabinet, tension dancing along her nerves. Okay, so far she was on target, although it had probably taken her twice as long as it would have taken Maida. It was a good thing she'd decided to get up early this morning, Paula thought as she headed through the swinging door to the front of the house and up the stairs. Next on the agenda was to take the coffee to Alex's room.

The second-floor hallway was as big as the entire living room in the apartment she shared with another teacher back home. She pushed the thought away. If she let herself make comparisons like that, she'd be too intimidated to do her job.

She tapped first, then opened the heavy door—

more English oak. She remembered Maida showing her around the mansion on an earlier visit, explaining how one of Alex's ancestors had imported the paneling and brought artisans over from Germany to create the stained glass. Maida had been as proud as if it belonged to her.

"Paula, good." Alex strode into the bedroom from the bath, still buttoning his shirt. He stopped, looking at her. "Is something wrong?"

"No. Nothing." *Nothing except that I didn't anticipate how this much intimacy would affect me.* She forced down the flutter in her stomach and lifted the tray slightly. "Where would you like this?"

Instead of telling her, he took the tray, his hands brushing hers briefly. Her skin seemed sensitized to his touch, reacting with awareness in every cell. For an instant his gaze held hers. Was there more than business-as-usual in his eyes? Before she could be sure, he turned away and set the tray on the mahogany bureau. He busied himself pouring out a cup of coffee, his back to her.

She'd like to beat a retreat back to the kitchen, but Maida had said Alex would give his daily orders now. *Orders.* Paula swallowed a lump of resentment. She didn't take orders well; she never had. But she couldn't argue with Alex the way she would have with her father or brothers. In this situation, he was the boss, just as he had been when she was Jason's nanny. Their kiss hadn't changed that.

She pulled a pad and pencil from her jeans pocket. She'd taken the precaution of coming prepared, and the sooner this was done, the sooner she could escape. But Alex didn't seem to be in any hurry.

"Do you have some instructions for the day?" she prompted. Somehow "instructions" sounded fractionally better than "orders."

He glanced toward her, the lines around his dark eyes crinkling a little as he gestured with his coffee cup. "Let me get some of this down first. Then I'll be able to think."

She nodded, glad he couldn't know how dry her mouth felt at the moment. This was just too awkward—standing in Alex's private sanctum, watching him drink his morning coffee, noticing the way his dark hair tumbled over his forehead before he'd smoothed it back for the day. But she didn't have a choice.

She forced herself to stand still, glancing around the room to keep from staring at him. The heavy forest-green drapes and equally heavy mahogany furniture darkened the room, and the deep burgundy tones of the oriental carpet didn't help to brighten it. The room looked like a period set, in a museum. In fact, it probably was a period piece, but in a private home. She doubted that the furniture had been changed in several generations.

Had Alex had a colorful little boy's bedroom once, like Jason's? She smiled at the thought. She'd have to ask Maida. Somehow the idea of Alex with a cowboy or astronaut bedspread made him seem more like a regular person, instead of the blue blood who always stood slightly apart from the crowd.

Alex's cup clattered onto the tray, and he swung toward her. "Now, about the day's schedule—" His tone was businesslike, and her image of a little-boy Alex vanished.

"You'll need to see to Jason and the meals, of course. I won't be home for lunch, but I expect him to have a balanced meal. I'm sure Maida's talked to you about all that, hasn't she?"

"Yes." She tried to match his briskness. This was what she'd wanted, wasn't it? Brisk and businesslike, so she wouldn't imagine things she couldn't have. "And I have her schedule of the daily work, and when the cleaners and gardeners come." She poised the pencil over the pad. "I just need any special instructions."

"Hand me that tie, please."

For a split second she stared at the pad, confused, then realized what he meant. She took the striped tie from the dresser and handed it to him. He knotted it expertly, barely glancing in the mirror.

"Today I think it best if you concentrate on Jason. He's bound to feel a little apprehensive about Maida's absence. Try to keep him occupied.''

He held out his hand. This time she'd caught on, and she had the suit coat ready to put into it. Again their hands touched, and a faint tingle warmed her fingers. She snatched her hand away quickly.

''I may bring a business contact back to the house this afternoon,'' he went on, ''so please be sure there's coffee brewed and some sort of savories ready.''

Her mind went blank. ''Savories?''

''Cheese puffs, that sort of thing. Maida always serves something with coffee when people are here.'' He picked up his briefcase.

Pretzels or cookies probably weren't what he had in mind, she decided. ''I'll see what I can do.''

''I'll need you to pick up some dry-cleaning—'' He was already out the door, and she hurried to follow.

''You can do that when you go to visit Maida. And don't forget to check on shirts to go to the laundry.''

She scribbled on the pad, trailing him down the stairs. *Jason, dry-cleaning, laundry, coffee.* What else? Oh, yes, the savories, whatever they were going to be. Maybe she'd been just a bit optimistic in thinking this would be a breeze.

Alex stopped at the bottom of the steps, turning

suddenly. Their faces were on a level, only inches apart. Her breath caught.

"And tomorrow morning the coffee could be a little stronger."

"Stronger, right."

He turned away, heading for the dining room. She started to breathe again. So much for her idea that working for Alex could ever be cool and businesslike.

She'd really ended up with the worst of both worlds, she realized. As Alex's housekeeper, she would be in as close contact with him as a member of the family. But Alex would treat her like a servant, because in his eyes that was all she was.

Alex pulled into the driveway, sending a swift glance toward his passenger. He couldn't go so far as to say Conrad Klemmer's visit had gone well. The representative of the Swiss firm had been stiff, even seeming a little uncomfortable. Perhaps finishing their discussions in Alex's home would loosen him up a little.

It had better. Alex's stomach tightened. With any luck, a pleasant meeting in the library, sipping coffee and eating Maida's cheese straws—

But Maida wasn't here. Paula, quite aside from the totally inappropriate feelings she'd roused in him, was an unknown quantity when it came to running the house. This morning, in his bedroom, she'd seemed off balance. Or maybe he was projecting his own feelings onto her. It had certainly unsettled him to have Paula bringing him his coffee, handing him his tie. He hadn't anticipated the effect on him when she'd come in with his morning tray instead of Maida. He'd tried to act as if it were business as usual, but he probably hadn't succeeded.

Klemmer leaned forward, scanning the mansion from its pillared portico to the octagonal cupola on top.

"You have a lovely home," he commented in British-accented English. He glanced beyond the house, where the thickly wooded hillside swept sharply up to a saddleback ridge. "And a wonderful view."

"Thank you." Alex pulled to a stop and opened the door, surveying the landscape for any disorder and finding none. "We can finish our conversation in greater comfort here. My housekeeper should have some coffee ready for us."

He hoped. He led the way along the walk skirting the bank of rhododendrons, still heavily laden with flowers, that screened the front of the house from view. This meeting would be successful when he had a commitment from Klemmer to bring a full team in to negotiate the deal. Until then, the whole thing could fizzle away into nothing, and his last, best hope of saving the company would be gone.

"I'll get it!"

The shout from the front lawn startled him. They rounded the corner. Paula backpedaled toward them, a fielder's mitt extended. A baseball soared over her head.

He reached for the ball, seeing disaster in the making. He was a second too late. Klemmer caught it.

Paula, wearing her usual jeans and a T-shirt, skidded to a stop inches from them. Beyond her, Jason stood holding a bat, looking horrified.

They ought to be embarrassed. This was hardly the impression he'd expected to make on Klemmer. And it certainly wasn't the welcome he'd told Paula to prepare.

"I'm so sorry." She burst out, her cheeks scarlet. "I didn't mean… We were just practicing a little hitting."

"So I see." He bit off a retort. He couldn't say the words that crowded his tongue. Maybe that was just as well.

Klemmer was already reaching out to shake hands. "What a pleasure to meet your lovely family. This must be Mrs. Caine. I am Conrad Klemmer, your husband's business associate."

He wouldn't have thought it possible for Paula's flush to deepen, but it did.

"No, I—"

"Paula is my housekeeper." He kept his voice calm with an effort. "And this is my son, Jason."

Fortunately Jason remembered his manners. He dropped the bat, came quickly to them and extended his hand.

"How do you do, sir."

Klemmer darted a quick, speculative glance at Paula. Then he smiled. "It's a pleasure to meet both of you."

That speculative look only added more fuel to Alex's anger.

"Jason, will you show Mr. Klemmer to the library? I want to speak with Paula for a moment."

Jason nodded. "This way." He scampered up the steps and opened the door. "I'll show you."

The instant the door closed behind them, Alex turned to Paula, anger making his voice cold.

"Is this your idea of entertaining my business associate?"

"No, this is my idea of entertaining your son." Her green eyes sparked with answering anger. "That was my priority for today, remember?"

There might be some justice in her comment, but he was too annoyed to admit it at the moment. "I distinctly remember telling you I might be bringing an important business associate back with me this afternoon. I didn't expect you to greet him with a fly ball."

He saw her stubborn jaw tighten. "The coffee is

ready, and I found some of Maida's cheese straws
in the freezer. Why shouldn't I play ball with Jason?''

''I don't care what you play with Jason,'' he
ground out. ''But the back lawn is the appropriate
place for baseball, not the front. Jason should know
that, even if you don't.''

He knew how condescending it sounded the instant the words were out. But before he could say
anything else, Paula had turned toward the door.

''I'll bring your coffee to the library.'' The words
were coated with ice. ''It will just be a moment.''

The library. Klemmer. Alex followed her
quickly. The Swiss businessman had to be his major
concern right now. He had to salvage what was left
of this meeting, if he could.

Then he'd worry about straightening things out
with Paula. He wasn't sure which of those would
be the more difficult.

Paula resisted the urge to clatter the baking sheet
as she pulled cheese straws from the oven. That
would be immature and childish. But it would feel
so satisfying.

Using a spatula, she slid the straws onto a wire
rack to cool for a moment before she took them in
to the library. The cheese straws weren't the only
things that needed to cool off. If she didn't get her

temper under control, she wouldn't dare face Alex and Mr. Klemmer.

Well, she had every right to be angry. Alex had spoken to her as if she were beneath his consideration. As if only a barbarian would play catch with a child on the front lawn.

A reluctant smile tugged at her lips. Alex should see her neighborhood. Kids played ball anywhere and everywhere, including in the street.

The smile faded. Things were different here. She'd known that from the start. She'd known, too, that it was her responsibility to fit into Alex's world, and not the other way around.

Maybe, if she'd stopped to think about it, she'd have realized that the manicured front lawn wasn't intended for a game of catch. But it had been the first thing she'd suggested all day that brought a spark of enthusiasm to Jason's eyes, and she couldn't ignore that.

She wouldn't apologize for it, either. She arranged the coffee and cheese straws on a heavy silver tray, then picked the tray up, suppressing a nervous flutter in her stomach. She'd show Alex that she could be the perfect housekeeper, if that was what he wanted. But she wouldn't apologize for playing with his son. Jason could use a bit more play in his life.

The militant mood carried her down the hallway and right up to the library door. Then she paused, again needing to push down the apprehension that danced along her nerves. If Alex was still angry...well, he'd just have to get over it. She was doing her job. She tapped lightly, then opened the door.

The two men sat in the leather armchairs on either side of the fireplace. Was it just her imagination, or did Alex look worried?

She dismissed the thought. Alex, with his air of always being in perfect control, didn't worry about anything.

"Just put the tray here, please." Alex nodded to the inlaid coffee table between them.

She set the tray down, sensing Alex's quick assessment of it. Apparently satisfied, he nodded.

She poured the coffee into fragile china cups, careful not to let even a drop fall on the gleaming surface of the table. It wasn't until both men were served and she took a step back that she realized she'd been holding her breath.

Ridiculous, she scolded herself. She was being ridiculous to put so much pressure on herself to do this perfectly. And equally silly to imagine Alex would notice, or care.

"Will there be anything else?" she asked.

"That's fine, Paula." Alex's tone was cool and dismissive.

Well, all right. She could take a hint. Maybe he

expected her to bow her way out of his presence, like a servant of a medieval king.

She nodded briskly and spun away. The sooner she got out of here, the better. If they wanted more coffee, they could pour it themselves.

A couple of hours later, she hadn't exactly forgotten her irritation as she started supper, but it had been reduced to a slow simmer. Cooking, she'd discovered, was good for her disposition. Intent on Maida's chicken casserole recipe, she heard the kitchen door swing open. She turned, expecting Jason. But it was Alex, apparently back from delivering Klemmer to his hotel.

Her temper bubbled up again, as if their disagreement had been moments ago instead of an hour ago. "If you're here to deliver a lecture, don't bother." She dried her hands on a linen tea towel.

"Lecture?" His dark brows arched. "What lecture did you have in mind?"

"I got the message. No ball playing on the front lawn."

He held up his hands as if surrendering. "No lectures, I promise. I just came in to see if you had any more hot coffee."

The mild response took the wind out of her sails. It was tough to stay angry with someone who seemed to have forgotten the quarrel. She managed a smile. "This is a Norwegian kitchen, remember? There's always coffee."

Alex took a heavy white mug from the shelf and filled it. He took a long swallow, then stood staring down at the mug. "I owe you an apology."

That was the last thing she'd expected to hear him say, and it left her momentarily speechless.

He turned toward her, the faintest of smiles curving his firm lips. "I take it you agree."

"I..." She didn't seem to have anything to say. Her anger had slid away, and she didn't know what to replace it with. Maybe it was easier to hold on to the anger, because it provided a protection from feelings she didn't want to recognize. "You don't need to apologize to me. I work for you. If you have a problem with what I'm doing, you have to tell me."

He leaned back against the counter, and the lines of worry in his face were unmistakable. She'd told herself the richest man in town didn't have anything to worry about, but clearly she'd been wrong.

"The point is, I hadn't told you not to play ball on the front lawn. And I certainly shouldn't have spoken to you so sharply." He shook his head. "It wasn't your fault."

She wanted to tell him that it wasn't anybody's fault, that it was perfectly normal for a little boy to play ball on his own front lawn, but she couldn't. Obviously what was normal in her world wasn't in his.

"I hope your guest wasn't upset." She tried a smile. "At least I didn't give him a concussion."

Alex's face relaxed a fraction. "Thanks to his quick reflexes. I hadn't warned him he'd need a batting helmet when he came."

"Seriously, if you think I should apologize to him, I will." And what had happened to her fine conviction that she didn't owe anyone an apology?

"Not necessary. He has other things on his mind, anyway."

She wondered if expressing concern was beyond the limits of her job. "You look as if you do, too."

For a moment she thought he'd tell her it wasn't her business, but then he shrugged.

"Is it that obvious?"

"Pretty much." She could hardly say that she'd made a profession of studying him the last time she was here, or that she still remembered his every mood as if it had been yesterday.

"I suppose..." He frowned, then shook his head. "Maybe it's best if you know what's going on. What did Maida tell you?"

That Jason was lonely. That you were lonely. No, she couldn't say that, either. "About the business? She said you had some big deal going on, something that would happen this summer. She was worried about entertaining the visitors."

"I wish that were all I had to worry about." The

lines between his brows deepened, and again she had that ridiculous longing to smooth them away.

"What is it, then?" It had to be something serious, to make him look like that.

"If this deal doesn't go through—" He paused as if he didn't want to say anything else. "If it doesn't, I'm going to lose the company."

"But..." She grappled with the idea, trying to get her mind around it. It seemed impossible. "But you've always been the biggest employer in the county. How could this happen?"

"Changing markets, bad decisions." His face was grim. "It doesn't take much, not in today's economy. If this deal with Dieter Industries goes through, it will open up a whole new marketing opportunity for us. If not, the company will go under."

"But so many people count on Caine Industries." That probably wasn't the most comforting thing she could have said.

"Half the town." His hand tightened on the coffee mug until the knuckles turned white. "Half the town directly, and more than that indirectly. If I can't pull off this deal, I'll let all of them down."

The pain he was trying to hide caught at her heart. "It's not just your responsibility. There are other people involved. No one will blame you."

He shot her a skeptical glance. "You can't believe that, Paula. If Caine Industries goes under, everyone will blame me—most of all I will blame me. And there won't be a company to leave to my son.''

She didn't have any words to deal with something like this. Apparently the prince in his castle wasn't safe from the world's problems, after all.

''I'm sorry,'' she said at last.

He shrugged, pushing away from the counter. ''I thought you should know what's at stake, because you're a part of it. These people from Dieter have to be entertained, and they expect it to be in my home. That means you have to keep things running properly.''

No more ball games on the front lawn, in other words. Why hadn't Maida explained all this to her? Because she'd been afraid Paula would run at the thought of it?

Or because she knew one little boy was in danger of getting lost in the midst of all this high-powered business.

Paula realized Alex was waiting for some response from her. She looked up, meeting his gaze. ''I'll do my best,'' she said. *My best for Jason, and for you.*

Chapter Five

The prince in the castle, the man who had everything, stood on the verge of losing it all. *No, not
all,* Paula corrected herself, drying the silverware
from breakfast the next morning. The Caine family
fortune would probably survive the loss of the company that bore its name. But for a proud, private
man like Alex, the blow would still be severe.
When he'd said there might be no company to leave
to his son, she'd glimpsed a secret agony in his eyes
that he probably didn't guess he'd revealed.

He wouldn't like it that he'd exposed so much
of his inner life to her. She knew that instinctively.
He wasn't a man who confided his troubles willingly or easily. Probably no one in Bedford Creek
understood just how important this business deal of
Alex's was to all of them.

Paula stared absently out at the June sunlight slanting over the mountain, gilding the pool. Aunt Maida didn't know how crucial it was. She'd never have kept that from Paula. *"Take care of Jason."* Maida's voice rang in Paula's mind. *"Find out what's bothering that child."*

Paula found herself counting the number of times Jason had smiled. Twice the day before, when they'd been playing ball. Once today, when she'd made a happy face with syrup on his pancake.

She clasped wet hands on the edge of the sink. *Dear Father, if Maida's right, if you do have something for me to do here, please show me my task.*

"Washing-up prayers," Maida called them. She always said she could feel as close to God standing at the sink as she could in church.

Movement on the patio caught Paula's eye. Alex skirted the pool, then headed for the empty cottage the gardener had occupied, back in the days when estates like this one had live-in gardeners. As she watched from the window, he opened the door and went inside.

She'd probably never have a better chance to catch him where Jason couldn't overhear. Maybe God was answering her prayer already, giving her an opportunity to talk to Alex about Jason's needs. She dried her hands and hurried out the back.

Curiosity overtook her as she approached the cottage. What had brought Alex here? She knocked.

The door swung open promptly, but before she could see inside, Alex's tall frame blocked the space.

"Paula." He didn't sound particularly welcoming. "I'm rather busy. Can this wait?"

"I'd like to talk with you before you leave for the plant. May I come in?"

She took a step toward the door. Alex didn't back away. Instead, he stood like a solid barrier, his frown a warning signal.

"We can discuss whatever it is this evening. I really don't have time now." His tone suggested that anything she might wish to discuss was far less important than his agenda.

She fought to control her temper. She wanted to involve him in making plans for Jason, not alienate him. "I want to talk with you about Jason, and I'd like to do it where there's no chance he'll overhear." Again she made a slight movement toward the door, and again his immobility stopped her. For a moment he just looked at her, frowning.

Then he stepped out of the cottage and pulled the door closed behind him. She heard a lock snap.

She lifted her eyebrows. "I wasn't planning to break in. You didn't need to lock it."

His frown deepened. "I keep some plans I'm working on in there," he said. "The office stays locked so they won't be disturbed."

In other words, he didn't get away from work

even when he was at home. She wondered if he had any idea just how compulsive that sounded.

He took her arm, leading her a few steps away from the cottage, and her skin warmed as if she'd walked into the sunlight.

"All right, what's so important?" He shot back his shirtsleeve to consult his watch. "I have to be down at the plant in less than half an hour."

"I want to talk with you about Jason."

"You already said that. What about Jason?" That faintly defensive tone she'd noticed before threaded his voice.

Carefully, she thought. Say this carefully. "I'm a little concerned about him. I know this is a difficult time for him with Maida in the hospital, but he seems so withdrawn."

"Withdrawn?" She had the sense that his muscles tightened. Hers seemed to clench, too, as if preparing to fight or run. "My son is not withdrawn."

She tried to force herself to relax, tried to smile. "You make it sound like a communicable disease."

He didn't smile back.

"Alex, I'm just afraid he's worrying too much about things, instead of talking them over with people he trusts."

"You can't expect him to trust you immediately. He probably barely remembers you from the last time you were here."

"I realize that." *Even though I remember him, and you, as if it were yesterday.* "I didn't necessarily mean me. Is he talking to you about Maida, or about anything else that worries him?"

His face hardened. "I've already told you, I don't think it's wise to discuss illness with him. I don't want him to worry—that's why I protect him from such things."

"But—"

"He is my son, Paula. These decisions are mine to make, and I'm raising Jason the best way I know. Now if that's all, I really have to get to the plant."

She was losing him, losing the chance to make him see that Jason needed something he wasn't getting from the people in his life. There had to be something, some positive step she could take right now for that child. Maybe it was time, as her brother Keith, the football player, would say, to drop back and punt.

"What about his friends?" She blurted the words out before Alex could walk away. "I haven't seen any of Jason's friends since I've been here."

"You've only been here a couple of days." He looked harassed, as if she were a small dog nipping at his heels. "Jason has friends."

"Where are they? Wouldn't it be good for him to be playing with them every day to distract him from Maida's absence?" She had to press whatever advantage she had.

"He has friends at school."

"It's summer vacation. What does he do for friends during the summer?"

Alex gave an exasperated sigh. "We don't exactly have neighbors to run in and out, Paula."

True enough. The Caine mansion, sitting on land that seemed carved out of the hillside above the town, was alone and isolated. A steep, winding lane led from the mansion to the nearest street, far below.

"Then we ought to be making an effort to get him together with his friends, even if I have to drive him. Don't you agree?" A plan, somewhat hazy and amorphous, began to take shape in her mind.

"Yes, I suppose so." He took a step away. "Look, I have to go. You're right, Jason needs to see his friends. I'll trust you to arrange it. Do whatever you think is best."

She nodded, the plan becoming clearer by the moment. "You can count on it," she said, watching as he strode away, obviously eager to get to work. Well, she was just as eager to get to her work, now that he'd given her a green light.

Alex might be a little surprised when he found out what she thought was best for his son—and maybe for him, too.

He had just enough time to swim his laps before dinner, Alex decided as he arrived home that afternoon. He tried to ignore the pain that radiated down his leg, but it demanded attention. He might succeed in denying weakness to everyone else, but he couldn't deny it to himself.

Too much stress, too little exercise. He knew exactly what Brett would say, whether he spoke as a doctor or a friend. And Brett would be right. Alex had too many people depending on him to let physical weakness get in the way of doing what he had to do.

"Jason?" He called as he entered the center hallway, but no one answered. Perhaps Jason and Paula had gone somewhere.

He started upstairs to change, trying to push away memories of that conversation with her that morning. She'd been persistent, he'd give her that. Her face, intent and serious, formed in his mind before he could block it out. In fact, her presence seemed to linger in the house even when she wasn't here, refusing to leave him alone.

All right, he was too aware of Paula Hansen. He accepted that, he admitted it. But that didn't mean he was going to act on it. There wasn't room in his life right now for anything other than his son and the business deal that might save them. His relationship with Paula would stay strictly business. That was what he'd promised her, and that was the way it would be.

Ten minutes later, towel over his arm, he walked

out to the pool area. Paula and Jason hadn't gone anywhere; they were in the pool.

Paula glanced up, saw him and waved. Sunlight glinted on her blond hair and turned her warm skin golden. She wore a green swimsuit that matched her eyes. He swallowed with difficulty.

Hiding any suggestion of a limp, he crossed to the pool.

"This is a surprise. Jason doesn't usually like the water."

"Sure I do, Dad," Jason said quickly. But the tight grip he had on Paula's hand gave him away.

"If you want us to get out…" Paula began.

"No, of course not." He dropped the towel and stepped into the water. "There's plenty of room for all of us. I'd better get my laps in before Brett Elliot sends the exercise police after me."

Her face relaxed in a smile. "He is a good doctor, isn't he. He's been in to see Maida so much, and every time it perks her up."

"He cares." He could say more, could tell her how only Brett's determined intervention had brought him as far as he'd come in recovering from the effects of the crash.

He could, but why would he? Where had it come from, this longing to confide in Paula? She was his housekeeper. Listening to his personal troubles wasn't part of her job description.

"Well, I'd better get at it." He turned away

quickly, before he could give in to the impulse to share anything else with Paula. Before he could let his gaze linger on her smooth, honey-colored skin or the freckles that splashed across her cheeks.

Stroke, kick, stroke, kick. The familiar pattern soothed him, and he felt tight muscles gradually relax, responding to the repetitive motion and the massage of the water. When he swam, he could block out everything but the movement and the water.

At least, usually he could. Somewhere about the fifteenth lap, he realized that he wasn't letting his mind float clear. He was listening to Paula and his son.

She seemed to be coaxing Jason to trust the water to hold him up. If she succeeded, she'd be doing a better job than Alex ever had. He'd tried to get his son interested in swim lessons, but Jason had always held back. He'd finally realized the boy was afraid, and he hadn't known quite what to do about it. His own father would have bullied him into conquering the fear, but that wasn't the way he wanted to raise Jason.

"There, see?" Paula had kicked off and pushed herself through the water to Jason, then grabbed his hands. "I trust you to catch me. You want to try it?"

Alex stood at the shallow end of the pool, half

turned away from them, not wanting Jason to think he had an audience, and listened.

"I guess so."

Jason sounded reluctant. Alex wanted to intervene, wanted to tell Paula not to push the boy. But just this morning he'd told her to do what she thought was best for Jason. He shouldn't second-guess her already.

He glanced toward them. Paula didn't even seem to notice that he was there. All her attention was focused on his son. Her smile encouraged Jason, and she held out her hands to him.

"I won't let you sink, honest. I promise."

Jason nodded, shivering a little as a breeze swept across the pool. Alex saw his skinny chest rise as he took a breath. Then, his gaze fixed on Paula's face as if it were a lifeline, Jason launched himself through the water.

"All right!" Paula grabbed his hands and helped him upright. "You did it, Jason. And you didn't sink one little bit."

"I did it, didn't I." Jason grinned. "I really did it."

"Good job, Jason." There was, unaccountably, a lump in Alex's throat, along with maybe the smallest bit of jealousy that Jason had tried for Paula something he'd never tried for his father.

Jason glanced at him, startled, as if he'd forgotten

his father was in the pool. Paula held out her hand, inviting Alex to join them.

"Maybe Jason will float to you, if you promise not to let him sink." The faintest stress suggested that *promise* was the operative word.

Alex didn't need Paula to tell him how to react to his own son. He hoped his look made that clear. "Jason knows he can trust me." He held out his hands. "Come on, Jason."

His son seemed to mentally figure the distance between them. "Come a little bit closer, Dad."

He almost coaxed Jason to try it, but Paula's eyes held a warning that might as well have been shouted. He swallowed his resentment and took a giant step forward. "How's that?"

"Okay." Jason bounced a little, as if working up his nerve. Then he pushed off, face screwed up, hands reaching toward Alex.

Alex grabbed him. "Way to go, son." He grasped a small, wet shoulder. "Good job."

Jason looked up at him, all the reserve gone from his dark eyes, at least for the moment. "I did it!" He turned, reaching out for Paula, and she swam a stroke or two closer to take his hand.

"You sure did." She stood, water streaming from sun-warmed skin, and smiled at them.

The smile went straight to Alex's heart and lodged there, making one thing abundantly clear. Ignoring Paula would not be an easy thing to do.

* * *

Paula's breath caught in her throat. Did Alex have any idea how devastatingly attractive he looked at that moment? He and Jason wore identical, laughing expressions, and the tenderness in his gaze when he looked at his son made her want to cry. As for the expression in his eyes when he looked at her—no, she must be imagining that.

She had to keep her mind on her job. Right now, that meant unlocking the puzzle that was Jason, and part of the answer had just played itself out right in front of her. One of the things Jason needed, maybe the most important thing, was a closer relationship with his father.

She didn't doubt that Alex loved his son—loved him more than life itself, probably. He just didn't seem to know how important it was for a seven-year-old to feel love, not just hear the word. If only Alex were willing to listen to her, she could help him understand.

"Alex, I—"

The telephone rang, so close it startled her. Then, as Alex turned and swung out of the pool, she realized he'd brought his cellular phone out with him.

"Just one minute," he said, drying his hand and then picking up the phone.

In an instant she knew that playtime in the pool was over as far as Alex was concerned. His gaze turned inward as he concentrated on the call, and she could almost see him donning his corporate armor. Without looking back at them, still talking, he went into the house.

She tried to swallow her disappointment. Alex had business to take care of; she could understand that. It didn't have to spoil Jason's afternoon. She held out her hand to the boy.

"How about another try, Jason?"

But all the interest and happiness had gone out of Jason's small face. Shivering, he climbed out of the pool. "Don't want to."

"We don't have to go in yet," she said. "We could play a game of water polo."

"I don't like water polo." He grabbed a towel and started for the house. "I don't like swimming at all." He ran inside, slamming the door behind him.

Paula climbed slowly out of the pool. Jason might say he didn't like swimming, but she had a pretty clear idea what was bothering him. And it had much more to do with his father than with the pool.

She toweled her hair, feeling it curl over her fingers as it began to dry. She'd look like a poodle if she didn't blow-dry it, but she probably should have started dinner already. She pulled on her terry robe and headed for the kitchen.

Paula had no sooner gotten in the back door than Alex came hurrying toward her. Somehow he'd found time to pull on jeans and a knit shirt, and his dark hair was slicked back, still damp from the shower.

"Paula, thank you. That's the most interest Jason has ever shown in swimming. I'd about given up."

She clutched the robe around her, embarrassingly aware of how disheveled she must look. "I'm glad." She edged past him. "I really have to get changed and start dinner."

He shook his head, smiling. "Why are you embarrassed? I saw you in your swimsuit in the pool."

She didn't know why there was a difference between playing in the swimming pool with Jason and standing so close to Alex in the narrow hallway, but there was. And she didn't intend to say that to him.

"It's not that," she said. "I just don't want dinner to be late." She managed a smile. "My boss might not like that."

He touched a wet curl, turning it around his finger. His hand came within a millimeter of her cheek, and her skin tingled as if he'd caressed it. "Right now, your boss is very happy with you." His tone teased her. "You could probably burn the biscuits, and he wouldn't say a thing."

She wanted so badly to lean toward him. Just the slightest movement would bring them together. Her treacherous memory told her exactly how his hand would feel against her face.

She stepped back, instead. "I'll remind you of

that when I put dinner in front of you. Now, I really need to get started.''

His hand closed around her wrist. ''Just one second. I wanted to tell you that your success in the pool with Jason gave me an idea for something that might make this time a bit better for him.''

''That's great.'' Was she really going to get her wish so easily? Had Alex seen how much it meant to Jason when the boy felt his father's encouragement?

''One of the high school coaches gives swimming lessons to kids in the summer. I hadn't even considered hiring him, since Jason wasn't interested, but now I think that's just the thing.''

''Swimming lessons?'' Her heart fell. Jason didn't need lessons from a stranger. He needed his father.

''It's perfect. Lessons will give him something to think about and keep his mind off Maida.''

''Alex, I'm not sure that's what Jason needs right now. Maybe it would be better if you taught him.''

''Me?'' He looked at her as if she were crazy. ''I don't have time to do that now. Besides, kids usually learn better from someone other than a parent.''

''Jason was excited because you were there. I'm not sure he'd be equally happy about swimming with someone else.'' In fact, given the way the child had left the pool, she was sure he wouldn't.

But Alex wasn't listening. He turned, headed toward the front of the house. "I'll try and reach him now. Thanks, Paula."

"Alex, I don't think…"

It was too late. He'd already charged through the swinging door.

Typical, so very typical. If Alex approached his business with that energy and directness, he'd undoubtedly saved the company several times over. He hadn't even heard anything she'd said.

She ran her hand through wet curls, seeming to feel again Alex's gentle touch. She forced her mind away from that moment in which they'd stood so close. She couldn't afford to let herself think about that.

She'd asked God to show her what she was supposed to be doing. And now God had given her the answer, in language so clear she couldn't possibly ignore it.

God had given her a chance to make up for the mistakes she'd made the last time she was here. Maybe that was why her memories had come back when they had. God had known she'd need them to accomplish her task.

No matter how difficult it was, she'd have to put her own needs and feelings aside for the time being. She had to help bring the prickly, private father and son closer together. And she suspected she really had her work cut out for her.

Chapter Six

"Are you sure this is going to be all right with my dad?" Jason's dark eyes filled with concern the next afternoon.

Paula tried to push down her matching concern and speak with a confidence she didn't feel. "Your dad won't care one way or the other if I have a pet in the cottage. And I need something to keep me company while Aunt Maida is in the hospital." She opened the door to the animal shelter. "Come on. You've got to help me pick out just the right puppy."

The long room was filled with kennels on either side, and their entry signaled a chorus of yips and howls. Every dog there seemed to be proclaiming, *Pick me, pick me!*

"So many dogs." Jason's tone was awed. "How can you decide?"

She ruffled his hair. "That's why you're along. When we find the right one, we'll know."

And when Alex found out about this, what would he think? She tried to assure herself that what she'd said to Jason was true. Technically, this puppy was going to be hers, at least until Alex saw that it made a difference in his son's life.

Besides, he'd said she should use her own judgment about getting Jason together with friends. Somehow she felt a puppy might be just the right friend for Jason now—a creature that would depend on him and love him unconditionally.

And if she ended up having to take the dog back to Baltimore, she'd deal with that when the time came. But with that in mind, maybe a small breed would be best. She could just imagine what her roommate would say if she came home with a huge dog.

"Oh, Paula, look." Jason leaned against a large pen filled with puppies of every description, all barking and tumbling over each other.

The attendant smiled. "Shall I let the two of you into the puppy pen to make your choice?"

Paula tried to dismiss the image of Alex's frowning face. "Let's do it."

They were engulfed in a melee of puppies the instant they entered the pen. Laughing, Paula removed a beagle from her shoe. The little cocker spaniel might work. It shouldn't get too big. She looked at Jason. "What do you think?"

Jason was on his knees. A fluffy yellow pup had planted suspiciously large paws on his shoulder and was licking his face. The boy looked up, his eyes filled with longing that clutched her heart and wouldn't let go. "This one, Paula. Please, this has to be the one."

"What is it?" she asked the attendant, a sense of foreboding filling her.

The girl grinned. "A yellow Labrador. Great dogs."

"Large dogs." She banished Alex's face firmly from her mind. "Okay. He's the one." Jason's joy was worth any number of confrontations with his father.

A few hours later, she wasn't so sure. She hurried to finish dinner preparations, her stomach tied in knots over Alex's impending return. Jason and the puppy, playing on the kitchen floor, slowed her down, but she didn't feel comfortable letting them out of her sight yet.

She scooped the puppy out of her way as she bent to open the oven door. "Here, Jason. Keep him away from the hot stove. We don't want him to get hurt." She lifted out the casserole dish. "Have you thought of a good name yet?"

Jason frowned, forehead wrinkling in an imitation of his father. "Goldy would be nice, 'cause of his color. But that sounds like a girl's name, and he might not like that."

She suppressed a smile. "What about Nugget? You know, like a gold nugget."

"Nugget." He tried the name, then tickled the puppy. "You like that, boy? You want to be Nugget?"

The puppy wiggled, licking his face.

"He likes it!" Jason declared. "His name is Nugget."

Paula's heart turned over at the sheer happiness in his face. She hadn't seen Jason look like that since she'd come here. His closed-off, somber expression had vanished. Now he looked like any normal seven-year-old should. Surely Alex would see that and would understand what she was trying to do.

"I'm going to carry this into the dining room." She picked up the casserole dish. "You hold Nugget so he doesn't get out."

Two things happened at once. Paula pushed through the door between the kitchen and the dining room, and Jason lost his hold on the puppy's collar. Paula felt a brush of fur against her legs, then lifted the casserole out of the way as Jason charged after the puppy.

"Grab him, Jason!" She deposited the casserole

dish on the waiting trivet and dived after the golden blur. "Don't let him get out."

She skidded across the marble floor of the hallway in Jason's wake. Her feet tangled with the throw rug; she lost her balance and sat down heavily. Nugget danced just out of her reach—his paws scratching a pair of highly polished brown wingtips.

Alex, who'd just come in the front door, bent over and picked up the wriggling puppy. He held it at arm's length, and his expression looked just as ominous as she'd imagined it might.

"What, exactly, is this?"

The glib explanation she'd prepared died in her throat. "A puppy."

His frown deepened. "I can see that it's a puppy. Whose puppy is it, and what is it doing in my front hall?"

She scrambled to her feet, trying to find some reasonable words.

"He's Paula's, Dad." Jason gathered the fur ball carefully into his arms. "I helped her pick him out. His name is Nugget."

"Nugget." Alex's expression didn't lighten, but she thought she saw him ruffle the puppy's ears before he pinned her with that frowning gaze. "Tell me exactly why you need a dog *now,* of all times."

"Well, I..." All her assurance shriveled at that frown.

"Paula gets lonesome in the cottage by herself at night," Jason piped up. "She needs Nugget to keep her company."

"She does, does she?" Alex's gaze softened slightly as he looked at his son. "Well, why don't you take Nugget out on the lawn for a while. Paula and I have to talk."

"Okay." Laden down with puppy, Jason trudged to the swinging door. "I'll get his leash, Paula. And I'll be really careful."

"I know you will." Suppressing the urge to run out the door after them, she turned to Alex. "If there's a problem with my having a pet in the cottage…"

His dark brows lifted. "But he's not in the cottage, is he?"

She couldn't deny that. "He's so little, I didn't want to leave him alone. He and Jason were playing in the kitchen while I cooked supper. I never intended for him to get into this part of the house."

Alex leaned a little closer, and she had the sudden feeling that he was using up all the air in the hallway. How else could she explain her sudden breathlessness?

"You're lonely in the cottage at night?" His tone made it a question. "Ms. Independence, the woman who's not afraid of anything?"

She shrugged. "Everyone's afraid of something." *What are you afraid of, Alex, besides losing the company? What keeps those barriers between you and the rest of the world?*

He studied her, his gaze so probing that it was as if he could see right through her. "Who picked out the puppy?" he asked abruptly.

"Jason did."

He lifted an eyebrow. "I see. And who named the puppy?"

She had to stiffen her muscles to keep from fidgeting. "Jason and I both did."

"I see," he said again. His expression didn't change, but she realized that was amusement lurking in his dark eyes. She was right—he did look straight through her. At least he wasn't demanding she take the dog back.

"Really, Alex, he won't be any trouble at all," she said quickly. "I'll keep him out of your way. I promise." She held her breath.

"I did tell you to do whatever you thought best for my son, didn't I? But this wasn't quite what I had in mind."

She chose her words carefully, not wanting to imply that she knew better than he what Jason needed. "I just thought it might help to take his mind off things right now. There's nothing like a puppy for occupying a small boy."

A smile tugged the corners of his lips. "And then there's the little matter of keeping you company at night." His voice dropped. "We don't want you to get lonely."

"N-no I won't," she stammered. He was too close, way too close. With the spicy scent of his aftershave teasing her senses, she could hardly think coherently. She took a step back, putting some space between them. "And I will keep him out of your hair."

Alex gave a quick nod. "I don't like disorder in my life, Paula. See that the puppy doesn't bring any, and we'll both be happy."

She wanted to point out that disorder was a chronic and even desirable state when it came to puppies and small boys, but she was afraid to press her luck. At least Nugget could stay. "I'll see to it."

Alex stopped her as she started toward the kitchen. "One other thing, Paula. I have a church committee meeting here tonight at eight. I'd like you to serve coffee and dessert." He raised his eyebrows. "Unless you'll be busy puppy-sitting then."

"Coffee and dessert, right." Her mind scrambled among the possibilities, coming up empty. "I'll take care of it. And dinner will be ready in five minutes."

When Jason and the puppy came into the kitchen in answer to her call, she was frantically leafing through Maida's wooden recipe box. How could

Alex calmly expect dessert to be served to guests, just like that? What would her aunt have done?

"I'm ready for supper," Jason announced. "What are you doing?"

"Looking for a dessert I can fix in no time flat. Your dad wants me to serve something to a committee he has coming here tonight." She hoped she didn't sound as panicky as she felt. If she'd known ahead of time, if she hadn't spent the afternoon at the animal shelter...

Jason rinsed his hands at the sink. He grabbed for the tea towel and knocked the recipe box over.

Paula caught it. "Careful. I don't want that to get broken."

"It's just an old box. We could get Maida a new one."

"I couldn't do that." She ran her hand along the box's polished surface. "I gave this to Maida when I was about your age. I did chores for a month to earn enough money to buy it."

"Really?" The concept was obviously out of his experience.

"Really. And I hoped just now I'd find a fast, easy dessert recipe in it, but I didn't."

"Why don't you call Ingrid's?"

She looked at him blankly. "Who's Ingrid and how can she help?"

Jason giggled. "Ingrid's a bakery. It's the one Maida uses for stuff like that. You just call and tell them what you want, and they bring it to the house. Then you put it on a nice plate and serve it.''

You put it on a nice plate and serve it. ''That sounds like a terrific plan.'' Always assuming the bakery would still be open, of course. But during tourist season, every shop stayed open late. She wasn't sure whether she was happier over the answer to her problem or the fact that it had come from Jason. ''Thanks, Jason. You've really helped me.''

''It's okay.'' A faint flush colored his cheeks. He bent to say something to Nugget, then scurried into the dining room.

The puppy sat back on his haunches and stared at her, his tongue lolling in a silly doggy grin.

''I think we're making progress, Nugget,'' she told him.

With Jason, anyway. As for Alex...well, that was another story. The memory of those moments in the hallway flooded over her. If she could keep her feelings under control, she'd be better off. But that seemed impossible where Alex was concerned.

Alex pushed chairs into a semicircle in the library for the church fund-raising committee. He ought to be concentrating on the agenda for the meeting or on the appropriate amount for the donation he'd undoubtedly be expected to make. Instead, he was thinking about Paula.

Those moments in the hallway had gotten totally out of control. He seemed to stand back and look at himself in surprise. He'd been *flirting* with her— there was no other word that fit. It was the last thing in the world he should have been doing.

He saw again the wave of warm, peachy color filling her cheeks, saw the way her eyes sparked with indignation or clouded when she tried to think up a reasonable explanation for an unreasonable action.

He was spending entirely too much time thinking about Paula Hansen, he decided. All right, granted she had an appeal for him that he couldn't begin to explain. He still couldn't risk giving in to that attraction.

His mouth tightened. When his wife had walked away from their marriage and from their son, she'd made it clear that his small-town life wasn't what she'd expected from a rich man. He hadn't measured up for her, just as he'd never measured up for his father. He could accept that, and he could build a life without a romantic relationship.

And even if he wanted to expose himself to that kind of hurt again, he wouldn't risk Jason's happiness. His son had had too many people disappear from his young life. Jason wasn't going to be put in a position of learning to love someone and then having that someone leave.

Maybe Paula wouldn't leave, a treacherous voice whispered in his mind.

She did before, he reminded himself.

His rational side assured him this was the right decision. Anything between Paula and him had to be strictly business, for all their sakes. He'd put a guard on his emotions, and that little incident in the hallway wouldn't happen again.

The doorbell rang, and he went to let his guests in.

An hour later, the fund-raising committee had made progress on plans for the new campaign, and he had begun to wonder what had happened to Paula and the coffee. Almost as soon as the thought formed in his mind, the door opened. Paula, burdened with a large tray, entered.

"Why don't we take a break," he suggested. "I see Paula has brought some refreshments."

He had to smile. Paula, apparently determined to be the perfect hostess, had changed from her usual jeans to a skirt and blouse. He couldn't help noticing that the sunny yellow of the blouse brought out the gold flecks in her eyes.

You weren't going to notice things like that, he lectured himself. Before he could move, Mitch Donovan had leaped to his feet to take the tray from Paula.

"Let me give you a hand with that." Mitch balanced the tray while she cleared a spot for it on the cherry table against the wall. "It's good to see you again, Paula."

Paula looked a little startled at suddenly being the center of attention. Maybe it didn't fit in with her idea of a housekeeper's role. If so, she'd forgotten something about Bedford Creek, Alex thought.

"I think you know most of these people," Alex said. "You remember Gwen Forrester."

The older woman smiled. "How is Maida doing?" Her voice was warm with sympathy. "I just heard about her surgery. It's just like her to keep it a secret. She never wants to accept help. I plan to go and see her tomorrow, if you think she's ready for company."

Paula barely had time to nod before Pastor Richie interrupted. "I'm sure she'd love it, Gwen. I went in today but she'd like to see someone besides me. And Paula, of course."

"You know Pastor Simon Richie," Alex went on. He'd gotten used to interruptions with this group. "And you remember Mitch Donovan, our police chief."

Mitch smiled as he helped himself to a cup of coffee. "I remember Paula from when she was Jason's nanny."

"And this is Ellie Wayne, our church organist." As people got up and moved toward the coffee service, Alex introduced the last member of the committee. Ellie nodded, her wary manner with strangers disguising her generous heart.

"You'll be coming to worship with us on Sunday, I hope." Simon Richie sugared his coffee generously. "Maida never misses, and she'll want to know everything that happens."

Before Paula could respond, Gwen Forrester began giving her suggestions for Maida's therapy. Alex exchanged a smiling look with Mitch. Since Gwen's daughter had married Bedford Creek's only doctor, she had begun to consider herself an authority on all things medical.

Mitch crossed the room to join him. "Nice to have Paula back again, isn't it?" he said softly.

Alex tried for a neutral tone. "I'm sure it's eased Maida's mind, having her here."

"Maida's, huh." Mitch lifted a quizzical brow. "Actually, it wasn't Maida I had in mind."

Most people in Bedford Creek wouldn't probe into a Caine's personal affairs, but Mitch wasn't most people. He'd saved Alex's life, once upon a time. Maybe he felt that gave him the right to ask what others wouldn't.

"She's good with Jason," Alex said, gaze fixed on Paula. She was laughing at some comment of Simon's, and he felt a stab of what seemed like jealousy. "Irrational." He stiffened with annoyance when he realized he'd said it aloud.

Mitch eyed him with some amusement. "What's

irrational? The fact that she's good with Jason? Or are you talking about her effect on you?''

"Neither.'' He turned his back on the small group by the fireplace. "Paula's an employee, nothing more.''

"Try that on someone who doesn't know you as well as I do,'' Mitch said. "You're attracted to her.''

He knew Mitch would see through anything less than the truth. "I shouldn't be,'' he said.

"Why? She's free, you're free. There's no reason—''

"Alex!'' Gwen's call was peremptory, and he swung toward her. "You have to convince Paula to come to the church picnic Saturday. After all, you and Jason are coming. She can come with you.''

Paula's cheeks were flushed. "I'm not sure that's a good idea.''

"Nonsense,'' Gwen said briskly, her gray curls bouncing with emphasis. "You'll have to fix something, anyway, so you might as well come and enjoy it.''

Paula glanced at Alex, and he wasn't sure what was in her eyes. Embarrassment at being singled out? He spoke before the silence could become awkward. "We'd like to have you join us, if you want.''

"There, that's settled.'' Gwen beamed. "I'm going to make my apple-crumb pies. Ellie, what are you bringing?''

Alex glanced toward Mitch, to find his old friend regarding him with amusement.

''Is that a date?'' Mitch asked softly.

''Certainly not,'' he said. He saw Paula slipping out of the library and knew he had to speak with her before the situation became awkward. ''Excuse me.''

He caught up with Paula at the kitchen door. She looked at him somewhat distantly.

''Is there something else I can bring you?'' she asked.

''What? No, that's fine.'' He frowned, not sure how to say what he felt he must. ''Look, I know Gwen's friendliness can be a little overpowering at times. If you don't want to go to that picnic, you certainly don't have to. I can make some excuse.''

She looked at him steadily for several moments, and for once her usually readable face didn't give anything away. ''Does that mean you don't want me to go?''

''Of course not!'' He always seemed to say the wrong thing to her. Or maybe she always took what he said the wrong way. He grasped her arm, and immediately knew he shouldn't have. He could feel her smooth skin warm at his touch. ''Look, I didn't mean it that way at all. I just meant that you shouldn't feel obligated. It's not part of your job.

But Jason and I would enjoy having you come with us. Please.''

A dimple appeared at the corner of her mouth. ''I guess we should leave Nugget at home.''

''Definitely.'' He smiled. ''We'll give him a dog biscuit to make up for it.''

''It's a deal.'' Still smiling, she turned and disappeared through the swinging door.

He stood for a moment, not yet ready to go back in the library and face Mitch's inquisitive gaze. What exactly had just happened here? He'd intended to keep his distance from Paula. He'd assured himself that what happened before wouldn't happen again. And instead, he'd committed himself to a social event with her.

It's not a date, he repeated to himself. He was just being hospitable to someone who was, after all, a stranger here.

He had to believe that was all there was to it.

Chapter Seven

By the next afternoon, Paula had been over the events of the previous day a hundred times in her mind, and she was no closer to deciding what they meant. One moment Alex had barked orders at her, the next he'd seemed to want...what? Friendship? Something more? She just didn't know.

"Come on, kids." She waved to Jason and Kristie, Gwen Forrester's granddaughter; they were playing with Nugget on the lawn near the pool. "You can go back in the water now. Jason, better put Nugget in his pen."

Having Kristie join Jason's swim lessons had been a stroke of genius, if Paula did think so herself. If Alex wouldn't teach his son, at least Jason would have the company of a playmate. Kristie, a year younger than Jason, was quick and adventurous. She'd stayed after the lesson to play, with the promise that they'd go back in the pool again later in the afternoon.

Paula sat on the pool edge, dangling her feet in the water, and watched the children play with a float in the shallow end. Timing was everything, she decided. Alex had arrived home moments before, and, true to his routine, he was changing to swim his laps. When he got to the pool, he'd discover he had company.

She stretched, enjoying the sun's heat on her back. Maybe she couldn't, and probably shouldn't, do anything about Alex's attitude toward her. But she ought to be able to influence how he behaved with his son.

This will work, Lord. Won't it? If I can just involve Alex with Jason, help him to loosen up and relax with the boy, it would be so good for both of them.

Her prayers lately always revolved around the Caine family, in one way or another. She watched Jason pull the float through the water, making motorboat noises and sending ripples across the surface. Jason seemed to be keeping his word to her. There had been no incidents with matches. And he certainly smiled much more since Nugget had come into his life. Now if she could build a few bridges between him and his father, she'd feel she was accomplishing something.

Alex came out the back door, saw them in the pool, and hesitated for a moment before striding toward them. She suppressed a smile. Did Alex realize just how predictable he was? He treated swimming the way he did every other task in his life, approaching it with a determined work ethic. Of course, his swimming was therapy, but there was no reason why it couldn't also be fun.

He crossed the patio toward her, and a familiar tingle swept along her skin. *Keep your mind on the task,* she ordered herself.

"Hi." She looked up. He loomed above her on the pool deck, blocking the sun. "You have some company in the pool today. You don't mind, do you?"

"It's fine." To her surprise, he dropped his towel and sat down next to her. "I didn't know Kristie was coming."

Was there an undertone suggesting he should have known? He had told her to make arrangements about Jason's friends, she reminded herself.

"Gwen and I talked about it when she was leaving last night," she said. "She'd been looking for something to occupy her granddaughter now that school's out, and she thought swimming lessons would be perfect."

Alex's face relaxed as he watched the little carrottop try to balance a beach ball on her head. "She's a cute kid."

Her breath caught. That was how he'd looked with his friend Mitch the night before—off guard, as if he'd put away for a while the burden of being who he was. Why couldn't he seem to do that with his own son?

Maybe because it mattered too much. She thought again of those moments when he'd confided his concerns about the company. Alex was so intent on providing the proper lifestyle for his little boy that he didn't have time to play with him.

She remembered only too well the formal, intimidating presence of Alex's father. She'd been terrified of earning the elder Caine's disapproval on her visits. He certainly hadn't provided a role model for relaxed parenting. And like Jason, Alex had grown up without the softening presence of the mother who'd died when he was young. Maybe he just didn't know how to be closer to his son.

"Come on," she said, sliding into the water, cool after the heat radiating from the flagstones. She held out her hand in invitation. "Let's help the kids practice what they've learned."

For a moment she thought he'd follow her, but then he shook his head. "I have to get my laps in."

Of course he did. She tried not to feel disappointment. Changes wouldn't come in a day.

He walked toward the deep end, then paused, looking at her. "By the way, did the puppy serve his purpose?"

The sudden change of topic startled her, particularly since she'd been busy noticing the breadth of his shoulders. "What do you mean?"

"Your loneliness," he said. "Remember? You needed the puppy so you wouldn't be lonely in the cottage by yourself."

"Right." She couldn't stop a grin. "I'd have to say, he is a mixed blessing. He yipped until I gave up and let him spend the night on my bed."

He glanced toward the pen, where Nugget slept curled up on a rug. "It sounds as if that puppy knew how to get exactly what he wanted." He dove into the pool.

Maybe she could stand to cool off a bit herself. She submerged, then came up beside Jason's float, tilting her head back to let the water run off her hair.

"Why don't we practice your swimming," she suggested. Maybe when Alex saw what was going on, he'd be drawn in, just as he had their first time in the pool.

For the next few minutes she worked with the kids, careful to keep it fun. Kristie was more adventurous in the water than Jason, and her presence pushed him. He wouldn't want a girl, especially not a younger girl, to do something better than he did.

"Okay, let's practice blowing bubbles." She dipped her mouth under the water's surface, watching them closely.

Kristie put her whole face in, then came up sputtering. Jason, a little more cautious, screwed his eyes closed before trying.

"Good job!" Paula said when he'd come up again.

"Very good." Alex's voice, close behind her, made her jump. She'd been so intent on the children, she hadn't noticed his approach.

"I think putting your face in the water is the toughest part of learning to swim," she said, determined not to let him rattle her. "You two are doing great after just one lesson."

"I want to swim like you and my dad," Jason declared, bouncing on his toes. "I want to do regular strokes and go in the deep water and dive."

"You will." She pushed wet dark hair back from his eyes. "Give yourself a little time. Everything takes practice."

"Is Paula a good swimmer?" Alex gave her an innocent look. "I haven't seen her do anything but blow bubbles."

"I could probably give you a run for your money," she said.

"Is that a dare?"

"A race!" Kristie hopped up and down, clapping. "Have a race!"

"A race," Jason echoed. "Down to the end and back."

"Willing to put it to the test?" Alex's dark eyes held a challenge.

"You bet." She mentally measured the distance to the end of the pool. She might have overreached herself. "Jason, you be the starter."

Jason pulled himself to the pool deck and stood above them, raising his hand. "Ready, set, go!" he shouted.

Paula plunged into a shallow dive, surfacing with a strong, smooth stroke. It would take more than her best race to beat Alex. She churned through the water, glimpsing him from the corner of her eye. He didn't seem to be exerting himself at all.

They reached the end in nearly a dead heat, flipped and started back. *Outclassed,* she thought, watching him forge ahead of her effortlessly. She was definitely outclassed.

By the time she reached the end, he was standing there, smiling at her. She came up beside him.

"No fair," she gasped. "You're not even out of breath."

He seized her wet hands and pulled her upright. "Why is that unfair?" He grinned. "Because you lost? Maybe you'd like a handicap—say, three strokes?"

"More like five or six." She clung to his arm for a moment, getting her balance and her breath. Beyond Alex, she saw the children watching them. Kristie was grinning and clapping her hands. But

Jason—Jason wore an expression she couldn't interpret.

She glanced up at Alex, to find he watched her equally closely. His expression was just as difficult to read, but whatever it meant, it made her heart contract.

"I don't want to!" Jason ran out of the kitchen the next afternoon, slamming the door behind him.

Paula sighed and bent to ruffle the puppy's ears. "Looks as if we've lost our charm, Nugget."

He woofed softly, and she almost thought his eyes reflected her own disappointment.

She'd been so sure she was on the right track with Jason. Now she regretted that her daily reports to Maida had been so optimistic. She'd hit a roadblock with the boy, and she didn't know what to do about it.

Since she and Alex had raced, since she'd caught Jason watching them with that odd expression, the boy had been difficult—sullen, locked away from her as if their growing friendship had never been. He didn't even seem to take pleasure in the puppy. Everything she'd suggested, including time in the swimming pool, had been met the same way. *"I don't want to."*

She heard the front door open and close—*Alex*—and bent to put Nugget back in his pen. The puppy whimpered a bit, then began to chew on a toy.

I know how you feel, she told him silently. *I have to do something I don't want to do, too.*

But Alex had a right to know things weren't going well with his son, and she had a responsibility to tell him. She walked slowly to the swinging door and pushed through to the front of the house.

Alex stood in the wide center hallway, leafing through the mail she'd put on the heavy mahogany table. He glanced up at her step and smiled.

That smile had a regrettable tendency to take her breath away. "You're home from the plant early," she said, determined not to let him know his presence had an effect on her. "Is something wrong?"

"On the contrary." He dropped the envelopes back onto the table and came toward her. "Everything is remarkably good."

He looked lighter, as if a burden had been lifted from his shoulders.

"Really? What's happening?" She could use some good news to distract her from her worries about Jason and from her dread of telling Alex.

"I finished up my talks with Klemmer today."

Klemmer. It took her a moment to remember the representative of the Swiss firm—the man she'd nearly hit with a fly ball.

"And that's good?" she asked.

"More than good. He liked the plans I presented to him and recommended the firm to his company.

His boss will arrive next week to negotiate the deal.''

"Alex, that is good news." Without intending to, she reached out to him. He held both her hands in a firm, warm grip. For a moment they stood, hands clasped, very close together. Then she took a step back.

He released her immediately. "Yes, it is good. Not settled yet, of course, but they wouldn't come all this way if they didn't like what we have to offer."

"If it goes through—"

"It has to go through." His eyes darkened. "It's our last chance. So everything has to go perfectly."

She felt her nerves tense at his tone. Somehow she thought she was about to meet a hurdle. "Which 'everything' did you have in mind?"

"Among other things, I have to entertain them. I thought a small dinner party a week from Friday. Nothing too large, no more than twenty people."

She managed to keep herself from gasping. "Twenty?"

"We'll use a caterer, of course."

She could breathe again. No one expected her to cook for twenty.

"And we'll have the cleaners here an extra time," he went on. "Come to the library, and I'll give you all the information you'll need."

She followed him, trying to swallow her apprehension. She'd said she could do this. Now she had to live up to her word.

Alex riffled through a file before holding it out to her. Naturally he would have a file on entertaining. She thought again of her method of having guests, which usually consisted of ordered-in pizza. No, she was definitely out of her league now.

"That should have all the information you'll need, but if there's anything you don't understand, please ask me. I don't want any mistakes."

She held the folder, trying to think of a question to begin with, out of the many that crowded her mind. "Where are we going to seat that many people?"

He beckoned her to follow him again, and she trailed after him across the hall to the dining room.

"With the leaves in, the table seats sixteen. If there are more, the caterers will set up small tables. We'll talk about place cards and table arrangement when it gets a bit closer." He frowned at the heavy mahogany chairs, large enough to dwarf a normal human. "This room is tricky to arrange. I've always hated this furniture. The pieces we're making at the plant now are much more attractive."

She stared at him for a moment. "I don't understand. If you feel that way about it, why on earth don't you replace this…stuff?" She'd almost said *ugly stuff,* but caught herself in time.

"I couldn't do that." His response seemed almost automatic.

"Why not? It's your house."

His gaze lingered on the heavy oil portrait of his grandfather that hung over the dining room fireplace. "Sometimes I find that hard to believe."

His words were so quiet, he almost seemed to be speaking to himself. She wanted to argue, but instinctively she knew it wouldn't do any good. She'd been wrong. It wasn't his house, not in the way she understood those words. It was the Caine mansion, and right now Alex looked as if that were a heavy burden.

She frowned down at the folder. She had come into the hall intending to confide her worries about his son. But Alex already had his hands full. Maybe she should hold her tongue and try to handle this herself. Perhaps in another day Jason would regain his smile. *Coward,* a small voice said in her mind.

"I'll get started on this." She waved the folder.

Alex turned toward her, seeming to shake off the clouds that surrounded him. "Thank you." He reached out to clasp her hand again. The warmth of his grip shimmered along her skin.

"For what? It's my job." It was hard to sound casual when her heart clenched at his closeness.

"For being here. For helping me." His fingers moved caressingly along the back of her hand. "I'm glad you're back."

She wasn't sure she actually walked back to the kitchen. It felt much more like floating. She didn't want to look too closely at what she was feeling, because that might make it vanish, like mist on the mountain burned off by the sun.

Clutching the folder, she pushed through the door into the kitchen—and came to a halt. Nugget slept in his pen. The sauce she'd started for dinner simmered on the stove. But Aunt Maida's recipe box lay in the middle of the floor, broken into pieces.

Alex put another weight into place on the machine and slid onto the seat, hooking his legs behind the padded bar. Maybe if he pushed his body hard enough, he could keep his emotions at bay.

Ten repetitions later, he knew it wasn't working. His injured leg complained at the added weight, but that wasn't what bothered him.

Paula had caught him off guard. He'd told himself he had neither the time nor the inclination to get involved with her. He'd promised her that what happened the last time she was here wouldn't happen again. But each time he was near her, it became more difficult to keep that promise.

He forced himself into another set of reps, gritting his teeth against the pain. Brett would say Alex was pushing too hard. But Brett, newly married to the physician's assistant in his office, wasn't fighting a wave of longing for something he'd never have. He tried to remember feeling this way for his wife, but he couldn't. This was something new.

Is it so impossible? The treacherous question slid into his mind and refused to be dislodged. He'd convinced himself that happily-ever-after didn't exist, but his closest friends seemed to have found it.

He concentrated on his exercises, trying to bury the thought. It refused to be buried.

"Alex?"

The weights clanged down as he swung toward the sound. He hadn't heard Paula come in, but there she was, looking around the exercise room his friends had created in the old conservatory.

"I'm sorry. I shouldn't interrupt you when you're working out." She looked as if she wanted to back right out the door.

"Don't worry about it." He slid off the machine, willing his knee not to waver at the punishment he'd been dealing it. He grabbed a towel, feeling a wave of embarrassment at being caught this way. "I was about done anyway."

"I... There's something I need to talk with you about."

Whatever it was, she clearly didn't want to bring it up. He could almost see the reluctance surrounding her.

"All right." He tossed the towel over the machine. "If it's something about the party, we can go over the notes together." He was astounded at the amount of pleasure generated by that thought. Paula hadn't just caught him off guard—she'd gotten under his skin.

"No, it's not the party. It's this—"

She held something out to him. Frowning, he crossed the room to her.

"That's Maida's recipe box, isn't it? What happened to it?" The wooden box that always sat on the counter next to the stove had been broken into several pieces.

"I'm afraid Jason broke it."

Her gravity seemed all out of proportion to the event. He took the pieces from her, turning them over in his hands. "I'd say, get a new box, but I know Maida prized this one." He smiled at her. "Because you gave it to her, as I recall. I think it can be fixed."

"That's not the point." She looked at the box, then up at him. "When I said Jason broke it, I didn't mean it was an accident. He broke it on purpose."

For a long moment he could only stare at her. Then anger kicked in. "What are you talking about? Why on earth would you think that?"

"I don't think it, I know it."

There was no matching anger in her face, only sorrow.

"Alex, I'm sorry. I feel like a talebearer, but I didn't think I should handle this on my own. Jason was angry—he's been angry all day. And he broke the box deliberately. He told me.''

He wanted to say he didn't believe it, but he couldn't. "Why? Why was he angry?''

She took an audible breath. "He wouldn't tell me, but I think I know.'' Peachy color flooded her cheeks. "He was watching us yesterday, in the pool. When we were…when we were close to each other. I think it bothered him. He's been angry ever since.''

"I can't accept that.'' The words were out before he thought about it. "You must be wrong, about all of this. My son doesn't behave that way.''

A spark of anger lit her eyes at that. "Why? Because he's a Caine? Because Caines don't have normal human feelings?''

Whatever softness he'd felt toward her was wiped from the slate now. He leaned toward her. "I know my son better than you do. He's been taught what appropriate behavior is.''

"Appropriate—Alex, he's a little boy, and he's hurting.'' Her voice rose, impassioned. "For some reason, he was bothered by seeing us together. I don't know why, but I know we can't ignore it.''

"I don't intend to ignore it.'' His grip tightened on the pieces of the box, but he kept his voice cool and controlled. "Jason is my responsibility, not yours. I'll take care of the situation, if it exists. I don't care to discuss it with you any further.''

She jerked back as if he'd struck her. "Fine." She was as pale now as she'd been flushed earlier. "I'd nearly forgotten. I'm just the housekeeper. You handle it."

She whirled and nearly ran out of the room.

Chapter Eight

This picnic was going to be no fun at all, Paula decided as she sat next to Alex in the car. At least, not if her enjoyment depended on the status of her relationship with Alex.

She glanced across at him, but if he felt her gaze, Alex didn't respond. Meanwhile, Jason moped in the back seat.

No fun at all.

"I'll bet lots of your friends will be at the picnic," she told Jason, trying to sound cheerful. After all, somebody had to.

"I wanted to bring Nugget." His lower lip came out in a pout. "He'd like a picnic."

Alex had flatly refused to bring the puppy, with good reason.

"Don't you think a picnic would be too exciting

for a puppy?'' she asked. ''I know you'll enjoy it, but Nugget is still just a baby. He might be frightened of all the noise and people.''

Jason clearly hadn't considered that. His gaze met hers in the rearview mirror. ''But he'd be with me. He wouldn't be scared if he was with me. Besides, there'd be lots of good stuff to eat.''

''For people, not for dogs,'' Alex pointed out. ''Remember what the vet told Paula. Only puppy food is good for puppies.''

''That's right.'' She welcomed the opportunity to agree with Alex on something, after the battle royal they'd had several days earlier. ''You wouldn't want him to get sick.''

''I guess.'' Jason acted reluctant to give up his grievance. ''Can I give him a treat when we get home?''

''Sure.'' She smiled at him in the mirror, and after a moment got a hint of a smile in return.

At least her relationship with Jason had settled down. He wasn't quite as open as he'd been, but now he played with the puppy and went back in the pool. Whatever had been bothering him, whatever had led to his breaking the recipe box, he seemed to have gotten control of his feelings. Like his father, Jason always had to be in control.

Control was certainly the defining word when it came to the Caine men. Alex had been rigidly polite to her since their quarrel. Maybe if she apologized for her outburst, things would get back to normal.

No, she couldn't do that. She probably hadn't been very tactful, but she'd said what needed to be said, and there was no one else to do that.

Alex stopped the car at the bottom of the steep lane, waiting while a cluster of tourists crossed the street, heading for the parking lot along the river. One woman carried a handmade quilt encased in a plastic bag over her arm, while another juggled three bags from Ellie Wayne's gift shop.

"Now you see why we have the picnic in the evening." Alex nodded toward the tourists. "The shops will close soon. No one would want to risk losing business during the tourist season."

It was the first conversational thing he'd said to her since their argument. Maybe that meant he was ready to put the disagreement behind them.

"I guess if you run a shop like Ellie's, you probably have to make money while you can."

He nodded. "There's not much market for handmade baskets and dried flowers in the middle of winter." He shot a sideways glance at her that was almost a smile, and the tension inside her began to ease. "Bedford Creek tends to hibernate in the off-season."

He turned up the steep street that led to Grace Church. From the Caine mansion, the church steeple was clearly visible across the narrow valley.

Maida had told her that an earlier Caine had do-
nated the land for the church and even paid for the
steeple, so he could have a good view of it from
his windows. It took a bit longer to drive there,
down and up the narrow, hilly streets, than it would
take a sparrow to fly.

Bedford Creek seemed crammed into its tight
valley, spreading upward from the river because
there was no other place for it to go. Above the
town the mountain ridge, dark with hemlocks, cut
off the sky.

Paula looked out at narrow clapboard houses
whose colorful window boxes were filled with pan-
sies and ageratum. Bedford Creek dressed in its finest for the tourists who came to enjoy the mountain
scenery and buy at the quilt store, the basket shop,
the bakery, the candlemaker's. In addition to Alex's
factory, tourism was the town's only source of in
come. Could it get by on that if the factory failed?
She doubted it. No wonder Alex felt such a burden.

He pulled into the church parking lot. "Looks as
if we'll have a good turnout." His unexpected smile
erased the last vestige of tension from their quarrel.
"Enjoy yourself, Paula. You're not here as part of
your job, remember."

She smiled back, her spirits lifting. She just
might enjoy herself at that.

Tables had been set up under the trees on the
park-like grounds surrounding the church. To her

relief, she saw some faces that were familiar from other years, other visits.

Alex took the picnic basket she was holding, then leaned close. "Don't let them overwhelm you," he murmured. "They're good at that."

She nodded, not trusting her voice. She was in danger of being overwhelmed, all right, but not by friendly church members.

But by the time she started through the buffet line, she wasn't so sure. She'd already given updates on Maida's condition to at least a dozen people and had promised to deliver get-well wishes. She tried to remember names, knowing her aunt would want to know who'd asked about her, but they began to blur in her mind.

As she reached for a scoop of fruit salad, Gwen bustled up to her, bringing the line to a halt. "Now, Paula, I have several quarts of homemade soup in the car to give you. Don't get away without it."

Paula looked at her blankly. Why was Gwen giving her soup? Was it something Maida had ordered and forgotten to tell her about?

"It'll do for lunches, and as soon as Maida comes home, we'll start bringing in suppers, too," the woman went on. "You'll have your hands full, running that big house and looking after Maida."

"You don't have to do that," Paula began, but Gwen went on as if she hadn't spoken.

"Probably I should line up people to stay with

Maida right at first. Yes, that would be best. I'll let you know when I have a schedule set up.''

"I don't need any help,'' Paula protested, but it was too late. Gwen had bustled away again, looking like a busy little brown wren on her self-appointed errand.

"You may as well let them help.'' The amused voice came from behind her, and she turned to find that Pastor Richie was the next person in line. The rotund, white-haired man smiled with sympathy. "I know Gwen can be overbearing, but everyone wants to help.''

"But…'' *I want to do it myself.* That would certainly sound ungracious, but it was what she felt. "The doctor wants Aunt Maida to go into rehab, so she won't be home for a couple of weeks at least. And I'm sure I can handle things, even when Maida comes home.''

"Of course you can, but that's not the point, is it?''

She looked at him blankly. If that wasn't the point, what was?

Pastor Richie helped himself to a heaping spoonful of scalloped potatoes, then sighed. "I might be able to lose weight, if I could bear to turn down one dish. But then someone's feelings might be hurt.''

It took a moment to realize what he was saying.

"You mean people's feelings will be hurt if I don't let them help."

He nodded, and his bright blue eyes were intent. "That's true, of course. People here love Maida, so they're quite ready to love you, sort of by extension. But it's more than that. If you don't let them help, you might do them harm."

"Do them harm?" she echoed. Why on earth would her being independent harm anyone else?

"People need to be of service to others," he said. He added a dollop of cranberry salad to an already overflowing plate. "It's a spiritual blessing, you see. You wouldn't want to deprive anyone of a spiritual blessing, would you?"

"No...no, of course not." Like Aunt Maida, the pastor clearly saw the world in spiritual terms.

He beamed. "Then you'll let them help. You can always tell yourself it's for Maida, not for you, if that makes you feel better."

She looked at him with surprise and respect. How had he known that was what she'd do? And what else did his wise eyes see when they looked at her?

"Paula, over here." She glanced toward the voice, to discover Mitch Donovan, seated with a group at one of the folding tables, waving at her to join them.

It wasn't until she reached them that she realized Alex was there. She hesitated, not sure whether he'd consider this appropriate. He'd told her she wasn't on duty at the picnic. Did that mean he'd prefer not to socialize with her?

He answered that by pulling out the chair next to him. "Join us, please."

She sat, very aware of his movements as he adjusted her chair and handed her a napkin. Would she ever get over this hyper-awareness when it came to Alex Caine?

"I think you know some of these people. Mitch, of course, and Brett."

Paula nodded to Brett. If she'd thought about it, she'd have realized Alex would be sitting with these two men. They'd long been his closest friends.

"This is Mitch's wife, Anne."

A beautiful, dark-haired woman looked up from the toddler on her lap and held out her hand. "Welcome to Bedford Creek, Paula."

"And you know Brett's wife, Rebecca. She's the physician's assistant at the clinic now."

"I'll see you often once your aunt is discharged from the hospital." Rebecca had a warm, sunny smile to match her auburn hair and peaches-and-cream complexion. "You'll be bringing her to the clinic for her checkups, I'm sure."

Paula nodded, a little overwhelmed with all this friendliness. They acted as if she were Alex's guest, instead of his housekeeper.

Anne seemed to sense her discomfort. She turned

the conversation to the current tourist season, urging Mitch to tell a story about the enterprising young man who'd tried to set up a souvenir shop in the town's park.

With the focus off her and the talk bouncing comfortably around the table, Paula tried to sort them all out. Anne was an attorney, she remembered hearing, and the toddler on her lap was adopted. Rebecca was Gwen's daughter, little Kristie's aunt, and she'd inherited her mother's warmth.

Paula noticed something else after she'd listened to them for a few minutes. With these people, Alex was at ease. With everyone else, as far as she'd been able to observe, the Caine shield stayed in place, marking the boundary between him and the rest of the world. But with Brett and Mitch, and perhaps with their wives, he was himself.

She saw his firm mouth relax, his eyes crinkle with laughter, and her heart seemed to cramp. If he ever reached that point with her...but there was no sense imagining something that would never happen.

Anne leaned across to her under cover of the general conversation. "That's our foster son, Davey, kicking the soccer ball with Jason and Kristie."

The lanky preteen towered over the smaller children, but he kicked the ball gently enough so that Jason had a shot at it. "He seems like a very nice boy."

Anne smiled with maternal pride. "He's come a long way, believe me. Mitch is terrific with him."

"I imagine you have something to do with it, too."

"I try." She stroked the soft curls of the sleepy toddler on her lap. "How are you doing with Jason? I know from Maida he can be a little difficult."

The urge to confide her concerns to a sympathetic ear was strong, but she resisted it. She didn't have the right to say anything about Jason, even to someone who was Alex's friend.

"I think we're getting along pretty well. I'm sure he misses Maida, though." Surely it was all right to say that much.

"Maida's been like a grandmother to that child." Anne seemed to read between the lines. She touched Paula's hand lightly. "Jason's had too many losses in his young life. And it can't be easy living up to the Caine name."

It was so near what she herself thought that she had to clench her teeth to keep from blurting something out.

Anne smiled. "If you ever need someone to talk to, just give me a call."

"Thanks." She had the sense that, improbable as it might seem, she'd made a friend. "I'll do that."

Nobody seemed able to make him as angry as Paula could with just a word. Alex smiled wryly as he walked slowly across the patio. Perhaps he needed to remind himself that the rest of the world wouldn't treat him with the deference most people in Bedford Creek did. Certainly Paula didn't. He suspected only her desire to keep her job had prevented her from saying even more than she had.

She seemed, without being aware of it, to have joined the select group that actually looked at him as just another human being. Certainly Brett and Mitch knew his weaknesses as well as he did himself, and didn't hesitate to call him to order if they felt he needed it. Now Paula had come on board, and he didn't know how to handle that.

He'd watched her at the picnic. He'd seen her fitting into his town, fitting into his life, as if she belonged here.

Nonsense. He tried to reject that idea out of hand. Paula worked for him. She neither wanted nor would welcome anything else.

She was the only woman willing to defy him. Maybe she was also the only woman who could really accept him.

That was a dangerous thought. He wasn't ready to take that kind of risk again. He—

A cry echoed through the gathering dusk, startling him. Was it a bird of some sort? Then it came again, and he knew instinctively what he'd heard. *Paula!* He began to run toward the garage, toward that panicked cry.

His heart thudded in his ears as he rounded the building. She was in trouble, she was hurt, she—

An errant flame, stirred by the breeze, licked upward from the brush the lawn service had been burning earlier. He'd have something to say to them about that. Then he saw Paula's face, and her expression banished every other thought from his mind.

She was terrified. She stood backed against the garage wall, clutching the puppy in her arms. She looked unable to move, and she stared, eyes wide and frightened, into the flames.

''Paula!'' He grasped her arm, pulling her away from the fire. Another dry branch caught, flaring up. He couldn't stop the images that flooded his mind—the flames rushing toward them, working frantically to free Paula from the seat, knowing that at any moment it could be too late...

That must be what Paula saw, too.

''It's all right.'' He turned her toward him, frightened at her reaction, and held her face between his hands. His heart still pounded, but he willed his voice to stay calm. ''Paula, look at me, not the fire. It's all right, do you hear me? You're safe.''

For several seconds she didn't respond, as if she couldn't hear him. Then, finally, she blinked. The terror was still in her eyes, but she focused on his face.

''You're safe,'' he said, longing to pull her into

his arms and not daring to. "Can you stay right here while I get the hose and put that out?"

She swallowed, the muscles in her throat working. Then she nodded. The puppy wiggled and yelped, but she gripped it tighter.

"Good." His voice nearly betrayed him, but he wouldn't let it. He couldn't let her know how shaken he was by her reaction. "I'll just be a minute."

He let go of her tentatively. She took a gasping breath, then nodded again.

Alex hurried around the garage, grabbed the coiled hose and twisted the tap on. He ran back to Paula, ignoring the throbbing in his injured leg, and aimed the nozzle at the flames. Moments later, only a blackened circle marred the grass.

He brushed his hands on his pant legs as he went back to her. "The lawn service should never have left that brush pile behind the garages." Maybe talking would erase the shock from her face. "It's out now, and no harm done."

That had to be the stupidest remark he'd ever made. He desperately wanted the tension to be over. He wanted them both to smile and walk away.

But that couldn't happen, not now. This was one time when keeping a stiff upper lip and smiling through the pain wouldn't cut it. He put his arm around her gently and felt her tremble.

"Come on." He led her a step. "Let's go in the house. We need to talk."

She tried to pull away, embarrassment flooding her face. "No, I…I don't need to do that. I'm fine." Her voice seemed to gain strength as she spoke.

A few days ago he'd have accepted that. He'd have used it for an excuse to back away from a conversation that had to be painful for both of them. Now he couldn't. Paula's return had changed things. Her agony forced its way beneath his protective barrier, wrenching his heart. Pretending everything was all right was no longer an option.

He caught her hand, holding it firmly. "You're not fine, and we need to talk." He brushed his thumb over her knuckles, as gently as if she were a child.

She looked away from him. "There's nothing to talk about. I just have this stupid fear of fire."

"I can see that. And we both know why."

"I was chasing Nugget," she said, ignoring the reference to the accident. "When the flames flared up in front of me, I just panicked for a moment."

"Paula—"

"That's all it was." She tried to pull away.

He tightened his grasp on her hand. She was doing what he always did—tamping down the pain, ignoring it, ignoring anyone who brought it up. He was just beginning to realize how futile that was.

"I'm not satisfied with that explanation. You

might get away with it with anyone else, but not me.''

She looked at him then, and he read the pain in her eyes so clearly.

''I don't...''

He shook his head. ''Don't even try, because I'm the one person in the world you can't fool on this subject. I was there, remember?'' He never talked about the crash. He was going to. ''Like it or not, we shared something terrifying and lived to tell about it.''

Somehow those didn't seem to be the right words.

''No, not 'tell about it,''' he amended. ''You haven't been talking about it, I'm sure of that. And maybe you need to.''

''Talking won't make it go away.''

''Nothing will make it go away, but we have to deal with it.'' Her pain was forcing him inch by painful inch from behind his own protective barricade. ''I've got scars on the outside from the crash. But you—you're carrying your scars inside. And like it or not, we're going to talk about this.''

Chapter Nine

Paula wanted to argue, to insist that she was all right, but she couldn't. Her stomach still churned, and the metallic taste of fear lingered in her mouth. She wasn't all right, and both of them knew it.

She let Alex pilot her into the house. He seemed to hesitate for a moment, as if trying to decide where to go, then led her into the sunroom that adjoined the kitchen.

The gathering dusk seeped into the room through the wall of windows, chilling her. Alex switched on a table lamp, and its golden glow banished the darkness.

''Sit down here.'' He pushed her gently onto the chintz sofa, then ran his hands down her arms. ''You're cold. I'm going to make a cup of Maida's herbal tea for you.'' He shoved a hassock under her feet. "I'll just be a minute. Do you want me to take the dog?"

"No." The word was out before she had a chance to think about it. She stroked Nugget's soft fur, taking comfort from his warmth. "I'll keep him with me. You don't need to—"

But he was gone. She leaned back against the overstuffed cushions. The couch gave under her, cradling her body, offering further comfort. Maybe that was what she needed. Her legs still trembled, as if she'd run a marathon. She'd just relax a minute; then she could assure Alex she was fine and leave.

The small room, so out of place amid the formality of the rest of the mansion, welcomed her. Its soft colors were feminine and restful, and the dried flower arrangements and faded chintzes would have been appropriate in her parents' house. It hardly seemed possible that the same person who'd chosen mahogany bedroom suites suitable for Buckingham Palace had decorated this cozy haven.

She heard Alex's steps in the kitchen, their faint unevenness the only hint of his injured leg. Then he was back. He put a white pottery mug in her hands, sat down next to her and moved the sleeping puppy from her lap to a spot between them.

"Drink that. Maida's chamomile tea is guaranteed to make any trouble better."

She remembered all the times she'd sat across

from Maida at the kitchen table, drinking her aunt's special brew, talking about anything and everything. Steam curled from the pale liquid, and she sipped cautiously.

Warmth suffused her, calming the quaking inside. Her muscles relaxed as the tension seeped away, leaving her limp and exhausted. As the last shadow of the nightmare vanished, she looked across at Alex, seeing him with a clarity she'd never before experienced.

He leaned back, his long fingers absently stroking the sleeping puppy. He seemed perfectly at ease, as if willing to wait all night, if need be, for her. Even the lines around his firm mouth had relaxed, erasing the formal reserve he normally projected. He was watching the puppy, and his dark lashes hid his eyes from her. His skin, tanned from his hours in the pool, contrasted with the white knit shirt he'd worn to the picnic.

He looked up suddenly, and their eyes met. Awareness of him shimmered along her skin and took her breath away.

''Better now?'' His dark gaze probed.

''Yes.'' Her heartbeat accelerated, the tension returning. He was going to push her for answers, and she wouldn't be able to withstand him. He'd drag her weakness out into the light for both of them to see.

"This is a nice room, isn't it?" He ran his hand along the rose chintz arm of the sofa.

She blinked, surprised. That certainly wasn't the question she'd expected. He was giving her time, she realized. The hard questions still lurked, held in abeyance until he thought she could handle them.

She took another swallow of the tea. "It's a cozy room." She tried to smile, suspecting the result didn't look very convincing. "I've always thought this spot doesn't match the rest of the mansion."

"That's because my mother decorated it. My father insisted the rest of the house be left in its turn-of-the-century grandeur, but this room was hers." He touched the faded blossoms of a dried flower arrangement, his long fingers gentle. "She loved flowers. That's one of the few things I remember about her—the scent of flowers."

His words reached out and clutched her heart. Alex was exposing feelings he usually kept hidden. Maybe he did it because that was what he expected from her. He'd consider that fair. She might deplore Alex's arrogance, but she'd never doubted his fairness.

"I'm sorry." Her throat tightened. "It must have been hard, not having a mother when you were growing up." Her thoughts flickered to her mother, then Aunt Maida—two very different female influences in her life.

"Now my son is going through the same thing."

The lines around his eyes deepened. "The Caine family doesn't seem destined for 'happily every after.'"

"Jason will be fine." She answered the doubt under his words. "He just needs…" She stopped, not sure she should go on.

"What do you think Jason needs?" The usual defensive note was missing from his voice. He asked as if he really wanted an answer.

He needs the same thing you do. "He needs to open up to someone." She took a breath and waited—for an explosion, for him to freeze her out or give her that superior look that said her opinion wasn't worth hearing. For him to retort immediately that his son was fine, as he always did.

Instead, he put his hand over hers. "Isn't that what you need, Paula?"

There it was—the question he'd been waiting to ask, the question she knew she had to answer. "I don't know." The words didn't want to come out, but she forced them out, anyway. "Maybe I need courage. Maybe I'm really a coward, letting myself panic over a simple thing like fire." Her mind flickered to Jason and the matches. But he had been asleep for hours. He couldn't have had any thing to do with this.

"The accident—"

She swept on, the words suddenly rushing out now that she'd started. "You don't know, do you?

I don't even remember the accident! It's wiped right out of my mind. So why should I have this stupid panic when I see flames? It doesn't make any sense.''

"You don't remember anything about the accident?''

"Nothing.'' Her mouth twisted. "My family insists that's lucky. Maybe they're right.''

He stroked her hand, in much the same way he'd stroked the sleeping puppy. "I'm not so sure. Maybe your conscious mind doesn't remember, but something inside you does.''

She hadn't thought of it that way, but, of course, he was right. Something in her remembered and was terrified. "I feel like it's hiding there, in my mind.'' She took a shaky breath. "Just waiting to jump out and grab me.''

"I'm sorry I didn't know.'' His fingers wrapped around hers. "I asked Maida how you were so many times, but she didn't tell me this.''

"It makes me feel like a failure.'' The words tasted bitter. "I try to be strong, but in this…'' *But I'm not.* She choked, and couldn't go on. She'd run out of steam, with her pitiful weakness laid out for both of them to see.

Alex took her hand and held it between his palms. His warmth and strength seemed to flow along her skin. "Paula, that's nonsense. You must know it. Nobody can go through what we went through and not have scars. Believe me. Do you think I don't have nightmares about the crash?''

She blinked rapidly to hold back hot tears. ''You're functioning. You don't let your fears paralyze you.''

''Maybe not, but everyone is different. You take any group of people and put them in a life-threatening situation, and each one of them will respond in a unique way.'' His hands tightened on hers. ''Believe me, I know. I've been through it twice.''

''Twice?'' For a moment she didn't know what he was talking about, but then half-forgotten words came back to her. ''I remember.'' She shook her head. ''A little, anyway. I overheard Aunt Maida talking to someone about you. But then when she saw I was there, she changed the subject.''

''She probably didn't want you to think about imitating our stupidity.''

'' 'Our'?''

''Brett's, Mitch's and mine. We came close to wiping ourselves off the planet on a class camping trip our senior year in high school.''

His words were light, but the rigidity of his jaw muscles belied that. He was trying to help by telling her this, but it was costing him.

''What happened?''

''A flash flood. You know how fast the streams can go up when we've had heavy rain.''

She nodded, unable to suppress a shiver. The valley was so narrow, there was no place for the water to go. "You were trapped, weren't you?"

"We were stupid. Or maybe just too immature to be let out alone. Each group in our class was supposed to find its way through the woods with a compass and a map. Instead, we got lost and ended up in an abandoned quarry with the water rising around us."

His voice sounded perfectly calm, but his hand clenched hers so tightly it hurt.

"You could have died." Just as they both could have died that rainy night at the airfield.

He gave a tight nod. "I slipped into the water. If Mitch hadn't grabbed me, within minutes I'd have been just a memory."

"But you did get out, all three of you." If he was trying to make her feel better about her pitiful weakness, he hadn't succeeded. "You survived that. You survived the plane crash. You didn't let either of those things keep you from moving on." If he did have nightmares, as he claimed, he'd beaten them into submission.

He seemed to realize how tightly he gripped her hand, and loosened his hold with a small, apologetic smile. But he didn't let go.

"I'm not making my point very well. All of us were affected by what happened. In the long run it made us stronger, but at the time it wasn't easy. For you, it's flames. For me, it's rain. I can't hear rain on the roof without breaking out in a cold sweat.'' He shrugged. ''Other people didn't help after the accident. They either acted as if we were heroes for getting out or stupid for getting into the situation in the first place.''

That brought her startled gaze up to his face. ''No one would blame you for an accident.''

''No?'' Something faintly mocking appeared in his eyes. ''You don't remember my father very well if you think that.''

Yes, she remembered that rigid autocrat. ''What did he say to you?''

''Just the usual sort of thing.'' His tone was light, but pain threaded through it, sharp and hard. ''That I'd failed. I hadn't lived up to my responsibilities. I should have gotten excused from the trip, should have had better sense than to go in the quarry. My position as his heir was too important to risk on childish adventures.''

His words pierced her heart. Alex wasn't invulnerable, after all. He might try to convince himself that it didn't matter, but his father's harshness had damaged him. She actually found herself feeling pity for the man who had everything.

And she felt something else, too. Something she'd been trying to deny but couldn't any longer, even if she could never say it aloud.

She was still in love with him.

* * *

Alex heard the pain in his admission, and it shocked him. What was he doing? He was saying things to Paula that he'd never said to anyone, not his closest friends, not even his wife. The lessons he'd learned early had been too deeply ingrained. A Caine didn't feel weakness. And if he did, he certainly never admitted it.

Paula was different. Karin had bought into the whole Caine mystique, but Paula never did. She saw him as a person, not just the Caine heir. He wanted to tell Paula the things he'd kept hidden in his very soul. He wanted to give in to that fierce attraction he felt every time he was near her. He wanted to stop thinking about what he should do or shouldn't do, and follow his instincts. For once in his life, he wanted to put his intellectual side on hold and just feel. Maybe, for the first time, he'd found someone with whom he could let down all the barriers.

She was looking at him with a mixture of emotions in her clear-as-glass green eyes—sympathy, tenderness, caring. Those feelings drew him in. They pulled him closer and closer to her. Close enough that he could feel the warmth that emanated from her skin. Close enough that he could smell the fresh, flowery scent she wore. Close enough that their lips could meet...

For once he wouldn't stop and analyze this. His hand moved, almost without volition, and he stroked her smooth cheek. He brushed back a strand of golden hair, and it clung to his fingers as if to pull him even closer.

Her breath went out in a soft sigh, moving across his cheek. He turned her face toward him, overwhelmed with a rush of longing and tenderness. His lips found hers.

She was soft, so soft. She moved closer, nestling into his arms as if this was the most natural thing in the world. The kiss deepened, saying all the things he couldn't find words for.

Finally she drew away. "Alex." She sighed his name, her cheek warm against his.

His breath came out unevenly. "That's been a long time coming."

She pulled back, looking into his eyes, and her hand rested over his heart. "Not for me."

He looked questioningly at her.

"That's another thing Aunt Maida didn't tell you. What happened then, when I was here before," she paused, as if preparing herself for something. "I didn't remember any of it. Working here, being Jason's nanny—it was all wiped out. I know my parents wanted me treated at the bigger hospital in Baltimore, but I didn't remember going back. My memories started again in the hospital there. I didn't remember that summer until Aunt Maida asked me to come back. And it was as if a door fell open in my mind, and there it was."

He frowned, trying to assimilate her words. "You mean, all this time, you hadn't remembered anything from that summer?"

She shook her head. "I didn't remember. I still don't remember the actual crash—" She broke off sharply.

Her eyes widened, and the hand that had rested over his heart gripped his shirt.

"Paula, what is it?" She'd turned sheet-white. "What's wrong?"

"The...the a-accident," she stammered. "I didn't remember it. But now—" She stopped again, her pupils dilating.

"Paula." He gripped her arms. "You've remembered. Is that it?" Something—maybe that kiss, echoing the one two years ago, or maybe talking openly about the accident at last must have brought it back.

She couldn't seem to answer. Then she nodded. Her eyes focused on the past, dark with pain.

He knew what she was seeing. He'd seen it often enough himself. The ground rushing toward them, the grinding crash, the crumpled seats and panicked passengers. The flames.

"Paula, it's all right." She didn't respond. He pulled her against him, wrapping his arms around her as if that would protect her from the images in her mind. "It's all right. It's over. You don't have to think about it any more."

"I don't want to." Her voice choked with tears. "I don't want to! All this time I couldn't, and now I can't get the pictures out of my head."

"I know, I know." He stroked her hair, and her pain surrounded his heart. "But it's a long time ago."

"Not for me!" She sounded almost angry, but her hands clung tightly and her voice was muffled against his chest. "It's right now."

He understood then. Time had blurred his memories of the crash. Bad as they were, the jagged edges had been smoothed away, eased by layers of other events, happier memories.

But not for Paula. Paula was experiencing it now as he'd experienced it those first few days in the hospital, when he couldn't close his eyes without seeing it all again.

He cradled her against him, rocking her as gently. Her hot tears soaked into his shirt. "Hush, it's all right." They were the words he'd wanted to hear someone say to him. "It was terrifying, but you're all right. There's nothing to fear."

Her pain pierced his control. *Lord, help her.* He so seldom asked God's help for himself, thinking that surely God expected him to handle his own responsibilities. But help for Paula was different. *Give her peace, Lord. Please. She's in such pain.*

All he could do was hold her, tightly, as if he could absorb the pain. He let her cry, and her sobs ripped through him, shaking him in ways he didn't begin to understand.

One thing was clear, though. His feelings for Paula couldn't be tidied away as convenient or unsuitable. Like it or not, she roused emotion in him that he wasn't prepared to handle.

Why not? Why couldn't he and Paula, like any other two people, find a way to build something together? He'd told himself he didn't believe in happy endings. Nothing in his experience had led him to think one could exist for him. But maybe, with Paula, things could be different.

They didn't have to be just employer and employee. They didn't have to fall into the roles life had assigned them. Paula was an intelligent, giving, lovely woman, not the child who'd looked at him with hero worship in her eyes. They could start again, put the mistakes of the past behind them, and begin as equals.

Gradually her sobs trailed off. The death grip she'd had on his shirt relaxed. Next, he thought, she'd become embarrassed. Independent Paula never wanted to admit that she'd shown what she'd call weakness.

She eased back, still in the circle of his arms, and rubbed her eyes. "I'm sorry."

He had to smile at the predictability of the words. "Don't be sorry. You've relived a terrible experience. Of course you cried—anyone would."

"I didn't just cry." She touched his wet shirt. "I bawled like a baby. You must be ready to run for cover."

"Not yet." His heart lifted. She was past the worst of it. *Thank you, God.*

"Right." She mopped her eyes with her sleeve. "Men hate it when women cry."

"Depends on the man." He touched her cheek lightly, brushing away the tear that sparkled there. "And the woman."

He felt the warmth rise in her cheeks at his words, and it made him want to kiss her again.

"I don't like behaving like a baby," she said stubbornly. "Especially—" The words broke off, and her gaze evaded his.

"Especially in front of me? Am I that much of an ogre?" He needed to make her smile again.

"No." A smile trembled on her lips. "Not an ogre. But you are my boss, remember?"

"That doesn't mean I can't also be..." He shouldn't push it, not when she was so fragile. He had to smile at the thought of her probable reaction if he called her "fragile" aloud. "A friend," he finished. "Haven't we always been friends?"

The word seemed to reassure her, and he sensed some of the tension leave her.

"A friend," she agreed. "You've gone above and beyond the call of friendship tonight."

"I've been there," he reminded her. "I know what it feels like."

She nodded. Her eyes narrowed, as if she approached the memory again, very cautiously. "I always wondered about it, even when I tried not to. What it was like, how I got out."

"Now you know." He moved a little away from her. "It will be easier now. You remember, so you can let the memories start to fade."

She frowned. "Is that what yours have done?"

"Most of the time." He had to be honest with her. "Sometimes the thoughts bother me, but most of the time, even if something reminds me, I can put it aside and go on."

How long? he wondered. How long until he could stop being the supportive friend and move to being the interested male?

Her forehead was wrinkled, her gaze focused on the past. "Put it aside," she echoed. "Not hear it, not see it." She shivered. "Not smell it. That's the worst. Maybe that's why I get so panicked around fire. I smell it, and I want to run. But I can't. I'm trapped..."

Her eyes widened as she stared at him. "That's true, isn't it? I was trapped."

Reluctantly he nodded. He didn't want her to think about that, but it wasn't in him to lie to her. "You were trapped."

"The flames. I couldn't get the belt loose. I couldn't move."

She was reliving it again; he could see that. He reached for her, longing to wipe the memories away, and knowing he couldn't.

"But you did. We both got out."

She shook her head as if trying to shake the image away. "I was trapped." She focused on him suddenly. "You got me out. I remember now. You came—you got me out of the belt."

"Paula..." What could he say? That he didn't want her to go there?

"You dragged me to the hole in the cabin." A shudder passed through her. "People were crying. You took my hands and lowered me out of the plane. You told me to get away."

"Everyone got out," he reminded her. "It could have been so much worse. Everyone got out alive."

"But you saved me." She reached toward him. "You saved me."

He realized what was happening, and the hope he'd felt moments before turned to ashes. Paula wasn't looking at him like the woman who'd returned his kisses. She was looking at him like a starry-eyed, hero-worshipping child.

He drew back, fighting the fierce disappointment that swept through him. He couldn't do it. He couldn't pursue a relationship with Paula when she thought of him as some kind of a hero. Not when he was only too aware of how often he failed to measure up. They couldn't build anything on that.

Chapter Ten

"Come on, Jason. You can do it." Paula waved her mitt. "Throw it right in here."

Jason looked doubtful, but he pitched the baseball. His expression turned to astonishment when the throw made it across the makeshift plate and thunked into Paula's mitt.

Smiling, she stepped back and motioned one of the other peewee baseball players to take her place. When she'd learned the group of youngest kids from the church had no one to coach them, it had seemed a golden opportunity to involve Jason. And when a chance remark from Mitch at the picnic had informed her that Alex had been a pitcher on their high school team—well, that was too good to pass up.

She glanced at her watch. Alex should be home

from the plant soon, and this time they were playing where he could have no objection. The grassy lawn behind the garage was perfect for games, and even the most wildly hit ball couldn't damage anything. Or anyone. She thought of the Swiss businessman and winced.

But she wanted more than Alex's approval. She wanted his presence.

For Jason, she hurriedly reminded herself. This was for Jason, not for her. She stood back, watching the children, and tried not to think about what had happened between her and Alex on Saturday night. But it was useless. The memory wouldn't be denied.

Her cheeks heated at the thought of his kisses, and she could almost feel his strong arms around her, holding her protectively close. *Protected*—that was a good word for it. At a moment when reality had shattered around her, Alex had been a secure anchor.

That was all he had been, as far as he was concerned. She had to accept that. He'd been kind, and they'd both been a little carried away by the emotion of the moment. Maybe, for a few minutes, she'd dreamed their connection was something more.

But Alex's behavior in the days since had shown her the truth. He'd withdrawn from her, going back to his usual cool, urbane manner. The very tone of his voice had told her clearly that he regretted what had happened between them and had no intention of repeating that mistake.

At least he hadn't apologized. Her face burned at the thought. That would have been the final humiliation. He'd simply ignored the whole incident. Now she had to do the same.

She had to concentrate on the two people she'd come here to help. Aunt Maida would be home from the hospital soon, and Paula would have her hands full even with the aid of the church volunteers. And just as important, she had to make more headway with Jason.

She watched him toss the ball to Kristie, who promptly ducked. Jason had begun to smile again. Certainly that was progress. But she couldn't kid herself; the boy was worried about something. She could see it so clearly in the sadness that filled his eyes in unguarded moments. Whatever it was, he wasn't ready yet to confide in her. Maybe he never would be.

She wouldn't give up, she told herself as she went to help Kristie catch the ball. She'd come here to help Jason, and that's what she'd do, no matter who stood in the way.

"What's going on?" Alex's voice, coming so appropriately on the heels of her thought, startled her. Her heart cramped, and she took a firm grip on her emotions. *Be natural,* she ordered herself. *Pre-*

tend it never happened. She swung around, looking for signs of annoyance in his face. But he was smiling.

"Baseball practice."

"So I see." He came closer. He wore his usual white shirt, but his jacket was thrown over one arm and his striped tie was loosened. She reminded her heart not to feel anything.

"Aren't they too small for this?"

"Not according to my brothers. They put a baseball in my hand when I was three." She grinned. "I'm not advocating that, you understand. This is the peewee team from the church. They want to start playing, but they don't have a coach."

He raised an eyebrow. "How are they?"

She lowered her voice so the kids couldn't hear. "Well, they can't throw. They also can't catch or hit. But they have lots of enthusiasm."

"In that case, I wish you luck. Sounds as if their coach will need it."

"I didn't volunteer myself as coach." She braced herself for an explosion. "I volunteered you."

"Me!" For the moment he looked too dumbstruck to be angry.

"Mitch told me what a good player you were in high school. He thought this was a great idea."

"He would." Alex looked as if he was thinking up a suitable punishment for his friend. "I'm afraid it's out of the question." He turned away.

She wasn't going to let him off that easily, not where his son was concerned. "Why?"

He looked at her blankly. Apparently that was something people didn't often ask Alex Caine.

"Why?" she repeated. "Why is it out of the question? The kids need someone to work with them. You have the requisite skills."

"I've already made a donation to the program."

"The kids need someone to give time, not money. You have a son who wants to play. Why shouldn't that someone be you?"

"That should be obvious." He wore the expression she thought of as the *royal look*—the calm assumption that anything he chose to do wouldn't be questioned.

"Not to me, it isn't." Somewhat to her surprise, she realized that Saturday night's events had made her bolder where Alex was concerned. She wasn't sure why, but it seemed a step forward. "Explain it to me."

He sent a harassed look toward the children, who'd begun to gather around Paula. "You should know why. The business I'm working on right now is important. It requires all my concentration."

"All the more reason why you should be getting some physical activity and relaxation," she said promptly, ignoring a twinge of caution. She was pushing hard, and she'd probably have her head bitten off for her trouble.

He raised his eyebrows skeptically. "And you recommend coaching small children for relaxation?"

"Are you going to coach us, Dad?" Jason's eyes widened. "Will you?"

Kristie, carrot-colored ponytail bobbing, threw herself at his legs. "Please, please, please," she chanted, clearly not awed by his status.

Over the mob of small children, Alex shot her a look that was both laughing and annoyed. "I'll get you for this, Paula. You and Mitch both."

The tension inside her eased, and she smiled. "I'm not intimidated by threats. Let's see what your fastball looks like after all these years."

"Too fast for a bunch of seven-year-olds," he said. "Even at my advanced age. Suppose you start with batting practice, while I go change."

She nodded, starting onto the field as the children hurried to grab bats. But as she passed him, he caught her arm, drawing her close to him. His dark eyes sparkled with laughter, and her heart seemed to turn over. He didn't often look like that, and when he did, the effect was devastating.

"I meant it, Paula. You and Mitch are in trouble."

She willed her body not to betray the effect he had on her. "At least that means I've got the police chief on my side," she retorted.

Laughing, Alex headed toward the house, his suit

jacket slung over one shoulder. Paula kept her smile in place as she turned to the kids. Nobody was going to guess what she felt.

She'd created an opportunity for Alex and his son to grow closer, she reminded herself. That was what she'd intended. She hadn't intended to prove so clearly to herself that her feelings for Alex were completely out of control.

Paula had turned his world upside down, Alex thought as he raised the window shades in the old gardener's cottage the next afternoon. His studio flooded with light. Sunshine splashed across the wide, uneven oak flooring and touched the half-finished wood carving on the workbench.

He moved toward the carving of Jason he'd begun working on, his eyes assessing it, even while his mind continued on the by-now-familiar track. Paula, and the changes she'd brought to his life.

It was just like the last time she'd been in his house, he realized. She had a knack for turning the mansion into something other than the museum it so often felt like. She filled it with laughter, noise, small children. With Paula around, his son smiled.

The thought clutched his heart. Why hadn't he realized how little his son smiled? Jason's sober expression had become so habitual that Alex had begun to take it for granted—until Paula changed things.

He couldn't stop the smile that tugged at his own lips when he thought of that baseball team practice yesterday afternoon. She'd done it to involve him with Jason, of course, and she was remarkably good at not taking ''no'' for an answer.

But he'd had a surprise for her. If she wanted him to work with the children, she'd have to be involved, too. He wouldn't do it alone.

It was almost frightening, how much pleasure the idea of working with her gave him. He'd told himself there couldn't be anything between them for so many reasons, but she seemed to be breaking those walls down, one by one.

Unfortunately, the biggest wall still stood irrevocably between them. As long as she looked at him with hero-worship in her eyes, any other relationship was impossible.

He ran his hand over the grain of the carving, itching to get back to work on the piece. Carving soothed him, letting his mind wander while his fingers brought the wood to life.

A foolish waste of time. You have better things to do. It was remarkable how often the voice of his conscience sounded just like the voice of his father.

The knock at the door startled him. Quickly he tossed a cloth over the half-finished piece and went to answer.

''Paula.'' Somehow he wasn't surprised. He

hadn't satisfied her curiosity the last time she came to the cottage, and she wasn't one to give up.

She held Maida's wooden recipe box in her hands. "I found this on the kitchen counter. You've had it fixed." Her dimple flashed. "I'm so grateful. I hated the idea of explaining to her what happened."

"No problem."

He wanted to be happy for her, but the box was a reminder of her insistence that Jason had broken it deliberately. He'd thought of that each time he'd worked on it, and the accusation had leached the pleasure from the delicate repair job.

"If that's all…"

He should have closed the door more quickly. She moved past him as easily as if he hadn't spoken.

"Where did you have it fixed? I didn't realize there was a shop in town that did this sort of work."

He shrugged, groping for an answer. It was ridiculous to be so reticent about his hobby, but he couldn't seem to admit the truth to her.

In another second, the admission wasn't necessary. She saw the workbench. Her gaze shot from it to him.

"You repaired the box yourself, didn't you." She frowned. "I don't understand. Why didn't you tell me you were doing it?"

"I didn't think you'd be interested. What difference does it make who fixed it?'' He took a half step toward the door, trying to ease her out. Having her here brought her too far for comfort into his inner life.

Paula ignored the hint, moving toward the drafting table. Her eyes widened as she took in the papers scattered on it. ''Are these designs for the factory? I didn't realize you actually designed the furniture you make.''

He swept the sheets together, unaccountably embarrassed. ''It's nothing. I don't do all the designing, just a few of the lines.''

She touched the top sheet. ''That's the one Dieter is interested in, isn't it?'' She looked up at him, perplexed. ''Alex, I don't understand. Why are you so reticent about it? If I had a gift like this, I'd be proud.''

''The designs are part of my job. Nothing to be excited about.'' He frowned down at the drawings. ''It's true they're an aspect of the attraction our business has for Dieter, but certainly not all of it. Don't get the idea that I'm the Michelangelo of the furniture world.''

He couldn't suppress his embarrassment that she'd found out. People at the plant knew, of course, but they'd learned not to comment. He'd started tinkering with designs when he was just a kid. He'd quickly found that his father didn't consider that the proper role for a Caine. He was sup-

posed to run the plant, not play at being a drafts-
man.

"If you don't mind, Paula, I really have to get
back to work. I'm a little short on time, especially
since someone seems to have involved me in baseball practice."

He rather enjoyed the way she flushed and
looked away.

"That's all I wanted. Just to say thank you."

She picked up the box, which she'd put on the
table, and her elbow brushed the carving of Jason.
Before he could grab it, the covering slid off.

Paula could only stare. She'd thought she understood Alex. She'd assumed she knew who he was—
a rich man with no interest in anything other than
his company and his family name.

But in the last few days she'd discovered facets
of him she'd never expected. She'd seen the hero
who had rescued her at the risk of his own life.
She'd seen the gentle comforter who'd held her
while she wept. And now she saw yet another side
to the man she only thought she knew.

"It's beautiful." She reached out tentatively to
touch the carving. Jason's face looked out of the
warm, smooth wood. The piece was clearly not finished, but Alex had somehow suggested that lingering sadness that seemed a part of his son. She
wondered if he even realized he'd portrayed that.

"It's not finished." Alex snatched up the cloth as if to hide this example of his artistry.

"No, I see that. But you've already caught his expression. That must be the most difficult thing." Her fingertips smoothed the figure's cheek. It was almost like touching the real thing, and her heart caught at the beauty of it. "Has Jason seen this yet?"

"No."

He flipped the cloth over the head, ignoring the fact that she still touched it. She took her hand away reluctantly.

"You want to wait until it's done, I suppose. But I'm sure he'd be fascinated at seeing his face appear in the wood."

Alex frowned, straightening a row of tools on the tabletop that didn't seem to need straightening. "I don't know that I'll show it to him. It's just something I've been playing around with."

"Not show him!" She reached out impulsively to touch his arm. "But it's wonderful. Any child would be thrilled." Didn't he realize that his love for his son came through in every line?

"It's more important that I provide properly for him, rather than wasting time on something like this." He looked as if the words tasted bitter in his mouth.

"Who said that?" she asked with sudden insight. "It sounds like a quote."

He shot her a look that was almost angry. "My father." He turned away from the workbench. "He had very little patience for wasting time. And he was right."

She wasn't sure how to respond to that. Probably she didn't have the right to say anything, but she couldn't seem to stop herself.

Lord, show me what to say to him. I didn't understand.

"It's not a waste of time to do something just for the love of it," she said.

His mouth tightened until he resembled the portrait of his father that hung in the library. "It is when there are more important things to be done. Like saving the company, for instance—"

For a brief instant she saw the pain reflected in his dark eyes.

"If this deal doesn't go through soon, I'll be letting down a great many people, in addition to my son."

She tried to find the words that would comfort him, but she didn't have any. She couldn't spout platitudes in the face of his pain. Had she been wrong to push his involvement with Jason?

No, I can't believe that, Lord. Important business deal or not, a son needs his father's attention far more than he needs status or money.

"You can't hold yourself responsible for the welfare of the whole town," she ventured.

His swift gesture of rejection told her that had been the wrong thing to say.

"I am responsible." His hands tightened on the edge of the table until the knuckles whitened and the tendons stood out like cords. "Bedford Creek has always depended on the Caine family for its livelihood. Nothing's changed. If the factory goes under, half the town will be unemployed. That is my responsibility."

"I'm sorry." It was all she could say. "I know you're doing your best for them. Everyone must know that."

But did they? Did anyone, outside of Mitch and Brett, perhaps, really look beneath the surface to see the real Alex Caine? Or did they look at that polished, cool exterior and envy the man who had everything?

The way she had, she had to confess. All these years she'd seen him as some sort of privileged being, immune to the struggles that beset ordinary people like her.

Now, for some reason she didn't understand, he'd given her a look at the man beneath the shining surface—the person whose life was a constant struggle to do what was expected of him.

The saddest thing was that he didn't see that being perfect was impossible. And he didn't see the barriers that it put between him and everyone else in his life, especially his son.

Chapter Eleven

Why wasn't her plan working? Paula had been so sure God had brought her here to help Jason. She'd been convinced it was her opportunity to atone for leaving so abruptly two years ago. But if this was what God intended, why was she failing? With a sudden flare of temper at her own inadequacy, she kicked one of the two-by-four boards she was using to build a temporary ramp to the housekeeper's cottage.

"Is that a new construction method?"

Her heart thudded into overdrive at the sound of Alex's voice, and she turned to annoyance in self-defense. "Must you sneak up on me that way?"

He crossed the grass from the pool. "You were too busy beating up that defenseless piece of wood to hear me. What's going on?"

"That's the question I wanted to ask you. What's going on? Why didn't you keep your promise to Jason?"

She could see in an instant that he'd forgotten it completely—a blank stare, followed quickly by comprehension, then embarrassment.

"You forgot." She knew she sounded accusing, and she didn't care. "You made a promise to your son, and you forgot." He had told Jason at breakfast he'd be home before supper to practice with the team. But four o'clock came and went, and no Alex.

Dismayed by the children's pensive little faces, Paula had tried to engage them in batting and fielding practice. The other children had responded, but Jason had thrown his glove down and walked off the field. She hadn't had the heart to reprimand him, knowing the depth of his disappointment.

"Where is he?" He looked around, as if he expected to find Jason still waiting. "Was he very upset?"

"Of course, he was upset! What would you expect? Don't you remember what it feels like when the most important person in your life lets you down?"

She knew she'd gone too far, and she regretted the words almost before they were out of her mouth. Given what Alex's father had been like, that had to be a sore spot. But it was too late to call her hasty words back.

Alex's mouth tightened. "I'll tell my son I'm sorry, Paula." His implication was clear—he didn't owe an apology to her. "Where is he?"

"Brett and Rebecca took him out for pizza with Kristie. They should be back in about an hour." She sounded like a sulky child, even to herself. She tried to be honest. Was her sharp retort on Jason's behalf? Or was she thinking of her own disappointment? Her newfound empathy for Alex had become frayed around the edges the last few days. His preoccupation with the business to the exclusion of everything and everyone in his life had become so intense that all her efforts to bring him and Jason together were evaporating. Jason withdrew; Alex withdrew—she seemed to be the only person in the house who was actually *there*.

She glanced at her watch. "Or sooner. I've been working on this thing longer than I thought."

"What exactly are you doing?" He picked up the two-by-four, sounding as relieved as she was to get away from the difficult subject on which they'd probably never agree. "Are you and Jason taking up carpentry?"

Now that she had the opportunity, she was reluctant to ask Alex for help. She folded the instructions. "The physical therapist said I should rig up a temporary ramp to the porch, for when Maida gets home. So she won't have to tackle the steps every time she wants to get out.''

He held out his hand. She fought down a flare of resentment at the imperious gesture and gave him the paper.

He scanned it quickly. ''This doesn't look too difficult.''

''That's easy for you to say.'' Actually, it probably would be easy for him, given the unexpected skills she'd discovered he had. For that matter, she had yet to find the thing he didn't do well. ''I'm afraid I must be mechanically challenged.''

''I'll take care of the ramp.'' Alex slipped the paper into his pocket before she could snatch it back.

''No, you won't.'' She planted her fists on her hips. ''Aunt Maida asked me to handle this.''

He looked annoyed. She ought to be familiar with the expression by now, since he so often wore it when he looked at her.

Not when he kissed you, a small voice in her head reminded her. *Not when he held you.*

''I'm sure Maida expected you to take care of this by turning it over to me,'' Alex said. ''She'd know I'd have the ramp installed properly.''

''You mean, I can't do it the way you want it done.'' The fact that she probably couldn't only added to her frustration.

''That's not what I meant. This isn't a good use

of your time, with the dinner party coming up. I'll have one of the carpenters from the plant stop by and do this.''

''Maida is my aunt. I'd rather provide for her myself.'' She was using anger as a shield, and she knew it. But anger was the safest emotion she could feel where Alex was concerned. At least when she was angry with him, she didn't have to remember what his arms felt like around her.

Alex studied her for a moment. His dark eyes were as intent as if he studied a business plan. ''The cottage belongs to me,'' he said finally. ''I will modify it for Maida's needs. Why is this so important to you?''

His question pierced the shield of her anger, and she struggled to get it back. ''Because I'm used to doing things myself, not ordering someone else to do them. Some of us didn't grow up having all this—'' Her gesture took in the grounds, the pool, the mansion, maybe the whole town.

He didn't say anything, and she braced herself for an eruption. No, not an eruption. Alex was too cultivated to erupt. He'd give her the look that suggested she'd just crawled out from under a rock.

But he shook his head, suddenly looking tired. ''That's not quite what you imagine it to be, Paula. I won't try to convince you of that, because I probably couldn't succeed.''

His calm, even tone brought a wave of embarrassment to her cheeks. Whether she was right or wrong, she shouldn't have spoken that way to him.

"I'm sorry. I—"

"You don't have to apologize for saying what you think of me. But I don't think you should be so proud of not accepting help, not when other people will have to pay the penalty for your pride."

"What are you talking about? What other people?"

"Maida, for one." He didn't sound angry, just matter-of-fact. "You'd rather build something you know won't work as well, so you can say you did it yourself."

His words stung, and she could tell he wasn't finished yet.

"And you won't let me help, even though I love Maida, too. I suppose that means my love is tainted by whatever privilege it is you imagine I possess. That's an odd kind of caring, Paula. I'm not sure Maida would approve."

She stared at him, her defenses crumbling and her eyes filling with tears. How could he cut her to the heart with a few words?

Alex's heart contracted when he saw the expression on Paula's face. He hadn't intended to hurt her, but he'd gone too far.

Maybe he was the one who needed to understand. He hadn't made any effort to find out why Paula felt as she did. He'd simply considered her stubborn independence an obstacle to what he knew was best. Did that mean he was as arrogant as she thought? He decided he didn't want to know the answer to that question.

''Paula.'' He reached out, wanting to touch her, knowing it was unwise. ''I'm sorry. I don't want to hurt you. I want to understand.''

She shook her head stubbornly, but her mouth trembled. ''There's nothing to understand. I'm like everyone else.''

Suddenly he didn't want to impose his will on hers or get his own way, even though he was convinced he was right. He just wanted to know what drove her.

''Tell me what's going on with you. Make me understand.'' He tried a smile. ''In spite of the handicap of my imagined status, maybe I can.''

He went to the steps, sat down and patted the spot next to him. That first night she'd done the same thing. Jason had sat next to her and connected with her in a way Alex still didn't quite understand.

The image of Jason's small face sent a twinge to his heart. Paula had been right about one thing: Alex had let Jason down tonight, and that was something he'd promised himself he wouldn't do. But Jason wasn't here now, and Paula was—a suddenly vulnerable Paula.

"Tell me what makes Paula Hansen tick," he said, trying to keep his voice light.

"Nothing out of the ordinary. Nothing important." She shrugged, obviously making an effort to sound casual, but she sat down next to him.

"It's important to you." For both their sakes, he had to stay detached. He had to be a friend, and nothing more. "Come on, Paula. Who are you really rebelling against?"

He knew at that moment that his shot in the dark had gone home. She crossed her arms over the Towson University T-shirt she wore, as if in self-defense. "I'm not. Not anymore, anyway."

"Why do I find that so hard to believe?" He tried to keep his voice gently teasing.

She shook her head. "Maybe I am a little overly independent. I don't think you'd understand why."

"Why wouldn't I?"

"Because you didn't grow up with four older brothers determined to protect you." There was a flicker of a smile at that.

"Doesn't sound so bad," he said, sure she hadn't yet reached the heart of the matter.

"Oh, really?" She did smile now. "Did you have an older brother who insisted on taking you to your first dance? Or one who threatened to beat up anyone who teased you? It got so bad, boys were afraid to smile at me."

"They loved you."

"They drove me crazy." She shook her head. "I had to fight them every step of the way. But it taught me to stand up for myself."

"And your father? Did you fight him, too?"

She rubbed her arms, the smile fading. "My father has some very old-fashioned ideas of what boys do and what girls do. Boys go places, they play sports, they get football scholarships if they want to go to college. Girls stay home. Girls are protected." Something in the timbre of her voice changed, betraying the emotion she seemed determined not to show. "I remember…"

He leaned a little closer, afraid to touch her because that might break the slender thread of connection between them. "What do you remember?" he said softly.

"I must have been about Jason's age." She looked down, her face soft and defenseless. "I had a teacher who really encouraged me. She recommended me for a special program for gifted kids. I remember coming home from school carrying the paper, so proud." Her hands clasped together.

He could almost see the little girl she'd been, blond braids to her shoulders, face alight with eagerness. "What happened?"

"My father refused to enroll me." Her face tightened. "The teacher even came to talk to him, but he wouldn't budge. I sat at the top of the stairs and listened. 'A waste of money,' he called it. He wasn't going to throw good money away on foolishness. It wasn't worth it.''

The vision of that little girl, huddled at the top of the stairs, hurt his heart. He knew what she'd felt when she'd heard those words. She'd felt *she* wasn't worth it.

Now, she'd reject sympathy. She'd interpret it as pity. "He sounds like quite a reactionary. He and my father probably would have had a lot in common.''

She looked up, startled. Then, quite suddenly, she smiled. "I don't know which of them would have been more shocked at that comparison.''

The tightness around his heart eased at her smile. "I'd say you turned out remarkably well, considering the obstacles. You got your degree in spite of him, didn't you?''

"With Aunt Maida's help. You should have heard the battle between them over that. On second thought, if you'd been listening, you might have been able to hear it from Bedford Creek.''

"Maida is a special lady, isn't she. She's done as much, or more, for me over the years.''

Paula raised her eyebrows. "Meaning you ought to be allowed to build the ramp for her?''

"I did have that in mind,'' he said. He sensed that she was eager to move away from the subject of her past.

Tears brightened her eyes for an instant, and she

blinked rapidly. "I guess even a rich man ought to be allowed to give a gift of love."

He ought to say something light in response, but he couldn't. He'd been wrong. He couldn't go this far into her life and stay detached. Like it or not, he'd begun to care for her too much. All he could think was how close they were, and how much he wanted to close that gap and kiss her.

She looked at him, and she had to be able to read the longing in his face. Her eyes darkened, and he seemed to hear her breath catch.

Car doors slammed, and children's voices echoed from the driveway.

Paula pulled away from him, her cheeks flushing. "They're back."

His first thought was that Brett had rotten timing. His second was that Brett actually had pretty good timing, because in another second Alex would have moved his relationship with Paula in a direction he'd promised not to go.

"Paula, how nice to run into you."

Paula, arms full of packages, stopped, surprised to be greeted by name on Main Street. Anne Donovan was just coming out of the candle shop. "I went to see Maida yesterday," Anne continued. "She's really doing well, isn't she?"

"The therapist says she'll be able to come home soon."

It felt like a deadline to Paula. The days were passing, and with them went whatever opportunity she had to do some good for Jason and his father. She'd thought that if she understood Alex better, she'd be able to help his son. Instead, she seemed only to have put her own heart in jeopardy. The memory of those moments on the steps the day before shimmered in her mind like a bubble about to burst.

"I'm so glad she's doing well," Anne said warmly. "Do you have time for a cup of coffee? We haven't had a chance to talk since you've been here." She nodded toward the café across the street.

Paula juggled packages to glance at her watch. "I do have half an hour before I pick up Jason. But I should get Alex's shirts—"

"Nonsense." Anne grabbed one of the bags. "You look as if you could use a break. Let Alex pick up his own shirts."

Paula couldn't help smiling as she followed the other woman across the street. Anne looked intimidating, with her glossy black hair and elegant clothes. But her easy friendliness was hard to resist.

Besides, she thought as Anne pushed open the door to the Bluebird Café, Anne's husband was one of Alex's closest friends. If anyone understood him, it was Mitch.

Anne dropped the packages on a blue-padded bench and slipped into the booth. Almost before

Paula sat down, an older woman slid coffee mugs in front of them and poured with a deft hand.

"What'll you have with the coffee? I've got some currant scones fresh from the oven." The woman poised a pencil over a pad.

"No, I—"

"Two currant scones," Anne said quickly. "Cassie, have you met Paula Hansen?"

The woman nodded briskly. "Work up at the big house, don't you? I'll be right out with those scones."

She whisked away toward the kitchen, and Anne gave Paula an apologetic smile.

"Sorry about that. But Cassie takes offense if you don't eat something. And given the way she talks, you don't want her annoyed with you."

"I guess there are some interesting pitfalls to living in a place as small as Bedford Creek."

Anne nodded. "I've been here nearly two years, and I still don't understand all the ins and outs of it. People imagine living in a small town is simple, but actually it's very complicated."

"Because everyone knows everyone else?"

"Even back a generation or two." Anne stirred sugar into her coffee. "Take Alex, for example. Everyone in town knows his family history."

"They've always been the people living in the big house on the hill," Paula agreed. *Where they can look down at everyone else.* She couldn't help the thought.

Cassie reappeared and put plates in front of them. Paula broke a corner off a feathery light scone. Still warm, as Cassie had promised.

"It can't be easy," Anne continued, slathering butter on her scone. "Having everyone in town interested in what you're doing. It might make you put a shield up for protection."

She looked at Anne with increased respect. "Yes, I guess it might."

"A few people probably get past that, if they try hard enough."

"Maybe." She could hear the doubt in her voice. She'd tried, hadn't she? But each time she got too close, Alex pulled away.

She seemed to see him leaning toward her on the porch steps. He'd have kissed her, if Brett and Rebecca hadn't arrived when they did. But that hadn't been regret she'd seen in his eyes when he pulled away. It had been relief. He'd been glad they were interrupted.

"Trust me." Anne smiled, dropping the pretense that this was a theoretical discussion. "Alex is worth the effort to get close to him. He and Mitch go back a long way. They—"

"Coffee and gossip?"

Paula looked up, barely able to restrain a gasp. She'd been so intent on what Anne was saying that she hadn't heard Alex come in. She probably looked guilty, but Anne just smiled and slid over on the seat.

"You can join us, if you want. We aren't bashing men, I promise."

Alex sat, then looked enquiringly across the table at Paula. "Where's Jason?"

"At the library story hour." She gestured toward her packages. "I was picking up a few things we need for the dinner party."

"She's allowed a coffee break, Alex." Anne's voice was silky. "You don't want to get a reputation as a slave driver, do you?"

"I'm finished," Paula said hurriedly, deciding she really didn't want to sit across from Alex with Anne looking on. The woman saw too much. "I'll take the scone with me to eat later." She wrapped a napkin around it.

"I'll walk out with you." Alex stood, putting a bill on the table before Paula could open her bag.

Once they were on the sidewalk outside, she expected Alex to head down toward the plant. Instead, he walked beside her as she made her way uphill to the tiny library. In Bedford Creek, it seemed you were always going either uphill or down.

When he didn't say anything for half a block, she began to feel nervous. "Is something wrong?"

He looked at her blankly. "Why should anything be wrong?"

"Well, I thought you were on your way back to the office."

His rare, charming smile was like the sun coming out on a cloudy day. "I should be. But I'm playing hooky, just for the moment."

She smiled back, the tension inside her relaxing. Alex was treating her like a friend, instead of a housekeeper. That was the most she could expect, and she shouldn't let herself have silly dreams of something more. But there was something unresolved between them, and maybe this was a good time to bring it up.

"There's something I've been wanting to say to you all week, and I've never had the chance."

"What?" His dark eyes grew wary, as if expecting the worst.

"You don't need to look like that." She smiled. "It's not anything bad. It's just...I wanted to tell you how much I appreciate what you did in the accident. 'Thank you' doesn't seem enough to say to someone who saved your life."

"That's not necessary." His tone was curt, and he turned away almost before the words were out. "I have to get back to the plant." He strode off, leaving her staring after him.

One instant he'd been smiling down at her, warm and approachable. The next he'd turned into a cold, distant stranger.

Chapter Twelve

By the next day, Paula had had twenty-four hours to think about that exchange with Alex on the street, and she still didn't understand his reaction. She stood at the linen closet, counting out napkins for the dinner, trying to concentrate on anything but the memory of the look on Alex's face when he'd turned away from her.

She clenched the napkins, as if she could use them to wipe away the image. It didn't work. Nothing would push it out of her mind, not even the rush and tension of the dinner preparations.

The linens stacked carefully in her arms, she started down the stairs. She hadn't taken two steps into the downstairs hallway before the caterer grabbed her arm, nearly sending the clean linens to the floor.

"Ms. Hansen... Oh, sorry." The woman caught the stack as it toppled. "I have to talk with you."

"Is something wrong?" Judging by the expression on Janine Laker's face, something was amiss, and Paula braced herself. Janine and her brother were supposed to be the best caterers in town, in addition to running the finest restaurant. They'd do a wonderful job, everyone said, but they had high expectations of the resident staff. Meaning her.

"The cleaning people are supposed to be finished in here." Janine glared at the man running a vacuum in the dining room. "And the flowers haven't arrived yet. We can't finish the tables without the flowers."

"I'll take care of it." Paula tried to sound soothing. "The cleaners will be finished momentarily, and I'll see to the flowers."

An answering glare from the cleaner suggested he wouldn't welcome any advice on finishing his job, and Janine didn't look as reassured as she hoped.

"We want everything to be perfect when we do a dinner," Janine said. "Everything."

"I'm sure it will be." Paula hoped she sounded calmer than she felt. "You can leave the dining room to me."

Looking only partially appeased, Janine disappeared into the kitchen.

Cleaners, florist, table settings. She shook her

head, remembering the moment in which she'd assured herself that this would be easy. Give her thirty rambunctious five-year-olds, and she knew what to do. Making the arrangements for a formal dinner party was something else again.

Finally the cleaners were finished and out the door, taking their equipment with them. The florist had delivered the centerpiece, and delightful aromas had begun to float from the kitchen. Paula stood back, looking with admiration at the long table. Pristine white linen covered it, with not an errant crease in sight. Bone china reflected light back toward the chandelier, and cut-glass tumblers glistened.

Her gaze lingered on the massive chair at the head of the table. Alex would sit there, elegant and in control. Candlelight would flicker, while soft music played in the background. With a guilty start, she realized she was picturing herself seated at that table, too. Firmly putting that image from her mind, she began folding napkins.

Just as she finished, Alex came in. His swift gaze assessed the room.

"Is everything ready?" He frowned, looking at the table as if he expected a flaw.

"Everything is coming along fine," she said. "You don't need to worry." At least, she certainly hoped that was true. She ran her mind over her lists again, nervously checking to see that everything had been done.

"I don't see any place cards." Alex strode to the table, his frown deepening. "I told you we'd need place cards." His tone suggested that only the most inept of housekeepers would neglect something so important. And maybe that he hadn't expected any better from her.

Paula snatched up the calligraphy place cards she'd left on the window sill and handed them to him. "Place cards," she said.

He had the grace to look embarrassed. "I thought you'd forgotten them."

"You didn't tell me how you wanted the seating arranged, so I was waiting until you arrived to put them out."

She tried to feel resentment, because that was safer than looking at her true emotions. Unfortunately she knew what they were—longing, hurt, love.

Alex looked down at the place cards in his hand, because that way he didn't have to look at Paula's face. She'd hand-lettered each card in graceful script, and his guilt deepened. She'd done more than he'd asked, and all he'd done in return was bark at her.

"I'm sorry." *Sorry I snapped at you because I*

wanted to keep some space between us. "Let's decide how best to arrange the table."

"Fine."

Her back was stiff as she walked to the long table, her tone making it clear that he wasn't forgiven yet.

"I assume you want Mr. Dieter on your right."

He nodded, handing her the card. He'd thought he knew what his attitude toward Paula had to be. But unfortunately, just seeing her had thrown his careful, well-ordered plans into disarray. He'd been so aghast at the surge of feelings she produced that he'd barked at her in self-defense.

Yesterday he'd let himself get too close, again. He'd almost let himself think a relationship between them might work. Then she'd brought up the crash and looked at him as if he were a hero. That attitude wasn't a recipe for happiness—it was a recipe for disaster.

"It's just not going to be perfect," Paula said. He gave her a startled look, then realized she was talking about the table.

"The arrangement?"

She shrugged. "Too many men and not enough women. Even I know the table should be balanced, but you just can't do it."

He didn't know what to say to the implicit self-criticism in her words. He hadn't intended to make her feel inadequate. She was doing a good job, and he hadn't realized before how difficult it was. Maida had always made things look easy.

"Do you think this will work?" She put the last card in place.

He saw the concern in her eyes, and it touched his heart. "It will be fine." He had a sudden picture of Paula in a soft evening dress instead of her usual jeans and T-shirt, sitting across from him at the table, the candlelight reflected in her deep green eyes. "If you—"

A commotion erupted in the hallway, composed of thudding feet and puppy yelps.

"Nugget, come back here!"

It sounded as if Jason had jumped down the last three or four steps, Alex thought. Jason had never come down the steps that way before Paula entered their lives. Why hadn't it ever occurred to him that a small boy wasn't supposed to be decorous?

Paula reached the hall a few steps before him and bent to corral the golden fur ball that was Nugget. She knelt, holding the puppy, until Jason reached her and grabbed Nugget's collar.

"Hey, Jason, I thought we decided Nugget would stay outside today." Her voice was soft, her face on a level with his son's.

Jason's lower lip came out in a pout. "Why can't he be in here? I want him to."

Paula stroked the puppy. "Well, mostly because there are a lot of strangers in and out today. That's upsetting for a puppy. And we put candy out in dishes for the guests. What if Nugget got some of it? Did you know it could make him sick?''

''I wouldn't do anything to let him get sick.'' Jason's pout disappeared. ''Come on, Nugget. Let's go out back and play. I'll throw the ball for you.''

Boy and dog pounded toward the door, not even noticing Alex, who tried to swallow the lump in his throat. Paula was so good with his son, so easy and unaffected. Jason responded to her better than he had to anyone in a long time.

''You must be a very good teacher,'' he said.

She looked up, as surprised as if she'd forgotten he was there, and got up quickly. ''I am, as a matter of fact.'' She smiled, and the tension between them vanished. ''But what brought that on?''

''You're good with Jason.'' He wanted to say more—to say she'd brought laughter back to his son—but he couldn't form the words.

Paula shrugged. ''I like him. I think he likes me.'' Her gaze slid away from his, and he knew she was hiding something.

''And?'' he prompted.

''I guess…'' She hesitated. ''I guess I feel I let him down, going away so suddenly the last time I was here. I'd like to make up for that, if I can.''

Regret was a cold hand around his heart. He'd been the reason she'd left so abruptly then, he was sure of it. He didn't want to make the same mistake again. But he wanted to show her how much he appreciated her efforts for Jason. For him.

"About the dinner tonight—" He stopped. Was he doing the right thing? A wave of rebellion swept over him. This might not be the proper thing, but he felt quite sure it was right. "Will you do me the honor of joining the guests?"

Either she'd heard him wrong, or she'd misunderstood him. It almost sounded as if Alex were inviting her to be a guest at his dinner. "What did you say?"

"I want you to join us." Alex gestured toward the table. "You can easily fit another place setting there, since Dieter didn't bring as many people as I thought he might." He paused. "Can't you?"

"Well, yes." Pleasure swept through her. Alex wanted her to join in something that was important to him. *Don't read too much into this,* some part of her mind cautioned. "But why do you want me to attend?"

For a moment he looked disconcerted, as if he hadn't expected her to ask the question. "You said yourself the table was unbalanced. Not enough women."

"You could have asked another woman from the office."

"Yes, I could have, but I didn't." He gave her

that rare smile. "I want you to come, Paula. Please."

A wave of warmth flooded her. "In that case, I'd like to." She turned back to the table, to hide any trace of embarrassment. "I can add another setting here."

She felt his gaze on her as she rearranged the place settings, and her hands became clumsy in response. What did he see when he looked at her?

"Paula, there's just one thing." He was frowning again, looking at her jeans. "You do have something else to wear, don't you?"

Well, that seemed to be the answer to how he saw her—as someone who didn't know how to dress. Before she could respond, someone did it for her.

"Alex, that's not a question to ask a woman." Anne Donovan came in through the kitchen door, amusement filling her deep blue eyes. She gestured toward the kitchen. "The caterers let me in. I hope you don't mind."

Alex smiled, kissing her cheek lightly. "You're always welcome. Is that for me?" He nodded toward the sheaf of papers in her hand.

"No, it's for Paula. A list with phone numbers of people who are going to bring food in or help out when Maida comes home. I thought she might be feeling overwhelmed at the moment." She shot a teasing glance at Alex. ''And your insults don't help.''

He raised his hands as if to shield himself from attack. ''I just thought Paula might not have come prepared for a dinner party.''

Paula did a quick mental inventory of the clothes she'd brought with her. Was there anything suitable for dinner with Alex's business associates? Did she even *own* anything suitable?

''That's not a problem,'' Anne said. ''If she doesn't have anything with her, we're about the same size. But Alex, if Paula is going to attend this business dinner, she has to have time to get ready. You can't expect her to make all the arrangements, take care of Jason, and then scramble into her clothes.''

Paula tensed for one of Alex's polite putdowns, but it didn't come. Anne, like her husband, seemed to be one of the few people who could treat Alex like a human being. He shook his head, smiling.

''You're right as always. Paula, please take all the time you need. I'm sure the caterers know what they're doing, and I'll see to Jason.''

''And the puppy,'' Anne prompted.

''And the puppy,'' Alex agreed. He shook his head. ''I don't know how Mitch managed to survive before you came to town.''

''Not as well as he does now,'' Anne said, her mouth softening at the mention of her husband. She linked her arm through Paula's. "Come on. Let's decide what you're wearing tonight."

Bemused at Anne's management, Paula let herself be led through the kitchen and out onto the patio. There she stopped, common sense reasserting itself.

"Alex was right. I really don't have anything with me to wear." She looked down at her jeans. "And even if I did, it wouldn't be suitable for Alex's high-powered business types."

"Relax." Anne patted her arm. "We really are about the same size, and I have a closet full of clothes from when I used to work with some of those high-powered business types." She smiled. "Believe me, those clothes don't get much of an outing in Bedford Creek. I'll find an outfit for you to wear."

"But I couldn't. What if I spilled something on it?"

"Everything can be cleaned." Anne didn't seem concerned. "I'll run home and bring a couple of choices back. Meanwhile, you go run yourself a bubble bath." Her face lit with laughter. "We're going to knock Alex for a loop, believe me."

Paula still found the turn of events hard to believe two hours later, when she stood in front of the full-length mirror in Maida's cottage.

"That's it." Anne, sitting behind her on the twin

bed, beamed with satisfaction. "That outfit was never quite right for me, but on you it's absolutely perfect."

Paula ran her hand down the length of shimmering aqua silk. "Are you sure you want to lend this? It's so lovely." It was the kind of dress she'd look at in the windows of the most exclusive shops— look at and walk on, knowing she couldn't afford it.

"I'm positive." Anne got up, a small box in her hand. "I brought the jewelry I wore with it, since you probably don't have much with you for the summer."

"What a tactful way of putting it." Paula smiled.

Anne held the dangling crystal drops at Paula's ears. "What do you think? They're the perfect touch, aren't they?"

Paula looked again at the image in the mirror. If she blinked, that elegant stranger might disappear. She laughed suddenly. "Aunt Maida would say, 'Fine feathers don't make fine birds.'"

"In this case, the fine feathers are just bringing out the beauty that's already there." Anne gave her a quick hug. "You really will dazzle them."

Paula glanced at the clock, and a wave of pure panic swept over her. "It's almost time. What on earth am I going to say to those people? I don't know anything about business."

"They're just people," Anne said. "Encourage

them to talk about themselves, and they'll be happy.'' She turned toward the door. ''You can't back out now. Alex is counting on you.''

''Right.'' Paula took a deep breath. She could do this. Anne was right—they were just people.

They walked back to the mansion together, but Anne stopped at the back door. ''I'd better get home. Wish I could be a fly on the wall, though. I'd give anything to watch Alex's face when he sees you.''

Hand on the door, Paula paused, thinking about Anne's words. That was why she stood here, half eager, half afraid. Because she wanted Alex to see her in a new way. Not as a housekeeper, not as a nanny, not as his assistant baseball coach. She wanted him to see her as a woman—a woman he could love.

Chapter Thirteen

W here was Paula? Alex wondered for perhaps the twentieth time, as he stood in the front hallway, greeting his guests. She'd done a wonderful job of organizing this affair. The old house shone with an unusually welcoming air. He tried to analyze the change. Perhaps it was the bowl of fresh-cut flowers on the hall table—from the garden, he realized, not the florist. Or maybe it was the way Janine circulated, at Paula's suggestion, offering shrimp and cheese puffs from a tray as guests arrived.

Paula had put her own stamp on this affair. The only thing missing was Paula herself.

He silently counted heads. Everyone else had arrived, including Christian Dieter and his staff. Dieter, a rotund elderly man whose cherubic expression was belied by a pair of shrewd ice-blue eyes, seemed genuinely pleased at being entertained in Alex's home.

Alex pressed down a wave of apprehension. No one must know from his demeanor how important this night was to him. He should be concentrating on Dieter, not worrying because Paula hadn't shown up yet.

Maybe she'd lost her nerve at the thought of participating. It hadn't occurred to him at the time that he might be putting additional pressure on her with his invitation. He'd just wanted to show her how much he appreciated her, not put her on the spot. She might have balked at the thought of coming to an elegant dinner party in a hand me-down dress.

Just then, the door to the rear of the house swung open, and Paula walked into the hallway. She stopped directly under the crystal chandelier his great-grandfather had brought back from Germany.

The breath went out of him. She was beautiful. The blond curls that usually tumbled around her face had been swept back into a sophisticated style, and crystal drops dangled from her ears and around her neck, rivaling the chandelier for brilliance. The dress, an elegant length of aqua silk, molded her slender form, making her skin glow with a golden sheen, as if she'd brought the sunlight in with her.

He wasn't the only one she'd struck dumb, he realized. Dieter stood silent, interrupted in the midst of a story he'd been telling. With a brief nod, he dismissed the aide at his elbow and moved toward Paula.

It was high time Alex stopped staring, too. Anyone who'd been watching him would have known that Paula Hansen had just made him feel like an awkward kid instead of the company president.

He arrived at Paula's side in time to hear Dieter introducing himself.

"I am Christian Dieter." The man captured Paula's hand and held it in both of his. "I regret that I have not yet been introduced to you."

Paula's smile looked a bit strained. "I'm Paula Hansen, Mr. Dieter. It's a pleasure to meet you."

Dieter raised his eyebrows as he looked at Alex. "Where have you been hiding this lovely lady since our arrival?"

"I'm Alex's—"

"I'm afraid Paula has been very busy lately." Alex put his hand lightly on her waist, identifying his feeling with some surprise—possessiveness. He shouldn't feel that way about her, but he couldn't deny it. "Paula is a friend who's been helping me this summer."

"Lucky man," Dieter murmured, "to have such a lovely helper. And what do you do, Ms. Hansen, when you are not helping your friends?"

"I'm a teacher."

Paula drew slightly away from Alex, as if to put some space between them, but he increased the pressure of his hand, unwilling to let her go. He thought the faintest flush touched her cheeks.

"I teach kindergarten at a school in Baltimore."

"Inner Harbor," Dieter exclaimed, beaming. "I visited your city once on business. It's lovely."

Alex wondered, a little sourly, if there was anything Dieter didn't find lovely. Janine arrived at his elbow with a tray, distracting Dieter. As the man began asking Janine to identify the various tidbits, Alex drew Paula away from them a step or two.

She looked up at him, her eyebrows lifting. "A friend?" she asked softly.

He thought there was a slightly edgy undertone to her voice. "Aren't you a friend?" he countered, enjoying the way her green eyes sparkled.

Her chin tilted at a stubborn angle. "Maybe. But I'm also your housekeeper, remember? Are you embarrassed to tell Mr. Dieter that?"

She tried again to pull away from him, but he captured her hand. "Not at all. But tonight you're not my housekeeper. You're my guest."

Her hand twisted in his, and he tightened his fingers. They were engaged in a battle, locked in a private circle, just the two of them. The buzz of conversation in the hallway only served to isolate them together.

Paula looked up at him, emotions warring in her face. "I don't want people to get the wrong idea. They might think—"

She stopped, as if afraid to put it into words.

"They might think we're together," he finished for her. "Would that be so terrible?"

"I don't know." She met his gaze with a challenge in those clear green eyes. "Would it?"

Alarm bells seemed to be going off in his mind, and he ruthlessly suppressed them.

"Not at all," he said softly. He raised her hand, holding it in both of his. "Besides, if I don't lay claim to you, every man here will be trying to impress you. Then how will we get any work done at all?"

"That would be a problem." Her gaze never left his, and the things they weren't saying hovered in the air between them.

"We can't have that," he said. He brought her hand to his lips and kissed it, feeling her smooth skin warm to his touch. The others receded into the distance, as vague and insubstantial as flickering images on an old newsreel.

He heard her breath go out in a little sigh.

"No." She barely breathed the word. "I guess we can't."

Paula was adrift in an ocean in which only she and Alex were real. She knew the others were there, of course. She heard the murmur of polite conversation and the quiet background music she'd started. But all she really felt, all she really knew, was the touch of Alex's lips against her skin.

"Ms. Hansen." Janine's voice was low but insistent.

Paula forced her gaze away from Alex, made herself turn and smile. Janine, neat in a black skirt and white silk blouse, didn't look convinced. Her dark eyes held a certain speculative expression. Paula stiffened. What was the woman thinking?

For that matter, what was everyone else thinking? The whole room could have noticed the byplay between her and Alex. She took a cautious look around, but the others seemed engrossed in their own conversations.

"Dinner is ready to serve, Ms. Hansen."

Paula tried to look as if she received messages like that every day. She suspected Janine wasn't fooled.

"We'll be right in." She turned to Alex, trying to keep from blushing as her gaze met his. "Will you get people moving to the dining room?"

"I will." He touched her arm. "And you'll go in with me."

The wonder was that she actually arrived at the table without tripping over her heels. And she couldn't blame it on the fact that she'd been wearing sneakers all summer. Alex's grasp was sending messages tingling along her skin, distracting her so that the simplest action seemed difficult. Luckily she'd seated herself along the side of the long table, where she wouldn't have to meet his gaze throughout the meal.

But Alex led her to the chair opposite his, quietly indicating places to his guests as he did so. He pulled out the chair, and she shook her head.

"This isn't mine," she murmured.

He nodded to the place card. "It is now," he said.

He must have changed them around, and she could hardly try to rearrange the seating at this point. She slid into the seat he held out, very aware of his strong hands brushing her shoulders. He bent over as he seated her, his face so close to hers that she felt the warmth radiating from his skin.

"You're my hostess," he said softly, his breath caressing her cheek. "Naturally you'll sit opposite me." Then he straightened, and her skin felt cold where his breath had been.

She sat very straight as he went to the head of the table, trying not to watch him. How she was going to get through this evening without everyone there knowing she loved him, she couldn't imagine.

Love. The word echoed in her mind, shaking her. No, she couldn't let herself think things like that. Resolutely she turned to the man seated on her right.

Dieter's second-in-command looked far too young for his position, and much too stiff to carry on a conversation with her. After several futile attempts to find something they had in common, Paula remembered Anne's advice.

"Do you have a family back in Zurich?" she asked, not sure whether it was common for European men to wear wedding bands.

He beamed. "My wife and I have a baby daughter. She is just six months old."

It took very little prompting to get him going then. As he told her story after story designed to show that young Elissa was surely the brightest baby who'd ever been born, Paula decided that Anne had been right. He was really just a person.

He produced photos of a round-faced, solemn infant, and talked about how much he missed his family when he had to travel with Uncle Christian on business. She nodded, made encouraging noises and tried not to watch Alex.

But it was useless. She couldn't prevent her gaze from being drawn to him, any more than a compass could prevent its needle from pointing north.

She forced herself to look away, glancing around the table. Janine and her brother had outdone themselves, and the salmon *en croute* had been an inspired choice for the entrée. Dieter ate and gestured, his face growing more relaxed by the moment. He leaned toward Alex, nodding, and she could tell by the smallest of things—the set of Alex's mouth, the movement of his hand—that he was pleased.

Where had it come from, that unconscious ability to read his mood? When had every line, every gesture, become familiar and dear to her?

Love, she thought again, and this time the word didn't seem quite so frightening. Alex looked up just then and caught her watching him. He gave her a small, private smile.

Something strong and tangible seemed to run the length of the table between them. The connection was so palpable that she felt everyone at the table must have been able to see it. It was so strong it gripped her heart as if it would never let go.

"It has been a great pleasure. Thank you again." Dieter beamed at Paula, clasping her hand, as he and his entourage finally headed out the door.

She'd felt stiff, standing next to Alex in the gracious center hallway, telling his guests good-night as if she and Alex were a couple. But Alex had made it clear that was what he expected, and no one else seemed surprised. Of course, Dieter and his people didn't know what her true position was here, and those who worked for Alex apparently accepted what he did without question. It was his house, his company, his town.

When Alex finally closed the door, she should have felt relief, but she didn't. All she could think was that they were alone together, and there were too many conflicting feelings bouncing around inside her for comfort.

"I should check the kitchen," she began, but Alex caught her hand before she could move in that direction.

"Janine and her crew will leave everything spotless. They always do, and she wouldn't like the suggestion that you had to check on her."

"No, I didn't mean that." *I meant the excuse would get me out of your presence until I figure out what's happening between us.*

Alex loosened his tie. "It went well tonight. Thank you, Paula. For everything."

She nodded. Did "everything" include the way he'd teased her? The moment when he'd kissed her hand? Her skin tingled at the memory. Maybe she'd better find a safer topic of conversation.

"What about Dieter? I saw the two of you talking at dinner, and he looked receptive."

"Very receptive." His face relaxed in a smile. "I'm beginning to think we might pull this off. And if we do, I owe you thanks for that, too. I don't know how I'd have gotten through these past weeks if you hadn't been here."

"I was glad to fill in for Aunt Maida in any way I could." That sounded hopelessly stilted, and it wasn't what she wanted to say at all. What she wanted to say was that she'd do anything for him.

But how could she, when she didn't know how he felt?

She glanced at her watch. "Well, maybe I'd better go." She gestured to the silk dress. "I think it's time for Cinderella to turn back into a pumpkin."

"That isn't how the story goes, is it?" He still held her hand loosely, and she didn't want to pull away.

"Close enough," she said.

"I'll walk you out."

His hand was warm against her waist as they pushed through the swinging door into the back of the house. From the kitchen came the clatter of pans and the sound of voices. Alex guided her out the back door to the patio.

The nearly full moon sent a silver path along the surface of the pool, and the stars clustered thickly, far brighter than they ever were when seen from the city. She walked beside Alex, hearing the faint unevenness in his steps that was the only hint of his leg injury.

They stopped at the end of the pool. The kitchen window cast a golden oblong onto the flagstones, but other than that everything was dark and quiet. The silver birch bent gracefully opposite them, its white bark sketching a ghostly figure against the gazebo.

"It's a beautiful night," she murmured. Maybe

speech would interrupt the flood of feelings that surged through her. She shivered a little.

"You're cold," Alex said instantly. Before she could object, he'd shed his suit coat. "Put this on. Lovely as it is, I don't think that silk is going to keep you warm."

He draped the coat over her shoulders. It fell around her, still warm with the heat of his body. The fine wool carried a faint, musky scent that seemed to say his name.

She looked up. Alex was a dark silhouette against the darker night. She couldn't make out his expression, but whatever she imagined of his face took her breath away. She wanted to put her palms on his white shirt front, feel his heart beating....

"I should go in." Her voice sounded soft and uncertain, not at all like her.

"Maybe you should," he murmured, but his grip tightened on her hands.

"Jason will be up early. I really..." She lost whatever she'd been about to say when Alex drew her slowly against him.

His shirt was smooth against her hands, and through it she could feel the warmth of his body. For a heartbeat he just held her close. Then he stroked her face, his fingertips gentle against her skin, and emotion ricocheted through her. She cared so much for him. She'd tried to deny it, but it was no use.

He tipped her chin back, his touch insistent, and then his lips found hers. Gentle, so gentle. The kiss was tentative, questioning, as if he gave her every opportunity to draw away if that was what she wanted.

But she couldn't. Her arms slid around him almost without conscious volition, and every cell in her seemed to sing. She drew him closer. Paula's heart pounded, so full it seemed it could hold no more. She loved him, and she wanted to stay in his arms forever.

He pulled away, tearing his lips from hers. "No."

She could only stare at him, trying to read his expression through the gloom, trying to understand through the tumult in her heart. It was what had happened before. He'd kissed her in the moonlight, and then he had pulled away, apologized, tried to pretend it had never happened.

But he couldn't get away with denying it this time. Two years ago she'd let him, but not now. Not when she saw how he wanted to hold her. That gave her courage.

"Why?" She caught his arms when he would have pulled away, held him close. He couldn't break free without hurting her, and she knew he wouldn't do that. "Just tell me why. You can't say you don't want this, because I don't believe it."

His breath sounded ragged. "Maybe I do. But I'm not the hero you think I am, Paula. I'm not."

Her first impulse was to argue, to point out that he'd saved her life at the risk of his own. But some instinct told her that was the wrong thing to say. For whatever reason, he couldn't see himself in that light. And it was important to him. She could feel how important in the tension under her hands.

"That's good," she said quietly. "Because I don't want a hero. Just you, Alex. Just you."

Chapter Fourteen

Paula came awake slowly, trying without success to hold on to the fragments of a dream. She couldn't remember what the image had been, but she knew it was happy. She still felt warm and protected in its aftermath. Automatically she reached out for Nugget, but her hand didn't encounter a furry object in the puppy's usual sleeping spot.

She opened her eyes. Nugget wasn't there. Then she remembered. Alex had said the puppy could spend the night with Jason, so she could concentrate on the dinner party.

She sat up, memories flooding her—last night, the dinner, those moments on the patio when Alex had kissed her and she'd felt as if she'd come home.

Be careful, a faint, cautious voice urged in the back of her mind. *Be careful with your heart. It's*

*a long way from kisses in the moonlight to happily
ever after.*

That was probably good advice. Unfortunately,
she suspected it was far too late for her to heed it.

She glanced at the clock, then swung off the bed
and reached for her clothes. She was late. Alex and
Jason would be expecting their breakfast.

A few minutes later, she hurried into the kitchen,
half expecting to find Alex already in search of his
morning coffee. But the kitchen was spotless and
empty. One of Maida's refrigerator magnets held a
note in Alex's bold hand.

She snatched the paper, unable to prevent a silly
little catch to her breath. But the brisk message,
saying he'd had a meeting and had left early, didn't
give any indication its writer had been thinking of
late-night kisses.

Paula pressed down a surge of disappointment.
She'd better get Jason up and have him take Nugget
outside while she fixed his breakfast.

The front area of the mansion, back to its usual
silence, seemed to reject the memory of yesterday's
hustle and the evening's elegance. She went quickly
up the stairs to Jason's room and called out his
name, tapping as she opened the door.

But Jason wasn't there. And when she went to
the window that overlooked the pool and the back
lawn, she still saw no sign of boy or dog.

Paula had just started down the stairs when she

paused, listening. Something disturbed the stillness. Then she heard it—the smallest yelp, instantly shushed. The sound came from the circular staircase that led to the cupola on top of the house.

She went quickly to the steps and looked up, squinting against the sunshine pouring toward her through the windows of the octagonal cupola. "Jason?"

Nugget barked in answer. What was going on? Surely the puppy hadn't gone up there alone. She hurried up the steep, tight spiral.

She reached the top step and stood on the cupola floor, then instantly regretted it. The tall windows on every side of the octagonal chamber gave views of the town, the river far below, and the mountain ridges soaring above. Standing there was like flying above the valley.

Jason sat scrunched into a ball, his face turned away from her. She sat, scooting close enough to Jason to touch him.

Please, Father, please. Show me what this child needs from me.

"Hey." She touched his shoulder gently. "What's going on? You can tell me."

He moved slightly, then buried his face again, but not before she'd seen the tears in his eyes.

"Jason, what is it? Are you hurt?"

He shook his head, holding out against her for another moment. Then, quite suddenly, he looked up. "I saw you." He hurled the words at her accusingly.

"You saw me?" What on earth had him so upset?

"I saw you," he said again. "Last night. From my window. You were kissing my daddy."

Her heart turned over. Jason's bedroom windows overlooked the patio. He'd obviously been looking out. What he'd been doing up that late wasn't the point. He'd seen them, and he was upset.

She tried to respond calmly, not making too much of it. "Your dad walked out with me after the party. Yes, we did kiss. Grown-ups do that sometimes when they like each other. It doesn't mean…"

She couldn't make herself say that kissing Alex didn't mean anything, because that wouldn't be true. His kisses had meant a great deal to her. Whether they meant the same to Alex was still to be determined.

"It's just like before." Jason's face was blotchy with tears. "That's what you did before, and then you went away."

His words pierced her heart. Jason was right—although he couldn't possibly know or understand the reasons. She'd kissed Alex, and she'd left when he made it clear that kiss had been a mistake. What else could she have done? After all, she had a little pride—

She stopped, the word resonating to her very soul. *Pride.* Was that what it had been? Was that what had put her on that airplane, intending to scurry back to Baltimore? She didn't want to believe that about herself.

Jason's the important person now. Do your soul-searching later.

"Jason, I'm sorry I went away." She spoke slowly, choosing her words carefully. Each one should be as true as she could make it. "I made a mistake, and I let you down. I'm sorry."

He shook his head violently. "Everybody goes away. It's my fault."

She stared at him, appalled that this precious child could think it his fault people had let him down. *His mother. Then me. I let him learn to rely on me, and then I left. I ran away because I couldn't face the emotional pain of staying.*

"Jason, it's not your fault. Please, believe me. Talk to me about this." She tried to touch him again, but he shook off her hand and scrambled to his feet.

"I won't talk to you!" He shouted it, the hurt in his eyes turning suddenly to anger. "I won't! You'll just go away again!"

He turned and thundered down the steps.

She sat where she was, trying to grasp what was happening. Nugget stood at the top of the steps, whining, then came to her and nudged her hand.

She gathered him into her arms, understanding why Jason had been up here hugging him. Comfort. The child had been looking for the comfort he wasn't getting from the adults in his life.

Is that what I've been doing, Lord? Asking the question was painful. *Have I been running away? Has my pride in being independent just been a cover for being afraid?*

She felt as if God had taken her heart, with all its pitiful little secrets, and held it up to His sunlight, pouring through the high windows. She wasn't very happy with what she saw.

She'd hurt Jason through her cowardice. She'd run away when she should have faced things. Faced Alex. If he hadn't cared for her then, if he didn't care for her now, she had to face it and go on. And right now Jason's needs had to come first.

Certainty pooled in her. She knew what God expected of her. The child was hurting, and he was trying to hide that pain, probably because he saw his father do the same thing.

It's my fault. Jason's words put a lump in her throat. He wouldn't tell her what he meant or why he believed that. His father was the only one who could possibly get to the bottom of this.

She had to make Alex see the truth about his son. Her heart seemed to cramp. It didn't take much imagination to know how Alex would react. Confronting him could put an end to any hope she might cherish that he returned her love.

She didn't have a choice. She had to do this, and soon, no matter what the cost.

Alex walked into the house, realizing he half expected to hear the noisy thud of Jason's feet on the oak stairwell or find Paula chasing an errant puppy across the Italian marble floor. But the Caine mansion preserved its silence, just as it had before Paula came back.

How had she managed to make such a difference in this place in a few short weeks? How had she managed to make such a difference in their lives? He'd told himself he no longer believed in happy endings. But Paula had begun to make a believer out of him.

If they shared many more moments like those out on the patio last night, he'd no longer have a choice about it. He'd tried, in the quiet hours of the night, to apply reason and logic to his reactions. But reason and logic didn't seem to fit the emotions Paula roused in him.

He carried his briefcase into the library, telling himself to concentrate on business. The meeting with Dieter had gone better than he'd dared hope. The man's assistant had even dropped a hint that they'd enjoy an opportunity to become acquainted with a number of community leaders—perhaps an informal social event at the Caine mansion?

Alex had quickly agreed, making mental lists to line up the caterers and have his secretary send invitations. Town council members, business owners, police chief, doctor—he'd have to include them all. Dieter and his associates wouldn't suggest such an event, he felt sure, unless they were on the verge of signing the agreement.

He heard Paula's steps sounding in the hallway. A moment later she walked into the library, and he knew moonlight had had nothing to do with his feelings.

"Paula." He rounded the table, wanting to eliminate the distance between them. "I'm glad you're here."

She stopped in the middle of the oriental carpet, reminding him of the day she'd stood there telling him he had to let her stay. She looked just as determined now as she had then.

"I need to talk with you." She seemed guarded, folding her arms across the rainbow design on the front of her T-shirt.

"That's good, because I want to talk with you, too." His news would wipe that concerned expression from her face. "About last night."

A warm flush brightened her peaches-and-cream skin, and he knew she was thinking of those moments on the patio. Suddenly he was there, holding her in his arms and wanting never to let her go.

"The dinner party," he added quickly. "I wanted to thank you for everything you did to make it a success. Dieter was pleased."

"That's nice." She shrugged her shoulders, as if to dismiss that as of no importance. "But—"

"Nice? It's more than nice." He closed the gap between them with a quick stride. "I've told you how important this deal is to the company's survival." He wanted to take her hands, but her body language set a barrier between them. "I think they're almost ready to sign."

The enthusiasm and encouragement he'd anticipated weren't there, and it annoyed him. Didn't she understand how important this was?

"They've asked for an opportunity to meet community leaders. That has to be a prelude to announcing a deal." Energy surged through him. He was going to pull this off. For an instant he imagined he'd look at the portrait of his father over the fireplace and read approval there. "I want to hold a reception here next Saturday. My secretary will take care of the invitations and schedule the catering. You'll handle it the way you did the dinner party."

Again she responded with the briefest of shrugs, as if the most important deal of his life were a trifle. "Yes, good." Her mind was obviously elsewhere.

"I'm glad it's working out, but I need to speak with you about something else."

Apparently he'd been wrong. He tried not to feel disappointment at her attitude. Paula didn't share his triumph. Apparently she didn't see this as anything more than just another job.

"What is it?" He took a step back, hearing his voice harden. "What's so important?"

"Jason." The muscles in her neck moved, as if she struggled to swallow. "I'm worried about Jason."

"Is he ill?" He glanced toward the hallway. "I assumed he was out when I didn't hear him."

"He is." She shook her head. "I mean, no, he's not ill. Rebecca picked him up to play with Kristie for the afternoon."

"Then what is it?"

"He's upset. I found him crying this morning." She hesitated, glancing away as if she didn't want to look at him. "He saw us last night. When we were on the patio. When we were kissing."

So that's what this was all about. "Paula, I'm sorry he was upset about it, but that's hardly surprising. I haven't...there hasn't been another woman in our lives since his mother left."

"It's not just that. I wish he hadn't seen us, but that's a minor part of the problem. He was genuinely upset, even angry." Color flamed in her cheeks. "He reminded me that we kissed the last time I was here. And then I went away."

Shame over Alex's behavior then reared its head, and he slammed it down. He couldn't let himself be sidetracked by past mistakes.

"Look, I know this is important, but I don't believe it's as serious as you're making out. I'll speak with Jason, explain it to him. He's a bright child, he'll understand."

Her soft mouth firmed in a stubborn line. "Alex, this is serious. You don't understand. Jason is troubled. He needs your time and attention right now."

Something in him tightened with annoyance. Paula was creating mountains out of molehills. Much as he appreciated her concern for Jason, she was letting herself get carried away. He tried reason.

"This summer hasn't been easy for Jason, I realize that. As soon as this business with Dieter is settled, I'll make more time for him. But this deal has to take priority. It will assure everyone's future, including Jason's."

She was shaking her head before he finished speaking. "Jason needs you now. He needs his father's attention."

His control slipped, and he felt himself reach for the protective barrier that was part of his Caine family tradition. "I'm doing what I have to for everyone, Paula, including Jason. I'm afraid you'll just have to accept the fact that I know best.''

Alex's arrogant words were like a match set to the tinder of her emotions, Paula realized. He knew best, according to him. Whatever was happening, whatever she thought and felt, Alex believed, just as her father always did, that he knew what was right for everyone.

''No.'' The word came out with the force of an explosion.

Alex looked at her, eyebrows lifting, perhaps at her daring to question him. ''What?''

''I said no.'' She took a breath, trying to hold on to whatever composure she had left. She had to make him understand. ''I'm sorry, but in this situation you don't know best. Not if you think your business deal comes before your son.''

He didn't move, but he withdrew. His frozen, superior expression told her she was losing him.

''My relationship with my son is not your concern.''

''Yes, it is.'' She tried not to think about those moments in his arms, because if she did, she'd be lost. ''I care about him.'' *And about you.* ''I can't just stand back and ignore it when I see him hurting.''

His dark eyes flickered, telling her that had touched him.

"I'm sorry." His voice softened. "Paula, I know you care about Jason. I shouldn't have said that. But you have to understand how important this is. The whole town will be affected by what I do in the next few days."

She knew he believed that. She could almost sense the heavy load of his responsibility for this town and its people. "Don't you see? The town needs you, yes. But not in the way your son does."

"Jason is just as affected as everyone else by the success or failure of this deal. It's his future I'm trying to assure."

He'd put up that shield that protected him from normal human emotions. She'd like to rattle him, but she knew that wasn't going to happen. Alex didn't get rattled. He'd just freeze her out, and she'd never be able to reach him.

"Is that what you think? That financial security is what Jason needs from you?"

He turned away, and despair gripped her. She looked from him to the portrait of his father, staring arrogantly out at the world as if he owned it.

"I suppose he'd approve of what you're doing?" She flung her hand out toward the painting.

Alex's jaw tightened until it looked made of marble. "My father's approval has nothing to do with this." The words were chipped from ice.

"Doesn't it?" She'd gone too far now. There was no going back. "Isn't that what this is all about, Alex? You're still trying to earn his approval, and you're doing it by repeating all of his mistakes. You're not thinking about Jason. You're thinking about the precious Caine family name!''

She stopped, suddenly breathless and exhausted. Alex stared at her as if from a very long distance. Then he walked to the library door and opened it.

It was over—that was all she could think. She walked out, passing him, trying to hold on to whatever composure she could. She'd tried to make him understand, tried to do what she thought God expected of her. And she'd failed. She wouldn't have another chance.

Chapter Fifteen

Paula's smile vanished as she closed the door of Aunt Maida's room in the rehab unit. She'd managed to maintain an air of normalcy during her visit, but she didn't think Aunt Maida had been fooled.

Leave it in God's hands, Aunt Maida had said as Paula was leaving. *Whatever the problem, leave it in God's hands.*

Unfortunately that seemed easier said than done. Paula stood for a moment, looking out at the courtyard of the rehabilitation unit, abloom with roses. She'd tried to turn her worries for Jason over to the Lord, just as she'd tried to relinquish her pain over the situation with Alex. But her rebellious spirit kept picking the burden up again. Surely there was something she could do—some way to make this right.

"Hi, Paula. How is she today?" Brett Elliot tucked a chart under his arm as he loped down the hall toward her. "Is she ready to get out of here and tackle the world?"

She had to smile, because that was an apt description of Aunt Maida's mood. "Just about. When do you think she'll be able to come home?"

"I'd like to hang on to her a few more days." He checked the chart. "Let's at least wait until after this reception Alex is planning. If we send her home before that, you'll have to tie her down to keep her from helping."

Even the most casual mention of Alex was enough to set the still-painful wound throbbing, but she managed to keep her smile on straight. "You know her too well."

"How is everything going with you?"

Brett's sympathetic tone was almost her undoing, and she struggled to suppress her worries. "I think the reception is under control." She deliberately kept the conversation superficial. He was Alex's friend, and she certainly couldn't discuss Alex with him, no matter how sympathetic he was.

"Alex tends to have a one-track mind about things like that," Brett said, his tone casual. "I've always thought he had way too much sense of responsibility. Of course, back in the old days, he said I had too little." He glanced over her shoulder. "Speaking of Alex, here he is now."

The warning gave her a moment to catch her breath and stiffen her spine before she turned.

"I didn't realize you were coming to see Maida this morning." *If I had, I wouldn't be here.*

Alex, dauntingly businesslike in a dark suit, came to a stop a few feet from them, as if he didn't want to get any closer to her than necessary.

"I had to come to town, anyway, to see an attorney about some business."

"I see." At least Brett was there, so they weren't alone.

"I'd better be off. Duty calls." Brett was halfway down the hall before she could react. "See you Saturday," he called over his shoulder, and left her alone with Alex.

Alex turned to her, and she tried to find some armor to protect her. There was something she had to say to him, if only she could get it out without betraying how she really felt.

"Brett says Aunt Maida can come home next week." She hoped that sounded as casual and cheerful as she wanted it to.

"Good. You can take off whatever time you need to get her settled." Alex glanced toward Maida's door, as if ready to move on at the earliest opportunity.

"I wondered..." She took a deep breath to still the quaking inside her. Was it better if his answer was yes or no? She really didn't know, so she'd better just get it out. "Once Maida is home, she might be able to supervise someone else doing the work. I'm sure we could work it out, if you'd prefer that I leave then."

He froze, but his well-bred mask didn't betray his opinion. "Is that what you want?"

Only the truth would do here, she knew. "No, it's not. If I leave now, I'll be doing the same thing I did the last time. That would just confirm Jason's fears, and I don't want to do that."

Do you? Talk to me about it, Alex. Please.

He gave a curt nod. "Fine. Stay until Maida is on her feet again." He turned toward the door. "I'll go in and see her now. Then I must get back to the plant."

It wasn't fine, but there also wasn't anything she could do about it. She'd stay until her aunt was well, and she'd try to ignore the pain that clutched her heart each time she saw Alex.

When Maida had recovered, when they'd had time to prepare Jason, she'd leave. And this time, when she left Bedford Creek, she wouldn't be coming back.

The reception spilled from the French doors as the crowd eddied through the downstairs of the mansion, out onto the sunlit lawn, across the patio. Alex made his way methodically from one group to another, encountering smiles and chatter. People seemed to be enjoying themselves, and that included the visitors from Dieter Industries.

A small group clustered around a table serving hot appetizers. He would have had the caterer set up a formal buffet in the dining room, but Paula had suggested a number of small serving stations, instead, scattered throughout the house and grounds. She'd been right. His guests mixed and re-formed again and again, and Dieter's people mixed with the rest.

He scanned the crowd—men in suits, women in colorful dresses that brightened in the sunshine like so many flowers. Where was Dieter? The man had proved remarkably evasive of late. Tension formed a knot in Alex's stomach, and he deposited the mushroom tart he'd been eating on the nearest tray. He'd expected, by this time, that Dieter would have—

"Dad?" Jason, wearing a dark suit and tie that replicated his father's attire, tugged on his sleeve and looked up at him questioningly. "Did you hear me?"

"Sorry, Jason." He tried to concentrate on his son, but his gaze kept straying to the surrounding crowd. Where was Dieter, anyway? "What did you say?"

"When is Maida going to come home?" Jason's small face tightened. "You said we'd talk about it, but we never did."

"Soon." Alex patted his shoulder. "The doctor says she can come home soon."

"But when?" Jason's voice took on a whining note. "When, Dad? I want to know now."

"Jason." He swallowed the tone of exasperation. "Look, son, I don't have an exact date, not yet. But she will be back. Just trust me on this, please."

"But what about Paula? Is she going to go away? I don't want her to." Jason's lower lip came out in a pout. "I want her to stay. Make her stay, Dad."

His tension went up a notch at the mention of Paula, until his very skin seemed to tingle with it. His hand tightened on the glass he held. Paula wouldn't stay long—he was sure of that. When they'd talked earlier, she'd made her feelings clear enough. She was staying because she felt Jason and Maida both needed her, not for any other reason.

"Da-ad!" Jason's whine was loud enough to attract attention.

He frowned down at his son. "Jason, this isn't the time or place to talk about this. We'll discuss it later. Everything's going to be all right, I promise."

For a moment Jason looked as if he'd flare up at him. Then he spun away and darted through the crowd.

Alex held out his hand, but it was too late to call Jason back.

Just as it was too late for a lot of other things.

He slammed the door on that morbid thought.

He'd make this up to Jason. As soon as the deal was completed, he'd arrange a weekend trip for the two of them. He and Jason would find a way to talk the way they used to—the way he and his father never had.

Paula would see that everything he'd done was for the best. She'd see—

The crowd around him moved toward a server with a platter of chilled shrimp, the ruffle of movement creating an open path along the grass. Looking down it, he saw Paula.

His throat tightened. She looked like a daffodil in the yellow sundress she wore, and the sunlight gilded her warm skin with gold. She looked like everything he'd ever wanted in a woman—everything he wanted now and couldn't have.

The open space between them turned into a gap—a yawning chasm he didn't know how to cross. They were too far apart; they'd said too many bitter things to each other. There was no way back.

Paula stared at him what seemed a long moment. Then she turned away.

He'd wanted her to stop looking at him as if he were a hero, as if he were the prince in a fairy tale. Well, he didn't need to worry about that any longer. Now she looked at him as if he were the frog.

Paula's heart thumped painfully as she turned away from Alex. This was so difficult—so much harder than she'd dreamed it would be. Her remembered emotions for Alex had been sharp enough to hurt when she'd come back. Now the pain had intensified a hundred times.

She'd thought, or at least she'd hoped, that he'd be able to pull down the walls he held against the rest of the world. She'd imagined she could get close enough to make a difference in his life. That was clearly impossible. As far as she could tell, even Jason's mother hadn't been able to do that.

This wasn't just about what was best for Jason. If it had been that simple, there might have been a way through it. But she'd been fighting three generations' worth of Caine family tradition, and she'd lost.

It was ironic, in a way. She'd always thought her choices had been restricted by her family's working class background. Now she knew that Alex's life had been just as restricted by his family's wealth.

She made her way through the crowd, automatically checking the serving tables as she went. In one way or another, all of these people depended on Alex. That very fact set barriers between them and Alex, whether they realized it or not.

She'd reached the pool area when she realized the crowd was falling silent. Alex and Dieter, surrounded by Dieter's colleagues, stood near the gazebo, and Dieter clinked a spoon against a glass.

The businessman beamed as he held up his hands. "I wish to make a small announcement to my new friends here in Bedford Creek," he said. "I am pleased to tell you that we have come to an agreement joining Caine Industries with the Dieter Corporation in a venture we trust will bring increased prosperity to all of us."

So, Alex had done what he'd set out to do. Paula joined in the applause, trying to feel some genuine happiness for this result. Of course she was pleased. This meant a great deal to Alex personally, as well as to the town. But it was hard to join in the general celebrating when her heart hurt.

People started moving forward to offer their congratulations. Mitch and Anne got there first, closely followed by Brett with Rebecca. The sight of that close little group surrounding Alex just reminded her that she wasn't part of it. She slipped to the rear of the crowd, swallowing hard. She'd better try to get her emotions under control before she did anything else.

The housekeeper's cottage looked like a haven. She'd give a great deal to be able to go inside and close the door. But she couldn't forget she had a job to do. She had to—

She stopped, frowning. Some foreign odor mingled with the aroma of food and flowers—something vaguely unpleasant. Her stomach lurched.

Smoke! She smelled smoke, coming from the old gardener's cottage Alex used as a studio.

Quickly she hurried around the small building to the door, pulse hammering, trying to reassure herself. She must be mistaken. There wasn't anything in the studio that could be burning. And she certainly couldn't start a panic. She'd have to investigate.

She grasped the knob, relieved to find it cool to the touch. This was nothing—she was letting her imagination run away with her. Besides, the building was probably locked—

The knob turned under her hand. She yanked the door open.

Fire! Panic crashed over her, stealing her breath in an instant. Flames shot from the trash can, and the draft from the opening door sent gray smoke billowing toward her. She clenched the knob. A cry ripped from her throat in spite of her effort to keep it back.

Run, the voice screamed in her head. *Run, run!* Suddenly she was back in the plane, the flames sweeping toward her, the twisted belt trapping her in the seat. She'd never get out, she—

Then she saw something that cut through her nightmare like a knife. The half-finished carving of Jason, covered by its cloth, sat on the workbench. Next to it lay the design plans Alex had shown her. Almost against her will, her mind assessed the risk.

They weren't in danger yet, but if the curtains caught, if she waited for help to arrive...

The fire extinguisher hung from a hook just inside the door. A prayer for help echoing in her heart, she grabbed the metal canister and advanced on the flames.

Please, God. Please. She wasn't trapped in the past any longer. A shudder ripped through her, but she shook it off. She wouldn't give in to the fear. With God's help, she never would again.

Chapter Sixteen

The moment Alex heard the cry, he knew it was Paula. Not stopping to wonder at the certainty that propelled him, he pushed his way through the crowd, ignoring their astonished stares. Paula was in trouble.

An acrid smell assaulted him as he rounded the pool. His stomach lurched. *Smoke!* He raced toward the studio, heart pounding, throat tight. Something was on fire, and Paula was there. She'd be terrified. He had to get to her.

The cottage door stood open. Gray smoke funneled out into the clean air. Behind him he could hear calls as others realized what was happening.

"Alex, wait!" It was Mitch's voice.

He couldn't wait. Paula was inside, maybe

trapped, flames reaching toward her—past and present mixed in a dizzying, terrifying scenario.

He ran to the door, throwing his arm up to shield his face, and stumbled inside. "Paula!"

She swung at the sound of his voice. Not trapped. Not terrified. Foam dripped from the extinguisher she held over the trash can. Even as he watched, the last wisps of smoke dissipated.

His mind seemed one huge prayer of thanks. She was all right. He went to her quickly, taking the metal canister from her hands.

"Are you hurt?" He clasped her hands in his, wanting to pull her into his arms, but not quite daring.

Paula nodded, coughing a little. "It's out. I put it out." Something like wonder filled her eyes as she looked at him. "I put it out," she repeated.

"You certainly did." He felt a long shudder work through her, and his hands slipped to her arms. Again he wanted to pull her against him. But heavy footsteps pounded on the porch, and the small room suddenly filled with people.

"Paula, how do you feel? Any trouble breathing?" Brett brushed past, elbowing him out of the way, intent on Paula. Mitch knelt by the soot-covered trash can. He picked it up gingerly and started toward the door.

Alex stepped back. His heartbeat should go back to normal now that the crisis was over, but that didn't seem to be happening. "Why didn't you call me?" He broke into Brett's series of questions. "You should have gotten out of here. You should have let someone else handle it."

Paula glanced toward the table, toward the carving of Jason. "I couldn't wait. I couldn't risk losing that." She looked back at him, and it felt as if no one else was in the room.

"Paula..." He let the sentence trail away. They were talking to each other without the need for words. They both knew what had just happened, whether anyone else did or not. Paula had faced the thing that terrified her most in this world, and she'd done it to save something important to him. His throat closed, and all he could do was look at her and think how dear she was to him.

"How did it start?" Mitch frowned at the remnants in the can. "I wouldn't think there'd be anything to spark a fire in here."

Alex tried to pull his gaze away from Paula. "It doesn't matter," he began, then became aware of a small figure in the doorway. *Jason.* His son shouldn't be exposed to this. It might frighten him. "Jason—"

"It was me!" Jason's face was white. "It was my fault. All my fault!"

Alex didn't know which of them moved first. He and Paula got to Jason at the same time. "No, Jason, no. It's not your fault, son. Don't think that."

Jason jerked away from his hand. "It is," he insisted almost angrily. "I did it."

Alex could only stare at the boy, totally at a loss.

"You were playing with matches." Paula said it softly, so softly probably no one else heard. "Is that what happened?"

A denial rose in Alex's throat, but before he could speak, Jason nodded. His small face crumpled.

"I'm sorry, Daddy. I didn't mean to. I'm sorry."

"Jason..." He stopped, reading the clear message in Paula's gaze. *Hold him.* She might as well have said it aloud. This wasn't the moment for analyzing or arguing. Alex knelt on the sooty floor. Feeling as if his heart might break, he drew his son into his arms.

For an instant Jason seemed to resist, then he flung his arms around Alex's neck, clinging as he hadn't in years. Sobs shook him.

"It's all right," Alex murmured, stroking his child's back. "It's all right, Jason."

His gaze met Paula's over Jason's head. The sheen of tears brightened her eyes.

"Is something wrong? What is happening?"

Dieter's voice had to be one of the most unwelcome things Alex had ever heard, when only moments before it had seemed so important. Aware of Paula watching him, he glanced up, not relaxing his grip on his son.

"Just a small accident," he said. His gaze caught Mitch's. "Would you?" He jerked his head toward Dieter.

Mitch nodded, not needing any further explanation. "Everything's under control now, folks." He began ushering people toward the patio, his large frame protecting Jason from curious eyes. "Let's get back to the party."

A murmur of voices, the shuffle of feet, and they were gone. Beside him, he felt Paula move, too.

"I should go. "

He shook his head. "Stay. Please." He stroked Jason's hair, his hand unsteady. "We need you, Paula."

That was as true as anything he'd ever said. He needed her. He loved his son more than life itself, but he didn't know how to reach him. If he didn't do this right, he'd probably regret it the rest of his days.

Please, Lord. Please. The prayer was almost involuntary. How long had it been since he'd begged God on his knees? The thought startled him. He'd been raised to be self-reliant. Somehow that attitude had extended to his faith, almost without his realizing it.

Paula nodded, seeming to understand all the things Alex didn't say. She moved closer, touching Jason's shoulder.

"Jason, it's okay. I understand."

Jason burrowed against his father's neck, and his voice was muffled. "I promised you."

"You didn't mean to break your promise," she said.

Her voice stayed calm, and Alex could only guess at the effort it took. He wanted to demand answers, but this wasn't the time. He could only try to understand.

"Tell your daddy what happened," she said gently. "He won't be angry."

Jason shook his head.

"Come on," she coaxed. "Were you mad?"

Jason sniffled. "Everybody was busy with this dumb party." A sob interrupted his words. "I just wanted someone to pay attention to me."

Someone. The word rang in Alex's mind. He remembered that exchange with Jason, how he'd brushed off his son's worries in his own anxiety over the business deal.

"So you were playing with matches in here." Her gaze ordered Alex not to react.

He felt Jason's nod, and then finally Jason raised his head, his gaze searching Alex's face. "I'm sorry, Daddy. I didn't mean to start a fire. I guess one of the matches wasn't clear out when I threw it away. I didn't mean it."

Alex gently wiped away the tears on Jason's face. "Fires are pretty scary, aren't they."

Jason nodded again, and his lips trembled. "I'm

sorry. I just needed to know. About Maida, and Paula, and everything.''

''I know, son. I'm sorry, too. But...'' He censored the automatic response that assured Jason not to worry. Obviously that did no good. Jason did worry, whether Alex wanted him to or not. ''You know I love you, don't you?''

''Mommy loved me.'' The words burst out, as if Jason had been holding them in for a long time. ''Mommy loved me, but she went away. It was my fault.''

''Jason, no. Why would you think that?'' Appalled, he could only stare at his son, feeling his heart shatter into pieces.

Jason hung his head, staring at the floor. He sniffled a little. ''I wasn't good enough. That's why she went away.''

How was he going to find the words? His son's pain wrapped around his heart, squeezing the life out of it.

Please, God. I've tried so hard to be the perfect heir my father wanted, but I've failed my own son. Please. Help me.

Paula watched the battle on Alex's face. His torment showed in his eyes so clearly. If he realized how much he was giving away, would he shut down again? Shut her out?

Alex stroked Jason's cheek. ''Jason, that's not it

at all. Of course your mommy loved you, more than anything. If she could have come back, I'm sure she would have. It wasn't your fault she went away. Mommy and I just couldn't seem to get along together. We made each other unhappy.''

A strong fist seemed to grip her heart. Alex was opening up to his son. Maybe for the first time, he was being vulnerable to the boy.

Please, Father, don't let him pull back now. Help him to tear down the barriers between them.

Jason shook his head as if he couldn't let go of the responsibility. He and Alex were so alike in that quality, and Alex had never seen it.

''Yes,'' Alex insisted. ''Don't you remember how she used to sing you to sleep at night?''

''She did?'' That simple idea seemed to break through Jason's absorption.

''Sure she did—''

Alex glanced at Paula, as if looking for confirmation he was on the right track, and she nodded, smiling through the tears that insisted on falling.

''And she made you that little stuffed dog that's on your dresser.''

Jason stared into his father's face. ''But she went away.''

''I know.'' She saw the muscles work in Alex's jaw. ''I'm sorry I didn't talk to you about it more. I guess I thought you were too little to understand.''

Jason straightened. "I'm big enough, Dad. I want to know what's going on."

"I see that now." Alex stood, holding out his hand to Jason. "Let's sit down and talk about it, okay?"

"Okay." Jason tucked his small hand into Alex's.

As father and son moved toward the bench against the wall, Paula slipped quietly out the door. Alex was doing it. He was taking down, stone by stone, the wall that separated him from his son. He could do that now without her.

She hesitated when she reached the patio. Snatches of conversation reached her ears, and the flurry of excitement was clearly over. Mitch stood on the pool deck, casually talking with someone, but his position was such that no one could go past him toward the studio. Brett had corralled several of Dieter's deputies near the gazebo, and Anne seemed to be keeping Dieter himself occupied.

She couldn't go back to the party, not until the last traces of tears were gone from her face. She moved softly across the grass and behind the shelter of the yew hedge.

The buzz of conversation turned into the merest background noise, quieter than the twittering of wrens in the hedge. Peace filled her.

Thank you, Lord. She glanced up, toward the

mountain ridge cutting into the sky. *Thank you. I think I understand now.*

She and Alex were more alike than she'd thought. He'd been trying to prove he was the perfect Caine heir his father wanted. She'd thought she had to earn the approval her father had never given. The truth was that neither of them had to prove their value in God's sight. They were accepted, just the way they were.

She wiped away another tear. She wasn't the starstruck girl she'd been two years ago, who ran away from rejection and told herself she didn't need anyone. She'd like to believe that, if not for the loss of her memory, she'd have dealt with that failing long ago, but this was her chance. Perhaps this had been in Aunt Maida's mind all along, when she'd pushed Paula into the situation. This time she wouldn't run away, no matter how difficult the future might be.

She loved Alex. If he didn't care for her in the same way, if the differences between them were too great, she'd deal with that. But she wouldn't run away from it.

"Paula."

She turned at the sound of Alex's voice, her heart thudding. "Is Jason all right?"

He nodded. "He will be. Thanks to you."

"I didn't do anything." Her throat was tight with

longing. "You're the one he needed." *The one I need.*

Alex shook his head. "I'd never have known that without you. I'd have kept on trying to protect him, not realizing I was closing him out." He moved closer. "You understood me better than I understood myself. If I succeed in being a better father, it will be because of you."

"I'm glad." She knew the love she felt for him was shining in her eyes, but she couldn't help it. There weren't any walls between them, at least not any of her making. Whether Alex could say the same, she didn't know.

His step closed the distance between them. He stood very close, not touching. "I don't think I'll ever be the perfect father I wanted to be."

"Jason doesn't need a perfect father. He needs you." It was much the same thing she'd said when he'd rejected the idea that he was a hero.

Perhaps he remembered that, because he smiled. "Not a hero," he said quietly. "Not a perfect father. Are you willing to take a chance on someone as fallible as I am?"

Her heart seemed to stop beating for a moment as she looked up into his eyes. It took a moment to find the words. "I've always been ready to take a chance. And in case you haven't noticed, I'm not so perfect myself."

He drew her into his arms, and she was home.

She rested her cheek against his chest and felt the steady beating of his heart.

"Will you marry me, Paula?" His breath stirred her hair. "Will you stay with us forever?"

She looked up at him, seeing the love so strong in his dark eyes that it took her breath away. Maybe they weren't perfect, but with God's help they could build a family that would last.

"I will."

He pressed his cheek against hers, and her heart overflowed. God had poured blessings on them, and all they'd had to do was open their hearts and hands. From now on the memories they made would be ones they could share, with God's grace.

*   *   *   *   *

Dear Reader,

I'm so glad you decided to pick up this book. The love story of small-town millionaire Alex Caine and his reluctant housekeeper, Paula Hansen, is one that has been teasing my imagination for a long time. I'm delighted to see it in print, and I hope you'll enjoy it.

Alex is the kind of person who thinks he has to be perfect for everyone, including God. It takes a near disaster to make him see the truth—that God's acceptance is already won for him. Once he understands that, he's finally ready for the happily-ever-after he always thought was an illusion. And he finds it in the surprise Cinderella who's right there in his own house.

Please let me know how you liked this story. You can reach me c/o Steeple Hill Books, 300 East 42nd St., New York, NY 10017.

Best wishes,

Marta Perry